The Temple Mount Code

CHARLES BROKAW

PENGUIN BOOKS

PENGUIN BOOKS

Published by the Penguin Group
Penguin Books Ltd, 80 Strand, London WC2R ORL, England
Penguin Group (USA) Inc., 375 Hudson Street, New York, New York 10014, USA
Penguin Group (Canada), 90 Eglinton Avenue East, Suite 700, Toronto, Ontario, Canada M4P 2Y3
(a division of Pearson Penguin Canada Inc.)
Penguin Ireland, 25 St Stephen's Green, Dublin 2, Ireland (a division of Penguin Books Ltd)
Penguin Group (Australia), 250 Camberwell Road, Camberwell, Victoria 3124, Australia
(a division of Pearson Australia Group Pty Ltd)
Penguin Books India Pvt Ltd, 11 Community Centre, Panchsheel Park, New Delhi – 110 017, India
Penguin Group (NZ), 67 Apollo Drive, Rosedale, Auckland 0632, New Zealand
(a division of Pearson New Zealand Ltd)
Penguin Books (South Africa) (Pty) Ltd, 24 Sturdee Avenue, Rosebank,
Johannesburg 2196, South Africa

Penguin Books Ltd, Registered Offices: 80 Strand, London WC2R ORL, England

www.penguin.com

First published 2011
1

Set in Garamond MT Std 13/15.25 pt
Typeset by Palimpsest Book Production Limited, Falkirk, Stirlingshire
Printed in England by Clays Ltd, St Ives plc

PAPERBACK ISBN: 978-0-141-04760-7

www.greenpenguin.co.uk

For my wife, with love.
You make it all possible.

Acknowledgements

Thanks to my excellent agent, Robert Gottlieb, at Trident Media Group, and to Libby Kellogg, who ably assists him there. Thanks also to my family and students, who are the light of my life.

Thanks are also due to the wonderful people at Penguin Books, including Alex Clarke, Nick Lowndes and Catriona Hillerton. I can't thank you enough for your professionalism and enthusiasm.

I

Jiahu Dig
Henan Province
People's Republic of China
July 21, 2011

'You've had quite a night, haven't you, Professor Lourds?'

Buckled into the passenger seat of the Bell helicopter, Thomas Lourds smiled. He was pleasantly tipsy and looking forward to his tent and the cot within it even more. 'Personally, I thought the evening ended rather abruptly.'

'It has a tendency to do that when you get thrown out of the bar.' Robert Anders sat in the pilot's seat, deftly handling the aircraft's controls. His voice was a pleasant baritone over the radio system. He was a burly Australian with an unkempt air. Tattoos of mermaids and dolphins danced along his forearms as he manoeuvered the helicopter over the craggy landscape below.

Lourds stared through the window at the ground. He knew they should be coming up on the Jiahu dig before long. After a moment, he saw the area, dotted with various lights, some coming from battery-powered lanterns and other areas lit by generator-powered strings of lights. Those camps were set up using private funding by corporations looking for tax shelters. Lowly universities, like Peking University, which Lourds was currently visiting, didn't have money to throw around. Instead, the crews – professors and grad students – worked from sunup to sundown.

Anders shook his shaggy head. 'I warned you not to hit on that woman.'

Lourds sighed. 'If the lady had worn a wedding ring or waited to come with her husband, I wouldn't have flirted with her so diligently. Rings were made for several reasons, you know, and one of those reasons was to keep a man from making a fool of himself.'

Working the stick, Anders dropped altitude and swooped down over the dig. Before they'd left the Peking University campsite, the Australian pilot had marked the makeshift landing pad with a fluorescent-painted sign. Lourds searched for it in the darkness.

'I don't think the fight started because you were flirting with the missus, mate.' Anders grinned. 'I think it was because you were on the verge of taking her home with you.'

Lourds smiled with genuine regret, which turned into a brief wince as his jaw twinged with pain. 'She was quite lovely, wasn't she?'

'Pretty as a pip, that one.'

'It wasn't just about the beauty, though. Marie had a wonderful way of listening.'

'That's 'cause you're a natural-born storyteller. I never seen the like.'

'You're too generous.'

'Just calling it the way I see it, Professor.'

'You can just call me Lourds.'

Anders nodded and looked out over the landscape again. 'How's Sleeping Beauty?'

Glancing over his shoulder, Lourds watched Professor Gao Kelu snoozing in the helicopter's backseat. The young man hadn't been able to go the distance with his older comrades. When they'd gotten kicked out of the club, after Anders and Lourds had gotten physical with the jealous husband and his brother, they'd had to carry Gao out with them.

'Still sound asleep.'

'Good.' Anders rubbed his face with a big hand. 'That bloke couldn't carry a note in a bucket.' He pointed through the Plexiglas. 'That's the campsite there, isn't it?'

Lourds leaned forward and stared through the cockpit windshield. His eyes were bleary from alcohol, days spent eating the yellow dust of the central plains of ancient China, and from long hours of studying text. He made out the signal with difficulty. 'It is.'

The landing strip had been situated on the other side of the dig Professor Hu had arranged for his students to work and for Lourds to visit. Lourds was initially visiting Peking University to deliver papers regarding protowriting to the professor's undergrad classes. Although Harvard was expecting him back in a few days, Lourds had managed to squeeze out extra time from the dean, which he was putting to good use here.

'Hang on, and I'll put us down.'

Lourds leaned back in his seat and felt the helicopter drop even closer to the ground. He'd lost most of the glow from the alcohol, but he knew he'd sleep well once he crawled into his cot. He wouldn't need any aid from the thriller novel he habitually carried.

Tall and lean, Lourds was in his early forties and kept himself in good shape with dedicated soccer as well as his international trips. His short-cropped goatee was in need of a trim, and his hair had gotten a little shaggy, but he knew it looked good on him. He was dressed in a chambray shirt over a white T-shirt, and brown cargo pants tucked into tall hiking boots to cut down on the amount of dust that crept into his footwear.

As the helicopter started its final descent, movement and a red flash near the one of the dig sites caught Lourds's attention. He grabbed for the spotlight mounted on his side of the helicopter, switched it on, and trailed the beam across the broken terrain.

'What is it?' Anders glanced in the direction of the beam.

'Thought I saw something.'

'What?'

The beam fell across the corner of the dig. The Jiahu was mostly undiscovered country for archaeologists. Even though over three hundred bodies had been taken from burial sites in the region, much of the area had yet to be explored. Lourds was a linguist, trained in dozens of languages, and a gifted translator.

Almost everything that was found at the dig was turned over to the Chinese government, but there was a fair market for stolen relics. Purloined antiquities remained a flourishing part of international business. Even though China dealt with black market trade in antiquities harshly, there were some who were desperate enough to risk the punishment versus the payoff.

Lourds trailed the beam across the ground and flicked across a man running with a pack on his back. 'Did you see that?'

'I did.' Anders flicked a hand out for the radio. 'I'll sound the alert.'

Lourds moved the spotlight around again and found another man. This one had a pack and a rifle, which he was aiming at the helicopter. 'Look out!'

Anders jerked the stick, and the helicopter side-slipped through the air. The muzzle flare below stood out bright orange against the black. At almost the same time, a bullet ricocheted off the Plexiglas bubble, and the sound of the shot penetrated the loud din of the rotors.

Startled, Anders swore and twisted the helicopter around. Lourds braced himself as he struggled to keep the spotlight on the grave robbers.

Another man emerged from the shadows and all three men ran for the outer fringe of the excavation, the light trailing after them flying across tents and other dig sites. Lourds doggedly stayed on them as Anders flew the helicopter after the men.

'Do you know what they might have gotten?' Anders heeled the helicopter around again, turning perpendicular to the running men.

'No, we're still exhuming bodies.' Lourds thought frantically. So much of what had been found at Jiahu was becoming ordinary, but who knew what extraordinary things were still waiting to be discovered? He knew it was more than possible the grave robbers had stumbled upon something irreplaceable. Lourds himself had done that when he'd located – and lost – Atlantis.

'There's a vehicle up ahead.' Anders shifted the spotlight on his side and pinpointed a pickup truck parked in the shadows of a ridge.

'Good eyes.' Lourds was impressed. He hadn't seen it, all of his attention focused on tracking the men.

'Have to have them in this business.' Anders glanced around. 'I'd've thought someone woulda noticed us by now, but I don't see anyone saddling up to come out this way.'

'We can't let them get to the truck. Whatever they have might be lost forever.'

'Okay, hang on.' Anders increased the throttle speed and leaned the helicopter forward.

'Can you put me on the ground?'

'You want to go down there after them?'

'Might give us a better chance. If you can put me

down near the vehicle, I might be able to disable it before they make their escape.'

'They're not going to just sit back and watch, you know.'

Lourds nodded and felt slightly sick to his stomach. He wasn't an action hero – he preferred to read about those kinds of people. And he was perfectly content to see any physical confrontation in his imagination as he turned the pages of a book. But he couldn't just sit by and watch as perhaps priceless artifacts disappeared before the world got a chance to see them.

Adroitly, Anders maneuvered the helicopter straight for the waiting pickup. 'I'm going to stay with the bird. For when you need to beat a hasty retreat.'

'All right.' Lourds took a couple of quick breaths to settle his nerves. It didn't work too well but helped clear his head a bit.

'I'm gonna drop you on a touch-and-go, mate – the moment I stop moving, you start. When you get out, keep your head low till I take off again. I don't want to decapitate you by accident.'

'No, we definitely *do* not want that.' Lourds unbuckled his seat belt and opened the helicopter's side door. He watched the pickup grow steadily closer.

'Don't forget they have guns.'

Lourds glanced at the starred imperfection on the cockpit nose. 'Trust me, there's no chance of me forgetting *that*.'

Slowing his forward momentum, Anders dropped the helicopter to a point a little more than three feet above the ground. He slapped Lourds on the shoulder. 'Go! But if you need me, run north. Put as much difference between them dingoes and yourself as you can.'

'Right.' Lourds clapped a hand on his Australian Outback hat and narrowed his eyes against the violent stir of dust kicked up by the spinning rotors.

'When you need help, I'll be there in a jiff.'

Lourds nodded, then hopped out of the rocking helicopter. He landed on both booted feet, gave thanks that neither of them twisted on the uneven ground, and got his bearings. The battered pickup sat about twenty yards away.

As soon as Lourds started for the vehicle, Anders throttled up, and the helicopter lifted into the air. The dust cloud stirred by the rotorwash grew huge, obscuring his vision and whipping into his face. Pulling his shirt over his nose and mouth to keep the dirt out, he ran for the pickup.

When he reached the vehicle, Lourds pulled a mini-Maglite from his pocket, switched it on, and peered inside. The flashlight was a primary tool for him to have out in the field, but he'd let the batteries go nearly dead. Only a weak light was emitted, but it was enough for him to see the that keys hadn't been left in the ignition.

Cursing the luck, Lourds turned to find where the tomb robbers were. Noting their arrival in just a few seconds, he reached inside the cab, popped the hood release, and ran around to the front of the vehicle, drawing his pocket tool as he shoved the hood up.

Lourds didn't know much about vehicles, but he knew enough to sabotage the pickup. He shined the Maglite over the engine and spotted the sparkplug wires immediately.

The men approaching the truck screamed curses at him. One of them fired, the bullet pinging off the truck's hood and sending a vibration stinging through Lourds's hand and arm.

Holding the Maglite in his teeth, he flipped out the tool's blade, grabbed a plug wire in one hand, and sawed at it, cutting through the plastic and wire.

Another bullet smashed into the engine and created a torrent of sparks. The pickup must have been leaking fuel through the carburetor because the exposed fuel immediately caught fire. The grave robbers yelled even more curses at Lourds.

Lourds dropped the severed wire and ran north, his long hours spent playing soccer paying off hugely. He streaked across the uneven terrain toward Anders and the helicopter, about a hundred yards away. The robbers were closing the gap and were about thirty yards behind him.

One of the men took a shot at Lourds as he ran. The bullet dug up a furrow in the ground right next to him, making Lourds put more effort into his stride.

Anders had put the helicopter down with the pilot side facing the three angry grave robbers. Shots slowly cracked, letting Lourds know that the men carried single-action rifles.

Running around the side of the helicopter, Lourds grabbed the door and pulled it open. As soon as he had one foot in the helicopter, Anders nudged the craft into the air.

Just as he was about to haul himself inside, Lourds's foot slipped on the landing gear. He fell and flailed for purchase. 'Help!'

Surprised, Anders threw out an arm, grabbed Lourds's chambray work shirt, and hauled him inside the cockpit. 'C'mon, Professor. I don't want you to fall and end up in a million little pieces.'

'Me neither.' Lourds clambered into the copilot's seat and buckled in.

The shots came again, another weak fusillade around the helicopter. This time, however, several jeeps topped the ridge, with armed men riding shotgun. Handheld spotlights caught the surprised thieves in their bright glare.

'Well, that's obviously not going to end well for them.' Lourds smiled, pretending that he did this kind of thing every day and that his heart wasn't jackhammering in his chest.

'You did good, Professor.' Anders smiled. 'You run a lot faster than I thought a professor could.'

'Thanks.' Lourds decided not to mention that the bullets fired at him had been one hell of a motivator.

Below, the three grave robbers scattered in different

directions, but it did them no good. Lourds watched the confrontations play out. The jeeps split up, each one pursuing a fleeing criminal. The thieves all gave up after a short run and planted their faces in the ground until the dig's security people arrested them.

Lourds happily clapped Anders on the back. 'Well, my friend, we're going to be heroes in the morning. After saving whatever it is we saved down there, I think people should at least buy us breakfast.'

At that point, Professor Gao woke up with a bleat. He'd slept throughout the encounter, but the intense jockeying of the helicopter hadn't agreed with his stomach.

'Grab him, mate!' Anders frantically dove toward the ground again, which only made matters worse. Gao bent forward, his face a sickly shade of green. Lourds unfastened his seat belt, then the one restraining Gao, holding the small man steady.

'*Don't* let him throw up in here!' Anders reached for his door with one hand. 'I don't need the stink for the next week.'

'Short of ramming a towel down his throat, I don't see how that's possible for much longer.'

'When I get us down, you get him out of here pronto.'

Setting the helicopter down on the makeshift landing pad, Anders reached across the passenger seat and shoved the door open. 'Get him out of here, now! No one throws up in my bloody heli!'

Grabbing Gao by one arm and his belt, Lourds

hurled the sick man toward the door. Gao went out unceremoniously, looking like a stilt-legged stork. He plopped onto the ground hard enough to make Lourds wince in sympathy.

Gao sat up and looked dazed. Then he threw up into his own lap.

Anders punched Lourds in the shoulder. 'Well, mate, if nobody recognizes you as a hero tomorrow, I will. That was a very near thing there.'

Lourds agreed as he watched the security vehicles hauling the three grave robbers into camp. 'Do you believe in omens, Robert?'

'Never had much use for them myself.'

'Nor have I.' But Lourds couldn't help feeling that something was coming. After days of relative peace and quiet, he felt certain he was on the verge of something big.

2

Jiahu Dig
Henan Province
People's Republic of China
July 22, 2011

'You have that whole "distracted professor" thing going on, Professor Lourds.'

Thomas Lourds glanced over his shoulder and smiled at the pretty, young Peking University student assigned to him by Professor Hu. Gloria Chen was a graduate student of linguistics with a minor in archaeology. The emphasis in both fields of study centered on the Neolithic Yellow River Period. Jiahu was one of the most important, and, until recently, largely unexplored sites that had been discovered. Lourds and Gloria were both there to further the study of evolutionary linguistics, trying to unlock the mystery of how human language was created over the millennia. In particular, Lourds hoped to find clues to some of the earliest protolanguages in existence.

'Sorry, Gloria. Still recovering a bit from last night.' Lourds spoke in Cantonese, which was Gloria's first language. He squatted at the soft edge of the grave he'd been contemplating. Dirt tumbled into the hole from his movement, and he slid his foot back, fearing the lip might crumble and send him sprawling.

The original resident lay inside the rectangular hole. The grad assistants working on the project with the Peking professors had partially excavated the skeleton, but the bones lay semisubmerged in dirt, dust, and debris.

'I heard about your little adventure.' Gloria's tone was neither fawning nor disapproving.

'Did you?'

'Oh yes, it was the talk of the camp this morning. This might help.' She joined Lourds and handed him a bottle of chilled water, which he took gratefully.

'What can you tell me about this person?' Gloria was slim and beautiful, in her midtwenties. She wore her black hair short, and it only brushed her shoulders. Prescription sunglasses covered her eyes, but Lourds had noticed they were a peculiar yellow hazel. She wore canvas pants and a T-shirt.

Lourds grinned, set the half-empty bottle of water down beside him, then lifted his battered Australian Outback hat and ran a hand through his black hair. 'I'm not a forensic anthropologist.' He replied in English. 'You'd have to ask Professor Chaoju or one of his grads for information like that.' He looked back at the skeleton. 'I can speculate that this was a man or a very young girl because the hips are too narrow for a mature woman. But I could be wrong about that. Probably am.'

The young woman laughed. 'Somehow, after the way

Professor Hu talked about you, I just expected you to know everything.'

'Not hardly. Professor Hu is too generous with his praise.'

'But you're the man that discovered Atlantis.'

'I also lost it. Never forget that.' Lourds had had the find of a lifetime in the palm of his hand, and it had slipped away to the sea bottom.

Lourds finished the bottle of water and slid it into the cracked leather backpack containing his tools, books, and cameras. Then he stood and stretched. Despite the fact he was tall and lean and stayed active, his body didn't always meet the demands he put upon it the way it once had.

Lourds looked around. A lot of people from all over the world were working the Jiahu dig. He'd already seen a number of archaeological teams he knew from past acquaintance and from reputation. As far as he knew, he was the only Harvard University professor currently on-site. And that had been at Professor Hu's express invitation, which Lourds hadn't hesitated to accept.

'Where's Professor Hu?' Lourds shaded his eyes with his hat as he scanned the various dig groups.

Hu had a tendency to wander off and socialize. The man was a Facebook demon and seemed to have the ability to keep up with the whole world. But it had been Hu's reputation that had pried Lourds free of Harvard and sent him off to Peking.

Gloria pointed. 'There. Why?'

'I want to get someone who knows what they're doing to exhume this skeleton.'

'I think they plan on doing it soon.'

'I know, but I'd rather they get to this one sooner.' Lourds walked in Hu's direction.

Professor David Hu was a small, slight man. His black hair had gone gray years ago, but hadn't completely given up. Strands of charcoal black threaded through the shoulder-length mop. He was talking quickly to a group of fellow archaeologists. Spotting Lourds coming over, Hu waved at him to join them.

'For those of you who haven't had the great fortune to previously meet my colleague, this is the world-renowned Thomas Lourds, Professor of Linguistics at Harvard, and the hero of the Jiahu dig, after his exploits of last night.'

The introduction embarrassed Lourds, but he'd learned to endure the attention. His translation of *Bedroom Pursuits,* a journal regarding the amorous adventures of a merchant in the fourth century, had garnered praise and damnation, depending on who voiced the opinion. However, the discovery of Atlantis had served him up into the public eye in a way he was still trying to deal with.

He shook hands all the way around, called by name the men and women he knew, and was introduced to those he didn't know.

The conversation quickly turned to questions directed at Lourds, but he held up his hands to deflect them.

'Ladies and gentlemen, I'd be only too glad to entertain you at our tent tonight if Professor Hu is all right with that – '

Hu nodded happily.

'In the meantime, I need to borrow Professor Hu.'

Good-byes were quickly said, and Hu fell into step with Lourds and Gloria.

'Sorry.' The professor looked a little embarrassed. 'I didn't mean to be away for so long, but I just got to talking.'

'Not a problem.' Lourds clapped the man on the shoulder and smiled. 'If I hadn't found something, I wouldn't have bothered you.'

Gloria looked surprised. She took a quick step in front of Lourds and put a hand on his chest. 'Wait. You found something? And you didn't mention it?'

'I didn't. I felt Professor Hu should see it first. And if the object turns out to be worthwhile, I don't want to disturb it until we can get a cameraman to record the event.'

'What object?' Professor Hu waved to one of the two-person film crews that had tagged along with the archaeological team.

The two-person crew, an Asian man and a young woman, broke free from shooting footage of the open graves and unhurriedly walked over. The young woman, Baozhai, seemed serious and intent, overdressed for the weather in long khakis and an olive drab button-up over a white tank, but she would look good on film. The guy carrying the camera wore a Green Lantern T-shirt, cargo shorts, and red Chuck Taylors. His hair fell down into his face.

'Hey, dude, what up?' He held up a hand for Lourds to high-five.

Lourds returned the high five and smiled. Jimmy Woo might have been born and bred Chinese, but he mainlined twenty-first-century American pop culture.

'Professor Lourds has some filming he'd like you to do.' Professor Hu waved the film team forward.

'Cool. What'd you find?' Jimmy resettled the camera over his shoulder.

'Show you in a minute.' Lourds headed for the grave.

Once more, Lourds squatted at the edge of the grave and stared down at the skeletal remains. At his direction, Jimmy took video footage of the grave and its grisly inhabitant.

'Now, Thomas, what did you find?' Professor Hu waved Jimmy and Baozhai away.

Carefully, Lourds reached down through the dead man's empty rib cage. After so many thousands of years, the bones were fragile and easy to destroy.

A smooth stone lay on the ground to one side of the spine. Lourds touched it with his fingertips, rocked it slightly, then redoubled his efforts to scissor his fingers and remain steady. With the stone caught between his fingers, Lourds withdrew his hand. He sat and crossed his legs, totally involved with his prize.

'What is it?' Hu knelt and peered closely, sliding his reading glasses on as he examined the stone.

'I don't quite know.'

'Then how do you know it's anything at all?' Gloria sounded a trifle put out.

'Because this stone is smooth.' Lourds twisted it in his fingers, showing off the smooth surface. Shaped something like a hen's egg, it was half the size of his fist. 'None of the other rocks down there are smooth.'

As one, the others peered over into the grave for a moment. Then they pulled back and looked at the stone in Lourds's palm.

'That still doesn't mean anything.'

Lourds remained focused on his perceived prize. 'Perhaps it doesn't. But do you know what?'

'What?' Hu looked at Lourds over the top of his glasses.

Lourds smiled. 'I don't think this is a stone at all. It's actually not heavy enough.' He looked around the ground beside him and found a rock that had a semiflat side. Laying the stone on the ground, he lifted the rock and prepared to bring it down.

'Wait!' Hu held up his hands. 'We can x-ray that – '

Lourds brought the rock crashing down.

3

Jiahu Dig
Henan Province
People's Republic of China
July 22, 2011

The 'stone' fragmented when the rock smacked it. Pieces shot out in all directions, several of the fragments hitting Lourds's bare leg hard enough to sting.

'Oh my.' Hu put his hands to his face in consternation. 'Thomas, do you realize what you've done?'

Lourds sorted through the pieces around him. 'Not yet, but hopefully soon.' He knew he was going to feel like an idiot if the 'stone' turned out to be nothing at all, and he was going to feel even worse if the 'stone' turned out to be an artifact they should have saved.

But he had a feeling about it. He'd learned to trust his gut over the years, and it had been telling him that the stone had been an important ruse.

'That "stone" was only pottery. A protective covering. You know, it's interesting all the things researchers have learned from Neolithic Yellow River pottery. I'm sure you've all heard about the alcohol recipe that was reconstituted from residue that had soaked into pottery jars?'

Hu nodded but looked decidedly anxious.

'As it turns out, the recipe was for alcohol fermented from rice, honey, and hawthorn, or as it's known in scientific circles, *Rhaphiolepis.* That particular species of evergreen has white or pink blossoms, and it bears a fruit, a pome, like a small apple actually, that can be made into a jam. Dogfish Head Brewery actually bottles that very recipe today. It's featured as one of their Ancient Ales series. They call the beer Chateau Jiahu. For the most ancient beer known to man, it's not bad, but I prefer one of the German darks.'

With a flourish, Lourds plucked a small, pale green-gray tortoiseshell from amid the debris and plopped it onto his palm. He smiled.

'Oh my.' Hu's exclamation this time was in a much different tone.

Several onlookers from nearby digs had come over, attracted by the commotion surrounding Lourds. He lit up at once, enjoying the attention. He loved being in front of a classroom.

'Tortoiseshells have been a mainstay of Chinese and Asian culture for thousands of years.' Lourds held the small shell up at the ends of his fingertips, delicately flipping it over to show the underside, and pointed to the sections. 'In ancient times, diviners used these plastrons to foresee the future. The Shang Dynasty is filled with stories about men who used them for those purposes. The process was to heat and crack the plastrons, then inscribe them.'

Jimmy Woo had his camcorder on his shoulder and was filming away.

Baozhai held a small wireless microphone in one hand and slid quietly into the shot. 'So the tortoiseshells were used in magic ceremonies?'

Lourds laughed. 'No. Histories were kept on the tortoiseshells. Historians wrote out stories of events and people on the plastron pieces. In fact, the oracle bones, as the pieces came to be called, gave historians the knowledge of the past and the complete royal genealogy of the Shang Dynasty, from Tian Yi to Di Xin.'

'Why did historians use the tortoiseshells?'

Lourds flicked the tortoiseshell with a forefinger, and the hollow note sounded loud in the quiet surrounding him. Punk rock music from one of the other dig groups sounded in the distance. 'I would think they used them because they were so durable. The Shang Dynasty ran from 1766 BC to 1122 BC, by Liu Xin's accounts. Liu was an astronomer in the Xin Dynasty. Another source, the *Bamboo Annals,* found in the tomb of the king of Wei, cites the time frame as 1556 BC to 1046 BC Papyrus wasn't invented and used by the Egyptians till the third millennium BC' He smiled again. 'It also helped that tortoises were so plentiful. Put a tortoise into a pot in the evening for a tasty soup, then you could note out the family history – including the previous night's family meal menu – the next morning.'

The crowd laughed.

'Sadly, thousands of years of history were lost

because no one realized the significance of these little bits of bone. Paper was invented in China in the second century AD or thereabouts. There is some speculation that it was used before then, but that seems to be the major point of entry. At the time paper was made, it was intended to replace silk in the Chinese culture, so that more silk could be traded and sold abroad. As you may recall, paper is counted as one of the Four Great Inventions of Ancient China. The inventions of the compass, gunpowder, and printing are the other three – for those of you taking notes.'

Professor Hu spoke up at once. 'There will be a test for my students.'

Mock groans mixed in with the laughter.

Lourds turned the tortoiseshell. 'Thousands of years passed, and people came to believe the plastrons held curative powers. Myths sprang up that all the broken shell pieces were dragon bones and could be used to cure various sicknesses or wounds. Apothecaries and shamans used the shell pieces whole or crushed to manufacture medicines and poultices for sicknesses like malaria and for injuries.' He shook his head at the thought of all that lost history.

Baozhai pushed the microphone toward Lourds again. 'You say thousands of years passed before anyone recognized that the tortoiseshells contained written records.'

'There was a scholar in the Qing Dynasty who figured it out. His name was Wáng Yíróng, and he didn't put it together until 1899. At the time, Wang was being treated for malaria. He and a friend, Liú È, spotted the engravings on the turtle shells and noticed they looked like the inscriptions on *zhong* bells and *ding* tripodal cauldrons from the Shang Dynasty to the Zhou Dynasty that they had been studying. They started to work on interpreting the glyphs immediately. That discovery of the glyphs on the plastron pieces changed the face of Chinese archaeology forever.'

'How?'

'At the time the oracle bones were discovered, Chinese professors had believed the Shang Dynasty to be a fabrication. A myth like other myths. Like Atlantis. As we now know, myths have a tendency to be true and show up now and again.'

The crowd laughed, and several clapped in appreciation.

Warming to his subject, Lourds rested his arms on his legs, felt the warm sun beating down on him, and thought of how Chinese teachers had probably sat among their students in this very way thousands of years ago. He projected his voice to reach all the listeners. 'These days, we've become accustomed to hearing the voices of history. We have any number of archives to hear the past march through our lives. From scrolls and books, to the audio and video recordings that are the mainstays of this generation, we're constantly confronted by the past. Television is full of reruns. You've all seen cartoons or shows that you first watched when you were children.

And they might have been old then. Memories, *your* memories, are archived with those reruns. They may serve as engrams that take you back to the day you first saw that show. Facebook is a kind of living history now. When I get on Facebook nowadays, what I look at is a kind of history scroll.'

'Lurk, you mean.' The feminine voice came from somewhere near the back of the crowd.

Lourds smiled. 'You see? Facebook has begotten its own language now. Before Facebook, *lurk* would have had a more physical meaning, more threatening, usually meaning the monster outside your bedroom door. Not some digital stalker.'

A female voice spoke up quickly. 'Oh, lurkers are still pretty scary at times.'

The group laughed good-naturedly.

'I'm always amazed at the wealth of history I find in a student's Facebook pages. As I flip through the photographs, I can watch that student literally grow up within a few moments.'

'Now *that's* creepy.'

Lourds smiled. 'Maybe. But I can remember my own youth when childhood was something your mother dragged out in dusty photo albums. I have to wonder what our descendants are going to think about all of this a hundred years from now.' Lourds tapped the tortoiseshell again. 'One thing I'm convinced of: they'll have a far better grasp of our history than any previous generation has of the one that preceded them.

'So, is there anything special about that tortoiseshell?' Baozhai asked.

'Tortoiseshells are important to the Jiahu site. Since it is part of the Neolithic Yellow River culture that occupied these central plains, every archaeologist I've talked to is convinced that we've barely touched the history that can be found here. Tortoiseshells are an important part of this dig. The Jiahu script contains sixteen markings that we've been able to recognize.'

'But, Professor Lourds, there are a number of historians and linguists who argue that the Jiahu *symbols* aren't a language at all. They're just drawings used to represent a concept.' That came from a studious-looking young man in the back.

Undeterred, Lourds leaned forward and inscribed a circle with an angled line through it.

Ø

'What is that?'

'A mathematical symbol for zero.'

'Is it?' Lourds raised an eyebrow. 'And if I were to inscribe a skateboard within its circumference? Or a gun? What would it be then?'

No one said anything.

Jimmy Woo looked around at the crowd. 'Dude, it would be a sign. No skateboarding. No weapons. You guys would suck at Pictionary.'

'Thank you, Jimmy.' Lourds smiled.

Jimmy shrugged and concentrated on his camera.

'That symbol, used in that context, becomes a message. When skateboarding first swept through the United States, and young hooligans made the sidewalks and streets unsafe for man or beast or vehicle, signs used to be written out.' Lourds trailed a hand through the air. '"No skateboarding." In time, a picture of a skateboard was added. For clarification, I supposed.'

'Or because they thought the great unwashed couldn't read.' That came from a particularly grimy young man at the forefront of the crowd.

'Ah.' Lourds smiled with pride as he successfully navigated the group into the lesson he wanted to deliver. 'So, city fathers, in their understanding of their populaces, chose to recognize that not everyone could read. Or, perhaps, take the necessary time to read a posting.'

'*Skateboarding* is a big word.' The young man grinned and high-fived the guy next to him.

'It is. So let's take that concept for a moment. You have a population that's largely uneducated and illiterate, what are you going to do to communicate with them quickly and efficiently?'

'And you don't have Facebook or Twitter?' The young woman at the front of the crowd looked appalled.

'Exactly. Think about the way silhouettes of men and women have replaced the designations men and women on public bathroom doors.'

Taking a new water bottle from his backpack, Lourds twisted the cap free and drank. 'Society tends to scale itself back to the lowest common denominator because the concepts are easier to pass along.' He held up the tortoiseshell. 'We know sixteen of the Jiahu symbols, and that knowledge was gained from tortoiseshells and bones. We know markings that compare to the oracle bone script for words like *eye*, *sun*, and *day*.

'From that, linguists and historians have to interpret what's written, what they know about the culture from other artifacts, and piece together as much of the language as they can.' He peered at the studious young man. 'So, in answer to your question, young man, some scholars may choose to view the Jiahu symbols as a type of protowriting, not a written language as we know it, but as a means of mass communication.'

'Do you think everything that's written is important?'

'I do.' Lourds nodded emphatically. 'Suppose you learned that the country you live in was settled by brave sailors who faced the unknown places on a map to seek out new lives. Then someone came along and took out the word *sailors* because the interpretation was wrong, and you were in fact descended from pirates. Would that change your view of yourself?'

A Chinese youth in the front looked hesitant, then spoke. 'It depends on how tight you were with your ancestors. How much that family history is used to build on.'

Lourds smiled and nodded. 'Exactly right. Again, it depends on how close a culture is to its past. There are still several cultures that are. One facet of language, one shred of new understanding, one reinterpretation or missed interpretation, has the profound ability to make a culture change its view of itself.

Baozhai took the conversation back to what clearly interested her. 'Do you see any new facets in that tortoiseshell you found, Professor Lourds?'

Peering at the tortoiseshell, Lourds took a penlight from his shirt pocket, illuminated the shell, and held it up to the crowd. Under the light, distinct lines gleamed through the patina. One of the symbols looked like a mountain that had been dyed blue-green. 'Actually, I think this is a map.' He held the tortoiseshell up to his eye. 'Isn't that interesting?'

4

Ma'an (Gaza City)
North Gaza Strip
July 23, 2011

'If I am caught talking to you, Professor Strauss, there are men who will kill me,' the shopkeeper said.

As he stood in the gloomy, dust-laden room, Lev Strauss felt perspiration trickle down his spine, and he had to quash the instinct to run.

'Men are already hunting me, Abu. I am also taking my life in my hands to be here. But here I am.' Lev stood in front of Abu Tamboura, dwarfing the small old man even though he was not a tall man himself.

Tamboura was an old-school smuggler who had made and lost small fortunes during the years of tight blockades and embargoes enforced by the Israelis. Things had since loosened up off and on, and he now owned several legitimate businesses, but he'd never left smuggling completely behind.

'You come to my place of business with men hunting you?' Tamboura knotted his fists and didn't try to hide his rage. His wispy slenderness emphasized his short stature, and he was bald as an egg, though bushy eyebrows stood at attention over his glasses. His suit was cheap but well cared for, indicating a frugal but fastidious man.

The 'place of business' wasn't much for show either. The small room was at the back of one of Tamboura's legitimate businesses. Cheap pottery and soaps lined the wooden shelves. A small card table and three mismatched chairs sat under a naked bulb that hung from the low ceiling.

'I didn't bring them here.' Lev hoped that was true.

After a moment of hesitation, Tamboura waved to the table. 'Sit.'

Lev sat, grateful to get his weight off his left leg. He'd lost everything below the knee more than thirteen years ago and, although the plastic-and-metal prosthesis that had replaced it served him well, he'd been pushing its capabilities over the last several days.

'What do you need from me?' Tamboura fidgeted as he sat.

'The same thing I have always needed. Information.'

Tamboura licked his lips and nervously drummed his fingers on the tabletop. 'What information?'

'Have you ever heard of a writer named Yazid Ibn Salam?'

Tamboura gave the name some thought, then reached inside his jacket and took out a small PDA. 'Should I know this name?'

'As an author?' Lev shook his head. 'I wouldn't think so. I only stumbled upon a book he'd written lately myself.'

'You are a language professor at the University of Jerusalem. Please forgive me for pointing out that books are your business, not mine.'

'I have reason to believe that any book written by Yazid Ibn Salam would be worth a considerable amount to anyone looking for it.'

Tamboura scrolled through the PDA. The ghost gray of the screen reflected against the hard planes of his face. 'If I had such knowledge, it might be costly.'

Lev smiled. Greed was a constant in Tamboura's world, as true as due north on a compass. 'I can pay.'

'I'll be the judge of that. Some of my contacts can be quite costly.' Tamboura searched his database. Several international art houses and insurance companies would have loved to know what was in that database. He glanced up and shook his head. 'I can find nothing about your author.'

Lev sighed.

'Perhaps I could continue searching for information about this author.' Tamboura put his PDA away and regarded Lev with his dark eyes.

'That might not be a good idea.'

When Tamboura's eyes glittered, Lev realized he'd said the wrong thing.

'Are other people searching for books by this man?'

Lev stood, and the pain in his leg throbbed to renewed life. He put money on the table. 'For your time, Abu.'

Tamboura looked at the money for a moment, then shrugged. 'I haven't done anything to earn it.'

'You confirmed something that I would have wasted time trying to find out.'

Tamboura scooped the money up in one hand. 'Then I'm glad to have been of service.'

As Lev turned to go, the doorway suddenly burst open, and a man stepped through with a pistol in his hand, followed by others.

Lev saw Tamboura already in flight toward the back of the building. Moving quickly, Lev slammed a fist into the naked lightbulb, shattering it and plunging the room into darkness. He ran after Tamboura. The wily smuggler always had a way out.

In the darkness, Lev collided with a wooden cabinet. Pottery splintered against the concrete floor in a kaleidoscope of noise. Evidently the man in the doorway thought he was being fired on because he began shooting.

'Stop shooting, you fool! He must be taken alive!'

Lev had an arm in front of him, fumbling at a run through the dark.

Then Tamboura pulled open a door almost hidden behind a wide bookshelf filled with boxes of soap. The little man scurried into the evening as traffic noises echoed inside the small room.

The doorway let out into a small alley that ran between stone buildings. To the left, a wooden fence barred the way. To the right, the alley opened up onto the street. Tamboura ran toward the street, and Lev was at his heels.

Before they'd gone a half dozen steps, a car turned down the alley and raced at them. Tamboura froze, trapped in the bright headlights. The doors opened, and men stepped out, all holding guns.

'Professor Strauss. We don't wish to harm you.' He spoke in English, but his accent was Arabian.

Lev turned immediately and ran in the other direction. Tamboura wheeled around as well and started to pull even with Lev, showing surprising speed. Then shots erupted, and Tamboura's head shattered into a bloody mess. His corpse managed one more faltering step and fell on the cobblestones without a sound.

Even with the prosthesis, Lev made good speed. He hurled himself at the fence and climbed as quickly as he could. Before he could top the fence, he felt something thud into it and thought that one of his pursuers had reached the barrier as well.

Then a man crested the top of the fence on the other side. He looked at Lev. 'I'm with Mossad, Professor. You're coming with us.' He thrust the snout of a wicked machine pistol over the top of the fence and fired strategic bursts.

Lev pulled himself over the top and dropped to the ground as bullets hit the fence behind him. The prosthesis buckled underneath him, and he fell, catching himself on his hands.

'Get up.' A man caught Lev by the arm and yanked him to his feet.

Lev stood and practically fell forward into a stumbling run. The man held on to his arm and tugged Lev forcefully. Two other men had joined the Mossad agent at the top of the fence. Bullets knocked one of them down, and he sprawled in the alley with blood covering his face. Lev yanked his attention forward to a van waiting across the street.

'Faster, Professor Strauss, if you want to live.' The Mossad agent was young and fierce-looking. He carried a pistol with an extended magazine in his free hand.

Men set up outside the van with weapons at the ready.

The sudden din behind Lev caused him to look back over his shoulder. The car that had stopped in the alley now roared through the fence. The two Mossad agents at the top of the fence flew backwards.

Immediately, the Mossad agents in the street opened fire. The van's side cargo door opened as bullets drummed against the vehicle. The man with Lev heaved him forward as another man caught his free arm and pulled. Lev sailed forward and landed on his stomach. The second man yanked him away from the opening as the other agent slammed the door shut.

The man who had pulled Lev to his feet and gotten him across the street slapped the driver's shoulder. 'We're secure. Go.'

The driver hit the gas, and the van shot forward as more bullets peppered its side.

Lev pushed himself to a sitting position and looked at the man beside him. 'You're Mossad.'

The man nodded.

'What are you doing here?'

'We came to get you, Professor.'

'Why?'

'The decision was made to bring you in and put you under protective custody. My superiors want to know where the book is.'

Lev looked at the grim-faced men around him. 'What book?'

The man shook his head. 'I don't know what book. But my superiors do. They want it – and you – protected. Too many people are after you. Including the Ayatollah.' He jerked a thumb over his shoulder. 'That back there should prove that to you. Trust us. We're your friends.'

Lev blinked. 'There's no book,' he said, shaking his head. *But if the book is true,* he thought, *and the world finds out, everything will change.*

5

Behesht-e Zahra (The Paradise of Zahara)
Tehran
The Islamic Republic of Iran
July 24, 2011

'You have no right to keep us from paying our respects!' Liora Ravitz stood at the front of the angry mob gathered at the cemetery entrance.

Reza stood at her side and raised his voice with hers. 'She is *our* martyr! We demand to be allowed entrance!'

The *Basij* militiaman in front of her ignored her as he stood behind his Plexiglas riot shield. He was young, as most of them were, dressed in military fatigue pants, jump boots, and a gray button-up shirt with the sleeves rolled to midforearm. His equipment belt held a baton, but he kept a hand on the folded-stock AK-47 assault rifle that hung at his side.

'Let us in!' Liora stumbled forward slightly as the crowd baying behind her surged forward. She felt frightened, and that spiked her anger even more. If she touched the *Basij*, the man would surely shoot her.

'Liora. Please be careful.'

She turned to face the young man she loved. Reza

was serious and intense, with a beard aging his baby face only a little. 'If we are careful, dear Reza, we will never be free in this country.'

'Let us in!' A man farther down the line spat on the Plexiglas shield of the *Basij* in front of him.

The *Basij* only spat and cursed at the man.

Two of the protestor's friends quickly hauled him back as he threw himself at his tormentor. The crowd collapsed on itself as the two men carried their friend farther back into the protection of friends.

Fear swelled Liora's throat. She was eighteen years old and was enrolled at Islamic Azad University. This was her first protest. Her mother had discovered her intentions and fought with her about it, but Liora had gone anyway.

When she'd first arrived, she'd been afraid, especially because she hadn't been able to find the other girls she'd agreed to join. She wondered if they had been forbidden to come, or if they had gotten too afraid to show up.

The protest had turned out much larger than she'd expected.

As she chanted and shouted, she wondered if this was how Neda Agha-Soltan felt the day she was shot for protesting the Iranian election two years ago. Liora didn't know how anyone could willingly face death. She didn't plan on dying, but then she didn't think Neda Agha-Soltan had either.

The young woman had been only twenty-six, with her whole life ahead of her.

But it was a life here, under the rule of a misogynist despot. Liora could barely stand the thought. Things had to change.

But even with the ascension of the new Ayatollah, things continued to be the same.

'We weren't allowed to pay our respects on June 20.' Another man railed at the assembled *Basij*. 'You cannot keep us from visiting her grave.'

Posters of Neda Agha-Soltan showed her as she had been in her best health, and as she'd lain dying on Kargar Avenue. In the one, Liora thought the woman looked like an angel. In the other, Neda looked broken and torn, blood running from her mouth and nose, her eyes unfocused.

Liora had first seen the videos of Neda's death at sixteen. She'd been young and impressionable, still smarting from a broken romance.

But Neda had given Liora someone to focus on, someone to hope to be. Neda Agha-Soltan had given her life trying to get the voice of women and reformists who stood against the Ayatollah's rule heard. Her memory deserved to be honored by those that loved her.

Taking a deep breath, Liora joined in the shouting again. 'Let us in! Let us pay our respects! We will not be silenced!'

Reza joined her, but he remained quieter than she though she knew his voice could be much louder.

A jeep cruised slowly through the crowd, protected by a circle of *Basij* carrying assault rifles. Protestors yelled imprecations and curses, but they all backed away from the armed men.

For the first time, Liora noticed the news cameramen gathered around the cemetery. *Basij* shoved through the crowd in an attempt to get to the cameras, but the crowd slowed the paramilitary people down just enough to allow the cameramen to get away through the crowd that opened before them.

A *Basij* officer's voice echoed over loudspeakers. 'You will leave this area at once. You have no right to assemble. This gathering is illegal and will not be permitted.'

An older man, flecks of gray showing in his beard, stood and raised a bullhorn. 'We're permitting it!'

The crowd roared its approval of the bold declaration.

'You could not silence Neda Agha-Soltan even after you murdered her!'

Another roar of approval followed, the crowd's unified voice growing even stronger.

'The Ayatollah called for three days of mourning after you butchers silenced Neda, but you tortured her fiancé. Caspian Makan had to escape and flee to Canada to avoid the same fate! You're all killers, and the Ayatollah is the biggest killer of all!'

'Stand down!' The officer's voice blasted over the crowd, but the protestors just grew louder and angrier.

'Let Iran decide its own fate! Let our voices be heard!'

The commanding officer turned to his men and waved decisively. The *Basij* pulled on gas masks as the crowd of protestors tried to back away, but there was nowhere to go. Their backs were against the line of *Basij* barring entrance to the cemetery.

The *Basij* threw tear-gas grenades into the crowd. A moment later, virulent yellow and green gas pooled on the ground and quickly lifted into the air.

Liora pulled her green *hijab* up over her lower face to block the noxious fumes. It didn't help much. The gas filled her eyes with tears and burned her nose and mouth.

Filled with terror and pain, the crowd became an animal in a trap, striking out at the source of fear and agony. Men pushed at the *Basij* in an attempt to break through their ranks. That was all the paramilitary men had been waiting for. As soon as contact was made, the batons came out. Blood flew into the air and coated their Plexiglas shields.

Coughing and nauseous, dizzy and barely able to stand, Liora swayed and tried to stay upright. She searched for Reza, but the crowd's fearful surging had separated them. Someone jostled her and knocked her into the line of *Basij*. The man she'd yelled at clutched his assault rifle in his fists. He raised the weapon and brought it down across her head and shoulder.

The impact drove Liora to her knees. Pain cascaded through her skull so badly that even her teeth hurt. Instinctively, she reached for the man ahead of her, caught his jacket, and started trying to pull herself back to her feet.

Wild with fear, the man turned and tried to push her

away. A baton smashed into his face and turned it to bloody mush. Broken teeth rained down on Liora, and she screamed. Blindly, the man staggered into the *Basij*, who thrust the barrel of his assault rifle into the protestor's stomach and squeezed the trigger.

The weapon's familiar staccato *booms* exploded and deafened Liora, but she heard the sudden mirroring of the sound all around her as the protest turned into a massacre. She shoved the dead man from her. His blood covered her clothing and her hands. Unable to stop herself, she screamed and cried out for Reza. She thought she might have heard his voice crying out for her, but she wasn't certain.

'Do you still want to pay your respects to Neda Agha-Soltan, girl?' The *Basij* grinned and pointed his AK-47 at her. 'Maybe they'll put you in the grave next to her.'

His finger tightened on the trigger. Liora never saw the gunfire. Pain screamed through her mind, then a black pit opened up under her. Her body felt like it was on fire, and she remembered Neda Agha-Soltan's final words:

'I'm burning! I'm burning!'

6

Ruling Palace of the Supreme Leader
Tehran
The Islamic Republic of Iran
July 24, 2011

As he watched the bloody mess the Neda Agha-Soltan protest had turned into on his plasma television, Grand Ayatollah Mohammad Khamenei's flushed with rage.

At least there was satisfaction in watching his *Basij* kill and maim the protestors. They were obstacles to all of the Muslim world reuniting and become one faith strong enough to stand against the West and bringing the cleansing faith of the *jihad* against all nonbelievers.

'Supreme Leader.' Allameh Rajai stood at the door. A tall man with a black beard and round-lensed glasses, he carried himself with military erectness. Most of the scars on his face were hidden by his beard, but others showed where he'd been hit by shrapnel and knife blades. A bullet had caromed through his left jaw and required reconstructive surgery. He'd been twelve at the time, already fighting for his faith.

The Ayatollah had been so engrossed in the television program that he hadn't heard his aide enter. He muted the news broadcast and waved the man over. 'What is it, Allameh?'

'Your son Vali awaits your audience.'

Khamenei smiled and stroked his graying beard. Vali had been an unexpected prize, and he enjoyed the boy's company immensely. So curious and so dutiful. 'Please show him in.'

'I also have news of Colonel Davari.'

'Give me the report first. My son will wait a few minutes. Patience is a strength.'

'I have had contact with Colonel Davari. He is on the ground in the Gaza Strip and expects shortly to be meeting with Commander Meshal.'

'Good, good. Everything is proceeding according to plan.' The Ayatollah clasped his hands behind him and took a deep breath as he centered himself. The images on the television continued to play.

Despite the violence and stupidity displayed there, he didn't like the idea of people dying because they were not well enough informed. If they only knew everything he did, if he had Mohammad's Koran, the violence between the different Muslim factions would end. God willing, he would have the Book soon.

He turned back to Allameh. 'What about the infidel?'

Allameh picked up the reference smoothly. 'Klaus Von Volker will meet with Colonel Davari in Lebanon. His people have brought another shipment in to Commander Meshal's people.'

'Instruct Colonel Davari to enlist Von Volker's aid in

the apprehension of that Jewish dog, Lev Strauss. He has gone to ground in Jerusalem, and our agents attract too much attention from the Mossad. They will never find Strauss in time.'

'Of course.' Allameh bowed.

'Send in my son. His smile is given to me by God, and he will brighten my day.'

A few minutes later, young Vali stood just inside the room. Seven years old, he stood straight and tall, and his father proudly took note of the warrior already blossoming in his son. His hair was thick and black, his eyes deep brown pools in his handsome face.

The Ayatollah motioned. 'Come to your father, boy. I would tell you a story.'

'Of course, Father.' Obediently, the boy walked to the Ayatollah's side. 'I have heard there were protests today.'

'It is nothing. My people are taking care of it even as we visit.' The Ayatollah smiled at his young son.

'I wish I were old enough to fight our enemies.'

'One day, my son, you will be. Until then, you will be your father's joy, and I will thank God for every day we have.'

'Yes, Father.'

'Join me in the garden.' The Ayatollah dropped a hand to the boy's shoulder and guided him into the private garden that abutted the rooms.

The rectangular garden contained an abundance of

flowers, shrubs, and trees. It was surrounded by a high wall, and closed-circuit television as well as human guards watched over every inch.

The Ayatollah loved the garden because it reminded him of the old stories in the Koran. The modern world, especially all Western things, were kept at bay. He sat at the edge of a fountain built on an artesian well. The flowing water burbled and sparkled on the leaves of the acacia shrubs that lined the fountain except in the sitting areas.

'I have told you the miraculous story of Mohammad before, my son.'

The child grinned. 'Many times, Father. But it is all right. I never tire of hearing you tell it.'

Leaning forward, the Ayatollah ruffled the boy's hair. 'It is one of my favorite stories, too. My father told it to me all my life. I wish that he had lived to tell it to you.'

'When we get to heaven, he will tell it to me then.'

The Ayatollah smiled. 'Yes, that will be so. However, you are in for a treat today, for I am going to tell you a part of the story I have never told you before.'

The child's eyes shone in expectation.

One of the Ayatollah's eldest wives – not the boy's mother – brought out a plate of fruits, honey, and bread, and a carafe of fresh water. She placed the plate between them without a word, then left.

The Ayatollah waved to the plate, and the boy chose a date and popped it into his mouth.

'And so it came to pass that God laid a heavy burden

on the soul of Mohammad.' The Ayatollah gave himself over to the story, picturing the events in his mind. 'During the night at Mount Hira, the angel Gabriel visited Mohammad, who was an old man living in Medina at this time.'

'Older even than you, Father?'

The Ayatollah chuckled. 'Yes, older than me, but not for much longer, I'm afraid. I'm swiftly catching up.' He paused. 'So Gabriel talked to Mohammad and told him it was God's command that he acknowledge God by telling everyone to read in the name of the Lord and Cherisher. He was to tell them that God created Man from a blood clot, that God was bountiful, and that God taught Man the use of a pen that he might teach Man other things that were not known. When these things were written down, they became the Koran.'

The boy plucked another date from the serving tray. 'That was only the first time Gabriel visited Mohammad.'

'That's correct, my son. After Mohammad set about the work God had tasked him to do, many obstacles were placed in his path.'

'Like the obstacles you have in your path, Father.'

'Yes. Exactly. I do not view my obstacles as tests of faith. I am strong in my faith. These obstacles only make my faith stronger. I am better for them.'

'And Gabriel visited Mohammad again.'

'Indeed, he did. This time Mohammad was near the Ka'ba in Mecca.' The Ayatollah listened to the birds chirping in the trees and the water burbling. The sun felt good on his skin. And he enjoyed his son's company. 'Gabriel returned and guided Mohammad through the Isra and Mi'raj.'

'On the winged horse, Buraq, who was named so because he is fast as lightning.' The boy's eyes shone brightly as newly minted coins.

'That's right. On Buraq, who was tall and white, bigger than a donkey but smaller than a mule. Off they flew into the Long Night.'

The boy stared into the fountain, and the Ayatollah knew Vali was imagining what that flight must have been like. The Ayatollah had done the same thing when his father had told him the story.

'The journey was only just begun. Gabriel took Mohammad to the "farthest" mosque.'

'To Al-Aqsa Mosque, right, Father?'

The location and the name of the mosque wasn't definitely listed in the Koran. The Ayatollah nodded. 'It was Temple Mount.' It could be no other. 'That is where God made the first man, though it was from blood, not dust as the Jews and the Christians tell their stories.'

'They do not know, Father. They are very stupid people.'

'Yes, and those that will not take the wisdom of enlightenment when it is offered to them will perish.' *I will kill them myself if I must.* 'While Mohammad was at Al-Aqsa Mosque, he visited with the other Prophets of God. With Moses, Joseph, and Christ – who was not the son of God but merely a man, though he was a Prophet. He talked of God's Will and the messages that must be carried throughout the world.'

'Such as how many times a day a man must acknowledge and give thanks to God.'

'Exactly. He also saw God in all his glory, surrounded by angels. Mohammad saw paradise, and he saw hell.' The Ayatollah took a deep breath. 'Now I will tell you a story that you must not repeat to anyone until the day I tell you that you may. Do you understand?'

'Yes, Father. I understand.' The boy's eyes rounded in fear and curiosity, and the Ayatollah knew his own must have matched his son's when his own father had told him the rest of the story.

'Do you swear before God?'

'I swear.' Vali nodded solemnly.

'While he was on the journey of the Long Night, which only took one night in our world, Mohammad had time to write his own Koran. The true Koran. From God's own sacred lips.'

The boy gasped.

'For all of these years, the Muslim faith has been split over what is Mohammad's teaching and what is not. But that Book, writ in Mohammad's own hand, tells the one truth.' The Ayatollah paused. 'Even better, Mohammad was given a Scroll that foretold the future of our faith, of the plans God has for us in this world before we go into the next.'

'The future, Father?'

'Everything, my son. God gave Mohammad all he would need to lead this world to its salvation. Unfortunately, on his way back to this world, Mohammad – overcome by all that he had seen and God's beauty – dropped his Koran and the precious Scroll.'

'How could he do such a thing?'

'Despite God's mission for him, Mohammad was only flesh and blood. He was stronger than men but weak in that moment, as men sometimes are.'

'Where did he drop his Koran and the Scroll?'

The Ayatollah took a breath and tried to decide how much to tell the boy. He knew his family was sequestered away from the rest of the world, that nothing he told them would make it outside the palace walls, but the knowledge was a burden. Finally, he made his decision.

'At first, my son, the few who knew of the loss – and even Mohammad himself – believed he had lost his Koran and the Scroll in the other worlds. If that had been so, we could never have gotten them back. However, as time has gone on, this has proven not to be the case. The Book and the Koran are here, in this world.' The Ayatollah ran a hand through his son's black hair. 'In fact, I nearly have them within my possession.'

'That is so wonderful.' The boy smiled.

The Ayatollah's heart softened at the sight of his son's excitement. 'When I get the Book and the Scroll, Vali, I will place them in your hands and let you know the truth.'

All his agents had to do was find the man who had

the book that revealed the whereabouts of Mohammad's Koran and the Scroll. They would. Of that, the Ayatollah was confident. They almost had him now.

The infidel Klaus Von Volker knew no master except profit, and the Ayatollah had taken advantage of that. The man's greed and ambition shackled him more completely than any chain.

Then the resulting *jihad* would unleash a rain of holy fire that would cleanse the world. The early Muslims had spread God's word with their swords. The Ayatollah had new weapons at his disposal, a nuclear arsenal that was being planned and built at that very moment.

And in time, by my hand shall the unbelievers perish, he thought as he gazed fondly at his son.

7

Deir al-Balah
Gaza Strip
Palestinian Territories
July 24, 2011

'Mr. Youssef.'

Colonel Imad Davari of the Guardians of the Islamic Revolution of Iran sat at a small table at an open-air café. Darkness filled the city just beyond its lights.

He felt naked without a sidearm, but getting one into the country with false papers was almost impossible and certainly lethal if he got caught. Thank God he was also trained to be deadly with only his hands. And he was a big, burly man used to fighting.

The speaker was a slim man with dark, intense features. He wore a thin cotton shirt and gray cotton pants. The only hidden weapon he could possibly have was a knife.

'I am Youssef.' Davari sat calmly at the table and sipped his coffee.

The man came forward. 'I am Lutfi. I was sent to get you.'

Davari pointed to the chair across from him. 'Sit. Have a cup of coffee.' He motioned to the waitress.

With obvious reluctance, Lutfi obeyed. 'I was told not to delay.'

'You need to relax.' Davari stared at the man. 'If not, you'll give us away to the two men following me.'

The man started to look around, then caught himself. 'You were followed?'

'They were at the airport waiting for me.' Even after twenty years of military experience, nine of those on the Quds Force, the extraterritorial operations arm of the Revolutionary Guard, sitting there with the men watching him had been hard for Davari. He preferred to do the watching, and he didn't like having to trust outsiders. He worked with a team of men he'd trained, whom he knew like the back of his hand. None of them were with him now. The Ayatollah had entrusted him alone with this vital mission.

Lutfi shook his head. 'This meeting is over.'

'If you leave so quickly, those men will follow you. Do you think there are only two of them?'

Frustration tightened the man's mouth. 'You should have warned me.'

Davari laughed. 'Your boss is the one that wanted no radio contact on the ground.'

'You could have waved me off.'

'Do you seriously think they wouldn't have noticed that?'

The man cursed.

'If I had warned you off, I would be facing them alone.' Davari sipped his coffee. 'I don't think they would have let me sit here much longer without taking me into custody.'

'Or killing you if they are Israeli.'

Davari shrugged. That, of course, was a possibility. He was confident that the men didn't know him or his work personally. Somehow they had intercepted Commander Meshal's communications.

'What are we going to do?' Lutfi didn't look happy.

'Now that you are here, and I have made contact, we're going to escape.' Davari finished his coffee. 'You have a car?'

'Of course. But I have no weapons.'

'That's fine. I'm sure they're carrying enough for all of us.' Davari stood. 'Let's get your car.'

'Do not glance around. If you alert those men that we are onto them, I will slit your throat myself.' Davari walked slightly behind and to Lutfi's right as they passed a half dozen closed shops.

'I do not care for this.'

'If you talk about anything other than the weather or sports, I will kill you.'

Tucking his head into his shoulders, Lutfi kept walking, choosing not to talk at all.

That suited Davari. The streetlights behind the two men trailing them allowed him to track them by their shadows, but it was good to be able to hear their movements as well. The men were good, probably Israeli, judging by how patient they were, but they'd grown confident and didn't try hard to mask their presence. They also didn't pull in the second unit, and Davari was certain there was a second unit. If the men had been Hamas, they would have seized him an hour ago and taken him to a torture chamber to find out why he was in the Gaza Strip.

If they were Israeli, they would be operating on foreign soil, as he was. This was in his favor, because they wouldn't want to draw much attention to themselves. On the other hand, they would be very good at unarmed combat, as the Mossad seemed to live and breathe *krav maga*. Davari smiled in anticipation of the coming confrontation.

'Where is your car?'

Lutfi nodded at the end of the alley. 'Around the corner.'

'When I step away from you, run for the car and bring it back here.'

'If I do not, you will kill me?'

'Most assuredly.'

'I do not like you very much.'

Davari smiled at that. 'Thankfully, you do not have to like me.' He heard the two men behind him exchange a brief conversation, then their steps quickened. Obviously, they felt they had waited long enough, and the alley was ending soon.

Davari immediately turned and ran at them.

They were good, he had to give them that. They separated at once to give each other room to maneuver.

Davari went for the bigger one first because closing with him would give the smaller man less room to position himself, and the bigger man would provide a better shield. The man set himself, obviously expecting Davari to pull up short. The colonel continued his headlong pace and slammed into the man's chest, giving his opponent no time to decide whether to shoot him with the pistol he suddenly held.

Using his weight and speed, Davari powered the man backwards till he was almost running, then slipped and started to fall. Instinctively, the man reached forward to grab him. Davari planted his own feet, caught the man's shirt in one burly fist, and snared his opponent's gun wrist with the other.

Yanking backwards, Davari spun the man around so his back faced his partner, then kicked him in the crotch. The man groaned in pain and threw up a little. Still, he clung stubbornly to his weapon as the second man sprinted toward him, leading with a silenced pistol.

Maintaining his grip on the man's shirt, Davari swung his elbow into the man's throat, then head-butted him in the face. His opponent's nose broke, and blood gushed. Nearly out on his feet and sagging heavily, the man's hold on the pistol loosened.

With a quick twist, Davari slid the pistol free and popped it into his hand. He raised the pistol and fired by instinct.

Three shots struck the approaching agent in the chest and threw him off stride. Davari fired two more rounds into the man's left leg as he came down on that foot and he fell, sprawling into the alley. The colonel placed the pistol silencer under the chin of the man he was holding and pulled the trigger twice, blowing the top of his head off.

Shoving the dead man from him, Davari strode toward the second agent. The man was trying to roll over onto his back and get a shot off. He managed to fire two rounds, but both missed, ricocheting off the alley wall.

Davari shot two rounds into the man's face and kicked the pistol away. Working quickly, he knelt and went through the men's pockets, taking their IDs, cash, and personal effects, and dropping it all into his jacket pockets. He found a spare magazine on the big man and quickly changed out the one in his captured weapon. He kept the half-empty magazine, then picked up the other pistol and the spare magazine for it and switched that one to full capacity as well.

He turned and headed for the end of the alley, thinking Lutfi had bolted and run and that he would kill the man if he ever saw him again. Then an ancient Russian sedan rounded the corner and headed toward him.

Davari stepped out of the way and fisted the pistols in his jacket pockets.

The car's brakes squealed as the vehicle shuddered to a stop. Lufti stared through the bug-spattered windshield as Davari opened the passenger seat and got inside.

'They're dead?'

‘Yes. Go.’ Davari relaxed in the seat as Lutfi shifted into gear and drove over the dead men in the alley.

Minutes later, Davari followed Lutfi into a pottery warehouse. They walked in silence to the back of the building, aided only by a flashlight Lutfi carried. Davari didn’t mind the darkness. He was armed, and he’d just emerged victorious from a confrontation. His blood sang.

At the back of the warehouse, Lutfi stood against the back wall, then stamped his foot in a practiced rhythm. ‘If I didn’t do that, you would be dead.’

A moment later, a section of the floor lifted, then slid noisily across the floor. Lutfi descended a narrow set of stairs into a small room. Three men armed with AK-47s stood at the bottom.

They all wore olive drab pants, khaki shirts, and red berets. One was in his early forties, sallow-faced, with acne scars and a salt-and-pepper hair and beard. Commander Ahmad Meshal calmly smoked a cigarette and studied his guest.

‘Colonel Davari?’

‘I am.’

Meshal stood his ground. ‘Commander Meshal.’ His eyes narrowed. ‘You have blood on your face and on your shirt.’

‘There was trouble.’

‘What kind of trouble?’

‘I was picked up at the airport by two men. They moved and acted like Mossad agents.’

Meshal glanced at Lutfi.

'They did not follow me.' Fear etched Lutfi's face. 'They were there when I arrived.'

'As I said, they picked me up at the airport.'

Davari glanced around. There did not appear to be any other exits. A wire shelf on the wall to his left held a small selection of food. Next to it, a curtain covered the far half of the wall. A laptop computer and other equipment sat on a card table in the corner. A stack of magazines sat on the floor.

'May I borrow your table?' He nodded at the card table.

'Of course.'

On the table, Davari spread out the IDs and papers he'd collected from the men he'd killed. 'These are probably fake, but we have experts who can tell who did the work. If I may use your computer.'

'Please do.'

Davari used the scanner to copy the IDs and papers onto the laptop, then used an encryption sequence from a Web site the Quds Force had set up for him. Then he uploaded the images to another Web site accessed by the Quds intelligence division. He probably already knew as much as they would find out, but confirming his suspicions would be good.

He turned to Meshal. 'I would guess that the two men I killed are here looking for the ones you have.'

'Probably.'

'When the Mossad finds those two agents dead,

they'll send more. Unless we give the two men back to them. Where are they?'

'In the next room.' Meshal walked over to the far wall and pushed the curtain back to reveal a glass window.

Inside the room, two men knelt in apparent agony. Both men wore plastic zip-ties that cuffed their hands behind their backs and to the chains that bound their feet together. Blindfolds covered their eyes and ears. One had wet himself, the dark stain showing on his beige pants. Their arms and legs showed evidence of burning, cutting, and assault with blunt instruments.

'These are two of the guards that were with Lev Strauss?'

Meshal nodded.

'What were they? Bodyguards?'

'Yes. For a time Strauss was here, in the Strip. We couldn't get to him, but we got to two of his men.'

'What was he doing here?'

'He spent most of his time at the library.'

'Doing what?'

'Reading old books.'

Impatient, Davari turned his attention back to the men. The Supreme Leader had told him about the Book he sought, and what he was convinced it was, but Lev Strauss was proving to be a unique quarry.

And now he had run back to Jerusalem, where he would be even harder to reach.

Davari didn't even consider interrogating the prisoners. From what they'd been put through, he knew they held no secrets. Otherwise, they would have already bartered them to keep the pain at bay.

Davari turned to the computer and sent an e-mail to Klaus Von Volker, requesting a meeting in two days. 'Kill them. Cut off their heads and hands and mail them back to their families.'

'It will be done.'.

8

Nangpa La Mountain Pass
Himalaya Mountains
People's Republic of China
July 26, 2011

At twenty-thousand plus feet, the world was bitterly cold and so bright that it hurt Lourds's eyes, even through his protective filtering lenses. He slapped his gloved hands together to get some feeling as he stared up at the mountain.

Only a few miles to the east, the 8,000-meter Cho Oyu, the sixth highest mountain in the world, stretched for the heavens. Clad in white snow, it looked beautiful.

The native Tibetans and Sherpas of Khumbu often made their way through these mountains regularly to trade. Less than a mile ahead of Lourds and his group, a few of the hardy mountain folk were coming toward them.

'Well, I guess we'll soon have a look at the neighbors.' Lourds smiled under his ski mask. Despite the protective layers, his face still felt frozen.

'We've traveled a long way, Thomas. Are you sure about this?' Professor Hu hunched over, resting his hands on his knees for additional support as he gasped for air.

'I'm as sure as I can be. You saw the map.' Lourds waved at the mountains. 'Cho Oyu translates literally into Turquoise Goddess, and there was a drawing of a suspiciously blue-green mountain on it.' He turned slightly. 'And there's Mount Everest, called Zhumulangma Feng, or "Holy Mother" by Chinese historians. The Tibetan name for it is Chomolungma, which means Saint Mother.' He felt the excitement of the expected discovery thrum through him again, always thrill him each time it happened. 'I think that's close enough to the drawing of the woman on the mountain to fit our map, don't you?'

'You know, while we were back at Jiahu, I felt mostly certain that you knew what you were talking about.'

'Of course I do.'

Hu shot Lourds an indignant grimace. 'So you say. Thomas, if I die up here, I am ordering you to drag my body after you and make sure I get partial credit for whatever you find.'

'What if it turns out there's nothing to find?'

'Drop my body into the first crevice you come across. I'll never be able to show my face at the university again.'

'Nonsense. Everybody has a setback once in a while.'

'Says the man who found Atlantis.'

Lourds laughed.

'You know, once you've uncovered a mythical land, you end up with a lot of street cred, my friend.' Hu took a water bottle from his pack and drank. 'The only reason

I agreed to come along is because you have the devil's own luck at finding things that have been misplaced for thousands of years.'

A slight chill that came from more than the frozen landscape around him shivered through Lourds. All he had to do was think back to Elliott Webster and what the man – or whatever he was – had almost accomplished in the Middle East to realize how his 'good fortune' cut both ways. Maybe Lourds had found a lot of things, but he'd also risked his life on a lot of those occasions to muddle through.

A lot of people had died, both during his trip to find Atlantis, and his more recent adventure in the Middle East.

'And at Jiahu, you managed to find a BBC film crew that would follow you up to this godforsaken piece of real estate. Want to tell me how that happened?'

Lourds shook his head. 'I got a call from Leslie Crane yesterday morning saying her company was willing to bankroll the expedition for an exclusive on the find.' Leslie Crane was a friend and a sometime lover. She'd managed to survive the Atlantis chase with him and had produced a nice documentary on the search. 'We needed transport and supplies, and if we'd had to beg it from Peking or Harvard, we'd still be trying to explain what we'd found to them.'

'I'd like you to take us through the discovery one more time, Professor Lourds.'

Lourds looked askance at the young man heading up the BBC crew. 'Ronald?'

'It's Rory, sir, actually.' He was a tall, well-built young man with carrot-colored hair and a freckled face.

'Of course.' Lourds stood with his back to a rocky outcrop where the group sheltered from the howling winds during lunch.

No one really felt like eating, but they did like sitting down instead of slogging through the snow.

Gloria Chen had gotten Professor Hu to allow her to come along. Lourds didn't know why she'd bothered. Since they'd taken up the expedition, she'd kept her distance, although she seemed to watch him constantly. She was doing that now, and the effect was somewhat unnerving.

'Rory, I've already told this story for the camera before.'

'I know, but my producer likes to have separate shots of some of the same material in different areas. When they edit the piece, I don't know which one they will choose. So I have to shoot a lot and wait to see how the story turns out.'

Reaching into his backpack, Lourds took out a rolled-up twelve-by-fifteen picture of the inside of the small tortoiseshell he'd found in the Jiahu grave. He tapped it with a forefinger. 'This is Jiahu. Professor Hu and I placed this location easily because of the proximity of the Yellow River.'

'How do you know that's the Yellow River if there's

no real language attached to the people who drew that map?' Rory asked.

'We don't know for certain. That's why this is what's called an educated guess. Logic dictates that if you were going to draw a map and leave it for someone to find, you would use local landmarks as a reference.'

'But the tortoiseshell wasn't left for someone to find.'

Lourds grinned. 'Really? Someone found it.'

The group huddled around the rock laughed at the young reporter's embarrassment.

'Honestly, Rory, I don't know how that tortoiseshell ended up in the grave if it was meant to be left behind. Or why it was encased in pottery, though it's possible the covering was there to protect it. Or maybe to disguise the shell from enemies. From that point, the shell might have been deposited in the grave by mistake. Thankfully, it was there for me, or I'd still be swilling the local brew in Jiahu.' Lourds looked around thoughtfully. 'Given the local weather conditions, maybe that wouldn't be such a bad thing.'

Even the reporter laughed at that.

'After we figured out the tortoiseshell was a map, Professor Hu and I had to figure out what it was a map of. As you can see up here' – Lourds tapped the jagged lines near the top of the tortoiseshell – 'these look like mountains. This is a tortoise.' He indicated the drawing of a circle with six extremities. 'Four legs, a head, and a tail. Although that was a source of debate for a time.

And this is a woman. You can tell that because she's – rather well endowed.'

The breasts were definitely enhanced on the stick figure.

'Assuming these were mountains, which – after a very spirited discussion – is what Professor Hu and I did, we had to figure out what mountains they were.' Lourds waved at their surroundings. 'Lots of mountains in China.' He paused. 'But not many that featured a tortoise and a woman.' He quickly explained about the origins of the mountain names.

'Now that we've found the mountains, what are we looking for?' Rory asked.

Lourds pointed to a small symbol on the map. 'This. A structure located somewhere off this pass.'

'What is it?'

'I have no idea. That's just part of the adventure.'

Less than an hour later, the Sherpas reached them. The group was friendly and used to outsiders coming to the mountains to climb. Most of them spoke rudimentary English.

Lourds explained the map to Gelu, the oldest member of the group. He was a short, stocky man with weathered, dark features, iron gray hair, and a scar along his left cheek. He liked to laugh and joke a lot, and was a consummate storyteller. For a time, in the lee of the stone and out of the wind, they swapped tales because business was something to be approached slowly.

He studied Lourds's map for a moment. 'I know this place. Very old place.'

'How old?' Excitement filled Lourds.

Gelu shook his gray head. 'Long, long time ago. This place has seen many people live and die. It is home to Tibetan monks who renounce the world.'

'Monks that renounce the world?' One of the BBC guys, Thompson, looked totally lost. 'For generations? Dude, monks don't reproduce. How are they going to keep people in some nearly forgotten temple? They'd die out from attrition.'

Lourds chuckled, and Gelu barked laughter. 'Many monks renounce world. Some say to study better. Others say so they not have to work.' He shrugged. 'Sometimes we bring them food. Monks not grow much up here.'

'I'd say not.' Lourds glanced at the white landscape.

'Snow not fill belly.'

'What's the name of the place?'

Gelu shook his head. 'Monk's temple. That's all I know. If you like, we can guide. Keep you safe during journey. We know way.'

Lourds knew from personal experience that the Sherpas didn't make much from their guide work. He also knew the group would be safer in the Sherpas' hands this far up in the mountains.

'If you have the time, Gelu, I would like that.' Lourds would pay them himself.

Gelu nodded and smiled. 'Sure, sure. Make time. Keep you safe. Maybe take more food to monks?'

'We're going to resupply only a little farther on. We can get food for them then.'

Gelu clapped Lourds on the shoulder. 'The gods will surely favor you.'

9

Fabios Restaurant
Innere Stadt (Inner City)
Vienna, Austria
July 26, 2011

Colonel Davari disliked the restaurant as soon as he laid eyes on it. From a tactical point of view, it was too open. Only glass walls separated diners from passersby walking along Wien Street. A coolheaded sniper could take out nearly half a dozen people before they knew they were being gunned down.

He also disliked the restaurant because it was so ostentatious. The black interior, the elegantly clothed servers, and the expensive ambiance all screamed decadent Western civilization.

Today he dressed the part of a European, in a dark suit without the *keffiyeh,* his hair and beard freshly cut at the hotel barber's, and swathed in cologne.

A maître d' met him at the door. 'May I help you, sir?'

'Yes, thank you.' Davari spoke German with an accent, as well as Romanian, and a handful of other languages. 'I am looking for Herr Von Volker. I am to be his guest.'

The young maître d' checked an electronic list at his

podium. 'Yes, sir, Herr Von Volker is dining with us tonight, and is already here. If you'll follow me, please.'

Davari followed the maître d' across the floor, ending up where he least wanted to be: at one of the tables in front of one of those windows.

'Herr Von Volker, your guest has arrived.'

The Austrian held a mobile to his face and listened, turning his head just enough to make eye contact with Davari. Von Volker was a big man with sandy blond hair going gray at the temples. His eyes were light blue and moved constantly.

Feeling even more irritated at the man for so casually dismissing him, Davari sat and waited. A server arrived to take his drink order: a water, and he had to select from a dozen different kinds. By the time the glass showed up at the table with a lemon wedge stuck to the rim, Von Volker was pocketing the mobile.

'I do apologize, Colonel.' Von Volker sipped his glass of champagne. 'Sometimes business waits for no man.'

'I understand. I appreciate your seeing me on such short notice.' With effort, Davari thought he managed to sound sincere.

'It's my pleasure. The food here is excellent. If you'd like, I'd be happy to order for you.'

'If you insist.' Davari wasn't there for the meal, but a soldier learned to eat whatever he could whenever possible.

The server returned, and Von Volker spoke quickly in German before turning back to his guest.

'I understand there was a problem during your last stop.' Von Volker's clear blue eyes held Davari's.

'Evidently our security has not been as tight as we had wished.'

'I'll bet that made the old man angry.'

Rage coursed through Davari, and he barely restrained himself. The Ayatollah wasn't a figure to be mocked. 'When you speak of that man, speak with respect.'

Von Volker shrugged. 'It's just a figure of speech. I intended no harm.'

Davari didn't believe the Austrian. Von Volker thought he was clever and untouchable, but he was no fool. While he'd walked to the table, the Quds colonel had identified five bodyguards sitting at different tables around them, and three more were questionable.

But it was Von Volker's ego that would get him into trouble. He sat in front of the window, requiring only one skilled sniper to assassinate him, in spite of his protection.

A small, covered plate arrived at the table. The server removed the lid to reveal hot sausages, the steam from them floating into the air.

Von Volker pointed to the plate with his fork. 'I know you can't eat them because of your faith, but I do love them.'

'Please. Enjoy yourself.' The meal just underscored the separation between them.

The Austrian pierced a sausage and put it on his plate, cutting it into bite-sized pieces. He showed no hesitation about eating in front of a stranger. Of course, as one of the leaders of the Austrian People's Party, Von Volker probably ate with strangers more often than he ate at home. In addition to the day-to-day business of politics, there were also the necessary meetings with 'invisible' constituents.

And then there was the illegal business Von Volker conducted. Companies hidden within companies running hired mercenaries that supplied the Islamic Republic of Iran with nuclear material and weapons of late. Publicly, Von Volker chastised the Ayatollah's cabinet for their repressive regime, while at the same time lobbying for Iran to have access to nuclear technology for power and peaceful pursuits.

No one in the Western world believed Iran would stop there. Davari knew they wouldn't. He'd already seen many of the plans.

The server returned and placed a green salad in front of the colonel. He made no move to touch it.

'Please. Eat.' Von Volker pointed at the salad with his fork.

'I ate before my arrival.' Davari suspected the man might have had something placed on the salad that would go against the Islamic faith. It was childish, but according to his files, the man was not above that. 'Thank you.'

With a shrug, Von Volker returned to his meal. 'As you wish. We are not enemies, you know.' He waved his fork to indicate both of them. 'We – you and I – hate the Jews. Our people, though some of mine are misguided and forgetful these days, hate the Jews. We share this, and this common enemy makes us friends.'

Davari didn't share that point of view, but he knew the Ayatollah trusted the anti-Semitic feeling in Austria. There were many problems in the Middle East, and not everyone favored Israel or held the Jews blameless in the conflict. The Ayatollah pumped money into the People's Party, and to Von Volker in particular. In return, the Austrian and his partners acquired fissionable nuclear materials and technology to give to Iran.

The server returned, carrying a large plate filled with steak, shrimp, and sautéed vegetables. He placed it before Von Volker with a flourish, then refilled his wine glass. Taking a piece of silverware in each hand, the Austrian surveyed his gastronomical battlefield with the practiced eye of an invading general.

'Your master told me there was something you required my help with, Colonel. I suppose this has something to do with the fiasco in the Gaza.'

Davari throttled his anger and kept his voice calm. 'Yes.'

'As I understand it, your friend on the ground there was looking for someone.'

'A university professor named Lev Strauss.' Davari took a snapshot of Strauss from his pocket and slid it facedown across the tabletop.

Von Volker lifted the picture and took a quick glance. Then he left the picture lying facedown. 'He isn't known to me.'

'There is no reason he should be. The professor has

had an interesting history.' Davari recited Strauss's background from memory. 'He was recruited by the Mossad while he was at Harvard in the United States. He continued working missions for them while he was at Oxford, then a plane he was on was booby-trapped over thirteen years ago. It blew up and went down in the Dead Sea region. Strauss lost his left leg below the knee in the crash.'

'No more missions.'

'He remains on active duty, but these days he spends his time in dusty libraries as a true scholar.'

Von Volker lifted his eyebrows and smiled. 'Except – something changed.'

'Yes.'

'What?'

'At this point, that information is restricted. On a need-to-know basis.' Davari knew that the Westerners liked their little spy games. The truth was that the Ayatollah did not want anyone told the nature of the prize they sought.

The Austrian sliced off a chunk of bloody meat. 'I would be better able to help if I knew what was going on.' He popped the piece into his mouth.

'Right now, we need Strauss found. That is all you need to concern yourself with at the moment.'

'He's not in the Gaza anymore?'

'No.'

'Where did he run?'

'According to the two guards my friend spoke with,

the professor has returned to Jerusalem.'

'You have people there.'

'We *had* people.' Davari had read the reports on the executions of those Quds agents only hours ago. 'They tried to capture the professor.'

'And got themselves killed?'

'Yes.'

Von Volker smiled. 'So the prey has already been spooked in the Gaza and in his homeland.'

'He is still there.'

'Sitting quietly in some sequestered hideaway while the Mossad watch over him, waiting for the rats to come to the cheese?' Von Volker shook his head. 'I don't think so.'

Davari remained silent.

'You're not painting a very appetizing picture, my friend.'

The colonel had run out of patience. 'I'm not painting anything. I'm offering you a job to perform, one my master believes you are in a position to accomplish. If you don't want to risk it, simply say so, and I will go to the next man on my list.'

Von Volker chuckled. He pointed his fork at Davari. '*You're* the next man on your list, aren't you?'

Davari glared at the man, but stayed silent.

'Yes, you are. You can't fool me.' The Austrian blotted his lips on his napkin. 'Well, let me tell you, my friend, you're not good enough to get into Jerusalem and get back out again. All you'll end up doing is getting yourself killed. Then your master is going to have to go to the next man on *his* list. Work with me, and we can both get what we want.'

Davari refrained from commenting with a supreme effort. What the Austrian said was true, and it angered him that the man knew.

'I can get to Lev Strauss.' Von Volker returned his attentions to his plate.

'Why are you so sure?'

'Because, just as you have a secret, so do I.' Von Volker smiled confidently. 'I will hand the professor over to you in a matter of days. And then we will talk about my bonus.'

10

Scholar's Rock Temple
Himalaya Mountains
People's Republic of China
July 26, 2011

'Look! There it is!' Gloria Chen walked slightly behind Lourds as he trudged through the snow, letting him do most of the work breaking through the frozen crust. The excitement in her voice drew his attention at once.

He'd been woolgathering, as he usually did when faced with physical drudgery and uninspiring surroundings, and a long walk up a mountain with more mountains around combined both those things.

The previous night, Gelu had persuaded them to rest and recuperate. The Sherpa guide had a good eye for people, and he'd told Lourds that several of the climbers, including Professor Hu, were all but worn-out. Gelu had promised they would comfortably reach their goal by the next evening, even after sleeping in.

Despite his anticipation and the urging of the BBC crew to keep moving, Lourds had agreed. They'd pitched camp there in the lee of the rocks, and the Sherpas had prepared the evening meal over a low fire. It wasn't as relaxing as a ski resort, but it had been surprisingly comforting to be cared for. Lourds had slept like a baby in his tent.

The stone building sheltered under an overhang of rock shelf, and Lourds wasn't surprised that no one had really known about the temple. At first he didn't know what had caused Gloria to become so enthusiastic, then a gust of wind blew a cloud of snow over the rock shelf. The setting sun caught the flying ice particles, and their prismatic qualities cast a field of rainbows over the temple.

'Rory?' Lourds raised his voice above the wind screaming through the canyon.

'Yeah, mate?'

'Tell me you're getting this with the camera.'

'You better believe it. If this works out, I think we're looking at our opening.'

Lourds's heart sped up as he watched the beautiful swirl with a huge grin.

'Wouldn't it be shorter to walk across the valley?' Lourds pointed his climbing staff at the circular depression between where they'd come up and the temple.

'Walk across not good.' Gelu shook his shaggy head. 'Much danger. Much frozen that.' He walked toward the depression, stood at the edge, and kicked away snowdrifts to reveal ice. He waved at the valley. 'All ice. Not good.'

'Come on, mate.' Rory pointed across the long walk

they had around the bowl. 'If we walk across, it's a lot shorter. Any ice up here is going to stay frozen.'

Gelu shook his head again. 'Much frozen. Not all frozen. Holes there. Deep. Sometimes fall through and no come back.'

'Ice is some of the most treacherous terrain up in these mountains.' Lourds adjusted his protective goggles. 'The snow blows, maybe melts a little on warmer days from the direct sunlight, and forms a thin crust over cracks and holes.'

'Yes.' Gelu nodded. 'Much deadly, you see.'

'With all the blowing snow shifting around, you might not see a crevasse until you went through it. You could fall a few hundred feet, and maybe your body would be found in a few hundred years.' Lourds turned to the reporter. 'Still feel like walking across now?'

Even with the cold turning Rory's face pale, his features turned even whiter. 'Nope. I can walk around just fine.'

Gelu assumed the lead once more, and they resumed their march.

'You said the monks don't get many visitors.' Lourds matched his stride to the Sherpa's.

'No. No many. Only men seeking to know what monks know come here.'

'What do the monks know?'

'I not know. I know Sherpa ways. I know trade. I know guide.' Gelu smiled. 'I know how to feed myself, not need others to feed me.'

'Have you ever gone to the monks to learn anything?'

'Father taught me all I need to know. Work hard. Live careful. Raise strong sons and obedient daughters. What more is there?'

'I suppose.' As he walked, though, Lourds couldn't help watching the gusting rainbows and wondering what lay inside the temple.

Professor Hu pulled at Lourds's elbow. 'You realize, of course, Thomas, that whatever made that temple special thousands of years ago could be long gone.'

'I do.'

'If it is, at least the BBC will have a lot of pretty footage of mountains and rainbows.'

'I reconcile myself with one thought.'

'What's that?'

'Even if a package is empty, many times you can learn a lot about what was there from the package itself.'

At Professor Hu's side, Gloria Chen shot Lourds an exasperated glance. 'Great thinking, but what if someone found a Big Mac wrapper? Do you really think that person could reconstruct how those two all-beef patties, special sauce, lettuce, cheese, pickles, onions on a sesame seed bun really went together?' She shook her head. 'I think we'd be better off if we found an artifact or two. So excuse me if I hope we find more than a wrapper up here.'

'Gloria!' Professor Hu studied her with a furrowed brow.

'I'm sorry, Professor Hu. I think I'm just tired.' Gloria

didn't look apologetic. She turned and headed back into the climbing party, Lourds watching her go with a puzzled expression on his face.

'Good evening.' Dressed in thick winter clothing, the young monk stood in the stone doorway and looked over the expedition with a beatific smile. 'This is the Temple of the Scholar's Rock. I am Ang. I bid you welcome.'

Gelu talked to the young man in Mandarin, explaining that the group was from Peking University and had come out all that way to see the temple.

Ang looked bemused as he turned to Lourds. 'Usually climbers find us by mistake on their way up the mountain. Or we sometimes discover them when they are lost or while we are walking. You are the first to come looking for the temple in a long time.'

'I hope our arrival and our curiosity won't be an imposition. We've brought food, enough to leave with you and your brothers when we leave, and we have our own tents.'

Ang smiled. 'Food is always welcome in the temple, and I'm certain we can find space for all of you. The temple is much bigger on the inside than it looks at first glance.' He moved to one side of the door and waved them in. 'Please. Enter. Our home is your home for as long as you wish.'

'When he said it was bigger on the inside than it looked, I thought he meant it was only a little bigger.' Rory stared in openmouthed wonder at the cavernous vault around them.

Lourds kept his own jaw in place with effort. The Scholar's Rock Temple was huge and ran back deep into the mountain. His explorer's instincts flared, and his hopes rose.

The walls looked natural in most places. The original builders had taken advantage of the existing cave system. Some of the other rooms contained scars from tools when they had been widened and deepened. Oil lanterns filled the rooms with a golden glow.

'I am Brother Shamar. Please sit.' A wizened old man waved at the small rugs adorning the smooth stone floor around him. He wore an orange saffron robe and sat cross-legged with an easy grace. Age had wrinkled his face so much that it looked like a raisin. Still, his dark eyes looked full of life and mischief.

Lourds and Hu introduced themselves. The audience was semiprivate. Rory and the BBC crew filmed from the doorway and used only the natural light coming from the oil lanterns hanging on the wall and the fireplace behind the old monk.

'Why have you come to our temple?' Shamar's excellent English had a British accent.

'Seeking knowledge.' Lourds sat cross-legged and felt the heat from the fireplace melting into his body. The cold that had leached into his bones seemed like it was finally leaving.

'You're not here to investigate our faith, Professor

Lourds. Your soul is too restless to travel quietly through this life.'

'No, we're not here about your faith. We came hoping to get information about this temple.'

'What do you wish to know?'

'First, let me give you some information.' Lourds brought out the picture of the tortoiseshell map and explained how he'd found it and how they'd located the temple.

'An impressive story.' Shamar seemed genuinely interested. 'I had no idea of the temple's history. It was already here when the first monks arrived. Our histories record no origin of this place.'

'It was like this?'

'Much as you see it now. Few changes have been made. Ours is a simple faith. We live within the world as it is and don't seek to change it to fit our desires. Monks come here to strip away the cares and concerns of the outside world so that we might become better teachers when we reenter that world. Our time here is spent in study and mastering our spirits.'

'Why is it called the Temple of the Scholar's Rock?'

'The temple was named so in honor of the many scholar's rocks found here.'

'Uh, Professor Lourds.'

Lourds peered over his shoulder at Rory.

'Maybe you could explain what a scholar's rock is. You know, for the audience back home?'

'Young man.' Shamar lifted his voice.

'Yes, sir?'

The monk smiled beatifically. 'Would you care to join us?'

'Uh, no. I'm good right here. Thanks.'

'If you would learn something, you must go to the feet of one who knows and talk, not bellow from the shadows.'

Rory scratched his head, then came forward reluctantly and sat cross-legged on one of the rugs.

Lourds answered the question. 'A scholar's rock is also known as a viewing stone. They've been around for a long time, but they were brought to prominence in the Song Dynasty. The Tang Dynasty defined the four main visual qualities of a scholar's stone: thinness, openness, perforations, and wrinkling. I'll give you the Cantonese words for those things later.'

'What do you do with a scholar's stone?'

Shamar laughed.

Lourds smiled. 'Well, you *appreciate* it.'

Rory's brow furrowed. 'Appreciate it? A rock? This isn't like a pet rock, is it? You aren't after having me on, are you?'

'No, not at all. Generally a scholar's rock is used for decoration in a garden. They have interesting shapes, holes, and perforations. The texture of the rocks is smooth. The smoother the better. The preferred method of getting them is simply finding them, but sometimes artisans *helped* nature along by cutting stones into interesting shapes and immersing them in running water or a lake so the sharp edges would wear away.'

Rory's brow furrowed. 'That would take years.'

'Of course it took years. But the texture was prized. A lot of scholar's stones come from lakes, such as from Taihu Lake, and they're used in gardens. Once the Chinese started using scholar's rocks, the Koreans picked the art form up in their country, as did the Japanese in their *suiseki* art.'

'The lesson, you see, is to learn to find and appreciate art in nature.' Shamar nodded in satisfaction. 'Now let me show you the cavern that gave this place its name.' With the easy grace of a child, he stood and walked toward one of the doors.

Ang took down one of the oil lanterns and fell into step with him.

Caught off guard, Lourds quickly scrambled to his feet, gave Hu a hand, and followed.

11

Scholar's Rock Temple
Himalaya Mountains
People's Republic of China
July 26, 2011

From the interview chamber, Lourds followed Shamar and Ang down a twisting passageway into the mountain. Lourds took a mini-Maglite from his backpack to add to the glow given of Ang's lantern. As the cold from the mountain surrounded him, he regretted leaving his coat behind. He'd assumed that since the monks hadn't bundled up, where they were going wouldn't be cold.

Hu slapped at his upper arms. 'Nothing like a brisk walk, eh?' His breath puffed out in small white clouds. 'Especially after the long trek up a mountainside.'

'I could have done with some more heat. And I honestly thought we were going to bed soon.' Lourds yawned and shined his light around. There were no tool marks on the wall, which meant the passageway was natural. 'I have to admit, I'm looking forward to sleeping in a warm bed.'

'So am I.'

They continued down for several more minutes

before the passageway widened into another cavern. When Lourds entered the new room, he saw dozens of scholar's rocks standing before him. They looked like a massive chess game set out to be played.

Stunned, he wandered among them, drawn by the enigma they presented. Nearly all of them were taller than he was and weighed several hundred pounds. He ran his fingers along many, discovering the same smooth texture.

Amazed, he turned back to Shamar, careful to keep the bright light out of the old monk's eyes. 'How many are there?'

'One hundred sixteen.' Shemar stood with his arms in the sleeves of his robe.

'Why are they here?'

'No one knows. This is one of the things the monks that arrive here for training are told to contemplate. We are still awaiting an answer.'

Overwhelmed, Lourds walked through the forest of stone figures. Many looked like people, the rudimentary shapes showing men, women, and children. He touched oval faces that held only the hint of features, eyes, nose, and mouth. Ears were conspicuously absent. The majority of the outer ring of statues depicted common people.

'This is a farmer. See his hoe?' Lourds traced the image of the hoe in bas-relief along the rock.

'All I see is a rock.' Rory stood on the other side of the large stone.

'That is because you choose to see with only your

eyes.' Shamar's voice echoed over the chamber, and Lourds knew the old man had chosen his spot because the acoustics in the cavern allowed him to be heard like that. Upon further inspection, Lourds saw the small platform cut from the stone floor. The area had been clearly marked.

'Who chose that spot?' Lourds pointed his flashlight beam over the low rise.

'The speaker's post was already inscribed when we got here.'

'Look! I found a pig!' Over to the left, Thompson pointed excitedly.

The lump of rock was definitely piggish in shape, with a snout and huge hindquarters.

'Here's a tortoise!' Gloria Chen strode through the figures and laid her hand on a low figure that was unmistakably that.

Lourds made his way to her, thinking that perhaps the tortoise would offer a clue as the other one had in Jiahu. The scholar's rock did indeed look like a tortoise, but instead of having a high, rounded back, it had a flat one. Still, the head, feet, and tail were all in the appropriate places. The creature even seemed to be smiling.

He got down on one knee and played his flashlight beam on the tortoise's underside. Gloria joined him, adding her beam to his. He hardly noticed the cold, even though every breath they breathed plumed out white. Her glasses were slightly fogged.

'You think there's another clue here, don't you?' Gloria didn't act angry now, but she seemed determined to find whatever might be there first.

Lourds smiled. Competition was something he knew all about. He flicked his light back and forth.

Unfortunately, nothing appeared to be there.

'Maybe something's hidden inside. Maybe there's a hidden space.' Gloria crawled under the massive tortoise and started pushing at the rock.

'You'll want to be careful under there. This thing has got to weigh a ton at least.'

'I got here first. If anything's here to be found, I'm going to find it.' Gloria shoved herself farther under the tortoise while on her back.

Lourds flattened himself as well and played his light over the tortoise. 'It would be poetic symmetry if this tortoise did, in fact, yield another clue, but the likelihood of that is small.'

'You're just trying to get me out of here, aren't you?'

'No, but I don't think this tortoise is going to tell us anything.' Lourds shoved himself out from under the tortoise and started to look around.

'This is a woman.' Professor Hu flashed his beam over a smaller figure with a thin woman's gentle curves a few rocks over.

'She's carrying a fan.' Hu flicked his beam down the rock's side and revealed the familiar fan shape in the woman's hands.

'A fan?' Rory walked through the figures to join them.

'A winnowing fan.' Lourds touched the stone fan and felt its sharp edges. 'The Peligang people, who lived in Jiahu along the Yellow River in 7000 BC, raised foxtail millet and rice to eat. After the millet was harvested and threshed, the grain was separated from the chaff by tossing it into the air. The wind blew the chaff away while the grain fell back into the fan.'

'Uh, Professor Lourds.'

Lourds looked up at the BBC reporter.

'I'm going to need you to repeat that in front of the camera.' Rory waved the cameraman over.

Sighing, Lourds shook his head.

'Look, whenever you feel like you're going to pontificate or go on about something, maybe you could give me a sign. It would save us both a lot of time and effort.'

Hu chuckled. 'Unfortunately, a professor is at the mercy of his own knowledge and interests. Poor Thomas never knows when he's going to launch into a presentation till he finds himself in the middle of it.'

'Rory.' Lourds clapped the young reporter on the shoulder. 'You're going to need to be a little more responsible for getting your material. I'm not going to stop at every moment and repeat myself. Take notes. When you get a spare moment, research things. *Learn* things. Trust me, you'll be much better at your job. Everyone needs an education, and most people never realize how responsible they are for their own edification. Do you understand?'

'Completely.'

'Good.' Lourds started to walk away.

'However, could you do the fan thing again?'

Deeper into the maze of scholar's rocks, the sculptures – and Lourds couldn't help thinking of them that way because so many of the figures couldn't have merely been found – changed significantly. The difference was immediate and disturbing.

'These men are armed.' Hu seemed rattled by the discovery as well.

Lourds played his beam over a large man carrying what looked like a stone axe, with a short haft jutting up from the man's big fist, and an oblong rock at the end.

'Those people living at Jiahu were peaceful, Thomas. We've found no evidence of wars among the bodies we've disinterred.'

'Only a little over three hundred graves have been opened. There may be surprises awaiting archaeologists. The big question is why these people, if they're indeed the same people who left the tortoise in the grave, traveled this far from their home.' Lourds moved to the next warrior figure, a man with a club held in both hands over his head.

'The flood could have done it. From all indications, the original settlement was surrounded by a moat they doubtless used to irrigate the millet and rice. But the Yellow River – China's Pride and China's Sorrow, in equal parts – has a habit of changing its course. During one of those changes, it flooded Jiahu.'

Lourds knew the process. Loess, formed of windborne erosion, filled the river with silt, sand, and clay that became naturally occurring dams solidified by calcium carbonate. The changes took hundreds and even thousands of years, but they occurred. The Yellow River, because of its elevated riverbed, was especially problematic.

'So did these warriors attack these people and cause them to migrate?' Lourds shined his beam into the nightmarish face of the club-wielding attacker. Less attention had been paid to the man's features, and he looked like a cipher. 'Or did these people attack the immigrants on their way to this place?'

'This cavern tells a story.' Lourds stood beside Shamar and looked out over the chamber.

The old monk smiled. 'Yes, we believe so, too.'

'The people who founded this place were desperate.' Lourds pointed his light at figures that seemed to cower from the approaching warriors. 'They'd lost their homes and were searching for another.'

He was slightly distracted by Rory's cameraman aiming the bright light in his face, but he persevered. The footage with the cave all around him would look terrific in the documentary. He'd chosen to stand on the speaking area, so his practiced voice thundered inside the cavern.

'But they couldn't live here. Not without a food source.' Lourds looked out over the scholar's rocks and contemplated the problem. 'Then why choose to live here if it was such a hardship?'

He answered his own question. 'Because they wanted to leave a message and tell their story.' Lourds was convinced that was the truth. 'Cultures want to leave something of themselves behind. Remember, these people had to have known the Yellow River overflowed their countryside. Look at the side of the cave.'

The cameraman swung around to survey the cavern walls. Hu had been the first to find the tool markings on the wall. Once they'd seen the first ones, the others had been found in quick order.

'These people inscribed the river on the walls. Those are river currents.' Lourds felt certain the wavy lines could be nothing else. 'The river, Mother River, had been important to their community, until she turned vicious and swallowed their homes.' He took a dramatic breath, the way he did sometimes to cement an idea in one of his classes. 'Then they came here to leave their story.'

'But what happened to them after that?' Rory stood at the forefront of the crowd.

Lourds shook his head. 'I don't know. Getting food here would have been hard. Enough to feed a large group, and I'm certain this was a large community, probably more than a hundred people, would have been even harder. They would have had to haul it in, or trade for it with the Sherpa or other people who traversed the mountains.'

'Why not go somewhere else? Somewhere easier?'

'All the arable lands, the lands where a people could live with relative comfort and assurance of a crop, would have been already inhabited around these mountains.' Suddenly Lourds realized something else. 'They knew they were dying. They knew their culture was going to be erased as surely as the Yellow River had erased their homeland.' He shook his head in wonder. 'Either they would die out from disease or a low birth rate, or they would be assimilated by stronger, more successful cultures.'

Rory focused on Lourds. 'How long did it take for those people to make all these statues?'

'Scholar's rocks, not statues. And the answer to that is decades. Generations.'

'They spent all that time looking for rocks that looked like people? Then hauled them to this cave? That sounds like a lot of work.'

'I'm sure it was, but one thing the Himalayas has besides a lot of snow is a lot of rocks.'

Everyone laughed.

But even as he said that, Lourds knew that wasn't the true answer. It was a possible answer – but not the correct one.

12

Schloss Volker
Vienna, Austria
July 27, 2011

'Will you be needing the car any more tonight, Herr Von Volker?'

'Yes, Hans. Keep it ready.' Von Volker strode past his liveried chauffeur and up the steps leading to his ancestral home.

Schloss Volker was a beautiful estate, built in the late 18th century by Erich Von Volker, Klaus's ancestor.

Erich had built his empire on two fronts. First, through transatlantic shipping and slave trade in Africa, backed by profitable gold and diamond mining on the continent. On the second front, Erich Von Volker had maintained a private standing army of mercenaries that protected his assets and fought wars for hire. Some of them had even fought for the Americans during the Revolutionary War, while Erich sold the young army weapons. He'd solidified his holdings through political favors and power.

Things hadn't changed much. Von Volker still maintained a few mining prospects in Africa, but the profits weren't as good as in the past. Getting gold and blood diamonds out these days was extremely difficult. If he'd chosen to live in South Africa, he could have lived well.

But his heart was here, in Austria, his ancestral homeland. Also contained deep inside him was the burning desire of one day reuniting Austria with Germany to make a large country that would successfully stand against the Jew-loving nations of the world. Not only reuniting the two countries, but leading them into a glorious new age as well.

The estate grounds around the *schloss* were immaculately maintained. The grass was green, flowers bloomed every day, and the fountains ran pure water.

Many other men, lesser men, would have been satisfied with what he already possessed. Von Volker was not. He wanted to be the head of a unified Germany and Austria that he dreamed of every day; he would accept nothing less. And once he'd accomplished that, he would use the newly allied nation to lead the rest of the squabbling, disjointed European countries as well. Either they would fall in line from economic pressure the new power could bring to bear, or else there were other ways of gaining their allegiance . . .

He walked up the steps, where the houseman held the large, carved wooden door open for him. Alice was not there, and that mildly irritated Von Volker. If he hadn't still been smarting from the casual disdain evidenced by Colonel Davari over dinner, he probably wouldn't have thought twice about her absence. She tended to be interested in her own pursuits these days, but she hadn't yet grown the guts to take a lover.

If she had, Von Volker would have had both of them killed.

'Where is my wife?' Von Volker handed his evening coat and walking stick to the houseman.

'With the piano, Herr Von Volker.'

Von Volker walked through the ornate front hall filled with a mural of significant images from Viennese history. Erich Von Volker had ordered pictures of early Rome painted on the walls, as well as images of the Battle of Vienna when the Ottoman Empire had been beaten back. Other images showed the Habsburg kings, with the Habsburg lion, red on a field of yellow, standing in proud prominence.

Von Volker passed through the formal dining room and turned left, opening the soundproofed double doors to enter his wife's music room. Just inside, he paused for a moment to listen. It was a classical piece, but that was all Von Volker knew for certain.

She sat in front of the piano in a dark blue lounging coat and played with her eyes closed. Von Volker didn't know if she was locked into the music or was imagining herself in happier times.

Alice played beautifully, making love to the piano with a passion she had never shown in the bedroom. In Von Volker's arms and beneath him, she only performed dutifully. He felt certain that her enjoyment of the act was a bit of theater on her part, nothing more.

Tan and fit from tennis on the clay courts and swimming in the Olympic-sized pool, Alice was a striking woman. At forty, she maintained a trim waist, elegant features, and, if her blond hair was anything but natural, only her hairdresser knew.

She stopped playing suddenly, then turned and looked over her shoulder. For just the barest moment, her face was frozen, then the familiar false smile spread across her features.

'Klaus. You're home. Why didn't you call me and let me know you were coming?'

'I thought I would surprise you.'

She kissed him thoroughly, but he still felt the distance between them that had always been there. He'd given up on ever being able to bridge it, settling instead for having a trophy wife who helped him on a political front.

'Why don't you play some more? I would like to relax.'

The smile she showed him then was genuine, and he could tell the difference in a heartbeat. 'Of course. What would you like to hear?'

'Something by Norah Jones, I believe.'

Some of her happiness dissipated then. Alice was happiest playing classical pieces, but she had learned the American tunes from Norah Jones, Diana Krall, Harry Connick, Junior because he had demanded it.

As his wife began playing, Von Volker recognized the opening strains of the American pianist's song, 'Young Blood.' He closed his eyes and listened, plotting how the rest of the evening was going to go. 'Sing the words. In English.'

'My voice isn't very good tonight, Klaus.'

'It is your voice. I will love it. Sing.'

She did, and her voice was beautiful as always. If he hadn't had malice in mind, he would have been soothed.

'Klaus, I'm sorry, but I'm too tired to continue playing. Perhaps another evening?'

Von Volker smiled at his wife. 'You played wonderfully.' She had, but he had been waiting for the sedative he'd slipped into her drink to take effect. 'This has been a most enchanting evening.'

'It's so late.'

It was. By Von Volker's watch, it was after one. She had sipped her wine instead of drinking it. Even though he'd requested American songs, some sung in English, others in French, and some in German, she had lost herself in the music, gotten off to a place that he could never reach with her.

'Of course.'

She stood and almost fell, catching herself on the piano bench. 'I'm sorry.' She pushed herself up. 'I guess the wine has gone straight to my head.'

That was exactly what Von Volker had intended. Over the twelve years of their marriage, he had drugged Alice before, but usually so she was passed out and much more pliable for whatever he wanted to do. That had been in the early years. Now he had mistresses willing to do those things. That was much more pleasurable.

Unfortunately, those willing mistresses didn't make good political wives. It was frustrating that married politicians seemed to do the best with their constituents, and that well-married ones from moneyed families, as Alice's was, fared even better.

He caught her hand and kissed her fingers. 'Allow me, dear Alice.' He folded her arm under his and guided her from the piano room to the lift. He didn't want to try to navigate the stairs.

Later, in the bedroom, they both lay winded and naked from Von Volker's efforts. She lay cuddled in his embrace, tucked up against his body, barely conscious.

'Alice.'

'Yes?'

Her lazy response led Von Volker to believe she was under the drug's influence as surely as she had been her music. In the early days, he had asked her if she loved him. Even under the effects of those narcotics, she had always said yes.

The present sedative was supposed to be much better at getting to the truth, according to the man who had given it to him. However, Von Volker wasn't even tempted to ask his wife if she loved him. He no longer cared. He controlled her, and that was all that mattered.

'Tell me about your college days.'

Alice lay with her eyes closed, her beautiful blond hair spread out over her pillow. 'College was wonderful.'

'What made it wonderful?'

'Everything. So carefree.' Alice smiled.

'Who did you know in college?'

She looked troubled at that.

'Who were your friends, Alice?'

'Thomas. Thomas was my friend.'

That surprised Klaus. It was the first mention he'd heard of anyone named Thomas.

'Thomas was the best lover I've ever had.'

Von Volker restrained himself from striking her. He cooled his anger with the prospect of success. More than he wanted to beat his wife, he wanted to wipe the smug look from Colonel Davari's face. The beating could come later, on another day, and the sex then would be wonderful – whether Alice enjoyed it or not.

'You knew Lev Strauss while you were at the Vienna School of Languages.'

'I did. Precious Lev.' She smiled dreamily.

'Did you love him?' The question fell from Von Volker's lips before he could stop himself from asking.

'No. Lev was my friend. A good friend.'

'Do you know where I can find him?'

'I haven't talked to Lev in a long time.'

Von Volker considered a fresh tack. He didn't have long before the drug pulled Alice completely under. 'Is Lev in Jerusalem?'

'I don't know.'

Stymied, Von Volker thought about his options. From everything Davari had said, Lev Strauss had disappeared into Jerusalem, somewhere in the City of David, the oldest section of the metropolis.

'Thomas and I visited Lev in Jerusalem.'

'Really?'

'Yes.'

'Where?'

'In the City of David. We went there for summer break. It was wonderful. Such a good time.'

Listening to his wife talk about those good times infuriated and pained Von Volker. The Ayatollah didn't know the extent he was willing to go to in order to succeed at his latest mission.

Or maybe the old man did, and that was why he'd sent Davari to speak with him. The Ayatollah knew that Von Volker didn't care for the colonel. Von Volker had made that explicitly clear.

'You were in the City of David. Where did you go? You and Thomas?'

'With Lev. We went with Lev.'

'Where did you stay?'

'With Lev. He had a wonderful little flat. His grandmother left it to him.'

Von Volker seized that tidbit of information. Property in Jerusalem rarely changed hands. Everyone – the Jews, the Muslims, and the Christians – all tried to hang on to as much of the land there that they could.

'Alice?'

'Sleepy. I want to sleep.'

'Where was Lev's lovely little flat?'

She didn't respond.

Gently, which was hard to do, Von Volker shook his wife. Despite his continued efforts, he got no response.

Angry but hanging on to his clue, Von Volker rose from bed, pulled on a robe, took out the picture of Lev Strauss Davari had given him, and went to his wife's library in one of the adjoining rooms.

Alice had her hiding places, just as Von Volker had his. The difference was that he knew where hers were and didn't care. Her secrets were very small. She was too afraid of him to do anything more than write about her discontent in her journal. Even there, she equally blamed her parents for her situation because they had arranged the marriage. They had wanted her to marry into nobility because they were of noble blood as well. However, their family fortunes had dwindled, while his had grown.

Even the hiding place Alice had chosen wasn't that imaginative. She'd found a loose board in her closet and had shoved her journals and other personal effects into the space behind it.

Von Volker knew about the journal because Alice had accidentally left it out one day. He hadn't asked her about it, and it had promptly disappeared. He'd had one of his security people come in the next day and find it while he'd taken Alice shopping.

Clever girl, she had tried to disguise what she was doing and writing by writing different passages in different languages. Having studied at the School of Languages,

Alice could read and write well in several different ones. Von Volker had simply had the pages photocopied, then translated.

At the time, he'd considered destroying the journal and other items. The only reason he hadn't was so he could do it some other day, preferably before Alice's eyes.

On his knees, Von Volker removed the board, reached into the space, and hauled out Alice's personal treasures. Selecting the college album, he left the others.

He crossed the room to her table, surrounded by leatherbound classical editions in foreign languages. When the piano couldn't soothe her unhappiness, she retreated to her books and their stories of romances. It was all foolishness. Power made a person happy. Nothing else.

Placing the picture of Lev Strauss on the table, Von Volker leafed through the album. Several of the pictures showed Alice with a dark-haired man in a goatee. The man was handsome, one of those types women invariably threw themselves at, and looked American in the ugly hat he wore.

Von Volker had seen the man before but had never known his name. Alice hadn't written more than the dates and places on the backs of the photographs.

Was this Thomas?

Von Volker decided he hated the man, and that it might be worth looking him up later to kill him.

But other matters were more pressing.

Only a few minutes later, he found pictures of a much

younger Lev Strauss. He looked confident and outgoing, exactly the kind of Jewish spy the Mossad would turn out. Von Volker turned the pictures slowly, looking at the trio in the dig sites, then in restaurants and market-places, then – at last – in a dwelling. Judging from the books and magazines strewn around the room, this was Lev Strauss's flat that Alice had mentioned.

A few of them listed the address.

Von Volker smiled.

'Elise, you look as radiant as ever.' Von Volker stepped into the expensive apartment and kissed his mistress exuberantly.

'Klaus?' Although she was surprised, Elise Feuer-stein smiled at his arrival and looked pleased to see him. She was a slim blond in her midtwenties, and resembled his wife as Alice had looked at that age. That was on purpose because Von Volker made her dye her hair and wear it in the same style. She wore a gauzy green negligee.

Von Volker ripped the thin material off her and dis-covered she was naked beneath. Already aroused, he picked her up and carried her to the circular bed. She laughed and giggled like a schoolgirl, and that made him harder than ever.

One of the best things Von Volker loved about Elise, in addition to the fact that she looked so much like Alice, was that she never needed foreplay. She was always ready because powerful men turned her on. After undressing, he sheathed himself, locked her hands above her head, and took her. She managed two explosions of her own before he reached his release.

Then stretched out comfortably atop the young woman, Von Volker reached for his jacket.

'That was certainly eye-opening, my love, but what's the occasion?'

'Can't I just be happy to see you?'

'Yes, but this was more than that.' Unlike Alice, Elise knew her place and took comfort in it. She never nagged at him to replace his wife because she knew Alice was important to Von Volker's political aspirations.

'I have something I want you to do.'

She laughed. 'You already know I would do anything I can for you. All you have to do is ask.'

'This man.' Von Volker flicked the photograph of Lev Strauss. 'I need you to contact him and play a little game with him.'

'Of course. Is that all?'

'Yes.'

With a strong push, Elise rolled him over onto his back and mounted him once more. She was almost as insatiable as he was. Knowing that he would soon have Lev Strauss where the Ayatollah and Colonel Davari had failed filled Von Volker's blood with passion. His immediate response surprised Elise, but she laughed, positioned him better, and started to ride.

13

Scholar's Rock Temple
Himalaya Mountains
People's Republic of China
July 27, 2011

Steam from the bath rose around Lourds as he lay back and tried to figure out what he was missing from the mysterious cavern and the scholar's rocks left by the immigrants from Jiahu. Something was there, pulling at the edges of his thoughts but never quite manifesting.

It was maddening.

At least the monks hadn't sworn off all creature comforts in the temple. They believed in bathing and bathing well. They'd carved baths from stone that were just deep enough for a man to sink down into. Shamar had said it was a trade-off with the outside world. People donated supplies to the temple more readily if they could get a warm bath and have private sleeping quarters. The meager guest quarters hadn't been enough for the whole expedition. Even though Lourds hadn't asked for special treatment, he certainly hadn't turned it down when it was offered.

He luxuriated in the hot water. A stone oven in the

center of the room provided heat. All he had to do was step out of the tub long enough to fill a copper kettle with water from the bath and reheat it. For the moment, the water was wonderful.

He took a breath and slid down into the tub till the water closed over his head. He closed his eyes and let the hot water soak into him. He felt sleepy and knew that he would do well to crawl into bed on the other side of the room when he got out. He was already feeling pruny, like he had spent far too much time in here . . .

And suddenly, just like that, it all made sense.

Lourds couldn't see in the darkness. He opened the stone oven, burned his fingertips enough to smart, and fed in a few pieces of wood. The orange glow brightened and pushed back the darkness. He spotted his pants, went to them, and started pulling them on.

Once his boots were on, Lourds fisted his shirt and headed for the door. Out in the hallway, he trotted over to Hu's quarters across the narrow stone hall. He rapped on the door. 'David. It's me. Time to get up.' He rapped on the door again. 'David.'

Hu's door opened and the professor filled it, standing there in Hawaiian boxer briefs, bedhead, and a perplexed expression. 'Thomas? What's going on?

Lourds took a deep breath and tried to control the excitement that filled him. 'We were wrong about the scholar's rock room. I was wrong about it.'

'What?'

'The room. That's what's wrong. All of it. There's no

way those people went roaming about the countryside for those scholar's rocks. And no way they could have smoothed them like that with hand tools. I should have thought of it sooner. My only excuse is that I was too tired to think properly. Grab some lights and help me wake the others. We're going to need help.'

'Mate, I hope you're right about the big reveal. We're wasting a lot of our generator fuel lighting this place.' Rory didn't look happy or convinced.

Lourds studied the room as the BBC production crew, Gelu and his Sherpas who had stayed to enjoy the respite, and the monks hung lights around the room. They'd put most of them on the east wall, where Lourds felt confident they would find the room's secret.

'Get your cameraman over here.' Lourds ran his fingers through his hair and reseated his hat. 'I only want to explain this once.'

One of the young monks pointed and whispered. 'Cowboy.'

Lourds grinned at that and shot the young monk with a forefinger pistol.

The monk laughed, then quickly took one of the staging lights Gloria gave him and started climbing the wall. He went up the craggy surface so easily it looked like he'd switched off gravity and flowed up.

Gloria looked at Lourds with a confused expression.

The cameraman switched the device on. 'Let's roll.'

Lourds hit his spot, straightened his hat brim, and

waited just a second. Then he waved at the 116 figures standing behind him. 'Yesterday evening, when I first saw these scholar's rocks depicting the migratory people who came here after Jiahu flooded, I was fooled. I thought those figures simply represented the struggles of those people to get to this place, the hardships they'd endured, and even the enemies they'd faced. I thought that was the whole story. I was wrong.'

Reaching out, Lourds directed the camera toward the figures.

'What you see there is only part of the story. It relates the history, and we've found some of the same symbols on those scholar's rocks. I thought that was the find, and I thought that was the vindication of those people. Then I started thinking, wondering why the tortoiseshell had been left behind at the grave.'

Lourds pulled the camera back to him and let his excitement show as it did when he was in the classroom.

'The tortoiseshell had to have been left behind with someone that would mark the way for others of the tribe. He was probably a wise man, a shaman. We'll know more when the archaeologists at the Jiahu site reveal their findings. Someone from this place had to return to Jiahu with the tortoise map.'

Lourds stepped back, allowing the cameraman to frame him and the cavern in the shot.

'When the Yellow River overflowed its banks in the past, the floods have always been horrendous. I feel confident in saying that the floods that struck in 5800 BC were terrifying. Added to that, the people living there had drawn the ire of an enemy. Maybe it was just a predacious encroachment. Robbers taking what they could from a peaceful community. Maybe it was a more hostile intent. That community was in a good spot until the flood. Their developed fields alone would have been worth a war to another people that had been uprooted by another flood. We may never know.'

Taking a breath, Lourds pointed at the scholar's rocks. The cameraman stayed locked on him, but Rory looked impatient.

'Possibly the people who came here thought their respite would be brief. Instead, they became stuck here because there was no home to go back to, or because the travel was hard, and they didn't want to chance it again if they could meet their needs here. We do know their lives were harsh while living here. But they concealed their greatest secret.'

As every eye in the chamber stared at him, Lourds hoped he was right. He'd piled on promises, and he was expected – like a magician – to pull a rabbit from his hat.

Now it was time to produce the rabbit.

14

Scholar's Rock Temple
Himalaya Mountains
People's Republic of China
July 28, 2011

Lourds grinned into the camera as nervous energy spiked his system. 'One hundred and sixteen figures stand in this chamber. Each of them weighs several hundred pounds at least. Some of them weigh a thousand pounds. My original thinking was that the people dragged the rocks into this cavern.' He turned toward the figures. 'Then I thought about all that work. And that didn't explain how all of them are smooth.'

Waving to the cameraman, Lourds walked down into the chamber while the expedition and the monks looked on. He felt like David Copperfield about to make an invisible elephant appear.

Except the elephant wasn't even in the room.

'As I considered the problem, I knew that the people needed a way to smooth the scholar's rocks. I also realized they needed a source of water and food. Lake water can smooth rock, but nothing wears down edges as fast as running water.'

Lourds stopped beside the scholar's rock of the flat-backed tortoise. He gestured to it, and the cameraman panned in for a full-frame shot.

'Professor Lourds.' Rory, his patience exhausted, trailed after the cameraman. 'Please. That camcorder battery is only going to last a little while longer. It takes hours working a hand generator to charge them.'

Ignoring the director, Lourds continued.

'Why make the tortoise with a flat back? I kept missing that. I mean, it was apparent. It looks like a serving dish. Or maybe a table.' He pointed to the extremities. 'Then it came to me. This tortoise was used as a staging platform.' He whirled and pointed at the surrounding figures. 'If you look at them, you'll quickly realize that *each and every one will fit on the back of this turtle.*'

In the back of the crowd, Brother Shamar smiled proudly and nodded. The old man hadn't known the secret before, but he was catching on quickly.

'If this tortoise is a staging platform, as I believe, then there has to be a support mount for a rope to run through somewhere on the ceiling of this cavern.'

Lights swiveled toward the cavern's ceiling. Hooking his fingers and toes into the craggy rock, Lourds climbed. The going was rough, and he wasn't nearly as graceful as the monks, but he reached the ceiling nearly twenty feet above the stone floor. Some of the monks and BBC crew climbed with him, and Gloria followed as well. They all held on one-handed and shined their flashlights around the uneven ceiling.

For a long few minutes, Lourds feared his hypothesis was incorrect.

Then Thompson shouted. 'There! Do you see it?'

He waggled his light over a thick stalactite, and the beam jumped through the hole that had been augured through the stone.

Lourds grinned.

Upon closer inspection – done while hanging from a climbing harness attached to pitons driven into the ceiling by the Sherpas – Lourds determined that the hole had been used for hauling.

'The lips and inside are worn smooth.' He hung upside down while talking to the cameraman. 'If you'll pass that camera up here – '

'He most certainly will not.' Rory stepped protectively toward the expensive equipment.

Lourds laughed and took a small digital camera from his shirt pocket. 'Your loss. These digital images will have to suffice.' With a quick, practiced pull on the ropes, he righted himself and took pictures of the hole. It was wide enough that he could have thrust both arms in and had room left over. And it was at least four feet deep. There had been plenty of leverage for the ropes.

At the top of the cavern, Lourds looked down. He had that much of the puzzle figured out, but where had the rocks come from? Then, on the eastern wall, he saw a crack near the top.

When he climbed up to the top of the eastern wall,

Lourds found the gap he'd spotted. It was only a few inches wide, nothing that would have been seen from the ground or by anyone not looking for it. Upon closer inspection, he found a seam that had been mortared into place. Cool air and the sound of rushing water sounded beyond.

A sandblaster couldn't have peeled the smile from his face.

'Wall is false.' Gelu pounded on the section of the wall with his pickax.

The rock sounded empty.

'Hollow on other side.'

Lourds turned in the climbing harness and shouted down to Rory. 'If your cameraman has a stout heart, now would be the time to get him up here. Otherwise you're going to miss that big reveal you've been waiting so impatiently for.'

When the cameraman was lashed securely in place to pitons, with a pair of Sherpas watching over him, Lourds and Gelu attacked the false rock with crowbars. Shamar had given his blessings to the endeavor.

'Rock made good.' Gelu growled as he shoved. 'Put into place much good.'

Lourds silently agreed and leaned more heavily on his borrowed crowbar. The rock broke, and he had to find a new leverage place. In the end, though, the mortar gave way to the crowbars. Lourds and Gelu tried to hold on to the piece, but it was no use.

'Look out!'

The carefully shaped section, eight feet wide and ten feet tall, toppled backwards and skidded down the twenty-foot slope. Thankfully, no one was standing that close, and the slab stopped well short of the first line of the scholar's rocks.

Lourds took out his mini-Maglite and shined the beam into the dark recesses on the other side of the opening. Another cave wall gleamed dully forty feet away. He climbed over to the opening and stood peering down into the darkness.

He couldn't estimate the distance for certain, but he guessed that somewhere around a hundred feet below was a rushing stream cutting its way through the guts of the mountain. Cold air seeped into the cavern from the closed-off area.

'The monks are going to hate us for all the draft we've brought into their homes.' As Lourds stood there, the beam reflecting off the water, he thought he saw another opening near the bottom. 'I need a flare.'

Gelu called out to one of his men, and an emergency flare was tossed up.

Lourds grabbed it, banged the end to set it off, then tossed it into the abyss. He counted the seconds of the fall as the brightly burning red star fell into the crevice, then into the water. A hundred feet was about right.

And there was another opening at the bottom near the waterline.

After the river carried the flare's light away, Lourds turned to Gelu. 'Can you get us down there?'

The Sherpa nodded. 'Sure. No problem. Is what we do.'

True to Gelu's word, the Sherpas quickly hammered in pitons and laid climbing ropes down the rock face.

Bundled up in cold-weather clothing again, Lourds rappelled down into the crevice. The BBC crew was more than a little put out that filming the discovery had gotten so difficult. To make matters worse, they'd had to stop filming except in bits and pieces to save the batteries.

Four of Rory's crew worked on the hand generators to power up the batteries. They looked like mad monkey dervishes as they kept winding and handing the units back and forth as they took breaks. The monks joined in, but the effort required a lot to produce a little.

Using a spotter light on his forehead, Lourds descended into the darkness. Except for the rushing water, everything was still. The rope sang through his gloves and the D-ring on his climbing harness. He caught himself on his feet, then pushed off and shot down at a controlled speed again.

He was on the cavern near the bottom of the crevice before he knew it. He overshot the wall and ended up sliding out of control into the cavern. His head whipped about, and he couldn't tell what he'd gotten himself into.

'Thomas!' Gelu bellowed behind him.

Half-in and half-out of the cavern, holding on with one hand on the rope and the other on the cavern mouth, Lourds yanked his head up and focused on his predicament. Fear gave way to astonishment as he peered inside the chamber.

'Thomas!'

'I'm here. I'm fine.' Lourds spoke more quietly to himself. 'My God, I'm fine.' He dug in his boots and climbed up into the cave as Gelu slid down beside him and perched expertly on the chamber lip.

The Sherpa grinned. 'Thought you lost.'

'Me too.'

'Water maybe bad. Take underground.'

'Yeah, you're probably right about that.' In the cave, Lourds pulled a flare from his backpack, banged it on the nearest stone wall, and held the blazing tube aloft.

Around him, the final resting place of several dozen Jiahu immigrants lay undisturbed. Desiccated remains lay in hollowed shelves in the walls.

Gelu stood at Lourds's side and gazed around in wonder. 'Not monks.'

'No, definitely not monks.'

The monks practiced sky burial, laying the bodies of the dead out in the wild for carrion birds and ground predators to take.

Slowly, Lourds walked forward. Tortoiseshells lay at the head of each body, and there were dozens of them in the tomb. Picking up one, he examined it in the spotter light. Nine symbols had been etched into the plastron.

Lourds only recognized two of them from the sixteen that scholars had found while digging at Jiahu. Not only that, beside the next body lay a delicate bone flute about eight inches long and half an inch in diameter.

The instrument alone was enough to make a career.

Hu handled the bone flute with reverence. So far it was the only one they had found. 'You know what you've done, don't you, Thomas?'

'What *we've* done, you mean?' Lourds smiled and looked at the chamber and at Gloria Chen organizing a quick cataloguing effort of the find. 'Yes, I know what we've done. Opened up a whole new field of study for people involved in the Jiahu dig.' He shrugged. 'I don't know if those people are going to love us or hate us. We've increased their workload considerably.'

'As long as they get additional funding to support their efforts, they'll love us.' The older man's hazel eyes gleamed with joy. 'You also realize we'll have to prepare a paper on this discovery soon.'

'I do. And we will.' Lourds yawned tiredly. Staying up half the night was wearing on him after the day he'd had. But he wouldn't have traded any of the experiences for anything.

Rory and the BBC crew had a very small area they could rove in, and they weren't happy about it, but the monks and the Sherpas enforced the restricted space.

'Seriously, Professor Lourds, we should be getting all of this on camera.' Rory fumed, but didn't try to bypass the Sherpas or the monks. 'We should be involved with aspects of this story. If it weren't for us, you wouldn't be here now.'

Lourds turned to the man. 'Rory, I like you. You're a good guy. You know your stuff when it comes to what you do. But this is what *I* do, and I know better than to let an amateur walk through what we have here. What we've found here is important. Maybe it seems like what someone found in an attic to you, but these are the kinds of finds that can teach the world a lot about how people lived thousands of years ago. Believe it or not, all those decisions all those years ago still have an impact on how we define ourselves as people.'

Rory scowled, but didn't object.

Lourds took the boon flute from Hu. 'This is a *gudi,* a truly rare find in the Jiahu dig. They're made from the wings of red-crowned cranes. They were used to make music, probably in sacrificial rites as well, and most certainly in bird hunting. But I'm sure you already knew that.'

Self-consciously, Rory dropped his gaze, then held up a hand in surrender. 'All right. Fine. Have it your way.'

'Thank you.' Lourds smiled. 'As we dig these things out, *carefully,* we'll show them to you. Take as many pictures as you want, as much footage. Interview me, Professor Hu, or any of these graduate-level students accompanying us.'

'The students?'

'Yes, the students. As of this moment, they're the foremost experts in the field on this find.'

15

Quarter Café
Tiferet Yisrael Street
Jerusalem, the State of Israel
July 28, 2011

'Lev, you know you shouldn't be here. It's dangerous.'

Smiling slightly, unwilling to admit how scared he was these days – not even to himself – Lev Strauss shook his head. 'I am here with you, Ezra. How could I not be safe?'

Ezra Goldstein sat on the other side of the small table at the back of the café. In his late-twenties, he was far too serious for his years. The Mossad made them that way these days, though. When Lev had been with the intelligence agency, they had still been solemn, but there were times when they could play.

'This isn't funny, Lev. The work you're doing, what you're looking for, it's important.'

'You really think so?' Lev tore off a piece of his bagel and popped it into his mouth. He chewed and swallowed, but these days he didn't taste much – his stomach always stayed sour with fear. He wasn't afraid of what might happen to him. Rather, he was afraid of what might happen if he failed at his self-appointed task. 'Because I don't think your taskmasters take what I'm trying to do any too seriously.'

'Whether they do or not, I'm here.' Ezra met Lev's gaze with an earnestness that almost shamed him. 'I'm with you, Lev, and I'm putting my life on the line every time you walk out of your flat.'

That made Lev feel bad because he knew it was true. 'I know, and I apologize, but I can't sit inside those four walls the rest of my life.'

'Don't think like it's going to be for the rest of your life. Think like it's just going to be for a few more days.'

'Is it? Is that all it's going to be? Because I've invested over a year of my life in this search so far, my friend, and I've got precious little to show for it. Even your superiors have doubts about this.' Lev sighed and dropped the remains of his bagel onto his plate.

'You should eat.'

'I can't. Nothing tastes right.'

'Don't taste it. Eat it. Your stomach doesn't care if anything tastes good. It just wants to be fed.' Ezra sat there, fit and trim, broad-shouldered, and probably with a gun tucked at the back of his waist under his long-tailed shirt.

He was a man of action, a man of possibilities, and in that moment, Lev resented the younger man for that. On days like this, when he was filled with anger and fear, Lev's missing left foot ached something fierce. He wanted to reach down to massage it, but he'd left it somewhere in the Dead Sea region.

'I have to get out and walk.' Lev tried the bagel again. He still couldn't taste it, but he didn't care. Eating it gave his hands something to do. 'I need to walk so my mind will work. Staying in that apartment causes me to freeze up.' He peered over Ezra's shoulder.

In the distance, the Western Wall stood at the foot of Temple Mount. The familiar gold dome atop the temple gleamed in the fading afternoon light. Pedestrians – many of the tourists, not citizens – walked along the sidewalks.

The way Ezra saw the world, all of them were potential assassins. It was a view that would keep him alive for a while.

'You were in the Gaza Strip only a few days ago.' Ezra sipped his tea and watched the café's diners.

'Under careful watch.' Lev shook his head. 'That wasn't like truly being out.'

Ezra started to say something, then hesitated.

'Tell me. You might as well. If you don't, you'll be around me the rest of the day acting like you've got something stuck in your throat.'

'You remember the men we had guarding you in the Gaza?'

A chill ghosted through Lev, and he knew something bad had happened. 'Yes.'

'Two of them went missing after we got you out of there.'

'What do you mean?'

Without inflection, Ezra went on. 'They were captured, tortured, and killed.'

'My God.'

'Their heads and feet were received by their families today.'

Sickness swirled in the pit of Lev's stomach.

Ezra leaned forward and tapped the tabletop. 'Some people know what you're after, Lev. And they believe what you're searching for exists. That has caught the attention of my superiors. That is why they won't believe I am letting you walk around the city today.'

'Why was I not told?'

'They did not want to burden you.' Ezra shrugged. 'I thought you should know. Maybe you will take the matter of your safety a little more seriously.'

Lev's head swam. 'I need to get out of here.'

'Back to the flat?' Ezra's firm gaze told him no other answer was acceptable.

'Yes.' Lev pushed up from the table.

'Have you paid attention to the television reports coming in from the Himalayas?' Ezra walked on the outside of the sidewalk, his eyes always roving and watchful. He was an excellent bodyguard. Lev knew the signs from having worked personal-security detachments.

'No.' Lev walked easily, with no trace of a limp. His prosthesis had been with him for more than thirteen years, and had become part of him long ago.

'According to your file, you knew Professor Thomas Lourds.'

For a moment, Lev's heart sank, thinking of the two guards in the Gaza whose names he couldn't remember. Thomas Lourds was one of the most vibrant men he'd ever met, and a good friend. The world was a better place with him in it. 'Has something happened to Thomas?'

'No, he's fine.'

'Then I still *know* him. Thomas and I are old friends.'

'Evidently he's had a bit of good fortune.'

Lev smiled a true smile then. 'Knowing Thomas, I'm not surprised. He was always the luckiest man I've ever known. What has happened?'

'He discovered some kind of forgotten temple in the Himalayas. The story has been all over the media. I'm surprised you didn't know.'

'I've been studying the books and the notes I've gathered for this last year. There's been little time in my life for anything else.'

'The news broke concerning the story three days ago.'

'He found something?'

'Ancient artifacts that date back to 5800 BC, according to the BBC reports I saw.'

'In the Himalayas?'

'Yes.'

Lev shook his head. 'Only Thomas could do something like that.'

*

In the small flat, Lev sat with Ezra and watched television. Lourds's find in the Scholar's Rock Temple was on the BBC news channels. The British were making the most of their scoop, but other media agencies had swooped in on the story as well.

Watching the raw footage of the temple caverns and the scholar's rocks, Lev was impressed. The find was already turning out to be one that would cause history books to be rewritten and launch future studies.

'I remember Lourds from the Atlantis discovery he worked on a couple of years ago.' Ezra sat on the low couch with his elbows on his knees. A pair of pistols lay on the coffee table in front of him. 'And there was that cache of books he found in Istanbul that no one knew about. He's an interesting man.'

'Thomas would laugh to hear you say that. He would act like it was nothing.' Lev smiled knowingly. 'But inside he would preen like a peacock.' He stretched out his leg and took the weight off the prosthesis. 'When I talk to him about this, I'm going to ask him why he didn't find this the last time we were in the Himalayas.'

'You were in the Himalayas?'

Lev nodded. 'A few times.' On some of those instances, he'd been there on Mossad business watching Indian and Pakistani troop movements. 'Thomas and I worked among the Muslim Chinese Uighur tribes. Both of us have linguistic backgrounds, and we documented a lot of information on the tribesmen. They served as the custodians of the Mongol Empire. Their records, once Thomas and I had them deciphered, gave us a lot of information about the Mongols, trade along the Silk Road, and the Uighur Khaganate.'

'And you lived in the Himalayas while you were doing this?' Ezra looked impressed.

Lev nodded. 'We did. On the southwestern side of the Himalayas.'

'Sounds like good times.'

'It was.'

'That was sarcasm, by the way.'

'I know.' Lev smiled. 'That was about fifteen years ago, when I was better equipped for getting around in mountainous terrain, before I lost my leg.' He continued watching the special, and for the time being, his own problems seemed far away.

That night, in front of his computer, Lev sorted through the digital images of illustrated manuscripts he'd assembled. He had read the translations so many times that he'd practically memorized them. Leaning back in his chair, he tried to gather his thoughts.

He was missing a key to the puzzle before him, and he couldn't for the life of him figure out what it was.

In the other room, Ezra watched ESPN on the television. European football filled the screen.

Thinking about Lourds, Lev accessed some of his off-site files and brought up photographs taken from the time he and his friend had spent among the Uighurs. Those had been good times. Both of them had been young and competitive, with each other as well as with their hosts.

And they had made friends. Over the years, Lev had kept in touch with some of them. A man who lived his life constantly on the go hung on to the friends he made even though he didn't see them for years.

Closing out the pictures, Lev stared at the image of Mohammad flying on al-Buraq. He clicked through the images, then saw the one that most disturbed him: the one where Mohammad had unknowingly dropped his copy of the Koran and the Scroll that foretold the future.

When he'd first heard that story, Lev hadn't been able to forget it. A united Muslim front would mean the end of Israel. The *jihad* would sweep across the globe, and the world would never know peace again.

No matter what he had to do, who he had to risk, the Book and Scroll couldn't fall into Muslim hands. He had sworn that when he'd found the first image of the falling Book and Scroll.

Lev had wanted to know if the story was just a fabrication. Or if it was true, he had wanted to find those things and save his people.

He frowned, displeased at how firmly he'd gotten stuck on the project. It wasn't his own hubris that kept him from seeking out help. The Israeli government hadn't wanted him spreading the knowledge that he was looking for Mohammad's lost Koran. Even admitting the Book might exist would be harmful to his people.

There were few people he could trust.

But he trusted one man. And maybe it was time to bring him into the fold.

If he would come.

Lev brought up Facebook and quickly went through his list of contacts.

Ziya Kadeer had been a young boy fifteen years ago when Lev had first met him. Now he was an import/export businessman in Artux, in the northeastern section of the Tarim Basin, the foothills of the Himalayas. They still exchanged letters, though these days they were more likely to be texts or Facebook messages.

When he checked, Lev found that Ziya was logged on to Facebook. He opened a dialogue box.

Ziya, how are you?

I am well, Professor Strauss! Good to hear from you!

They caught up for a few moments, then Lev made his decision.

Have you heard from Thomas lately?

No, but I see he is in the news! Again!!!

I know. He was always the lucky one.

Lev sent that, then immediately thought better of it and appended the message with another.

No, let me take that back. Thomas has put nothing ahead of his work. Those kind make their own good fortune.

And Lev had decided that what his own project needed was a little luck.

I have a favor to ask, my friend.

Anything.

Can you get someone to carry a message to Thomas for me?

You cannot call him?

I'd rather this be private. The only communications they have up in those mountains will be whatever the BBC provides. Or perhaps a short-wave radio.

Sure. But it will take a few days to get someone up there where they are.

I can wait. Thomas isn't going anywhere for a while if he can help it.

Lev felt guilty for what he was asking Lourds to do, but it couldn't be helped. Maybe if Lourds looked at the material for a day or two, he could help break the problem. Or at least provide a fresh perspective to work from.

I appreciate this, Ziya.

No sweat, prof. If it hadn't been for you, I wouldn't ever have been able to go to college. I owe you.

Thanks.

They talked a bit longer, then Lev passed on the message to Lourds, signed off, and returned to his work. At first, he thought he'd been too quick to send for Lourds, but tonight wasn't the first time he'd considered getting in touch with his old friend. The Israeli government people Lev was dealing with wouldn't be happy, though. They didn't want outsiders involved in this project.

Gazing back at the television in the living area, Lev saw another television spot about Lourds and the find at the temple.

The Israeli government definitely wasn't going to appreciate the way Lourds seemed to draw the public eye.

But Lev was convinced there was no other choice. He'd taken his search as far as he could on his own. It was time for new blood.

The cell phone on the desk vibrated. Lev picked it up and punched the button. 'Hello.'

'Lev?'

He tried to place the female voice and couldn't.

'I'm in trouble. I need help.' The speaker sounded hurt and afraid. 'Please, Lev.'

His fist tightened on the phone.

'Lev, it's Alice.'

Lev remembered her then. Alice Reinstadler had been Lourds's lover when they'd all been attending the Vienna School of Languages. He'd always had a crush on her, but he'd never acted on it out of respect for

Lourds. Then, after whatever had happened between Lourds and Alice had happened, she'd gotten married off by her parents to that racist imbecile, Klaus Von Volker.

'Alice.'

'Yes.' She choked back a sob, but sounded happy that he'd recognized her voice. 'I need help, Lev.'

'What's happened?'

'It's Klaus. I . . . He . . .' Her voice broke, and she couldn't go on.

Lev had never met Klaus Von Volker, but what he'd seen of the man on the news had convinced him that he wouldn't like the man. 'It's all right. Where are you?'

'In Jerusalem. I didn't have anywhere else to go. My parents wouldn't understand. I told you how they were when we were in school together in Vienna.'

Lev remembered. Whenever *Herr* and *Frau* Reinstadler showed up at the university to visit, Alice had always become incredibly tense and unhappy.

She went on. 'Maybe this was the wrong thing to do. So much time has passed. I'm sorry to have bothered you.'

'Alice . . .' Lev let out a breath. He'd been scared for months, knowing he had enemies out there, but Ezra's story about the two dead guards made him feel even more vulnerable.

'It's all right. I understand.'

Afraid she would hang up, Lev responded immediately. 'I'm coming to get you. Tell me where you are.'

She was quiet for a moment, and Lev feared she'd thought better of contacting him and hung up. Then she spoke again. 'On Saint Mark's Road. Near the Lutheran Hostel.'

'I'll be there. Give me just a few minutes.' Lev stood and took up his coat, already heading for the door.

16

Lutheran Hostel
St. Mark's Road
Jerusalem, the State of Israel
July 28, 2011

Ezra hadn't agreed to the rescue trip, but in the end Lev hadn't given him a choice. After Alice's call, Lev had escaped from the apartment. Unfortunately, Ezra had discovered his getaway and come looking, finding him through a tracking device in his prosthesis Lev hadn't known about. The young Mossad agent hadn't caught up to Lev until he'd reached his destination, though, and his argument had proven persuasive enough to stay.

Lev sat in the passenger seat and tried calling the cell-phone number Alice had used to contact him. She wasn't answering.

'Still no reply?'

'No.' Lev closed the phone unhappily.

'Perhaps she's in a place where she cannot talk.' Ezra handled the car smoothly, negotiating the light evening traffic with ease. His gaze shifted relentlessly, always tracking and evaluating their surroundings. A machine pistol lay between the seats.

Lev wore a bulletproof vest despite his protests. The heavy garment itched in the heat. 'You didn't hear her. She was beside herself.' Every time he replayed the conversation in his mind, Alice sounded more desperate.

Ezra shrugged. 'Maybe she and her husband made up. A lot of people have arguments. Too much to drink, a few harsh words, then they make up later.'

'Her husband is Austrian People's Party leader Von Volker. He wouldn't show his face in this city.'

'Ah.' Ezra shook his head. 'That man I do not like. Anti-Semitic with ties to Iran. A partnership forged in hell for certain. What is this woman doing with him if she is such a good friend to you?'

'Her parents arranged the marriage.'

'What were they thinking?'

'They wanted Alice to marry into nobility. They think the same way as Von Volker when it comes to a unified Germany and Austria.'

'Are you sure she's a friend?' Ezra braked, then turned right onto St. Mark's Road.

'I am.'

'With parents like that . . .'

'Alice thinks her own thoughts.'

'She just doesn't pick her own husbands.' Ezra shook his head. 'My apologies. That was uncalled for.'

'It's all right. You don't know Alice. If you did, you wouldn't wonder about this. She was coerced by her parents, and she'd recently had her heart broken.' Lourds hadn't meant to do that, and Lev never faulted his friend.

Anyone who knew Lourds should have known he'd never give himself to anything but his work. 'Alice was hurt, confused, and wanted someone to love her. I'm sure Von Volker looked like quite a prize at the time.'

'What does she look like?' Slowing the car, Ezra scanned the nearly deserted sidewalks.

Another car, this one also carrying Mossad agents, trailed after them. Ezra had called in the second line of defense, and Lev couldn't even imagine the flak the young man had endured to put that together.

'Blond. Petite. Very pretty.' Lev searched for her along the sidewalks as well.

'How long has it been since you've seen her?'

'Years. Her husband doesn't let her stray far.' Lev felt sad for Alice when he mentioned that, but there'd been nothing he could do.

'Maybe she's changed.'

A moment later, a feminine form stepped out of the shadows near a coffee shop whose neon signs still shone. The moonlight and neon highlighted the pale blond hair, but the darkness masked her face.

'There she is.' Lev pointed.

'I see her.' Ezra applied the brakes and reached for the machine pistol. He spoke into the headset comm he wore. 'I have eyes-on. The subject is in the alley by the coffee shop.'

'Understood. Do you want us in close?'

'No. Just play everything loose.' Ezra pulled the car into the alley only a few feet from the woman.

Lev popped the door open and got out, avoiding Ezra's desperate grab. 'Alice?'

She turned to him then, and the neon lights from the coffee shop took away just enough of the night to reveal her features in profile. Even then, Lev knew the woman wasn't Alice.

Before he could say anything, she turned and ran, and he knew something was very wrong. He turned to shout a warning to Ezra, but the young Mossad agent's neck blossomed bright blood that spattered Lev's face. Ezra staggered, managed to get the machine pistol in his hand, and went down.

The second car shrieked to a stop behind them. Before the two agents in it could get out, the vehicle exploded, leaping into the air and flipping over. Flames enveloped it, and the heat drove Lev backwards.

Three men dressed in black erupted from the alley. They bristled with weapons, but one man carried a curious pistol. The weapon hissed rather than detonated, and something sharp struck Lev in the throat.

Lev wrapped his hands around his neck and felt the small dart lodged in the hollow of his jaw. A warm lassitude filled his head, invaded his brain, and he was falling.

The men were good.

Watching from the shadows, Rayan Mufarrij appreciated the simple, brutal attack. If he'd had the manpower, the ability to manipulate the target as these men had, he would have done the same thing. The woman – not the one that had been there, but the one she was supposed to represent – meant something to Lev Strauss. She wasn't who she'd claimed to be, though. Strauss had started moving away before his attackers had struck. He'd recognized her as a stranger, or someone other than who he thought she was.

Mufarrij stayed where he was and kept watching. He was a patient man. A man in his calling either learned patience quickly or died. Muffarrij was forty years old, and twenty-five years into his chosen vocation.

If anyone intercepted him and recognized him, his life would be forfeit. The Israelis wanted him dead for assassinations of their people. The Shiites would kill him on general principles, and Colonel Davari had lost key personnel on operations that had brushed too closely to ones Mufarrij had been conducting. Al-Qaeda had placed a bounty on him for all the death and destruction he'd wreaked on their numbers in his native Saudi Arabia.

All in all, Jerusalem wasn't a good place for him to be, and an even worse place for him to get caught playing in the backyards of others.

He stood in the alley with the motorcycle he'd had waiting for him when he'd followed Von Volker's mercenary team to Jerusalem. Local contacts, men he trusted and had worked with before, had supplied him with it and his weapons.

Across the street, working in the light and twisting

shadows given off by the burning car, Lev Strauss's kidnappers gathered him up and carried him to a small cargo van at the back of the alley. Mufarrij knew the alley was a dead end from his earlier recon of the area.

Knowing the men would be back, Mufarrij pulled on his full-face helmet and climbed aboard the motorcycle. He pressed the ignition button, and the engine caught smoothly. The flat black motorcycle blended perfectly into the darkness. He wore black riding leathers, just another shadow in the city.

A small Fiat raced from the alley, followed by the cargo van and trailed by a second sedan. Von Volker's mercenary team had seven men. Three had been on the capture, two on the rocket launcher, and two more acting as lookouts.

Mufarrij engaged the clutch and dropped the shift lever into first gear with his left foot. He followed the caravan as it shot through the twisting streets. They were driving too fast, certain to draw the attention of local law enforcement. Mufarrij knew from that action that they didn't have far to go. If they intended to drive out of the city, they would have driven more slowly.

If they were acting quickly, he had to as well. He reached into his jacket and drew the Glock 18C from its shoulder leather. He smiled at the thought of using it. Glock had developed the vicious little 9mm machine pistol at the insistence of EKO Cobra, the Austrian counterterrorist force that was formed to protect Jewish immigrants chased through Austria by Palestinian militants. Mufarrij knew that Von Volker would not have approved the pistol's use.

Holding the motorcycle steady with his body, the cruise control on, Mufarrij removed the seventeen-round magazine and took one of the thirty-three-round magazines from the small duffel strapped to the handlebars. After sliding it into place, he held the Glock in his left hand and sped up alongside the rear car. He saw the two men inside – both Europeans – as he raced by.

They stared at him as he passed, and he knew they'd alert their teammates, but it was already too late. The motorcycle left him vulnerable to a degree, but he was nimble as a falcon in flight. He preferred the nimbleness.

The van driver swerved across the street in an effort to knock him aside. Mufarrij dodged the clumsy sideswipe with a smile. Pointing his pistol at the driver, he scared the man into moving away. The van's passenger shoved himself through the window on his side, hoisted himself into a sitting position so he could fire, but Mufarrij accelerated as he squeezed the trigger. The blast from the man's weapon stitched across a line of parked cars. Holes appeared in their fenders and windows blew out in clouds of flying glass.

Drawing abreast of the lead car, Mufarrij aimed the Glock at the driver from a few feet out. Panicked, certain he was about to die, the driver cut the wheels sharply left, trying to use the car as a weapon.

Mufarrij leaned left as well, heeling the cycle over as

he brought the Glock down and emptied the thirty-three-round magazine at the front tires. The bullets blew out the left-front tire, then he shifted his aim to the edge of the carriage, knowing the parabellums would ricochet off the street and tear into the passenger-side tire.

With both tires blown, throwing rubber in all directions, and the bare rims sparking on the stones, the driver lost control of the vehicle and it flipped onto its side. As Mufarrij wheeled the motorcycle around, the stricken car skidded across the street, sparks flaring all around it.

Mufarrij slid off the motorcycle and swapped the empty magazine for a full one, tucking two more full mags into his jacket pocket. He pulled the helmet off because it restricted his vision.

The two men in the overturned car never had a chance. Mufarrij executed them as they slid toward him, shooting through the cracked windshield into their faces. The car shot on past him, the grinding metal drowning out all other sounds.

The van driver tried to brake, but it was too late. He rear-ended the overturned car, the van slewing sideways in the road.

Mufarrij strode to the driver, shot him in the head, then thrust his gun arm through the window and unleashed a short blast that punched the second man through the passenger window. There was a third man in the van, but Mufarrij didn't have time to look for him. He changed out the magazine and raced to the back of the van as two men got out of the rear escort car. Taking cover behind the car doors, they opened fire, forcing him to hide behind the side of the van.

Momentarily pinned, Mufarrij reached into his jacket pocket and took out a grenade. Knowing he'd be traveling through the Jewish parts of the city, he'd come heavily equipped.

Pulling the pin, he slipped the spoon off the grenade, counted two seconds, then underhanded it toward the car, just before he ducked back under cover. His timing was perfect, and the explosion went off under the front wheels.

The car jumped up, and the antipersonnel fragmentation took out the legs of the mercenaries concealing themselves behind the doors. The blast also ripped through the tires, making the vehicle settle heavily onto the ground.

Mufarrij braced the pistol in both hands as he strode forward. One of the men struggled to get to his feet, but he was disoriented and bleeding profusely from his lower legs and feet. Mufarrij put a three-round burst through the man's head and searched for the second one.

The other man lay beside the car, bleeding out. A piece of shrapnel had sliced through the inside of his right thigh and cut the femoral artery. As Mufarrij watched, the man lost consciousness.

A squeal of terror came from inside the car. Blood

stained the blond woman's head as she tried to push herself up. Her face slashed and speckled by broken glass, she stared at Mufarrij with wide, shocked eyes.

'No. Please. Please, don't – '

Mufarrij shot the blonde twice in the chest, sparing her family the agony of her ruined face. She fell back out of view without a sound.

Ignoring the van's rear door, Mufarrij raced forward to the driver's door. Men used to working in groups tended to cover a single field of fire, relying on their comrades to cover the others. The final mercenary in the van would be panicked with all his teammates lying dead around him. And he still had to protect their kidnap victim. Expecting an attacker to come in through the rear doors, he would be completely focused on them.

Peering through the open driver's window, Mufarrij spotted the last mercenary crouched in the rear compartment. Lev Strauss lay on the vehicle's floor, barely stirring, still overcome by whatever narcotic they'd used on him.

17

St. Mark's Road
Jerusalem, the State of Israel
July 28, 2011

Mufarrij took one step away from the van and aimed at the vehicle's side. The sheet metal wouldn't deflect the bullets much. Squeezing the Glock's trigger, he spread a burst down the van's length, staying level at about where he thought the last mercenary's chest would be. When he finished, he sprang to the vehicle's rear and yanked open the cargo door.

Inside, the mercenary leaned up against the far wall, holding a bloody hand over one of at least two wounds in his side. As the door opened, the man tried to lift the submachine gun on a sling around his neck.

Mufarrij put two rounds into the man's face. The corpse stumbled back two steps and sat down heavily against the cargo mesh separating the compartment from the driver's area.

Pulling a miniflashlight from his pants pocket, Mufarrij stepped up into the van and played the beam over Strauss. Blood dotted the man's face, and at first Mufarrij feared one of the rounds had gone astray. Then he realized the spatter was from the last dead man. With a small sigh of relief, he squatted down beside Strauss.

'Professor Strauss. Can you hear me?'

Feeling drunk and confused, Lev Strauss tried to focus. A man was kneeling above him. The face seemed familiar somehow, but he couldn't place it. 'Thomas, is that you?' For a moment, he thought he was back at the plane crash in the Dead Sea. Things had been bewildering then, like this was. He thought maybe he was dreaming, but there was a sharp pain in the side of his head.

Then Lev's vision cleared a bit, and he saw it wasn't Lourds crouched over him at all.

This man's black hair was long and wild, and his beard was bushy. He almost looked like an American Hells Angel, but Lev was pretty certain that no Hells Angel had ever been born with those dark Arabic features. Or maybe he only thought about outlaw bikers because the man wore black riding leathers and a jacket.

'Professor Strauss. I'm going to get you out of here. I need you to help me.' The man tried to pull Lev to his feet.

Lev gripped the man's proffered arm and struggled to help get to his feet, but his limbs didn't work well. He had no strength in his arms and he couldn't feel if his legs were under him. 'Who are you?'

'A friend. You were in a car wreck. I'm trying to help get you to safety.'

As the man pulled Lev to his numb foot and held

him upright, he saw the dead man sitting against the cargo mesh. Two more sat on the other side of the wire in the driver's compartment. Blood was everywhere. Frantically, Lev fought against his 'rescuer,' remembering the fake Alice, the way the blood had jumped from Ezra's neck, and the dart hitting him in the throat.

'Take it easy. Go slow. I don't want you to get hurt any more than you already are.' The big man held Lev and talked in a soothing tone, and his words sounded true. 'I'm not one of them. I'm here to help you.'

'Where's Ezra?'

'Back at the abduction site.'

'Is he all right?'

The big man shook his head. 'I don't know. Everything happened too quickly. When I saw you had been taken, I came after you.'

'You were there?'

'Yes. In the alley across the street.'

Lev thought hard, trying to imagine the scene again, but found that it kept sliding through his mental fingers. 'I didn't see you.'

'You weren't supposed to.'

'The other team died in that car.'

'They did.' The big man pulled one of Lev's arms across his shoulder and walked him to the rear of the van. They had to move while stooped over.

'Are you Mossad?'

'Yes.'

Lev stared ahead of them, willing his wits to come

back to him. The drug had overpowered his system, and he knew he was lucky to be conscious at all. 'Where are you taking me?'

'Somewhere safe. Somewhere that you can work on the Book.'

'All right.' As Lev started to step down onto the ground beside the big man, 'Alice' rose in the backseat of the semiblown-up car in front of them. Blood covered her blouse and leaked from the corner of her mouth.

Lev frowned in confusion. 'That's not Alice . . .'

Startled, the big man looked up, but it was already too late.

'Alice' had a pistol in her hand, and bright yellow flashes burst in front of her. Something slapped Lev's skull hard, knocking him backwards. The big man's arm was no longer around him, and he was falling.

Mufarrij couldn't believe the woman wasn't dead, or that she would come up shooting instead of simply lying there hoping she would survive. The wild look in her eyes told him she was moving on pure adrenaline, which must have been the only thing keeping her alive.

He felt a bullet hammer the body armor under the motorcycle jacket, then Strauss jerked in his grip and started falling backward.

Whipping the Glock up, Mufarrij fired by instinct. Three rounds pierced the woman's chest, then a bullet hit right between her wide eyes. Her head snapped back, and she fell once more into the backseat.

Angry at the events and at the woman, Mufarrij crouched over Strauss. A single glance at the horrible wound in the man's face told the story. The bullet that had glanced off Mufarrij's body armor had crashed into the man's temple. Flattened from the body armor, the bullet had made a horrible, bloody mess of Strauss's face.

Miraculously, the man's mouth worked, and he had just enough strength to speak three words. 'Get . . . Thomas . . . Lourds.' Then the air went out of him, and he seemed to wilt there on the stone street.

Mufarrij was acutely aware of the seconds passing. It wouldn't be long before law enforcement arrived. Or maybe the Mossad. When the bodyguard teams had gone offline, that would have triggered a response on their part as well.

Knowing there was nothing else he could do here, Mufarrij ran to his motorcycle, righted it, and threw a leg over. The machine started at once, and the back tire spun for just a moment as he wheeled it around. Then rubber found traction, and he shot out of there.

Thomas Lourds. Mufarrij knew the name. The American's activities in Saudi Arabia only last year were well-known. Very few people knew the whole story of how Vice President Webster had gone missing and later turned up drowned during those hard times. When Mufarrij had heard the stories from his superiors, he hadn't believed it.

But now, thanks to all the television coverage, he

knew exactly where to find Thomas Lourds. Mufarrij stayed low over the handlebars and sped off into the night.

With Lev Strauss dead, he, the Mossad, and the Ayatollah's men were all scrambling for the next clue in the hunt for Mohammad's legendary Book and Scroll.

18

Schloss Volker
Vienna, Austria
July 29, 2011

Rage and pain consumed Klaus Von Volker as he watched the news footage from Jerusalem.

Controlled and outwardly calm, he sat at the big desk in his office. He loved it because it was solid and heavy, a prime piece of Austrian woodcraft made with maple and ebony parquetry, inlaid with mother-of-pearl, ebony, and exotic woods. It was the kind of desk that Prince Klemens Wenzel Nepomuk Lothar von Metternich or Napoleon Bonaparte might have sat at while planning the future course of empires.

Von Volker did that every day that he sat at the desk. The den was a man's room, redolent of fine cigars and brandy. One wall held a collection of weapons, swords and guns that spanned centuries. It wasn't a place that Colonel Davari found comforting.

On the large-screen television set into the wall, news footage showed the wreckage of the three vehicles that had carried the mercenaries Von Volker had sent to retrieve Lev Strauss.

'What happened?' Davari sat in one of the bentwood chairs in front of the desk.

'Lev Strauss was killed.' Von Volker backed up the film footage and froze the screen on an image. Two ambulance workers ferried Strauss's body to their waiting vehicle. 'See for yourself.'

'You're sure he's dead?'

'With a hole like that in your face, you'd be dead, too.'

'Perhaps.'

Von Volker sucked in a breath through gritted teeth. 'We have caught some luck at this point.'

'What?'

'The Israeli government has chosen to hide Strauss's identity for the time being. They're claiming this was a terrorist action.'

'Why?'

'You know the Mossad, Colonel. They like to control information.' Von Volker shrugged. 'That explanation will hold for a while before it comes apart, but it will eventually give way to the truth. For now, though, the explanation covers all the weapons and violence found at the scene.'

'Will the Mossad be able to track those men back to you?'

Von Volker smiled at that, but it was forced. He didn't like having his ability questioned. The question was in bad taste and offensive. He was certain Davari intended it to be the latter. 'No. I was careful.'

'If you really had been careful, we would have Lev Strauss now.'

'Perhaps. But perhaps the carelessness didn't come from my involvement.' Von Volker locked his gaze on Davari. 'The man who did this has a past history with you, Colonel. Not me.' He tapped the keyboard in front of him.

The television image changed from the newsfeed to a closed-circuit satellite feed that showed the rear of the van as the attack began. There were multiple views, from the front of the van as well as from the interior.

'What is this?'

'I had the van wired and uploading streaming video and audio feeds through a small satellite connection.'

'All of that hardware will be discovered at the site.'

'It won't matter. It won't lead investigators anywhere. My people know what they're doing, Colonel.'

'Yet, somehow, these men that you claim knew what they were doing managed to lose Lev Strauss.'

Stung, Von Volker clamped his jaw shut.

On the screen, the view shifted suddenly as the van collided with the overturned car. In the next instant, a man stepped partially into view and shot the van's driver, then the passenger.

Colonel Davari sat up straighter, interested in spite of himself. 'One man did all this?'

'Yes.' Von Volker shifted through the video feeds. He'd already marked the places he wanted to show the colonel. 'Make sure you mention this to the Ayatollah. I certainly plan to.' His words were a thinly veiled threat. 'The way he moves, the quick and professional way he kills, I thought he would be known to you.'

The image kept playing, showing the attack as it progressed. Despite the fact that the men in Jerusalem had all been hardened mercenaries who had seen action around the globe, the lone killer had cut a swath through them as if it were child's play.

When the man stepped into the van and shot the last mercenary there, Von Volker froze the screen. 'I had some of my computer people work with this shot. They tweaked the image until we got a good look at the man's face.' He pressed another button, and the cleaned-up image of the assassin enlarged and filled the screen in much clearer focus.

The man looked wild and elemental. Scars showed under his eyes and in the hollows of his cheeks. He'd been cut and shot, and the bottom of his right ear and the right side of his neck were covered in burn scars.

'Do you know this man?'

Colonel Davari looked for only a moment. 'No.' He didn't even bother to try to hide the fact that he was lying.

'His name is Rayan Mufarrij.' Von Volker spoke the words deliberately. 'Despite the best efforts of my intelligence people, not much has turned up on him. The man is a ghost. He's been a deep undercover agent working for Saudi Arabia's Emergency Force, the counterterrorist division of the General Security. For *years.* I'm surprised you don't know of such a man as this.'

Davari shook his head. 'They are simply terrorists by another name.'

Von Volker ignored that. 'This man, my sources tell me, reports solely to the House of Saud.' He advanced the footage, and on the screen, Mufarrij finished off the last mercenary, grabbed Strauss, and nearly got away with him.

If not for Elise.

Von Volker watched the woman push herself up with the pistol and fire at her killer. In his heart, Von Volker wanted to believe that Elise knew precisely what she was doing, that she was striving to complete the favor he'd asked her to do. In reality, he knew she was already dying and probably had no clue about what she was doing.

He was going to miss her, but he still couldn't help being angry with her because she hadn't killed Mufarrij. If only she'd been as good with the pistol as she was in bed. The situation was truly lamentable.

Switching off the television, Von Volker focused on Davari. 'You can tell the story any way you wish, Colonel, but I'm going to tell the Ayatollah that I've never had any dealing with Mufarrij. The only way that man could have found me was through you. You've got leaks in your organization. And don't try to tell me that Mufarrij found Strauss on his own. If he had, the man would have already disappeared.'

Davari couldn't argue with that, and Von Volker knew it.

'So, Colonel, what are we to do?'

'Our intelligence agencies are not entirely lax.' Davari stood. 'One of our computer technicians has already hacked into Strauss's computer.'

'From a remote connection?'

'Yes.'

Von Volker shrugged. 'Then you already know about the Facebook message Strauss sent to Ziya Kadeer?'

Davari wasn't quick enough to hide his surprise at that, but it went away quickly. 'Yes. We have agents en route to the Himalayas to find Thomas Lourds.'

'What are you going to do with him when you find him?'

'For the moment, nothing. We will wait and watch him.'

Irritated, Von Volker shook his head. 'You could tell from the Facebook message that Lourds doesn't know anything. Strauss was bringing him in to consult on this.'

'I know. And only days ago Thomas Lourds discovered a hidden civilization lost for thousands of years. He was also involved in that Atlantis business a couple of years ago. Such a man bears watching. So we will watch him.'

Von Volker wasn't happy with that. Watching was too passive, but at this point Davari had the lead. If Von Volker were in charge, things would go quite differently.

19

Scholar's Rock Temple
Himalaya Mountains
People's Republic of China
July 30, 2011

'These people came a long way to leave their mark. Can you imagine the hardships they faced? After being chased out of their own lands by flood and by warring factions, they faced the bitter, unforgiving cold of these mountains every day.'

Standing to one side of the American news team shooting footage of Gloria Chen as she recounted the story of the 'Scholar's Rock' immigrants as those people were currently being called, Lourds smiled. He leaned over to Professor Hu, who stood beside him. 'She's getting really good in front of the camera.'

Hu nodded. 'She shows a knowledge of her subject, yes, and she appears very confident.'

'Of course she's confident. She has a reason to be. At this moment, she's one of the foremost authorities on the "Scholar's Rock" people.'

Hu sighed and shook his head. 'We really need to find a different name to call them.'

'What?' Lourds shrugged. 'It's like with rock bands, all the really good names are already taken. We used a lot of them on the Native American tribes.'

'Of course. Well, back to work.' Hu patted him on the shoulder and walked away.

Lourds watched the man walk around the news crew and return to the temple. At the center of the crowd, Gloria grinned and answered questions from the rapt reporters like she'd been doing it all her life.

He laughed at the sight, then went back into the temple as well. There was still a ton of cataloguing to do.

'Rice?'

Lourds looked up from the Jiahu script he was attempting to decipher.

Gloria stood there with a steaming bowl in her hands. The spicy smell made Lourds's belly growl. She grinned at him. 'I suppose you missed lunch again?'

'It's lunchtime?'

'This is dinner.' Gloria placed the rice bowl on the floor next to Lourds.

He sat on the floor with his legs crossed, a notebook and pen in one hand and digital printouts of the Jiahu script in his other hand. He'd been sitting long enough that his legs had gone numb, and he hadn't noticed it. He stretched them out now, wincing as pinpricks of boiling pain flared along his thighs and calves.

'Honestly, Thomas, you need a keeper.' Gloria lay back on the bed and yawned.

'You're not the first to tell me that, you know.' He put down the notebook and pictures, then picked up the rice bowl. 'However, I believe I'm quite capable of taking care of myself.'

Gloria snorted.

'You looked good out there today.'

She rolled over onto her side and grinned at him. 'With the reporters?'

'Yes.' Lourds blew on a spoonful of rice and ate it.

'I was good, wasn't I?' She smiled, and it looked a little smug though he didn't begrudge her for it.

'Natural talent wins out.'

She gazed at him. 'I know you and Professor Hu have been pushing me in front of the cameras.'

'Maybe a little.'

'Why?'

'We wanted you to have a chance to shine. But to be honest, we also wanted to put a new face on our disciplines.'

'Someone younger?'

Lourds mock grimaced, but he wasn't totally unmarked by the observation. 'Yes. Seeing you answering questions, the audience – including people who fund the research we do as well as young college students looking for a field – believes doing what we do is really sexy.'

'Flatterer.'

'You're welcome.' Lourds ate more rice.

'You're kind of sexy, too.'

'"Kind of"?'

'You're also incredibly vain.'

'That's a failing I'll own up to.'

'Because people accept that from you.' Gloria smiled. 'I bet most women you've known wouldn't want you any other way, and at the same time they were irritated by the way you can be so involved with them and at the same time be so aloof.'

Lourds decided that was a topic best left unexplored. Gloria's evaluation of him was dead-on, though. His work was everything to him, and he couldn't fathom the day that anything – or anyone – would take him away from that.

'So how are you coming with your papers?'

'All right. I've been writing press releases for various news agencies as well.'

That surprised Lourds.

'You didn't know that, did you?'

He decided to be honest and shook his head. 'Been caught up in my own studies, I'm afraid. I haven't deciphered much of the new Jiahu script we've found, but I believe that's going to come. I just wish the progress would come faster.'

'It will. That's what you're good at.'

'I know.'

'I also got a book-deal offer.'

That really surprised Lourds. He finished up the rice and put it aside. 'That's fantastic.' His own agent was already putting together a submission to take to auction. His other books had been bestsellers, and there was no reason to think this one wouldn't be as well.

'I know you're going to do a book too.'

'Probably.' Lourds was going to do the book. He just didn't know whom he'd be doing it for yet.

'In a way, we're going to be competitors.'

'I wouldn't look at it that way. We've both got different things we're bringing to the party.'

'The old guard versus the new, is that it?'

Lourds's smile was wry this time. 'I'd describe it as youth versus experience. I'll be very interested in reading your conclusions when your book is published, Gloria.'

She rose to her feet and headed for the door. 'And I yours, Thomas.'

Lourds watched her go, his smile still in place. *Competition, indeed.*

Down in the hidden cavern the next day, Lourds was hunkered over a strange stone tablet that held not only the Jiahu script but a type of cuneiform he'd never seen before. It reminded him of Egyptian writing before the written language had fully developed there. But this wasn't Egyptian.

Kneeling beside him, Hu surveyed the stone tablet. 'We've never known the Jiahu tribes to use stone as a medium. Their writing tools were more suited to tortoiseshells and bone.'

'I know.' Lourds rubbed his beard thoughtfully. 'They

didn't remain static while they lived here. They progressed.'

'On their own? Or from contact with others?'

Lourds shook his head. 'Hard to say. Perhaps a combination of both. There's always been trade traffic through these mountains. These people could have met caravans, adopted members into their tribe from other cultures. We'll know more when DNA – if any – is processed. You and I know a lot of languages – especially written ones – were spurred on by trade. Original languages get bastardized and diluted, spun in different directions because of mutual needs.'

Hu nodded. 'There had to be an accounting of profits and debts, of stock and merchandise, of people traded with.'

'And of births and deaths and property.' Lourds stared down at the stone tablet. 'Those people lived in these caves for a long time. I wish I knew why.'

'Get those documents translated, and maybe you'll know.'

Lifting an arm, Lourds mopped sweat from his face. With all the bodies and high-intensity lights packed into the cavern, the ambient temperature had steadily risen. 'I hope so.' He paused. 'Did you know Gloria had gotten a book deal?'

Hu hesitated just long enough that he knew lying wouldn't work. He shrugged. 'Yes. One of the aggressive independent booksellers, as I understand. They're hoping to cash in on the youth market.'

Lourds nodded. 'It's a good angle. Why didn't you tell me?'

'It wasn't my place.' Hu studied Lourds. 'Does it bother you, Thomas?'

'No.' He knew that wasn't exactly the truth, but he was pretty sure he didn't know what the truth was. Things had gotten blurred.

'In some ways, my friend, Gloria reminds me of you.'

Lourds resettled his hat, conscious of the people around them, but no one was paying any attention. 'Me?'

'Yes. She's ambitious, driven, consumed by her passion for what she does.'

'I suppose.' Lourds wasn't sure how to respond to the remark, particularly given how accurate it was.

'Professor Lourds?'

Turning, Lourds spotted Gelu motioning to him from the cavern's entrance. Lourds walked over to the Sherpa.

'There's a man here to see you. He wants to speak only to you.'

Lourds shot a glance at Hu. 'My admiring public awaits.'

Hu waved to him.

At the cavern mouth, Lourds strapped into the climbing harness, then attached himself to the safety line that ran up the side of the chasm wall. Secured, he heaved himself up the pitons, climbing with ease even though there was some soreness. Repeated ascents and descents had taken their toll on him the last few days.

*

At the cavern mouth where the false wall had been, Lourds looked down at all the media people in the Scholar's Rock cavern. Many of them had left now that that the initial furor had died down, but several working on long-term projects – such as Rory and the BBC team – remained. Everyone here seemed busy.

Gelu heaved himself up beside Lourds.

'Which man, Gelu?'

'There.' The Sherpa pointed, singling out a tall, dark man in winter wear. It was obvious he'd come straight to the cavern. 'Say he know you.'

Lourds studied the man, but wasn't certain. Something about the his features seemed familiar. Then a younger face surfaced in Lourds's memory. He grinned and waved. 'Big Mike!'

The young man glanced up and smiled, waving excitedly. 'Professor Thomas!'

20

Scholar's Rock Temple
Himalaya Mountains
People's Republic of China
July 30, 2011

Known affectionately as 'Big Mike,' Turghunjun had been a smallish teenager with an insatiable curiosity the last time Lourds had seen him. Over the last fourteen years, Big Mike had grown into his nickname. Lourds had trouble gripping the younger man's large hand, and was swallowed up when Big Mike wrapped him in a bear hug and lifted him from the ground.

'You've gotten big, Big Mike.' Once he was returned to the ground, Lourds felt a little dizzy after being squeezed so hard.

'You've gotten small, Professor Thomas.' Big Mike grinned happily. 'But it's okay. Your hat still makes you look tall.'

'Thanks. I suppose you heard about the discovery, found out I was involved, and decided to come see me.'

Big Mike shook his shaggy head. 'Not really. That's a long climb to make even for an old friend.'

Lourds had also helped fund Big Mike's college, but

he didn't say anything about that. However, he was a little hurt by the Uighur man's honesty.

'So, if you didn't come here to see me, then why did you come?'

'To see you.'

'I don't understand.'

'Ziya asked me to give you a message from Professor Lev.'

'All right.'

'In private.' Big Mike looked around. 'There are too many ears here.'

'Sure. I've got private quarters. I've also got cold beer.'

Big Mike sat awkwardly in one of the canvas chairs Lourds had borrowed from one of the media teams. He sipped the bottle of Mongozo Lourds had given him, which he'd paid one of the supply teams to bring. Lourds had been pleasantly surprised to find the African beer brewed from bananas. He'd only had it a few times before.

'How is Lev?' Lourds uncapped his own bottle and took a sip. It was cold and clean and hit the spot.

'Ziya says he was doing good. They didn't talk long.'

'I haven't heard from him in over a year, I guess.' Lourds was surprised that so much time had passed. If people weren't in his everyday life, he tended to let an awful lot of time pass before he contacted them. It came with staying busy. Thankfully, most of Lourds's friends and associates led busy lives as well and understood. 'What are you doing these days?'

Big Mike shrugged. 'I guide people up and down the mountain, do some writing for magazines and documentaries on the side, and raise my kids.'

'Kids?'

'Yep. Two of them. Girls.' Big Mike smiled ruefully. 'At home I swim in an ocean of estrogen. I get breaks between guide assignments, but I'm always ready to go back into the mountains.'

Lourds laughed at the young man. 'Your English is fantastic.'

'I studied hard at university, and my wife makes it a rule that only English is spoken at home. She's British, and she's a pediatrician.'

'And living in the Tarim Basin?'

'Can you believe it?'

'No. You're a most fortunate young man.'

'I know. Really, I do. So . . . I don't suppose you've found a woman to make an honest man of you yet?'

'My work is my life, Big Mike. You know that from the time I spent with you.'

'I remember. First man up in the morning and the last one to stop telling stories at night.' Big Mike smiled. 'I don't know if you were aware of it, but all the village kids were in awe of you.'

'They were bored, and I was someone different.'

'So was Professor Lev. They gravitated toward you, though.'

Feeling slightly embarrassed, Lourds changed the subject. 'Let's see this message Lev sent.'

Big Mike handed over an envelope that contained a single piece of paper. Lourds opened the paper and read the printout.

July 23

Thomas, forgive the cloak-and-dagger approach to getting message to you. Thankfully, Ziya said he could get this to you.

I'm in a bit of a quandary, old friend. I think i'm on the trail of a find of a lifetime. Maybe even something as big as Atlantis, though I doubt you'll be willing to accept this. I can imagine you rolling your eyes about now.

'Professor Thomas, is there a joke you'd care to share?'

Lourds glanced at Big Mike. 'There's no joke. Why would you think there was a joke?'

'You were rolling your eyes like there was something funny.'

'Oh – no. Probably my eyes are just tired from being down here.' Lourds kept reading.

I can't tell you much in this missive, and I know that you're busy with your new find. I'll understand if you decide not to come, but if you could come – even for just a few days – I would deeply appreciate it. I've gotten stuck in the research and don't know where else to turn.

I also want to advise you to be careful. At least two men that have been involved with this project may have been killed because of it.

If you're too busy, please know that I understand. Sometimes our lives are not our own.

All best,

Lev

When he'd finished the note, Lourds read it again, wishing Lev had been more forthcoming. Then again, if Lev really was on to something that big, he'd be playing his cards close to his vest.

'Professor Thomas?'

Lourds looked up at Big Mike.

The young man looked troubled. 'Is something wrong?'

'No. I don't suppose you know what Lev is working on, do you?'

Big Mike shook his head.

Lourds drained his beer and stood. 'I guess there's only one way to find out.'

The telephone rang and rang. At first, no one answered. Lourds stood outside the temple on a nearby hill where the satellite phone's reception was better. He'd borrowed a boost from one of the media groups streaming live feeds back to their parent company.

Cold and uneasy, Lourds listened to the phone ring. He tucked his free hand up under his arm and stared out over the frozen landscape. Just as he was certain the line was about to go to the answering service, a woman answered.

'Hello?'

'My name is Thomas Lourds. I'm a friend and associate of Professor Lev Strauss. I'm trying to get in touch with him, and this is the only number I have.'

'Of course. I'm afraid Lev isn't here right now.' The woman's voice was cold and efficient, reminding Lourds of some of the secretaries at Harvard.

'I can call back. Do you know when you'll be expecting him?'

'I can't say at the moment.'

Well, scratch the efficiency. The secretaries and office managers at Harvard would have known exactly where their charges were and when they could expect them to return.

'Can I leave a number? Lev can call me at his convenience.'

'Of course.' Dutifully, the woman wrote Thomas's contact number down.

21

Covert Operations
Institute for Intelligence and Special Operations (Mossad)
Tel Aviv, the State of Israel
July 30, 2011

Katsas (Collections Officer) Sarah Shavit cradled the phone and stared at the image of the handsome man on the computer screen in front of her. She was familiar with him, of course. She'd read his file when getting acquainted with the operation involving Lev Strauss. More than that, she kept a copy of *Bedroom Pursuits* next to her bed.

'That was Lourds?'

Startled, Sarah looked up at her superior. Isser Melman was sixty and sleek, with silver hair and a weathered face. His prosthetic right eye didn't always track properly and sometimes gave him the appearance of looking in two directions at once.

Sarah nodded.

Melman entered the room and sat at one of the chairs facing the desk. He crossed one knee over the other and straightened the hem of his pants. 'You didn't tell him Strauss was dead.'

'He didn't seem to know. I saw no reason to scare him off at this point. I sent you the report regarding Lev Strauss's Facebook communication with Ziya Kadeer.'

'Perhaps telling Lourds his friend was dead might have made him come here.'

Sarah leaned back in her chair, trying to find a more comfortable position. Since Lev Strauss's assassination two days ago, she'd spent every waking hour poring over the files they had assembled on the man. She'd also ordered an additional layer, springing out from Strauss's known associates, to be gathered.

'Perhaps.'

'Then why not tell him?'

'We saw the note Strauss sent to Lourds, but Strauss was a master linguist – as well as being one of our agents – and Lourds is a clever man. There's a chance that Strauss communicated sensitive information in that message. I have our cryptographers going over it, but they've found nothing so far.'

'There has been some speculation that Lourds is a CIA agent.'

Sarah shook her head. 'I don't believe that.'

'Why?'

'Lourds isn't jaded enough or careful enough to be a CIA agent.' Sarah glanced at the image of the man on the computer screen. 'He's still an innocent. Despite his age, he's still very much a boy, more interested in his adventures and the puzzles he comes across.'

'Then let's hope he finds Lev's message puzzling

enough to lure him to Jerusalem. If Strauss's beliefs are correct, the world as we know it is in jeopardy.' Melman glanced at the desktop littered with files. 'Do we have anything on the mercenaries found with Strauss?'

'No. Those men all have spotty histories. Tracking them has proven difficult. We've connected them to operations by several corporations around the world so far.'

'So who runs mercenary operations?'

'Several international corporations have invested in those kinds of operations nowadays. Like any other corporate resource, those CEOs don't like to see assets idle when they could be out turning a profit. As a result, those mercenaries are often farmed out or loaned to smaller corporations that need black ops work done.'

Melman sighed. He already knew everything she was telling him. 'We saw this day coming, Sarah, where corporations would evolve into competition with intelligence agencies. Not only competition, but enemies.'

'Yes.'

'These are delicate games we play these days.'

Sarah nodded. 'I took the liberty of putting someone on Lourds.'

Surprise lifted Melman's eyebrow. 'Without consulting me?'

'Assigning someone to Lourds seems like overkill at this point, but I thought it might be a good training exercise for an agent we've been watching. Someone who can work in the shadows.'

Melman scratched his chin and smiled. 'That's what I like about you, Sarah. You're always thinking.'

'I try.'

'Who is the agent you put on Lourds?'

'Miriam Abata.' Sarah leaned forward and typed in the name. A moment later, Miriam Abata's file popped up on the screen. She turned it so Melman could see.

Miriam Abata was a pretty young woman. Dark hair hung in her face, partially obscuring one brown eye. In the picture, she was smiling, obviously amused. Her features were definitely Middle Eastern, with a hawk's nose, dark eyebrows, and dark coloration that was a mix of her Israeli mother and her Ethiopian father.

A frown deeply etched Melman's face. 'You sent a woman? With Lourds's record as a womanizer?'

'I made certain Miriam knows all about him. She's a good agent, Isser. She deserves a chance to prove herself.'

'What is she? Twenty-one, twenty-two? She looks like she just graduated university.'

'She's twenty-seven, actually, and she graduated university in New York just this year because she was getting a master's in Arabic languages and software design, specializing in encryption. Also, we were setting up a cover identity for her. She's one of the bright ones, a smart young woman. She can handle Lourds if she has to.'

'Let's hope she doesn't have to.' Melman's good eye narrowed. 'She's Jewish?'

'Yes. Her mother Sofia works in our cyber unit in the United States and is a citizen there, which Miriam is as well, but has a dual citizenship in Israel. Her father is Ethiopian, Beta Israel, and worked in Tehran as a field agent. His parents moved there when he was a small boy, and he grew up in Iran. He was killed by the Revolutionary Guard when Miriam was a teenager. You won't find anyone more loyal.'

'Where is Abata now?'

'At the temple site.'

'Has she made contact with Lourds?'

'No.' Sarah frowned. 'He's hard to get close to because he's involved in every aspect that's taking place there. Also, there's been no reason to contact Lourds directly.'

'She's a loose leash on the man.'

Sarah nodded. 'Very loose.'

Melman stood. 'As always, you've done well, Sarah. We don't yet have Strauss's research, and he saw fit to contact Lourds about it.'

'We assume.'

'I think it's a safe assumption. Keep Miriam on Lourds, and let's see what develops.'

'Yes, sir.'

'And let me know the minute you have any developments.'

'Of course.'

Melman left the room.

Sarah returned her attention to the screen. She tapped the keyboard again, and the screen returned to Thomas

Lourds. Why had Strauss reached out to the linguist when there were so many others he knew?

She didn't have an answer for the question, and that annoyed her.

On her desk, the encrypted satphone rang. The agent identification number assigned to Miriam Abata showed in the screen. Sarah scooped up the phone. 'Yes.'

'He's on the move.'

Sarah tensed, her thoughts sharpening. 'He's leaving the temple?'

'Apparently.' Excitement vibrated in Miriam's voice.

'How do you know?'

'I just walked past his private quarters. He's packing.'

'Does anyone else know?'

'Maybe his friend, Professor Hu. I'm not certain. I've been working in the lower level. Cataloguing.'

'Have you had contact with Lourds?'

'No. He doesn't even seem to know that I exist.' She sounded chagrined at that.

'That works to your advantage. If he's leaving the temple, I want you to stick close to him.'

'Of course. If he's intending to come to Jerusalem . . .'

'I'll make sure your cover identity has a ticket waiting at the airport and that you can switch it to Lourds's flight.'

'Thank you.'

Sarah thought about the brutal massacre that had left Lev Strauss, the unidentified woman, and the mercenaries dead. The man who had done that was still out there, still hunting. And they had no way of knowing what Strauss had told the man before dying.

'Stay close to Lourds if possible, but I want you to come back to us in one piece. Do you understand, Miriam?'

'Yes.'

'Good luck.' Sarah broke the connection and tried not to think about how young the woman was, or that she might just have sent Miriam Abata into harm's way.

22

Scholar's Rock Temple
Himalaya Mountains
People's Republic of China
July 31, 2011

'You're leaving?'

Lourds paused in his packing. Gloria Chen stood in the doorway of his personal quarters.

'Yes.' He tossed a shirt into the suitcase and tried to sort out his cleanest socks.

Without a word, she shouldered him aside, dumped all the contents from the suitcase, and started folding his clothes.

Feeling irritated and invaded, Lourds stepped back. 'Those are dirty.'

'Doesn't matter. They'll pack tighter and travel better if they're folded.' Gloria picked up a pair of jeans and started folding those as well. 'Want to tell me what's going on?'

'Honestly, I don't know.' Lourds cracked open a beer from the ice chest on the floor and offered her one. She accepted, and he gave her his, then reached for another, hooking the chilled bottle out with two fingers.

Finished with the suitcase, she zipped it closed and sat on the bed.

'I got a message from an old friend,' he said.

'Delivered by the guy the Sherpas brought in.'

'Yes.'

'Why didn't your friend call?'

'I don't know.'

'You could call him.'

'I tried.' Lourds sipped his beer.

'You're just going to walk away from everything we've got going on here?'

'I don't have a choice.'

'Yes, you do.' Anger tightened Gloria's face and darkened her eyes. 'Thomas, there's a lot of work to be done here. A lot of cataloguing, a lot of PR. If we play this right, we can interest enough universities or television-production-company deep pockets to fund our studies for years. Something like this *makes* careers.'

'I know.'

'"I know"?' Gloria looked exasperated. 'If you know, why aren't you staying?'

'Because I have to go.'

She studied him and shook her head. 'I've never met anyone like you. I've never seen anyone who could give himself to his work so completely.' She paused. 'It makes me curious about who could send a message and have you drop everything you're doing on a huge find like this. I mean, I know this isn't as big as Atlantis, but this is *something,* Thomas. You don't just throw something like this away.'

'I'm not throwing it away. I'm leaving it in very good hands. Yours and David's.'

'You know this isn't going to be the same if you leave. A lot of those people, especially the media people, are here to photograph Professor Thomas Lourds in his element, finding another mystery that history had kept locked up for so long.'

Lourds smiled. 'And now this place has been found.'

'So now you're through with it? Just going to ride off into the sunset?'

'It's not like that.'

'Who can just call you away like this?'

'A friend. An old friend.'

'A woman?'

'No. A man named Lev Strauss. He's an archaeologist in Jerusalem. We were friends, classmates, and competitors. Over thirteen years ago, we were on a plane that went down over the Dead Sea.' As he talked, Lourds remembered the screaming engines and panicked voices all around him. 'Everyone was certain we were going to die. A lot of people did.' The smell of burning flesh flooded his nose, and his heart was suddenly thudding in his chest as he relived those frantic moments. 'I hit my head when we crashed. Lev got me out of that plane, saved other people, and when the fuel tanks blew up, a piece of shrapnel cut off the bottom half of his left leg.' He took a breath and focused on Gloria. 'I wouldn't be here today if it weren't for him.' He shrugged. 'So when he calls for me, I'm going to go.'

Gloria held his gaze with hers. 'Even so, I can't believe you're walking away from this.'

'I know you can't, and I wish I could make you understand.' Lourds stood, slung his backpack on, slid his hat into place, and picked up the suitcase. Big Mike was already waiting.

He took a deep breath. 'You've got what you wanted, Gloria. You've got a great find, a book deal, a chance to continue your studies on something meaningful. You don't want anything else. Not really.'

'You want to know the saddest part?' She looked up at him with shiny eyes.

'What?'

'You're right. This is what I want. I'm not going to let go of this site till they pry my fingers off it. Nothing else matters. Just this chance to become something, to see something no one else has seen.'

'I know. Look, I'm taking copies of the language with me. If I get anywhere with it, I'll let you know. Please let me know how your work goes.'

'Sure.' Gloria crossed her arms. 'But there is a difference between us, you know.'

Lourds didn't say anything.

'You're weak enough to let a friend pull you away from this. I didn't think that would matter to you.'

Guilt flushed through Lourds, but he didn't say anything. He knew in his heart that it wasn't just the friendship for Lev that was drawing him to Jerusalem. It was the hint of the mystery, all the things that Lev hadn't mentioned, that was pulling Lourds from the temple.

Maybe he wasn't as good a friend as he should have been, or even the friend that Lev had expected him to be. Pushing those thoughts out of his head, Lourds walked out the door.

23

Namche Bazaar
Solukhumbu District
Sagarmatha Zone, Nepal
August 1, 2011

Because of the weather, the distance, and the ease of getting out of the high country, Big Mike took Lourds down the mountains into Nepal. As soon as they were low enough, they arranged for a jeep and drove into Namche Bazaar.

Lourds had been to the small town before. Residences ran in rows along the mountainsides, and the beauty of the Himalayan highlands was all around them. The permanent population was less than two thousand people, but there were a lot of transients. Hiking and climbing groups met their guides there, merchants who had traveled across the mountains to trade spread out their wares and made deals, and the locals counted their good fortune that so many people bought things while passing through.

The town also had the Shyangboche Airstrip, which offered charter planes to Lukla on most mornings when the weather was favorable. The five-minute flight cost hundreds of dollars, but it saved two days of hiking across the rough terrain.

Lourds sat in the passenger seat as Big Mike fearlessly drove down the mountain roads. A plume of dust followed them. Even though the snow had given way to brown earth again, the cold remained, and the jeep's heater wheezed more than it blew.

He worked in a spiral-bound notebook to decipher the new Jiahu language they'd discovered. As it turned out, he was more distracted by the terrain and the company than he'd thought he would be.

'You've been awfully quiet, Professor Thomas.'

'I think maybe hanging out with the monks has rubbed off on me. That whole solitude thing.'

Big Mike shot him a glance and shook his head. 'I don't think so. You've never been quiet. You've always had something to say.'

'Maybe I didn't relish the idea of trying to talk over the whining transmission or the tires grinding on this cow trail.'

Big Mike grinned at him and ran off the side of the road for a moment. He corrected their direction with a flick of his wrist. 'You know what I think?'

'What?'

'I think you need to get drunk.'

'And then climb on a puddle jumper tomorrow morning in those uncertain winds?' Lourds shook his head. 'That sounds like a recipe for disaster.'

*

That night, however, they ended up in a small, clapboard bar serving thin, overpriced beer. Big Mike regaled Lourds with stories of his recent life, then as they got deeper into the beer, they talked about the time when Lourds and Lev had lived among the Uighur.

Rough men hung out in the bar with them. Mountain guides boasted of their bravery and cleverness. Pilots talked about the treacherous winds that blew through the mountains. Experienced climbers told horror stories of past expeditions to newbies in exchange for drinks and to see their audience's eyes grow into saucers.

The scene felt good to Lourds. He sat there telling stories with Big Mike, listening to the languages, accents, and dialects swirling around him, and felt perfectly at home. This was what civilization ultimately boiled down to: people gathered and telling stories, genuine experiences as well as lies, and they used language to convey it all.

The logs in the fireplace crackled and spat and added a warm yellow glow to the rustic wood finish of the interior. A worn CD system pumped loud, raucous rock and roll throughout the room. Outside, the wind whistled through the mountains.

In the corner, however, a young woman was getting hassled by a couple of men who'd had too much to drink. She was dark and lovely, and probably in her midtwenties. Her winter clothes didn't completely hide her trim figure. Her hair, dark as a raven's wing, hung down into her face and brushed her shoulders. Her tanned skin was striking, smooth and unblemished.

One of the men spoke to her, then reached for her breast. The woman adroitly avoided his grasp by leaning back, but he only laughed at her and grew bolder.

By then Lourds was on his feet and crossing the floor. It wasn't until he was standing behind the other man that he realized how large he was. The guy must have been Scandinavian from the size of him.

'Excuse me.' Lourds stood his ground but knew he was swaying a little. The changes in altitude and the strong native beer had bollixed his motor control a bit.

The man swiveled his head and glared at Lourds. 'Go away.' He spoke German.

Lourds switched to that language without even thinking about it. 'I believe the lady has had enough of your company.' He spoke loudly, hoping that someone – in fact, several *someones* – in the bar would decide to become participants instead of bystanders.

No one moved except Big Mike, who seemed to be even more inebriated than Lourds.

Lourds scowled. Some Dynamic Duo. Still, he couldn't just walk away and leave the young woman in this situation.

'I said *go away*.' The man reached out to push Lourds.

Lourds stumbled back as the big hand shoved him in the chest, then he grabbed the man's hand, intending to grip one of the fingers and use it to control the man.

Before he could do that, the big man doubled up his other fist and smashed Lourds in the face.

Stumbling back again, Lourds tried to hang on to his senses, but they scattered like a covey of quail before a hunting dog.

Watching Thomas Lourds keel over on the floor, Miriam Abata couldn't believe her bad luck. She'd managed to be at the Scholar's Rock Temple for two days and remain invisible. She'd also followed Lourds and his companion down out of the mountains without being seen and had managed to arrive at Namche Bazaar slightly ahead of them once she was convinced that was where they were going. She'd even booked another plane leaving for the same destination at the same time as the professor's.

Katsas Shavit, her superior, had provided satellite support to watch Lourds's progress, so Miriam hadn't been too worried about losing the American professor.

Now he was lying sprawled on the beer-stained floor of a backwater bar after trying to defend her honor. If this hadn't been her first solo mission, she might have laughed.

But the bad news kept on coming. Instead of being chased out or even worrying the local police might come along to arrest them, the big man turned his attentions back to her. His foul breath pooled in her face, and she stopped breathing in self-defense.

'Hey, Franz, you laid that idiot out with one punch.'

The other man slapped the first on the shoulder and grinned hugely.

Franz flexed his right arm. 'See? I am a strong man. You would enjoy your time with me.'

Fear hummed through Miriam's nervous system, but she remembered the old martial arts instructor who had trained her. He'd always pointed out that, when used correctly, fear was fuel for an experienced fighter. Miriam wasn't terribly experienced in life-or-death situations, but she'd spent thousands of hours on those mats.

'I want you to go away.'

Franz laughed at her. 'No, you want Franz. You should know this by now. I have bought you drinks.'

'No. I bought my own drinks.' Miriam reached out for the beer bottle in front of her and casually twirled it.

Behind Franz, Lourds's Uighur companion Big Mike struggled to pull the professor to his feet. Unfortunately, Lourds was out cold, and Big Mike just wasn't sober enough for the task. Miriam had hoped that, between them, the professor and the Uighur would be able to limp back to their rented quarters.

'Now you are calling me a liar?' Franz glared at her.

'Maybe your memory isn't as good as you think it is.' Miriam watched as Big Mike had Lourds almost to his feet, then dropped the professor again.

'Oops.' Big Mike rocked unsteadily for a moment, then reached down once more for Lourds.

'Maybe I show you how I kick this guy's ass some

more.' Franz stood up from the table and headed toward Lourds.

Miriam looked around the room. Really? No one was going to get involved? She hesitated a moment, wondering if she should let Franz beat on Lourds. The problem was that Franz was drunk enough to do some real damage before he realized what he was doing. The man was probably mean when he was sober, too.

Franz swatted Big Mike backwards and the Uighur man crashed into a table with three men. All of them went down in a heap. None of them got up to fight Franz, though. They just saved their beers and looked around for another table.

Grunting a little, an anticipatory smile on his face that made him look demonic, Franz reached for Lourds.

Miriam gripped the bottle in her hand and stepped around the table. There was still enough beer in the bottle to give it a little heft. She halted just behind the big man. 'Hey. Franz.'

Franz turned around.

Swinging with everything she had, Miriam shattered the bottle across the big man's nose. Franz's head snapped back, and blood gushed from his nostrils. He didn't fall, though. He stood there with a surprised look, then clamped his jaw tight as crimson crossed his bared teeth.

'You shouldn't have done that, girl.'

The fear inside Miriam grew stronger. She dropped the broken neck of the bottle and almost drew the

Czech pistol she'd bought from a caravan of black market dealers going up into the mountains that day.

Franz reached for her.

Uncoiling, letting her body flow into the movements her instructor had taught her, Miriam batted the man's arm aside with her right forearm, reaching across her body and bringing her hips around automatically to load a side kick. She fired the kick into Franz's stomach with enough force to double him over slightly. Actually, he looked more dented than doubled.

Rotating on the ball of her left foot, Miriam lifted her right leg, loaded another kick, and swept this one across her opponent's face. The hard collision of cheekbone against the bottom of her foot jarred her, but she kept her balance.

Moving quickly, Miriam withdrew slightly, stepped to the side, then brought her left foot down in a stamp strike to the side of Franz's left knee. Something snapped, but she didn't know if it was bone or cartilage. Franz's left leg gave out under his weight, and he fell forward, landing hard on his injured knee.

As the big man yelled, Miriam stepped behind him and smacked the palms of both hands against Franz's ears. The concussive blows were enough to rupture eardrums. She didn't know how much damage she'd actually done because Franz tumbled forward face-first and lay there, unconscious.

Breathing hard, more from her fear than any physical adversity, Miriam wheeled on Franz's friend.

The man held up both hands in surrender and backed away.

Satisfied, Miriam looked back at Lourds and Big Mike. The Uighur man sat on his haunches and stared at her in amazement. Lourds sprawled inelegantly.

Miriam grabbed the professor's hat, then grabbed one of Lourds's arms. She glared at Big Mike. 'Get over here.'

'Sure.' He got to his feet with effort and grabbed Lourds's other arm. Together, with the unconscious man's arms spread over their shoulders, the pair carried the professor out of the bar.

Miriam cursed her luck but was secretly excited now that the danger was past. Outside, she swayed uncertainly across the uneven terrain toward Lourds's rented room and remembered how she had been so impatient while studying in New York. More than anything, she'd wanted to be an agent out in the field.

She'd gotten a more glamorized view of the job, though. As a Mossad agent, she was supposed to be saving Israel from her oppressors. Not carrying drunken professors home at night. She still didn't know why Lourds might be so important to the Mossad.

That night was, quite frankly, disappointing.

'Where'd you learn to fight like that?' Big Mike staggered and almost fell.

'Watching Jackie Chan movies.'

'Cool. I like Jackie Chan.' Big Mike seemed satisfied. 'I like Bruce Lee better. I like UFC better than WWE.'

Miriam didn't care to get into a discussion of martial arts with the man. She didn't want to be remembered in the morning and thought she still might have a shot at that.

As she trudged under Lourds's weight, she noticed two men closing on them. Both of them seemed professional, and they even pointed their pistols professionally when they drew them.

24

Namche Bazaar
Solukhumbu District
Nepal, Sagarmatha Zone
August 2, 2011

One of the two hard-faced men in front of Miriam waved his weapon. 'We'll take Lourds from here.' His words were clipped and efficient, with a German accent. 'No one has to get hurt.'

'Who are you?' Miriam glared at the two men and dropped her right hand behind Lourds's back to the pistol at her waistband. She did that without thought, but once she felt the cold metal in her hand, she had all kinds of doubts about what she was going to do next.

'The men who are going to take Lourds.'

'Wow.' Big Mike belched. 'This is turning out to be some night, huh?' He grinned, let go of Lourds, then threw himself at the nearest man.

Idiot! Miriam couldn't believe the big man wouldn't fight the guys in the bar, but he'd *throw* himself at men with guns.

The move either caught the pair off guard or they hadn't wanted to reveal themselves, because the man

Big Mike grappled with got knocked backwards and barely stayed on his feet. Pushing his opponent away, he snap-fired his pistol, the bullet tugging at Big Mike's sleeve as it passed through.

'Whoa!' Big Mike said, as the gunshot echoed off the buildings around them.

Hesitation gone, Miriam freed her weapon and brought it up, slapping her left hand around her right to set up the familiar push/pull hold she'd been taught. She flicked off the safety with her thumb, aimed at the shooter's center mass, and squeezed the trigger three times.

With three rapid-fire rounds in the man who had fired first, and him already stumbling backwards as crimson covered his coat, Miriam moved her pistol toward the other man. He was just getting his weapon up to fire.

Miriam stood her ground, centered her pistol on the man's chest, and squeezed the trigger, certain she was going to feel bullets rip into her flesh at any second. Instead, the man staggered as one of her rounds tore into his shoulder. Two of his shots went wide of her, and his face turned panicked, then slack as he stumbled and fell.

Heart hammering, afraid she was going to throw up because she was so afraid, and the adrenaline was sending her senses into overdrive, Miriam stepped forward, toe to heel, toe to heel, never crossing her feet to avoid tripping herself in case she had to move quickly.

She kicked the pistol from the dead man's hands, shifting her gun back and forth between the two men.

Kneeling, she checked the second man's pulse with her fingers. He was dead as well.

Voices sounded behind her. Glancing over her shoulder, she spotted the bar patrons crowding the open doorway, but none of them was brave enough yet to come outside. It wouldn't take long, though. They had liquor in them, tended to be men with too much testosterone and not enough common sense, and Miriam was willing to bet the bartender or one – or several – of them had a weapon.

She rifled the men's pockets, taking papers and personal items. This wasn't a random event. Her superior would want to know who they were, and who they were working for.

The crowd at the door grew bolder. 'What's going on out there?'

'What happened?'

Big Mike stared at her and looked dumbfounded.

Miriam stood and stuffed her haul into her jacket pockets. 'Are you all right?'

'Yeah, but that was wicked.'

'They pulled their weapons first.'

'I know. That's what makes it so wicked.'

In training, her instructors had commented on her natural proficiency and quickness with a pistol. When she'd been a child, her father had trained her to shoot. By the time she entered the Mossad training, she was very comfortable with weapons and targets.

Tonight was the first time she had knowingly shot – and killed – a man.

Kneeling once again, this time beside Lourds, Miriam checked the professor. The man snored peacefully though his nose had swelled, and one eye was already turning black.

She stood. 'Get him to his room. If you can't do it yourself, have someone help you.'

'Sure. Aren't you going to help?'

'No. I've done enough already.' Miriam shoved the pistol into her pocket and walked into the shadows. She couldn't stay. She had to hope those two men were the only ones who had been sent after Lourds.

In her rented room, Miriam paused only long enough to wedge a chair under the doorknob. Then she went to the bathroom and threw up. When she was finished, she washed her face, brushed her teeth, returned to the room, and sat on the edge of the bed.

Automatically, so suddenly glad for all the things her Mossad masters had taught her to do, finally understanding what all of the grueling hours of training had been about, she field-stripped the pistol and cleaned it with the kit she'd bought with the weapon. The familiar activity calmed and focused her.

When she was satisfied that the pistol was clean and battle-ready, when she was satisfied she was calm, she put the gun on the bed beside her and took out her sat-phone. She punched in one of the numbers she had been given for the cutouts.

'Hello. You have reached Best – '

Before the message could continue, Miriam punched in the code to break free of the answering service.

Another voice, this one calmer and in control, answered. 'May I help you?'

'I'm an agent.' Miriam gave the telephone operator her ID number. 'I need to speak to my field officer.' *Katsas* Shavit was another number. The connection was made quickly even though it was night in Israel.

'Is something wrong?' Even over the phone, Shavit wasn't going to use names.

'Two men tried to take the package tonight. They used force. I had to kill them.'

'Are you all right?'

'Yes.'

There was a moment of silence. 'This was an unfortunate occurrence.'

More unfortunate for the dead men. Miriam tried not to think about that, or the fact that the men might have had families that would miss them. In her job, she'd learned that usually even the worst of men were loved by someone. Someone's heart would soon break with the news.

'Are you there?'

Miriam realized Shavit had been speaking. 'Sorry. I am now.'

'Can you do this?'

'Of course.'

'I know this is hard. Something like this . . . it's always hard.'

'I am fine.' Miriam brushed at the tears that had started running down her cheeks.

'Has your situation with the package been compromised?'

'No.' Miriam didn't even want to go into the situation because it was ludicrous in light of what had happened. This terrible thing she'd done couldn't be linked to something so trivial. 'He still doesn't know who I am. I can make the rendezvous points without his being any the wiser.'

'We will pick him up at this end.'

'All right.'

Shavit's voice softened. 'Try to get some sleep if you can. Even though you are there, you are not alone. What happened tonight wasn't your choice. We put you in the position you found yourself, and those men decided their own fates.'

'I know.'

'You did well. I will see you soon.'

Even after Shavit hung up, Miriam clung to the phone a little longer, not wanting to let go of that human contact.

Standing in the shadows just outside the yellow glow spilling from the bar, Mufarrij let his frustration flow from him and disappear into the cold wind blowing around him. He had been close to getting his hands on Lourds, to finding out what the man knew about Lev Strauss's secret, but the German mercenaries had been hanging around too closely for him to snatch the man.

He'd almost interceded in the bar when Lourds had so stupidly risked himself over the young woman. She was a surprise, though. The way she'd handled herself in the bar had impressed him. Of course, taking out a drunken man was no great feat, but she had done it with no wasted movement.

She was young, though. A more practiced agent wouldn't have stepped into the limelight so quickly or so strongly.

In the street with her pistol, she had been death incarnate. In all his years fighting against hard, desperate men, Mufarrij had seen few people who possessed that kind of speed and accuracy.

The two dead men lay in the street beside the jeep used by the local police. Sullen-faced policemen carried assault rifles and asked questions of the bar's patrons. Most of the bar guests were only too willing to step forward and tell their stories. They were from out of country and this was probably the most exciting thing that had ever happened to them.

Mufarrij sipped his coffee and lamented that it had already gone cold. He also lamented the fact that the local police were taking Thomas Lourds and his Uighur friend into custody.

The chase was not over yet.

Lourds's head pounded as he sat on the uncomfortably thin mattress on the jail cot and looked in the metal mirror he'd finally been able to borrow from his jailer. His nose was swollen, and his left eye had a huge mouse underneath that promised a spectacular shiner later. He sighed and placed the mirror on the cot beside him. Having a hangover and a possible concussion was not how he'd wanted to wake up.

'It could be worse.' Big Mike sat on the other side of the room, lounging on the cot bolted into that wall. He'd rolled up one of his socks and was playing catch with it, throwing it up into the air and catching it when it came back down.

'How?'

'You could have gotten your nose broken. And you missed the whole gunfight.'

That was the part that really made Lourds's head hurt. He shook his head and regretted it immediately. 'Tell me again about that.'

Big Mike did, and this time the story grew even grander. By tomorrow morning, the young woman – whoever she was – would be plucking their attackers' bullets from the air and throwing them back at the men.

'I never saw anyone so fast.' Big Mike smiled dreamily. 'I thought I was a dead man. Truly. I threw myself at one of those men, intending to save you.'

'Save me?'

'They said they were there for you.'

'You heard them say that?'

'Yes.'

'You couldn't be mistaken?'

'No. They told the woman they were going to take you.'

Lourds took a deep breath and released it. He thought back over the last few months and couldn't think of a single reason why anyone would come gunning for him. He'd made some enemies over the last few years, over the Atlantis thing and the problems in Saudi Arabia, but those people had bigger problems than a relatively obscure professor of linguistics.

It didn't make any sense. And that was what scared him. He didn't know if he was leaving trouble behind or heading straight for it.

'Anyway, I threw myself at one of the men, intending to save you. He tried to shoot me, but this woman shot that man, then she shot the other. She was so fast, she was like Clint Eastwood.'

'Clint Eastwood?'

'Yes. You have seen his movies?'

'I have. This woman didn't look like Clint Eastwood, did she?'

'No, she was a very beautiful woman.'

'You're sure?'

'Of course she was. I'm sure that's why you were going to her rescue in the bar.'

Lourds barely remembered that. He didn't know if the memory loss was from the drink or from getting punched in the face. He couldn't remember the last time he'd gotten hit so hard.

'But there you were, on the floor.' Big Mike threw his

arms out and looked like he'd been run over by a steam-roller.

'Thanks for that visual. Really.'

Big Mike grinned.

'You know, I'm beginning to think you look entirely too comfortable on that jail cot.'

'I've had an exciting life since you left the village.' Big Mike folded his hands over his broad chest. 'Jails are all pretty much the same.'

'Are you sure you don't remember anything else about the woman?'

'She was beautiful. We are truly lucky, Professor Thomas.'

Lourds narrowed his good eye at his friend. 'How so?'

'The story would not be nearly so good if we'd been rescued by an ugly woman.'

Footsteps sounded out in the hallway, and one of the policemen reappeared. He wore a green-and-tan uniform and had a hat tucked up under his arm. Thrusting the key into the ancient lock, he worked the mechanism and pulled the door open.

'You're free to go.'

'Someone bailed us out?' Lourds grabbed his hat and clapped it onto his pounding head. He looked past the jailer, wondering if the beautiful young woman with the fast gun was waiting out there and wondering, too, if her presence was going to be a good thing or a bad one.

'No. You are just free to go.'

Lourds stepped out into the hallway, closely followed by Big Mike. 'Why?'

'You did not kill those men. All the stories have agreed on this. You were dead drunk when that happened, and your friend was barely able to stand on his own.'

'I wasn't dead drunk. I'd just been in a bar fight.' Lourds pointed to his injured eye and swollen nose.

'A bar fight.' The man nodded, obviously very unimpressed. 'One punch.' He blew a derisive raspberry. 'Then the woman knocked the man out. He's still in the hospital. We'll be talking to him, but we don't believe he was involved in this either.'

'Do you know anything about the men that attacked me?'

'They attacked the woman, and no, we don't know anything about them. Neither of them had papers.'

Lourds walked down the hallway. At the desk in the small, unadorned office, he recovered his personal belongings. His backpack and suitcase sat on the floor. The message was entirely clear.

A stolid man sat at the desk and eyed Lourds appraisingly. 'If you hurry, Professor Lourds, you can still catch your airplane.'

With his head aching so fiercely, the last thing Lourds wanted to contemplate was a hurried run to catch an airplane that promised five long minutes of torturous buffeting in the Himalayan winds. But he signed for his things.

'One other thing.' The stolid man reached into his

desk and brought out a well-worn copy of *Bedroom Pursuits.* 'Would you sign this for my wife? When she heard I had you locked up here, she made me promise I would get you to sign the book.'

'Sure.' Lourds took up his pen again.

'One more word of advice, if I may.'

'Certainly.'

'A man with a glass jaw should stay out of bar fights.'

'He hit me in the nose when I wasn't looking.' Even as he said that, Lourds knew that was almost a physical impossibility. All he could remember was the big man's even bigger fist rushing into view with the speed of a comet.

'Very well. A man with a glass . . . nose.'

25

HaRova
Old City
Jerusalem, the State of Israel
August 4, 2011

The heat hanging over the Old City was certainly a change from the frigid Himalayas, but it was evening now, and the night brought cooler temperatures. Lourds kept glancing over his shoulder as he trudged through the winding alleys. He told himself that he wasn't being paranoid, that there were actually people out to get him.

He just didn't know who they were yet.

He traveled the way from memory. He'd spent a lot of time with Lev off and on back in the day, and he regretted the fact that there hadn't been more time to spend these last few years. When he thought of how long it had last been, Lourds felt a little ashamed. Of course, not all of that was his fault. Lev Strauss stayed busy with his studies and teaching as well.

One of the things bothering Lourds was that he hadn't been able to connect with Strauss over the phone. He'd tried several times during layovers at the various airports during the two days it had taken him to get to

Jerusalem from Nepal, but the phone was never answered. He'd left several messages.

As always, pedestrians filled the cobblestone streets. The black and white clothing of the devout Jews mixed with the traditional Islamic garb, and all of that was interspersed by the obvious tourists, who walked around gawking at things. They were prime prey for the street vendors hawking their goods.

A few people stared at Lourds, then quickly looked away. One child even pointed at him and tugged on his mother's arm. As Lourds had feared, the black eye had turned out splendidly.

He entered Lev's building, then went up the stairs and stopped at his door on the third floor. Lourds knocked loudly. 'Lev?'

He heard no sounds from inside.

Lourds knocked again. 'Lev? It's Thomas.' Glancing around, he realized something was wrong. By this time, neighbors would have been peering from their doors. With the Jewish, Islamic, Christian, and Armenian people all living so close together in Jerusalem, everyone stayed on their guard.

Someone should have looked out at him by now.

Lourds shifted his backpack and took a fresh grip on his suitcase. He didn't know if Lev was putting him up or if he was going to stay at a hotel. Or if they were going to bolt in pursuit of whatever Lev was working on.

Two people stepped onto the landing from the stairs. The man wore a suit, and the woman had on slacks and a jacket over a tunic top. When they showed him their police identification, Lourds wasn't surprised.

'Professor Lourds? Professor Thomas Lourds?'

It wouldn't have done Lourds any good to deny his identity to the woman. Her partner was already comparing Lourds's face to a picture on his clipboard.

'I am.'

'I'm Detective Sharon Cohen. This is my partner, Detective Gabi Segalovitch. We'd like you to come with us.'

'Why?'

'We have some news of your friend Lev Strauss. Not very good news, I'm afraid.'

The detectives offered to drive Lourds to the US Embassy if he thought he would feel better there while being questioned. Stunned and greatly saddened, Lourds told them he would be fine talking to them at their headquarters. They split the difference and stopped at a sandwich shop not far from Lev's flat.

Lourds didn't have much of an appetite, but he made himself eat while he listened to Detective Cohen relate the shocking events of Lev's death. He barely tasted his corned beef on toasted rye.

'You people don't know who killed Lev?'

Cohen shook her head. 'Not yet. This is something we're working on very hard, Professor Lourds, but there are extenuating circumstances.'

'What extenuating circumstances?'

'We haven't been able, thus far, to identify anyone involved with Lev Strauss or anything that would get him killed. We were hoping to get some information from you.'

The woman was quiet, reserved and supportive, the perfect person to talk to. Lourds knew that was her role. Segalovitch watched Lourds like a hawk.

'I'm afraid I don't have any news for you. Lev called me here, and I came.'

'You came without knowing why?' Sarcasm and suspicion deepened Segalovitch's voice. 'And just left a media event in the Himalayas? Quite frankly, if you don't mind me being so bold, Professor Lourds, that doesn't sound like something a media hound like you would do.'

Lourds glared at the man, then felt foolish. The glare would have worked so much better if he hadn't been wearing a black eye. 'Lev Strauss saved my life. You don't forget a thing like that.'

'Is that enough to bring you to Jerusalem? Away from a find like what you had in the Himalayas?' Segalovitch paused. 'Or did Lev Strauss tell you what he was working on?'

Lourds took a breath, then let it out. Honesty, in this case, didn't hurt. 'Lev said he was working on something, but he didn't say what it was. He told me he'd tell me when I got here.'

'But that was big enough to bring you?'

'Lev said it was, and I believed him.'

Leaning back in his chair, Segalovitch seemed more

relaxed and more contemptuous. 'I told you this would be a waste of time, Sharon.'

The female detective ignored her partner, concentrating on Lourds instead. 'We do know that someone was providing Strauss with around-the-clock protection.'

'How do you know that?'

'Because we found the bodies of two of the men who were with him that night. The third was wounded, ended up at the hospital, and disappeared.'

'Lev didn't have the money to hire a protective service.'

'We know. We've seen his finances. Who do you think these people were?'

'Begging your pardon for pointing out the obvious, but guessing games like that aren't my department. Show me a document, I can tell you whether it's real or a forgery. I can translate it for you, given enough time. But something like this, Detective, that's just not something I do.'

Cohen looked at him for a moment, then nodded. 'There is one other thing you could do for us, if you feel up to it.'

'If I can.'

'We'd like you to take a look around inside Mr. Strauss's flat.'

Since he didn't intend to leave the city without doing that anyway, Lourds readily agreed.

'We've shot video of this whole flat, but we don't know what we're looking for.' Detective Cohen gestured at the rooms. 'We do know that some things were taken.'

'Stolen?' Lourds inspected the room quietly, juxtaposing how it looked with how he remembered from his visits. A historian always struggled to find a place to keep all his papers, documents, and books. Lev Strauss had fought the same losing battles.

Shelves lined the walls, filled with books that had bookmarks and flags through them. Magazines and bound papers filled neatly stacked boxes. A few museum-quality pieces, small artifacts from the Muslim, Christian, and Judaic worlds, occupied places of honor among the books.

Lev's study was even more jam-packed. Open books lay on top of open books, and the scholar inside Lourds cringed at the sight because it meant the bindings would eventually give way. He didn't know how many priceless books he'd seen that had been abused like that.

At the same time, Lourds knew that if anyone invaded his home study or his office at Harvard, they would find books treated in exactly the same manner.

'His computer is missing.' Lourds stared at the void in the middle of the messy desk.

'Who said you weren't a detective?' Segalovitch leaned against the doorframe and smirked.

Lourds ignored the man and looked at Cohen.

'His computer was missing when we got here.'

'Lev was in the habit of leaving files stuck out in cyberspace. Have you checked any of his on-line accounts?' Lourds asked the question trying to appear helpful, but he knew Lev would never have trusted anything worthwhile to a computer site.

'We've found some of them. We're searching for others. So far, everything we've turned up hasn't been helpful.'

'That's too bad.' Lourds put his hands on his hips like he was doing his best to figure something out, but inside he wanted to escape the detectives' scrutiny and get to the Wohl Archaeological Museum. If Lev had left him a message in the event something had happened to him, it would be there.

He hoped.

'What was here?' Cohen pointed at the bare wall near the desk.

Lourds walked over to the wall and ran his fingers along the dusty shelves. Patterns in the dust showed where some objects had recently stood. 'Your people didn't take these?'

'No. Those shelves were empty when we got here. Gone. Just like the computer.'

Lourds's heart hurt at the thought of all those things missing. 'These were Lev's special collections. He worked at a lot of digs, put in thousands of hours on different projects. He was an archaeologist and linguist who made a difference.' He looked at Cohen and spoke from the heart. 'He was a good man, Detective. He deserved better than this. Catch whoever killed him.'

Cohen nodded. 'We will.'

*

Once they were through with Lev's flat, Lourds accepted Cohen's offer to drive him to his hotel. He checked into the David Citadel Hotel, said good-bye to the detectives after exchanging cell phone numbers with them, and went up to his room.

There, he hooked up his computer and checked his mail. There were a few video clips from Gloria Chen and David Hu, regaling him with new thoughts on various pieces from the temple, and asking whether he'd managed to crack the language yet.

There was a lot of other e-mail as well, from his literary agent, his publisher, fans, the university staff – including the dean, and friends. He left them all for later.

After a leisurely shower, he changed clothing, then got back on the computer and found the nearest electronics store that carried a blacklight flashlight. He'd need it in the morning.

Stretching out on the bed, he lay down and took a nap. When his alarm woke him, it was 8 a.m.

Then he went out the hotel's back way and took off on foot. One of the many good things about Jerusalem was that it wasn't far to anywhere.

Normal operation hours for the Wohl Archaeological Museum were from Sunday to Thursday, from 9 a.m. to 5 p.m. But on holidays and Fridays they were open from 9 to 1.

Lourds went down the stone steps leading to the

underground complex and was completely blown away by the excavation work again. Many visitors to Jerusalem didn't know that the city existed on two levels. The modern-day city that everyone saw was referred to as the 'Upper City.'

In the days of Herod the Great (37–04 BC), the families of important temple priests had lived in mansions throughout the area. Excavations by the Institute of Archaeology of the Hebrew University of Jerusalem, the Israel Exploration Society, and the Israel Department of Antiquities (now known as the Israel Antiquities Authority) started in 1968, shortly after the Six-Day War.

From 1969 to 1982, those excavations were directed by Dr. Nahman Avigad. The archaeologist had also published one of the Dead Sea Scrolls, helped with the Masada excavation, and found the Broad Wall that protected the city during King Hezekiah's reign in the late eighth century BC. Lourds loved the man's work, but what fascinated him most was Avigad's study of Hebrew seals. One of the seals, according to Avigad, had belonged to Queen Jezebel. Despite peer challenges, Avigad had stuck to his guns in his claims.

The Burnt House had always captivated Lourds's attention as one of the most intriguing artifacts that had been discovered. It had been found under ashes, informing excavators that the building had burned down, but the ground floor was miraculously saved.

Lourds stood in the doorway for a moment and

imagined what it must have been like before the restoration efforts. Avigad and his people still had so many incredible finds ahead of them: the stone kitchenware that was used instead of pottery to keep the cleanliness by edict of the Halacha, the Roman-period oil lamps and inkwells, the perfume workshop tools that included measuring cups and bowls, an iron spear that might have belonged to a Jewish fighter, and the ghastly remains of a young woman's arm from fingertips to elbow.

That sight had stayed in Lourds's mind. The arm bones had been buried according to Jewish custom, but pictures of the find remained on display.

A short distance farther on, Lourds found the *mikveh,* the ritual bath used by men and women. Regulations varied widely among the different interpretations of the religion, but most agreed that the ritual baths had to be fed by natural springs and be deep enough to cover the person bathing.

The *mikveh* was constructed of stone and had two doorways at the top of the steps: one for entering and one for leaving. Lourds went down when no one else was there. He took the Black Scorpion blacklight he'd purchased from the electronics store from his pocket.

He stopped at the bottom of the *mikveh's* stone steps, then turned to his right and tracked the blacklight beam across the stones, counting as he went.

Thomas, if I ever have anything that is important and must be found, I will leave it where you can find it. Only you and I will know of this place. If, for whatever reason, I cannot finish my study of whatever this thing might be, I want you to promise me that you will look for it.

They'd been drunk at the time. It had been after Lev had gotten out of the hospital and been fitted with his prosthetic leg, after which walking with the prosthesis had proven both sad and hilarious.

As a boy, Lourds had fallen in love with the old Doc Savage pulps, and Lev had shared a love of them. In the stories, Doc Savage and his aides were forever leaving messages for each other written in ultraviolet chalk.

Over the years, Lev had occasionally left messages for Lourds in different places. Never the *mikveh*. That place was sacred, meant for only the holiest of things.

Lourds knew that if Lev had truly been working on something important, earthshakingly important, he would have left a clue there. He hoped there was nothing there.

Then the blacklight touched the message and brought it to vibrant life.

THOMAS
CENTRAL BUS STATION
B-34
GO WITH GOD, MY FRIEND

26

Schloss Volker
Vienna, Austria
August 5, 2011

Von Volker stared at Colonel Davari's face on the computer monitor. The telephone connection linking them was heavily encrypted, but they still remained careful.

'Thomas Lourds has arrived in Jerusalem.' The colonel's tone was accusatory, as if Von Volker himself were to blame for the professor's appearance in the city.

'I know. I have men watching him even as we speak.'

'Then why haven't they taken him into their custody?'

'Because we have to be careful. The police are watching Lourds, and somewhere out there you can bet the Mossad are also watching. I shouldn't have to remind you that if the Mossad finds out about me, they will also find out about you. Austria's political sympathies lie with the Ayatollah, at least for the moment.'

'What is he doing over there?'

That told Von Volker a lot, and he had to keep himself from smiling. Evidently Davari's intelligence sources didn't run that deeply into Jerusalem.

Or maybe he had pulled his people back to leave Von

Volker hanging as a Judas goat. That thought didn't settle quite so easily, and took away some of the superiority the Austrian felt.

'For the moment, Lourds seems to be sniffing around, looking for whatever crumbs might be left of his old friend.'

'I trust nothing was left that we need to worry about.'

'I had Strauss's computer and the artifacts by his desk smuggled out of the country. They've been arriving over the last couple of days. I've got people going through them this very moment. If there is anything to be found, any clue of the Book or the Scroll, they will find it.'

'And you will call me.'

'Of course.'

Without another word, Davari broke the connection.

Despite his casual conversation with the colonel, Von Volker was tense. If Davari was getting hard to get along with, Von Volker knew the Ayatollah would be even more so. If something didn't happen soon, blood would spill, and some of it might be his.

He rose from the plush leather chair and walked out of the office. In the hallway, he turned toward the former two back bedrooms, now one very large bedroom. When Lev Strauss's things had started arriving, Von Volker had hired a crew to remove the wall to allow more room for his specialists. After this project was completed, he would have the wall rebuilt.

He walked into the room.

Instantly, one of the older men got to his feet and approached.

'*Herr* Von Volker, it's a pleasure to see you.' The older man knew better than to offer his hand, and bowed his head instead.

'Have you any news to report, Professor Gustav?'

'We are proceeding according to schedule.' Gustav waved to the artifacts that lined the tables. 'There were many things in this collection, and the cataloguing takes time. If I may suggest, *Herr* Von Volker, your wife is a trained archaeologist, and many of these things are surely within her field of study.'

Von Volker glared at the man. 'Are you telling me that your skills are not up to this task, Professor Gustav?'

The old man paled. 'No. Certainly not. I was just thinking that another pair of hands would – '

'Then you presume to tell me my business.'

'No, *Herr* Von Volker. Certainly not. I will do as you wish to the best of my ability.'

'Good. Anything less will get you released.' *And your body dumped at the bottom of a lake.* Von Volker refrained from saying the last, so that it would be a surprise. Gustav and his group of experts were headed for the bottom of a lake anyway when the time came.

'It will not be a problem.'

'There are more deliveries forthcoming. They should arrive tomorrow or by Monday.'

'Of course. We will make room.'

Von Volker walked back out of the room and spotted Alice in the hallway in her lounging wear and a robe, a wine glass in her hand. He wondered if she had heard any of the conversation.

'How is your *secret* project going?'

'Fine.' Von Volker put on a small smile.

'You still haven't told me what it's about. Or why strangers stay so long at our house, or why the wall was torn out?'

'The wall was torn out to make room for the strangers. That should be obvious.'

She frowned at him and sipped her drink.

'As for the rest of it, that shall remain my secret for a time longer.'

'Whatever.' Alice lifted one slim shoulder and dropped it. She looked at him. 'Would you like a drink?'

'No. Thank you.'

'Are you coming to bed?'

Von Volker was almost tempted. It wasn't often his wife asked him to bed, but she did so every now and again when she wanted something. He supposed she might have grown tired of her car. 'I'm afraid I can't. Business, you see. There is the rally tomorrow night. I must make sure things are ready. People are depending on me.'

She nodded and even managed to look a little disappointed. She turned and walked away. 'Well, if you should change your mind . . .'

Watching her hips twitch so provocatively, Von Volker almost changed his mind. But he knew he had things to do. If the Ayatollah got his precious Book, and it even came close to doing what the man thought it would do, Von Volker knew the Austrian and German people had to be ready.

If the Ayatollah unleashed a global *jihad*, a brand-new powder keg lit in the Middle East would go a long way to paving the road for a larger, more powerful Germany. And Austria would be the crown jewel of that new unification.

And Von Volker was going to make sure that when the time came, he would be the man wearing that crown.

August 6

Alice lay in bed for more than two hours. First she heard her husband leave, watching out the window as his car drove into the night. Then she heard the men in the renovated bedrooms pack up their gear and leave.

The clock beside the bed showed 12:34 a.m. And they would be back no later than seven in the morning. Even though they were staying in one of the guest-houses and had no long drive ahead of them, she felt bad for them. Her husband worked them unmercifully.

She lay atop the bed for a while longer, thinking about the conversation she'd overheard her husband having with someone on his computer. Klaus had mentioned Thomas Lourds's name, something he'd never done in all their years of marriage.

For a moment, she thought back to the last time she'd

had sex with her husband. She didn't call it making love because it wasn't that. And it really wasn't having sex either, though sometimes his attentions were welcome because she was a young, healthy woman with her own needs.

That night, though, she was certain he'd drugged her. The way she'd felt, so hazy and out of control, and the spectacular headache she'd had the next morning had convinced her Klaus had given her something.

He'd done that before, though he never admitted to it. And each time, the next few days were always awful as her body recovered. When Klaus loosed his inner depravity, he was a beast.

No matter how much she struggled, though, she couldn't remember that night. They'd talked, she was sure of that, but she had no idea what they'd talked about or even what Klaus would be interested in talking to her about.

She got up, pulled on her robe, and went out into the hallway. She'd worn some of her sexiest lingerie, hoping to seduce Klaus. She did that to him sometimes, and when he was passed out in postcoital bliss, she went through his pockets, his phone, and his PDA.

There was always precious little to find. Klaus was very careful. Sometimes she wondered if he knew what she did and wondered if he thought the layers of duplicity was some grand game. Things like that delighted him.

Out in the hallway, she grew more afraid. This could

be some kind of game, too. Leaving the house unattended with the *secret* project here was enticing.

Of course, there was the possibility that he didn't think she could figure it out. Or that it wouldn't matter if she did.

He mentioned Thomas by name. There must be a reason. Alice screwed up her courage and walked to the doors at the other end of the hallway. A fresh security lock had been installed on the door. This one required a thumbprint.

She smiled at that. Klaus did love gadgets, but he wasn't nearly as clever as he thought he was. A thumbprint-recognition system in a house where he lived was foolish.

It only took her a moment to get a print off his electric razor with a piece of clear tape. Then she pressed the borrowed thumbprint to the door, watched the green bar cycle from top to bottom while it read it, and heard the locking mechanism pop open.

Her breath caught in her throat. If this *was* a trick planned by Klaus, this would be the point at which he would step forward and catch her in the act.

She remained alone in the hallway.

Trembling, she pulled open the door and stepped inside.

As she gazed in wide-eyed wonder at the artifacts revealed on the tables in the moonlight streaming through the windows, she wondered what it could all mean. How was Thomas mixed up in anything her husband might be doing? The only history Klaus was interested in was the German Confederation and how he might be able to bring Austria and Germany together as a large, imposing nation the West would have to acknowledge.

The news had been full of her old lover lately. Although she'd had to keep her interest hidden from Klaus, Alice had followed all the breaking reports about the temple Thomas had located in the Himalayas. She'd also heard that he had left the dig site a few days ago.

That hadn't sounded like the Thomas Lourds Alice knew. Wild horses and rampaging lions wouldn't have gotten him away from something like that.

But *something* had.

Alice studied the artifacts, realizing they were an impressive collection of Christian, Judaic, and Islamic pieces. There were centuries-old crosses, Stars of David, a sword-wielding figure that could only be a representation of Iblis, the Islamic devil, who'd been either a jinn and a devoted servant of God or a disobedient angel. That was just one of the many ways Muslim faith diverged. Iblis had been made of fire while Adam had been made of clay, and Iblis had refused to accept that Adam was better. God had thrown Iblis into hell and renamed him Shaitan. Since those days, Shaitan had devoted himself to turning men and women against God.

What did any of this have to do with Thomas Lourds?

As she touched the figure of Iblis, she thought of where she'd last seen a figurine like this. Lev Strauss had had one at his flat in Jerusalem. Only it had been his grandmother's flat at the time. The Iblis had been one of his first pieces.

Curious, Alice lifted the figurine and gazed at the bottom. There, on a piece of masking tape worn and faded with time, was the legend IBLIS, and it looked like Lev's strong, sure hand. She replaced the figurine and went to one of the computers on a desk. She didn't dare use her personal notebook computer because Klaus had loaded it with spy programs.

The computers in here had been left up and running. She went to the Internet and Googled Lev Strauss's name. She saw his handsome face, a touch of gray in his hair and beard now, and read the headlines that declared he'd been killed in a tragic terrorist attack on July 28.

Tears filled her eyes as she remembered the beautiful young man he'd been. For a time, after she and Thomas had parted ways, Lev had kept her company. She'd known he cared for her, but she was unable to return his interest. Every time she'd thought of him, she'd thought of Thomas.

In the end, not only had Alice lost Thomas to his treasure hunt for the Library of Alexandria, but she had lost a good friend, too. Now she'd lost him forever. How had she missed this story?

She knew the answer at once. Klaus kept her away from the world for the most part. She wiped the tears from her face. For just a moment, a piece of that drugged night of wanton sex surfaced in her mind.

Is Lev in Jerusalem?

She was certain that Klaus had asked her that.

And now Lev was dead, with his things somehow in her husband's control.

Desperate, she returned to the computer. If Klaus was going after Thomas next, he needed to be warned.

27

Central Bus Station
Jaffa Road
Jerusalem, the State of Israel
August 5, 2011

Walking like a man who belonged there, trying to ignore the little voice in the back of his mind that insisted he was stepping into a trap, Lourds entered the modern eight-story building that had replaced the old bus station in 2001. The building had five floors of office space above the three main levels and two levels of underground parking.

The new bus station also had a shopping concourse and a food court that had stirred up considerable strife among the Haredi community. Rabbis of the superconservative Orthodox Judaism had protested vehemently against adding more than coffee shops and magazine racks, the way things had been in the past.

Lourds missed the old bus station as well. He preferred it to the gleaming monstrosity that sprawled out around him. Getting big and modern had taken a lot of character out of the neighborhood. People had once been able to find small places and corners to talk over coffee and the newspaper, and even felt like they had some privacy. Now the food court was in plain sight, and everything felt hurried.

He took the bus locker key from his pocket. He'd retrieved it from inside an old prosthesis Lev kept in his closet as a hiding place. After all, who would think to look there?

Earlier that morning, Lourds had slipped into Lev's building through the back way, awakened Mrs. Hirsch, and listened to her complain about her bad hip the way she always had, even though it hadn't appeared to get any worse since the last time he'd seen her. She'd opened Lev's door with her spare key. Someone had to water the plants when Lev was gone. Mrs. Hirsch wasn't moving, so she'd been a good temporary flat sitter. They had consoled each other briefly over Lev's death, then Lourds had headed to the bus station.

At the locker area, aware that he was being watched by closed-circuit television, Lourds took note of the lockers and the way the numbers ran. The IDs held Hebrew and English markings.

He found B-34 with ease. He put the key into the lock and turned it, almost expecting someone to jump out of the small square space and shoot him. Relief filled him when he saw only a bound notebook inside.

Picking it up, he looked around to see if anyone was taking undue interest in him. Satisfied that he was safe for the moment, he walked out of the bus terminal. He hadn't slept a wink all night, and now – with adrenaline fueled by the discovery of the notebook – he was more awake than ever.

Dear Thomas,

If you're reading this, something unseemly must have happened to me. If I am captured, hurry and come save me because the people looking for Mohammad's Koran (more on that in a moment) are desperate to find it and bloodthirsty as well.

If I am dead – well, i hope it was quick. You know how I dislike pain.

Tears welled in Lourds's eyes as he read the last, but he chuckled as well. That was Lev, always a jokester. But the message reminded Lourds that he could be in danger as well.

He glanced around Jaffa Road as he sat in a coffee shop down the street from the bus station. He didn't see anyone watching him, and he felt quite certain that if anyone had been watching, they would have grabbed him when they saw he had Lev's book.

He resumed reading.

I'm not going to go into the whole story at this moment, but it's a great one, trust me on that. Rather, I'm asking you to try to find what I haven't been able to yet. Or quite possibly to find what I found that got me killed.

I found a most wondrous book in a little shop in Cairo. I

know you and I've been there together before, and probably either hungover or chasing women. Perhaps that's why we never found this book before, or perhaps the book didn't arrive till after we had gone.

I truly feel that I was fated to find this book and discover the truth of the legend in its pages. Even though i have had to call on you for help.

I was puzzled by the book because it was written in a dialect of Arabic that looked familiar, but that I couldn't quite decipher. Better minds than mine are obviously required.

So I thought of you. Not as a better mind, but as someone who might know one.

All kidding aside, as I'm sure I'm in dire jeopardy or dead at this moment and you're probably worried or grieving –

'If you only knew how much, old friend.' Lourds blinked to clear his eyes and focus on the page.

– I'll get to the problem straightaway.

The author of this book claims to know where Mohammad's personal Koran, written by him as God spoke it, is located. There's also talk of a scroll that foretells the future of the Muslim people. And of the need for all Muslims to join and raise a great Jihad that will strike down all who oppose them.

Pretty heavy stuff. Apocalyptic, even. It even sounds comic bookish, but maybe that's because we tend to trivialize that which will destroy us. Foolishness or a survival mechanism? I don't know. However, the problems of a unified Middle East cannot be overlooked.

Mohammad's Koran promises a way to provide that unification of the different Muslim faiths by delivering the true word of the faith. The scroll will describe a way for it to be done, though all these centuries later I have to wonder about that.

I translated that much of the book, but the location of the Koran and scroll evades me. I'm frustrated and stuck, and if anyone can think of something I haven't, it's you.

I've left you a message on the bottom of the 'gift of the magi' you gave me as a Christmas present one year. Your idea of a joke, which was pretty lame at the time, but I kept it anyway. I also hollowed out a section of it to keep messages in. Don't burn it!

I didn't want these two messages (the one in the mikveh you thought we'd never use!) to fall into the wrong hands at the same time.

Don't fail me, Thomas. I know you can do this, and it pains me to ask.

Love
Lev

The Magi's gift had been a candelabrum, given at Christmas, but in celebration of Hanukkah. It was intended as a joke, a holiday present wrapped in the most garish wrapping paper Lourds could find – a naughty

Santa showing his north pole to a group of young *Penthouse*-worthy women. The candelabrum was an artifact Lourds had received from one of the projects he'd worked on, not worth much more than sentimental value, but he knew Lev would appreciate it.

Evidently Lev had also worried that Lourds might have forgotten what it was, which was why he'd offered the 'burn' clue.

The thing that troubled Lourds most was that the candelabrum was among the artifacts missing from Lev's flat. He closed the book and placed it in his backpack.

Covert Operations
Institute for Intelligence and Special Operations (Mossad)
Tel Aviv, the State of Israel
August 6, 2011

Sarah Shavit picked up the ringing phone and tried to organize her thoughts in the space of a drawn breath. That was usually all the time she had to move from case to case. She placed the agent's identity number as one of the team currently riding Professor Lourds's coattails in Jerusalem.

'Our charge has evidently read whatever was written in the notebook he recovered from the bus station.'

Sarah opened the Lev Strauss file on her computer and made a note. She also made a note on Miriam Abata's file to check on her. The young woman was going through her psych eval this morning. Sarah wanted to handle the exit interview personally.

'What is he doing now?'

'Nothing. Sitting in a coffee shop. Do you want us to bring him in?'

Sarah thought about it, then decided against that. The Jerusalem police had already taken a run at Professor Lourds and come up empty. 'No. Stay on him. If he knew something, he would be up and moving. This isn't a man who sits around waiting for grass to grow. He's drawn by his own passions. Give him rope and give him time. See if he can produce anything if he's left on a long leash.'

'Understood. But perhaps our people would know more about whatever's in that journal than he does.'

'If this weren't that man, if this weren't tied to antiquity, and if the matter weren't so important, I'd agree with you. But it is that man and it's tied to a history that we've all but lost, and this is something that can potentially change the world as we know it. You have your parameters.'

'As you wish. It's time for a stress-free assignment anyway.'

The man's cockiness irritated Sarah. She made a note in his personal folder. 'I'd like to point out that the last agent assigned to this task left two dead men in her wake. Don't be too stress-free.' She broke the connection.

Acid burned in her stomach. Over the years, she'd learned to pay attention to that feeling. It was a manifestation of some sixth sense that let her know when a mission was about to turn critical in the worst ways.

She felt like she was on fire now. The pieces for this mission were scattered all over the board. Even Melman only had passing knowledge of what it was they were hunting, and no one knew if it truly existed.

Her secretary buzzed for her attention.

'Yes, Ben.'

'Agent Abata is about to be released from psych.'

'Thank you.' Sarah closed her files and went down to talk to her young charge. She hadn't been much older than Miriam Abata when she'd killed her first person, a man she'd been hopelessly in love with at the time. She thought she might have a unique perspective on the situation and repercussions and surviving the trauma that the psychologist couldn't deliver.

David Citadel Hotel
King David Street
Jerusalem, the State of Israel
August 6, 2011

The ringing phone dragged Lourds out of a deep sleep. Groggily, he brushed aside the pillow he'd used to block the light that even the drapes couldn't adequately filter. He had a headache and his face hurt.

'Hello.'

The voice at the other end of the connection brought him to full wakefulness quickly. 'Thomas?'

'Alice?' Not believing he was hearing her voice after so many years, Lourds sat up.

'Are you all right?'

'I'm fine. Just surprised to hear from you. You're not the last person I expected to hear from, but you would have been near the top of the list.'

She laughed and the sound was so pleasant it wiped away a decade and placed him at picnics and dig sites he'd gone to while at university in one country or another.

'I can't believe you recognized my voice so easily.'

'I will never forget your voice, my dear.' After losing Lev so suddenly and so brutally, being contacted by someone else from his past buoyed Lourds up for a moment. Then the probability of both things happening out of the blue brought him crashing back down. If he was having that kind of luck, it was time to go to Monte Carlo. 'How'd you get this number?'

'It wasn't easy. I managed to get hold of one of the film crews still in the mountains, then asked them to let me speak to Professor Hu. They did. I explained to him that I needed to speak to you on a matter of some importance and he helped me. Terribly nice man.'

'David's one of the good ones. So he gave you my number?'

'Yes. Thomas, I'm calling you about Lev.'

Lourds stood and paced. 'I'd only gotten the news yesterday.'

'The first I'd heard of it was this morning. Otherwise, I'd have called earlier because I knew the two of you were very close.'

'Yes.'

Alice hesitated. 'This isn't exactly a social call, Thomas. I'm afraid I've got some bad news. On the surface, it appears my husband had something to do with Lev's death.'

'What makes you say that?'

'Because many of Lev's things have turned up in our house. I thought maybe you'd like to come and have a look.'

Lourds immediately thought of the candelabrum. 'Yes, I would.'

28

Ringstrasse
Innere Stadt District
Vienna, Austria
August 7, 2011

Getting a flight from Tel Aviv to Vienna was pretty easy, as long as a passenger flew either by midmorning or late evening. EL-AL and Austrian Airlines both had regular flights out of the city, but they were gridlocked on their takeoffs and landings.

Lourds spent the rest of the afternoon and evening on his computer, researching everything he could find on Mohammad and a purportedly lost Koran written in the Prophet's own hand. There wasn't much. What he did find tended to turn up on the same sites that talked of a hollow earth and Lost Lemuria.

The long day and the hard rush after the Himalayas finally took their toll, and he'd slept. Then he'd gone to Ben Gurion International Airport and taken one of the scheduled flights to Vienna. He'd left his bags at the hotel and remained checked in there for the time being.

He was certain he'd be back to Jerusalem before the hunt was over. Lev had been there, not somewhere else.

Wherever the clue in the candelabrum led, Lourds was certain it'd be in the city.

Now, standing on the street that circled Vienna's old town, Lourds tried to remember the last time he'd been in the city. The *Wiener Staatsoper* looked beautiful. The state opera house's blue-green curved roof standing out against the dark blue sky.

He paid the taxi driver, shouldered his backpack, and strode to the Albertina Museum just behind the opera house. After paying the admittance fee, he went up to the open terrace where he was supposed to meet Alice. He was surprised at how rapidly his heart was beating, but he didn't know if it was from the coming reunion or the fact that his life could potentially be forfeit soon.

At the top of the steps, he stood in the shadow and gazed out across the terrace. The statue of Austrian Emperor Franz Joseph I and his high-stepping mount occupied a central location, and the old warrior gazed out over his city with sword in hand.

'You had quite the life, didn't you, old fellow?'

'Talking to yourself, Thomas? They say that's a bad sign.'

Startled, Lourds turned around and found Alice standing a short distance away. He hadn't even noticed her as the city's horizon had come into view because the sight was so breathtaking.

'Alice.'

He had just a brief impression of her dressed in an emerald green evening dress that was so light it seemed ready to blow away in the breeze. The flyaway halter top and thin spaghetti straps revealed an expanse of honey gold tanned skin, and the chiffon looked like fairy's wings wrapped around her curved hips. She held a flowered sunhat in one gloved hand.

Then she was in his arms, holding him tight, and kissing him hard enough to bruise his lips. Lourds's reaction was uncontrollable and immediate, and it made itself known as she pressed against him.

'Well, it appears some things never change.' She leaned back and laughed. Her expression sobered as she gently touched his face. 'Oh, Thomas, your poor eye.'

'It's nothing. You should see the other guy.'

'Seriously, Thomas. You were never a fighter. You were always a lover. Was it a soccer injury? Did you walk into a door? You've done that before, as I recall.'

Lourds didn't want to go into the whole story, but he knew Alice deserved part of it. 'I got this in Namchee Bazaar.'

'In the Himalayas?'

'Close enough. Two men tried to kidnap me. Fortunately, I had a guardian angel. Unfortunately, she killed them both, so no one knows who sent them. But . . . I don't think they were merely muggers. Then there's the second mystery of the woman that saved me.'

That sobered Alice up even more. She stepped back out of his arms, looking nonplussed. '"Woman"?'

'I never even got her name. I don't know who she was, either.' Lourds doffed his hat and ran fingers through his hair, then resettled it on his head. 'Everything about this affair concerning Lev has been mysterious, Alice, and I'm thrown from one confusing event to another. You have to believe me.' He paused. 'Your phone call was confusing as well. I have to admit, I didn't know if I could even trust you. I half expected to be snatched the minute I saw you.'

A sad look twisted Alice's full lips. 'Thomas, if there's one person in this world you can trust right now, it's me.'

Part of the knot in Lourds's stomach relaxed, but the sour taste at the back of his mouth hovered. 'I hoped I was right about that. That's why I came.'

'To answer Lev's mystery?'

'And to see you.' Lourds smiled. 'You look gorgeous, Alice. The years have been very kind to you.'

'That hasn't come without effort, I'll have you know.' Alice took him by the hand and led him to the terrace's edge. 'You were talking to Franz Joseph when I so rudely interrupted.'

'Casual conversation.'

'No discussion of history is ever casual with you.'

Lourds shrugged good-naturedly. 'Perhaps not. You are aware that his reign of sixty-eight years places him third, after Louis XIV and Johannes II, as the longest and most influential?'

'I was aware of that, but I didn't know the exact number of years. That's something you would know.'

'He was an impressive man. A warrior, a scholar. He

fought off Prussia's attempts to create a new German Confederation in their image. Survived an assassination attempt that would have taken his head off, and lived to see the completion of the church built to commemorate the event.' Lourds pointed off in the distance toward Votivkirche. 'That one, in fact.'

The two tall, slimline spires stood out prominently atop the church and towered over the buttresses, including flying buttresses and abutments. Many tourists mistook the Votive Church as Gothic, but the architecture was more modern by several centuries.

'He also survived an unhappy marriage with a woman he idolized, from all accounts. I actually translated several of his later letters, you know.'

'You've told me.'

'I suppose I have. I did that while we were at school here in Vienna.'

Alice gazed wistfully at the statue. 'You know the thing that I most remember about the emperor?'

'What?'

'That he forbade his son to marry the woman he loved and insisted on a marriage that the prince didn't want.'

Lourds nodded. 'Princess Stephanie of Belgium was the only royal of Roman Catholic faith who was considered the equal to Prince Rudolf in station. Who wasn't related too closely by blood, I mean.'

'They had to delay the marriage because she hadn't even gone through puberty. How could that poor girl be expected to know whom she wanted to spend the rest of her life with?' Wrapping her arms around herself, Alice shook her head. 'When a person marries, Thomas, it should be for love. At least Prince Rudolf and his seventeen-year-old mistress had the fortitude to kill themselves before they were made to separate.'

Lourds nodded again. The Mayerling Incident, as it was referred to, was a sad thing. Thirty-year-old Prince Rudolf and his lover had been so smitten with each other that they hadn't been able to separate. 'Some historians think that it wasn't a lovers' suicide pact, you know.'

'I know. They think it was an assassination because of Rudolf's arguments with his father or because of his pro-Hungary stance.' Alice looked up at Lourds. 'I prefer to think of it as two lovers strong enough to chart their own course.'

Placing his hands on Alice's shoulders, Lourds looked into her eyes. 'Are you that unhappy?'

'Terribly so, Thomas. You can't even begin to imagine the misery I've been through.' Sadness glinted in her sapphire blue eyes. 'How else do you think I can betray my husband to an ex-lover? This wasn't done frivolously. If Klaus finds out what I'm doing, I truly believe he will kill me. Then he will kill you.'

'If you didn't love him, why did you marry him?' Lourds sat across the table from Alice at an open-air café the way they had when they'd attended the university.

Around them, the Ringstrasse moved slowly. Fewer people lived there these days, and Lourds missed the crowds.

'I didn't have a choice.'

'Of course you had a choice.'

Alice took Lourds's hands in hers and smiled at him. 'Sweet Thomas, so immersed in the world of the past that you often don't realize how the real one works. Austria isn't the United States. People don't have the same liberties here.'

'Even so – '

She cut him off. 'I was fortunate that my parents allowed me to finish my extended education before they insisted on marrying me off.'

'Are they truly that backwards?'

'You met them.'

'Once.' Lourds growled at the memory. *Herr* and *Frau* Reinstadler had made it immediately and abundantly clear that they didn't care for their only daughter's infatuation. The weekend they'd spent in the Reinstadler estate home, in separate bedrooms, had been decidedly uncomfortable.

Alice smiled at him. 'And wasn't that enough?'

'It was.' Lourds shook his head. 'You could have left Vienna.'

'And gone where?'

Lourds had no answer.

'Before Klaus, before the arranged marriage, I'd been in love. When that ended, my confidence had been broken. In those days, the attentions of Klaus Von Volker had seemed a godsend. He wanted me in a way I thought I needed to be wanted.'

Lourds took off his hat and placed it on the table. 'I'm sorry, Alice. I never intended to hurt you.'

'I know. This isn't about you, Thomas. If I'd allowed you to take me off with you, I'd have been just as unhappy.'

Lourds grimaced, the hurt from her comment evident on his face.

Alice laughed at him. 'Don't be so fragile. It doesn't become you. I like remembering you as the aloof, self-centered young professor who once told me life was too big to live in one place.'

'Did I ever say that?'

She placed a hand over her heart, almost cupping one delectable breast. 'I swear. That was almost word-for-word.'

'I was something of a bounder, wasn't I?'

'No. You were young.' She studied him unashamedly. 'In many ways, you still are, and – I think – always will be. You'll always be the boy I fell in love with, always seeing the fascinating things and adventures in the world that no one else sees.'

'Still. If I had known – '

'You would have only made things worse for yourself and for me. I still cling to that memory of how we were. Some days that's my only solace. I would not have it destroyed.' Alice took a breath. 'The fault was mine. I hadn't planned for my own life. I had no place to go, Thomas. No money of my own to make a life anywhere. That was one of the keenest interests my parents had in arranging the marriage with Klaus. They hoped their fortunes would increase when they aligned with his.'

'Did they?'

'Of course not. Klaus is not a generous man. Not even with me. Though I do think he is more generous with the string of mistresses he's kept over the years.' She shrugged. 'Still, my parents have some consolation. They get to claim kinship with one of the most powerful men in the Austrian People's Party.'

'The man foments anti-Semitic behavior and calls for Austrians and Germans alike to rise against Israel. He lobbies for Iran to become a nuclear power, which would endanger all of the Middle East, and the Western world if the Ayatollah could make that possible. Various news agencies have accused Von Volker of supplying munitions to the Ayatollah, and have all but proven it.'

'I know. I live with the man. It's all true. Including the arms trafficking.' Alice pursed her lips in distaste. 'My parents idolize him for his opinions. They believe, like a lot of other Austrians and Germans, that Klaus Von Volker is the man who will bring about a new glory for a resurrected German empire.'

Lourds shivered at the thought. He looked out at the Ringstrasse. 'Austria has a long history of anti-Semitism.'

'Yes, but we're here to talk of the evils done by my husband.'

Lourds took her hand and kissed it. 'True, but we're not going to forget the evils he's done to you as well. Maybe – together – we can find a way for him to get his comeuppance as well.'

'There's a rally tonight. Klaus is speaking. We should go.'

'Why?'

'Because Klaus expects me to put in an appearance before he speaks.'

'I thought you said Lev's things were at your house.'

'The *schloss,* yes. But if I don't show up at the rally, Klaus might become suspicious that I'm snooping into his private business.'

'Perhaps I could go there myself.'

'You'd never get through the security. You'll need me.'

'Won't Klaus notice when you disappear from the rally?'

Alice shook her head. 'No. Once he's in front of his adoring audience, I cease to exist. He'll be swept away into the arms of one of his mistresses at the after-rally party while I go home to be the dutiful wife. Only tonight, I don't plan on being so dutiful.'

29

Stadtpark
Heumarkt (Hay Market Street)
Vienna, Austria
August 7, 2011

Klaus Von Volker had set up his rally near the north end of the Stadparkbrucke. The City Park Bridge, once known as the Karolinenbrucke, was a popular place. The bridge spanned the Wienfluss, and the Vienna River cut through the heart of Vienna.

When he'd gone to school in the city, Lourds had been fascinated by the river. People weren't allowed to walk or cycle along the concrete riverbed that had been laid. The headwaters in the Wienerwald sat on a bed of sandstone that saturated quickly. As a result, the *Wienfluss* could turn from a slow-moving creek to a roaring river pushing nearly 130,000 gallons of water a second. Even heavy equipment machines would get washed away in the deluge.

Von Volker launched his vitriol from an elaborate stage. The man was definitely a crowd-pleaser, if the reactions of the people gathered there to listen were any indication. Behind him, two large wide-screen projectors mounted on utility trucks showed 'Zionist oppression.' The footage was primarily of Israeli military rolling into contested areas, tanks crushing cars in the streets, soldiers shooting anyone who opposed them, and familiar politicians screaming.

'For too long, Israel has dictated the shape of the future in the Middle East. The Zionist government makes economic war on Iran, and their war has poured over onto us.' Von Volker walked the length of the stage like a rock star, touching the hands of his ardent supporters. 'The United States and other members of the European Union have reduced their trade with Iran, and they expect us to do the same. Not only expect it, for that is too genteel a word, they *demand* Austria's compliance as well. But the United States and her peers have alternate sources of oil.'

Lourds knew the argument held some validity. The sanctions the US and EU were trying to impose limited the amount of oil bought from Iran. That was primarily because the corporations outside countries dealt with tended to be – more and more – straw companies for the Revolutionary Guard, the Ayatollah's private mur der squad.

A few people in the audience dissented from Von Volker's claims, though most of them appeared to be tourists or young people. Bullyboys who evidently worked for Von Volker circulated through the crowd and ousted those people. The Viennese uniformed police appeared not to notice the semiphysical encounters.

'The United States allies itself with Saudi Arabia and other countries.' The PA system thundered Von Volker's words over the crowd. 'They can afford to cut back on oil because they have agreements with those countries to produce what they need. But what does Austria have? Do we have access to those other oil reserves?'

'No!' The crowd's response was deafening.

'The Zionists are seeking to hold our country back! They don't want to see Austria strong again!'

The crowd booed and hissed and cursed the United States and Israel.

'The United States has seen fit to pursue its "War on Terror" throughout the world. These days, it seems, the president and his advisers can find *terrorists* anywhere they choose to look!'

Another cry of protest filled the park.

'Could the previous American president find "weapons of mass destruction" in Iraq?'

'No!'

'And now they use their "War on Terror" to paint Austria's desires to advance her economy and her position in the global market. How long will it be before the United States tries to patrol *terrorism* in our country?'

An incensed howl went up from the crowd.

'If we do not stand together, if we allow Israel and her lapdogs to choose our allies, we will be defenseless before them one day. That is their agenda.'

More condemnation surged from the crowd, much of it directed against the United States.

Von Volker grinned like a wolf as he paced more furiously. 'Israel penetrated the infrastructure of the United States and took control a long time ago. Now they tell that greedy country what to do, commanding it like a lapdog trained to please its master. In these recent years, the United States has posited itself as the policeman to the world. Now they chase their shadows of terrorists around the globe. All the while, they continue consuming everything, becoming a monstrous leech that will suck the life from both the Western world and the Eastern one.'

More curses against the United States ran rampant through the crowd. As Lourds watched this time, he saw that the chanting was led by embedded cheerleaders, young, handsome men with strong Aryan features. They could have been poster children for Adolf Hitler's master race.

'How do you like the show?'

Lourds turned to look at Alice, who'd appeared from seemingly nowhere. 'Frankly, your husband makes me sick.'

'This is in a crowd. You should have to endure him at home.'

'I couldn't. This is the kind of blatant hostility and threatening posture that World War II was fought to stop.' Lourds shook his head. 'All that's missing is a martyr.'

Von Volker stood in front of the crowd again. 'The United States is inept. Look at how they poisoned the waters in the Gulf of Mexico when they lost control of the offshore oil rigs there. Millions of gallons of oil spewed into the ocean and killed wildlife in the waters and along the coasts for months. Did they take responsibility for their greed and destruction?'

'NO!'

Reluctantly, Lourds had to admit that Von Volker had plenty of ammunition against the United States.

'The oil spill in the Gulf of Mexico was disastrous.' Von Volker emphasized his words with a bunched fist. 'The world won't know the true cost of that blunder for possibly generations. In the meantime, all that oil the United States was counting on will need to be replaced. And do you know how they're going to replace it?'

The question thundered over the crowd, which responded in a disjointed burst of general unhappiness.

'By taking more oil from the Middle East! And in doing so, they will take more than their fair share. Austria will be like a homeless person begging for crumbs at the rich man's table.' Von Volker paused theatrically. 'Unless Austria rises up to take control of her own destiny!'

The furor rose to a fever pitch.

'Israel has already bemoaned Germany's dealings with Iran to the point that German business with Iran has been restricted. Iran has the oil we need. We have political support that country needs if it is to survive and move successfully into the twenty-first century. When the rest of the world is using nuclear power, Israel and her allies continue to lobby against Iran gaining that power to better maintain their nation and provide for their people.'

'As if that's all nuclear technology will be used for.' Lourds took a deep breath. 'He's a very dangerous man.'

Alice nodded. 'I know.'

'Together, Austria and Iran, we must rise up against the Zionist oppressors and kick the boot of the United States off the back of our necks.' Von Volker strutted before his constituency. 'We are a race of warriors!'

Cheering and whistling broke out.

'We are Austrian!' Von Volker roared his declaration. 'We will not submit like some meek schoolgirl in the face of a harsh taskmaster. All we need to do is rise up and stand our ground!'

Wild cries of support filled the park.

Alice touched Lourds's arm. 'Have you heard enough? He'll continue in this vein for another hour or two. If we leave now, we can reach the *schloss* just after his people leave the rooms.'

'Definitely.' Lourds took her hand and let her lead him through the crowd.

'*Herr* Von Volker.'

Von Volker finished mopping his face and glanced up at the bodyguard standing near him. He'd taken a break to briefly rest his voice. He wasn't finished inciting the crowd yet. Media people from all around the world were streaming the news footage live. CNN and Fox News were staying with the story as political analysts tried to interpret the coming worldwide reaction.

'Yes?'

'Your wife and Thomas Lourds are leaving the park.'

As he took in this news, Von Volker was surprised at the tiniest twinge of jealousy that flared through him. He quickly quashed it. 'Let them go. But make sure they are followed. Keep me apprised of where they're going and what they're doing.'

The man nodded and turned away to speak over the headset he wore.

Von Volker drained a bottle of water, then stepped back up on the stage. He had a rebellion to raise, and somewhere in there the Ayatollah's demands had to be met as well.

Ruling Palace of the Supreme Leader
Tehran
The Islamic Republic of Iran
August 7, 2011

The Eurasian lynx sat like stone in the shadows of the acacia tree and watched a young hare come closer. The lynx was young. Every now and again, its hindquarters twitched uncontrollably. The hare, like the lynx, lived in the lower portions of the Ayatollah's garden.

The beast was forty pounds of speed and muscle. Dark spots looked faded against the amber coat. The distinctive ears stood up in sharp points.

Hands behind his back, Davari watched the lynx with wide-eyed interest.

'Do you think the lynx will take the hare?'

Startled, Davari turned to face the Ayatollah. The older man had come up behind him without a sound, reminding Davari again that he had once been a warrior and had shed blood in God's holy name.

'Good evening, Supreme Leader.'

The Ayatollah nodded but never took his dark eyes from the lynx. 'You have not answered my question, Colonel.'

'My apologies.' Davari returned his attention to the lynx.

The animal's hindquarters trembled again as the hare came a little closer.

'I don't think so. The lynx is young.'

'He has speed and strength on his side.'

'True, but he lacks patience. He's letting his belly guide his instincts.'

'Yes.' The Ayatollah stepped up beside the colonel. 'You see the lynx's impatience, yes?'

'In the line of his body, the way he sits, of course.'

'Do you think the lynx sees these things?'

'How can he?'

The Ayatollah nodded. 'So we can agree that the lynx does not see these things in himself.'

'I don't see how he could, Supreme Leader.'

'I received your news that the professor – '

'Thomas Lourds.'

'Yes. Thomas Lourds is in Vienna. But you do not know why.'

'I believe it is because Von Volker has transported Lev Strauss's collection of artifacts to his manor home.'

'I am certain you are correct, but how did Thomas Lourds learn those artifacts were there?'

'I believe *Frau* Von Volker told him. As our investigation indicated, they were once lovers.'

The lynx gained momentary control over himself and was still again. The hare crept closer to the succulent blades of grass, almost within striking range now.

'It has been years since Lourds has seen *Frau* Von Volker.'

Davari nodded.

'So, why does he leave the search the Jew set him on to go to Vienna?'

'To see the collection of artifacts.'

'Does he know what he's looking for?'

Davari thought about that for the first time. 'I would assume so, Supreme Leader.'

The Ayatollah frowned. 'Assumptions will not find Mohammad's Koran and the Scroll for us, Colonel.'

'My apologies, Supreme Leader. I have failed you.'

'Not yet. I am merely adjusting your thinking.'

'I welcome your wisdom.'

'If Mohammad's Koran and the Scroll were among the Jew's things, we would have found them by now. Since we know Thomas Lourds is hunting those things as well, he wouldn't have gone to Von Volker's to find them. Therefore, he is seeking a clue.'

Davari nodded. That much he had already figured.

'The Jew will have been clever. Even if we found the clue, the Jew would have couched it in terms that would make it hard for an outsider to understand.'

The lynx's hindquarters twitched again as it readied itself.

'Thomas Lourds may solve whatever clues the Jew left for him. So we must be patient and give him room to work. Do you understand?'

'Yes, Supreme Leader.'

Coiled muscles exploded into action and thrust the lynx into motion. The big cat had misjudged his abilities, though. The hare had time to avoid him, then break away and seek shelter in the woodlands. Frustrated, the lynx yowled and stalked off.

'That lynx will go hungry, Colonel. Do not be that lynx as you proceed with your hunt. Give Thomas Lourds room to pick up the Jew's trail. God is on our side.'

'Thank you for your wise words, Supreme Leader.'

30

Schloss Volker
Vienna, Austria
August 7, 2011

As she watched Lourds's pained face, Alice knew he was reliving precious memories he'd shared with Lev Strauss. When she'd been with them, sharing their friendship while loving Lourds, she'd heard many of those stories. Only a few held special memories for her. She'd been along for the acquisition of only a handful of pieces and, sadly, she couldn't really remember much about them or how excited Lev had been.

At that time, she'd been so deeply in love with Thomas Lourds that little else mattered.

Studying him now as he worked his way through the collection, Alice felt those same feelings surfacing again. She wasn't sure exactly what the attraction was that existed between them, but she was more certain now that it was heavily weighted on her side.

She wanted him more than he wanted her.

It was a sad, hard thing to admit, but there it was. Thankfully, she was adult enough and experienced enough to recognize that.

Lourds was aloof, but it wasn't by choice. His work satisfied him on levels that no flesh-and-blood companion could ever hope to equal. That was frustrating and scary and addictive at the same time. What woman in her right mind could let such a challenge pass by without making an attempt to gain his attention?

Alice smiled to herself, but the humor was melancholy at best and painful at worst. She had been young and naïve when she'd fallen for him, but she was certain that even worldly women found themselves in a swoon over Lourds just as she had.

Lourds wasn't even aware of the effect he had on women. As far as she knew, he'd never taken the time to try to figure out why they were attracted to him. She knew from personal experience that he had an immense appetite for the pleasures of the flesh, and she'd come to suspect that making love only allowed him to take necessary mental-health breaks from his true passion.

He took what women willingly offered, but he didn't chase after them the way he did his mysteries. That had been a hard lesson to learn.

She had spent a few years thinking about everything that had happened to her in that relationship, trying to figure out what she'd done wrong. As she'd come to realize, she hadn't done anything wrong. If anything, she knew she should take solace and pride in the fact that their relationship had lasted through most of the two years they had spent together at the university.

According to Lev, no one else had ever occupied so much of Lourds's life.

'You're quiet.' Lourds glanced up at her.

'Just thinking.'

'Too hard, I'd wager.'

'Perhaps.'

'So what are you thinking about?'

'How good it is to see you again.'

Lourds grinned at her, that little-boy expression that was pure guile and mischief and innocence all at once. 'You're a married woman, *Frau* Von Volker.'

She frowned at him and felt a momentary flicker of anger. 'Don't call me that.' Her voice came out sharper than she'd intended.

Genuine regret marked Lourds's face. 'I apologize, Alice. That was inappropriate. Please forgive me.'

Just like that, the anger and awkwardness she'd experienced were gone. That was what it was like being with Thomas Lourds. He didn't judge her. He never had. He was only trying to be funny, to get a moment's respite during a hard situation.

'You're forgiven. I overreacted.' And she was way past feeling that her attentions to Lourds were in any way suitable for a married woman. She still loved him but at the same time she realized that she'd never be able to have him. That didn't keep her body from responding to his proximity, though. Every now and again, her breath caught at the back of her throat.

She was his for the asking.

And he probably didn't even know it.

Finally, he picked up a small candelabrum from one of the tables.

She joined him. 'Is that what you were looking for?'

His grin was all the answer she needed. 'Yes. This was something I gave Lev a long time ago. Evidently he put it to a new use.'

The candelabrum was a Jewish *menorah* for celebrating Hanukkah. Instead of the traditional six branches fanning out in an elliptical pattern around the main branch, this one had eight. It was supposed to be lighted during the eight days of the Jewish holiday. The *shamash,* the servant candle, was the candle that was used to light the other candles. Carefully, Lourds twisted that thin spire.

To Alice's surprise, the short candle base pulled free. A tightly rolled piece of paper occupied the hollowed area.

Lourds took the paper out, gently set the *menorah* aside, and opened his prize.

Standing on tiptoe, too aware of Lourds's clean, soapy smell and cologne, Alice peered over his shoulder and read the note.

Thomas, you'll have to see this from my point of view.

At the bottom of the piece of paper was a deftly rendered pictograph.

'Is that a Pegasus?'

Lourds smiled. 'It's a flying horse, all right. But this is al-Buraq, not the mount from Greek myth.'

'The flying horse that Mohammad rode?'

'The very same.'

'What does it mean?'

'It means I have to return to Jerusalem.'

Although she'd been expecting the answer, Alice's heart felt pierced. She didn't like the idea of getting Lourds back and losing him again so quickly. 'When?'

'The sooner the better. A lot of people are looking for this, and I'm not even sure what it is.' Lourds looked at her. 'Alice, I don't know how to thank you enough. Without you, I'd never have found this.'

Wordlessly, Alice gave in to the desire that had fueled her since she'd seen him that afternoon on the terrace of the Albertina Museum. She pulled him to her and kissed him soundly.

Lourds hesitated only for a moment, and she thought the fact that she was married – no matter how miserably – was going to stop him. Then he bent down and swept her up in his strong arms.

He smiled at her. 'I'm sure there are a lot of bedrooms here. Pick one and tell me how to get there.'

Anger flared through Von Volker as he watched the image of the American professor carrying his wife through the halls of his house. He watched them on the computer monitor. Their intent was unmistakable. In that moment, he wanted to go to the *schloss,* get one of his shotguns, and blow the American's head off his shoulders.

'*Herr* Von Volker, if you want me to stop this, I can.' The *schloss's* security chief looked uncomfortable.

They sat in the off-site security headquarters in one of the guesthouses. From there they could access the *schloss's* closed-circuit security system. Six computer monitors rotated views of the house. The central one tracked Lourds's progress through the hallway.

Evidently Alice was giving directions to one of the guest bedrooms. She wanted to avoid the one she shared with her husband. Von Volker took a measure of pride in that. If she wouldn't love him, he ensured that she feared him.

'No. Leave them alone. Let them have their fun. Because there will be no more of it after tonight.' Von Volker kept his voice calm. Von Volker was more angry about having to cut short his festivities at the after-rally party. He had whipped the crowd into a proper frenzy, and he'd gotten caught up in the pull of it all himself.

He was also angry because he could see how much his wife was in love with the American. Expectation glowed on her face. In that moment, he hated her in a way he'd never hated anyone.

On the screen, Alice and Lourds began removing each other's clothing. Von Volker made himself watch. Once they found out he had seen them, they would fear him even more. He would use that against them and enjoy every moment of it.

*

Alice lay beneath Lourds as he laved her breasts with kisses and his gentle tongue. Her breath grew shorter, and her needs grew stronger. Then his kisses drifted farther south until he was probing her sex yet again, driving her closer and closer to the edge – until she shattered and lost all control.

Her cries of pleasure filled the bedroom, and she knew she would have been mortified if she'd been in her right mind. Gasping, she lay back as Lourds raised himself above her and looked down at her, chuckling.

Finally, her breath returned, and she could feign a frown. 'You don't have to gloat.'

'This? This isn't a gloat. This is happy.'

'You're awfully proud of yourself.'

'Shouldn't I be?'

'Possibly. Of course, doing that to me has always had those results. You have always been a cunning linguist.'

Lourds grinned even larger. 'It's truly a shame that bit of wordplay only works in English.'

'Because you've been with so many women that don't speak English?'

He froze for a moment, and she could see that he didn't know what to say.

'My bad. Now I'm the one who's transgressed.'

'I forgive you.'

'How very gallant.'

'But I am going to exact a punishment.' Lourds adjusted his hips and sank into her.

Alice's breath grew short again. Then he began to

move, and the slippery, glorious friction made coherent thought all but impossible.

August 8, 2011

An hour before dawn, Lourds woke and started to get up so he would be gone before Von Volker's research team returned to the *schloss*. Alice grabbed him and slid on top of him. The lovemaking this time had more tenderness than desperation, and Lourds knew they were both resenting the fact that they had to part.

But the mystery wouldn't wait, and Von Volker wasn't a man to forgive trespasses.

Afterward, Lourds showered and dressed as she watched him. He didn't feel self-conscious about her watching, but he regretted the way his leaving was making her feel. On one level, he didn't want to go, but on all the others, he was excited to get back to Jerusalem and find out what Lev had left for him there.

And he thought he knew the exact place to look for the sign.

When he was ready to go, he leaned over and kissed her once more. 'While I'm gone, see if you can sort through Lev's artifacts. In case there's something else there we'll need to know about later.'

'I've already got a copy of the catalogue on the items that his people have compiled.'

Lourds nodded. 'That isn't all of Lev's collection. I

know of at least a dozen pieces that are missing. I sincerely doubt that Lev got rid of any of them. Concentrate on the ones representing the Muslim faith.'

'Like the figurine of Iblis?'

'Exactly.'

'I'll keep watch for them and let you know if and when they arrive.'

'In the meantime, you need to watch yourself. If Von Volker figures out I've been here – '

She put her warm fingers against his lips. 'I know, Thomas. This is a game I've played before. You're not the only lover I've taken since I've been married.' She smiled at him. 'I tell you that only so you don't have to feel as though you've been the one to help me break my marriage vows.'

'I was trying hard not to feel guilty over that.'

'Sarcasm?'

'It's a language-rich skill.'

Her beautiful eyes sparkled as she grinned mischievously. 'I'll also bet that I'm not the only married woman you've bedded.'

'A gentleman doesn't kiss and tell.' Lourds captured her hand and kissed her fingers.

'You're not a gentleman.'

'I do try to keep the tattered fragments in place.'

Alice picked up his hat from the bed and settled it atop his head. 'Go. Before you're caught and we're undone.'

Lourds kissed her and pulled back. 'If everything goes well, we'll see each other again soon.'

'Not soon enough.'

Lourds walked through the house, thinking about the night he'd just had and how familiar everything had seemed. It was as though they'd only been apart a few days, not years. All the moves were still there, and they still played each other's bodies like finely tuned instruments.

The main thing that occupied his mind, though, was what puzzles awaited him in Jerusalem. Lev had mentioned a book, so everything would start there.

As he approached the front door, movement to his left caught his attention. He started to turn, thought he saw a man, then an explosion opened a black hole in his head.

31

Jagdschloss Volker
Outside Vienna, Austria
August 8, 2011

Certain he was going to find his brains lying in a pool at his feet, Lourds cracked his eyes open against the harsh white light shining full in his face. The overpowering glare made learning any details about where he was being held difficult.

He was definitely being held, though. Leather straps bound him to a chair. He struggled against them, found they were more than strong enough to hold him in place, and succeeded ultimately only in making his already pounding headache worse.

Resigned, he leaned back against the chair and listened. The quiet told him that either the room was soundproofed or it was far from the neighbors. Either reason was bad.

A door opened. Tense, heart pounding, Lourds waited. He was pretty certain he knew who'd kidnapped him.

'Professor Lourds.' Von Volker's voice was immediately recognizable. 'Did you have a good time getting . . . *reacquainted* with my wife?'

There was no possible way that could be answered. Lourds didn't even bother to try.

'Come on, Professor Lourds. Surely you have some cutting remark to offer the man you just cuckolded.'

Fear made Lourds speak, but not for himself. 'Where is Alice? What have you done to her?'

Von Volker laughed, and Lourds hated the man for that.

'I've not done anything to Alice. She doesn't even know we're here.'

Lourds felt a little relief, but he was hardly in a position to be worry-free. 'If you're going to blame anyone for Alice's indiscretion – '

'I should blame you?'

'No, you pompous ass, you should blame yourself.' Lourds didn't know he was going to say that until he'd already spoken. But he remembered the fear and loathing he'd seen in Alice's eyes and couldn't hold back. He blamed the pain inside his skull, and the fact that he was possibly still addled.

Someone removed the light shining in his face. It took a moment for his vision to clear well enough to make out the small room and the three men in it.

Von Volker sat in a comfortable office chair. The room was small and barren except for a long counter that ran the length of one wall. A double stainless-steel sink with hose attachments occupied the center of the counter. The floor was concrete, and in the center of it was a large grill over a water drain.

The presence of the drain chilled Lourds's blood. The room was a kill room, a place where game was brought to be cleaned and dressed after being shot.

The two men with Von Volker were grim-faced hard-cases who wore pistols in shoulder holsters.

The Austrian glanced around the room and smiled. 'I surmise that you've fathomed the purpose of this room?'

Lourds remained silent.

'We're at my *jagdschloss*. You know the term, yes?'

'I speak German fluently.' A *jagdschloss* was a hunting lodge.

'Of course you do. That was one of the languages you used with Alice last night.'

Lourds couldn't believe it. 'You were watching?'

'Nearly the whole time.' Von Volker shrugged. 'I have to admit, watching her with someone else is quite interesting. The only time I ever get her so receptive to sex is when I drug her. During those times, she's hardly a scintillating conversationalist. To be equitable, you had her fairly speechless most of the time.' He grinned coldly.

'You're a sick, twisted bastard.'

A nerve high on the Austrian's face jerked. 'I'm tempted to have my men remove one of your fingers for such an insult.'

Lourds swallowed a thick ball of fear lodged at the back of his throat.

'Do I have your attention?'

'Yes.'

'Good. This will go much faster and be more rewarding for both of us.' Von Volker crossed one leg over the other. 'How did you find out I had taken Lev Strauss's little religious artifact collection?'

'Alice called me.' Lourds didn't see that telling the truth would get her in any more trouble than she was already in.

Von Volker nodded in satisfaction. 'Excellent. Having to fight you to get the truth out of you would be tedious. Although the thought of torturing you would be somewhat rewarding. On my part, at least.'

'Did you murder Lev?'

After a brief hesitation, Von Volker shook his head. 'No. I wanted him alive. His death was unfortunate. There is another man, a Saudi named Rayan Mufarrij, who caused your friend's death. Have you heard of him?'

'No.' Lourds was glad to be able to tell the truth. His mind had already started summoning awful images of what Von Volker's men would do to him.

'He's a very bad man, a dangerous man.'

'What does he want?'

'Presumably what we all want: Mohammad's Koran, the one given to him from God's lips.' Von Volker smiled mockingly.

'You sound like you don't believe it exists.'

'For me to believe that that version of the Koran exists, I'd also have to believe in a God. I don't. I believe in power. In the unity of the German and Austrian people. And in our destiny to become a powerful nation – a united nation – again. I also believe in me being the head of state of such a country. Anything else is unacceptable.' Von Volker paused a moment, then studied Lourds. 'Do you know where Mohammad's Koran is?'

'No.'

'Sadly, I believe you. Torture seems like such an ideal way for us to spend the morning, however.'

Trying to contain his fear, Lourds just stared at the man.

'You see, it's easy to believe you don't know where an imaginary object is. However, I do want to know what this means.' Von Volker held up the piece of paper Lev had left in the candelabrum.

Lourds shook his head. 'I don't know. I was on my way back to Jerusalem to find out.'

'That's too bad.' Von Volker put the piece of paper into his pocket and stood. 'Because I don't believe that.'

More afraid now, Lourds took a breath. 'Under the circumstances, if I knew, I'd tell you. You'll have to trust me on that.'

Von Volker studied him for a moment. 'Perhaps.' He looked at the two men. 'I'm going to return to Vienna. Give me time to establish an alibi, since it may come out that he's an old lover of my wife's, then kill him. Make it painful.' He turned and walked away, and the click of his heels against the concrete sounded loud and grim.

Alice tried to go about her day as if nothing had happened, but that was almost impossible because all she could think about was Thomas. Her body ached in pleasant ways from all the positions she'd found herself in during the course of the night.

She glanced at her watch again. It was after ten. He should have been at the airport already. She'd left six messages on his cell phone. She didn't know whether to be more afraid that he was deliberately ignoring her or that something had happened to him.

Seated in her office space, she had a clear view of the front gate, so when Klaus's private car pulled into the circle drive, she saw the vehicle immediately. Panic tightened her stomach, but she made herself breathe.

Leaning against the window, she watched her husband enter the house. She grabbed her keys from the nightstand beside the bed, flung open the window, stepped out of her shoes, picked them up, and scrabbled across the roof.

At the roof's edge, she hesitated. The drop was only fifteen feet or so, but it looked much farther. She tossed her shoes onto the ground, then lowered herself and hung by her arms. A moment later, she let go and dropped. When she hit the ground, she tumbled back into a yoga roll and came up on her feet.

She stepped into her shoes and ran to the front of her house. Her husband was still inside.

The driver stood outside the luxury vehicle and looked a little surprised to see her. '*Herr* Von Volker is inside the house, *Frau* Von Volker.'

Alice casually waved the news away. 'I'm going into the city. I'll talk to him later. I suppose the after-rally party ran late last night. Did you just get in from Vienna?'

'Yes.'

Alice started to continue on her way, then she spotted the hunting jacket in the backseat of the car through the open window. Her heart lurched into a furious beat as she headed for the long garage. She knew Klaus had been to the *jagdschloss* that morning. The last time he'd been out there, he'd left the jacket there. He'd complained about it for a week.

Thomas!

Swallowing her fear, Alice keyed the garage door and entered. She slid behind the wheel of a white Wiesmann two-seater sports car and took out her phone. She hesitated only a moment, then punched in the number for the police patrol around the *jagdschloss*.

'Hello. This is Alice Von Volker.'

The man at the other end of the connection responded immediately, obviously impressed with the name. 'Ah, *Frau* Von Volker. How may I help you?'

'Yes, I think so. Could you have someone check on my husband's *jagdschloss*? I drove by there only a few minutes ago and saw a strange car parked out front.'

'Of course. We'll get someone out there immediately.'

'Thank you.' Alice turned the phone off and dropped it on the passenger seat. She keyed the ignition and triggered the electronic garage door opener. Engaging the transmission, she shot out of the garage and roared toward the front gates.

The wrought-iron barrier pulled back just in time to allow her passage. She never looked in her rearview mirror to see if her husband had come out of the house or if anyone was in pursuit.

She had only one thought on her mind as she drove toward the *jagdschloss.*

Please don't be dead, Thomas.

32

Jagdschloss Volker
Outside Vienna, Austria
August 8, 2011

Thankfully, it was hot in the *jagdschloss* kill room. It hadn't taken long for Lourds to work up a sweat while shifting in the chair. The men watching over him didn't care that he occupied himself with trying to get away. The chair was bolted to the floor, suggesting it had been used for nefarious purposes before.

Bored, the men went to one of the other rooms. Every time they came to check on him, Lourds felt the air-conditioning in the other room invade the kill room for a moment and the noise of a television. Their visits had become more and more infrequent. Either the program they were watching was very good, or they didn't care if he was in need of a bathroom. The thought that he might escape probably hadn't crossed their minds.

Perspiration streaming down his neck and tickling his ears, Lourds leaned forward into the leather straps. Dampness from his sodden shirt had turned the leather a darker color. More importantly, the wetness had loosened the leather strap holding his arms to his sides and his hands behind his back.

In his studies, Lourds knew that American Indians and Mongols – both roving, nomadic peoples – had depended on leather to make their weapons. When they'd tied spearheads to shafts or made bows, warriors had first soaked the leather strands and tied them tightly, knowing the strands would draw up even more as they dried.

Of course, the reverse was true as well.

The door opened, and one of the guards stuck his head in. He surveyed Lourds, then flashed him a mocking smile and dangled a beer bottle from his fingertips. 'You miss party.' His English was heavy and accented.

'Is that an invitation?' Lourds smiled hopefully.

'No. We're going to kill you. No reason to waste beer.' The man laughed at him, then went to tell his partner what a fine joke he'd just played on the American professor and how stupid the man was.

Lourds heard the man braying his story even over the television. For a moment, he gave in to despair, but then he forced himself to focus again on his efforts. He was making headway with the leather. Because of the sweat he'd worked into the material, he could already tell it was stretching out, loosening.

He worked solidly, concentrating on each effort, grinding his sweat into the straps. Finally, it felt looser, and the leather around his wrists no longer felt as tight.

He dropped his left shoulder and raised his right, repeating the motion again and again. Gradually, the leather strap worked up past his shoulder. Long minutes later, it was past the point of no return because any visitation on the part of his guards would give away his game, and they wouldn't make the same mistake twice.

Finally, though, his shoulder slid free of the strap. His flesh felt abraded and raw, and he knew he'd be sore from the chafing, but if his luck held, he wouldn't be dead.

He tucked his head into his shoulder, emulating a move he'd read that Harry Houdini used to escape straitjackets. A few moves later, his head was free, too. When he stood, he walked to the sink, turned around, and carefully felt for the tap. He turned it on just enough for a trickle, then held his bound wrists under the flow. The leather binding him grew even looser. He stretched and pulled and applied pressure a dozen different ways.

After a few moments, his left hand slid free. He scooped his hat up from the counter, slid his wallet and phone back into his pants pockets, and started for the back door.

Footsteps sounded out in the hall, coming closer. 'I'm getting another beer. Want one?'

'Yeah. And check on the professor. He should be begging for his life right now.'

'Maybe I should slap him around a little. Provide a little encouragement.'

The other man laughed.

Lourds tried the back door, but it was locked. Obviously, Von Volker had made certain his 'guests' couldn't escape under any circumstances. Frantic, he looked around for a weapon, then spied a heavy iron frying pan on a woodburning stove. He hefted it and discovered it weighed several pounds. Moving swiftly, he positioned himself by the door and drew back the pan.

His knees trembled slightly as he thought about what he was going to do. He would have preferred to run. He was not a fighter. Fortunately, there wasn't much time to think or dread.

The man stepped through the doorway and Lourds swung with all the strength in his arms. The frying pan hammered the guard in the face, but the sound was much duller than Lourds had anticipated, more like a thump than a bang.

Knocked out or dead, Lourds wasn't sure, but there was enough blood from the nose and mouth that it could have gone either way, the guard dropped like a stone. The empty bottles he carried shattered against the stone floor.

'Walter?' The television sound muted immediately. 'Walter?'

Lourds thought briefly of searching the fallen man for a weapon more serviceable than the frying pan, but the flight instinct in him was strongest of all. The ring of keys on the man's belt made his choice obvious. Grabbing them, he abandoned the frying pan and tackled the back door again. It took him a moment to fumble through the lock.

'Walter!' Footsteps pounded toward the kill room.

Lourds got the door open just as the second guard stuck his pistol into the room and followed it around the corner. Just as Lourds charged through the door, two bullets smashed through the glass panes in it. Flying glass shards chased Lourds out into the woodlands behind the *jagdschloss.*

Aware the gunman could shoot him in the back if he stayed on a straight line, Lourds grabbed the first tree trunk he came to and veered to the left. The bark ripped free and tore at his palm, but he kept his feet under him and lengthened his stride.

In the distance, a road cut through the tree line nearly two hundred yards away at the bottom of the steep incline. Gnarled roots and the rocky soil challenged his footing as he raced down it.

The gunman pursued him, firing periodically. Every instinct Lourds possessed screamed at him to dive for cover somewhere along the way, but he knew that would only delay the inevitable. He was in shape. There was a lot of real estate in front of him. He had a chance to get away if he just kept running.

And don't break your neck.

An unseen rock rolled under his right foot. He tried to keep his foot straight, hoped he hadn't turned his ankle, and stumbled in the direction he almost fell in order to keep his feet under him. His rhythm was thrown off for a moment, and he crashed against a tree trunk, the impact driving his right elbow into his side and knocking the breath from his lungs.

Off-balance and in pain, he fell and rolled down the incline. The gunman fired a handful of rounds that kicked up fist-sized clods of earth around him. Still falling and rolling, Lourds managed to get back up on his feet while tumbling. Soccer games had taught him to fight for control and get back up as soon as possible if a whistle hadn't blown.

There was no whistle while he was running for his life.

Hoping to become a harder target, Lourds charged through the brush. Once, when he suddenly found a downed tree in front of him, and there was no way he could stop or change directions successfully, he stepped up the pace and leaped. Branches and bushes whipped at him, and he couldn't see what he was going to be landing in when he came down.

On the other side of the fallen tree, the incline plunged ten feet almost straight down. Lourds flailed his arms and tried to pick his landing spot, but he came down in a twisting, flailing fall that rolled him head over heels. As he got to his feet, banged up and sporting new bruises, he reflexively grabbed his hat and ran again.

He'd lost sight of the road, but he marked his passage by landmarks he'd chosen along the way.

The gunman had closed the distance, drawing to within twenty feet. He was still running, too, gaining steadily.

Why couldn't I have been held by couch potatoes with guns? Lourds ran as hard as he could, but he knew he was outmatched. He was going to die out here in this forlorn wilderness, and there was nothing he could do to prevent it.

Then the forest melted away in front of him, and the road was there. He ran out across it without hesitation, hoping to get across the narrow two-lane before the gunman had a clear shot at him. Gunshots echoed around him and bullets ricocheted from the road.

A car topped the hill and nearly ran him down. He threw himself forward and got clear. The gunman wasn't so lucky. He'd come out of the tree line totally focused on Lourds and hadn't seen the car until it was on top of him.

Brakes shrieked, but the grisly *thump* told Lourds that neither man nor machine had been able to avoid the collision. Out of breath on the ground, hurting and certain he couldn't run much farther, he looked back at the road.

A police car sat sideways in the road thirty or forty feet from the point of impact. Two young uniformed officers got out of the car brandishing weapons. The passenger held a shotgun.

Dazed and battered, the gunman drew himself up from the road. Bloody scrapes showed on his face, and his left arm hung crookedly at his side. But his right arm came up with the pistol.

'Stop! Police!'

The gunman fired at the police officers. The man with the shotgun fired once, and Von Volker's henchman lifted from his heels and fell backwards. He quivered and was still.

The second police officer sprinted forward with his pistol in both hands. He kicked the gunman's weapon away and hauled out a pair of handcuffs that couldn't possibly be needed.

Lourds stared up helplessly as the policeman with the shotgun walked toward him while aiming his weapon. The man looked grim and deadly.

'Professor Lourds?'

In disbelief, Lourds nodded but didn't move. His hands were in plain sight for the policeman, and he knew to keep them that way. 'I'm Thomas Lourds.'

'*Frau* Von Volker sent us.' The policeman lowered his weapon. 'Are you all right?'

'I am now. Thank you.' Lourds took the proffered hand and climbed shakily to his feet.

Hours later, after being grilled by two investigators and a lieutenant of homicide, Lourds was released on his own recognizance. The lieutenant told him they would be in touch if they needed anything more.

'I would caution you on one other thing, Professor Lourds.'

Lourds looked at the broad, clean-shaven lieutenant with sad eyes. 'Yes.'

'Based on your statement, and that of *Frau* Von Volker, we have issued a warrant for *Herr* Von Volker. But I must tell you, *Herr* Von Volker is an important person in

Vienna. He has many friends. Your continued presence in this city, perhaps even in Austria, will be perilous.'

'I plan on leaving as soon as I get out of here.' Lourds had already changed his plane ticket to the evening flight out of Vienna instead of the morning one.

'Good.' The lieutenant shook his hand, then showed him the door.

Alice sat in one of the chairs out in the hallway. She looked at Lourds for just a moment, then came to him and held him. Lourds wrapped his arms around her and felt her shaking against him.

'I hear I have you to thank for my life.'

She tilted her head and looked up at him. 'I was also the one that very nearly got you killed by bringing you here in the first place.'

Lourds smiled at her and kissed her. 'I wouldn't have missed it for the world.'

'But you're still going back to Jerusalem.'

'I've got to locate whatever Lev left for me to find.'

'You'd be safer going back to Harvard. If you had any sense, that's where you'd go.'

'I can't. Lev counted on me to help him.'

'I don't think he would hold it against you under the circumstances.'

Lourds just held her, relishing the way she felt and smelled and made him glad to be alive.

'You can't go till you figure this thing out, can you?' Alice looked disappointed.

'No.' The unknown was a siren call for him though he wished that call were safer sometimes. 'But we should be safer in Jerusalem.'

Alice shook her head. 'Not *we*. Not yet.'

That surprised Lourds. 'Alice, you can't possibly be thinking of staying here. Not with that madman still on the loose.'

'Lieutenant Krieger is going to help me get my things from the house. And by *things*, I mean Lev's collection. I can't just pop back across the border with those. I don't know how Klaus managed it, but I don't have the political clout he does. So, for the time being, I'm going to stay with that collection and research it.'

'Do you have somewhere safe to go?'

'Yes. And the means. In order to take advantage of various tax shelters, Klaus put a number of bank accounts in my name. I intend to avail myself of those while I deal with the collection.'

'You're a brave woman, Alice.'

'Perhaps it isn't bravery at all. Perhaps it's just curiosity.'

'There's a lot of that going around.' Lourds frowned. 'I think Von Volker is working with the Iranians on this.'

'Why?'

'Because the book pertains to Islam, and because Von Volker doesn't believe it exists. I think he's just making a token effort to get the book for the Ayatollah. I can't think of anyone else he'd be working with in this matter, and that would explain the extremes he seems willing to go to in order to find it.'

Alice shook her head. 'I don't know. I do know that a man from the Ayatollah's Revolutionary Guard has come to our house on occasion, and I've seen phone numbers for him on Klaus's cell phone.'

'What man?'

'Colonel Davari.'

Lourds considered the name but couldn't place it. 'Maybe I'll take a look into him too. Once I get back to Jerusalem. It would be good to know who all our enemies are.' He checked the time on a clock in the hallway. 'I'm sorry, Alice – '

'I know. The plane will leave without you. Go. I'll take care of things as best I can at this end. You just make sure you stay alive long enough for me to see you again.'

'I promise.' Lourds kissed her, then went to get his backpack and suitcase. The lieutenant had promised him a police escort to the airport.

33

Covert Operations
Institute for Intelligence and Special Operations (Mossad)
Tel Aviv, Republic of Israel
August 8, 2011

'We're fortunate, *Katsas* Shavit.'

Glancing up from her desk, Sarah waved Isser Melman into her office. 'Come in, please, and explain our good fortune.'

Melman entered the room and took a seat in front of her desk. He used his walking stick to lever one leg over the other.

'We have picked up Professor Lourds's trail once more.'

'In Vienna?' Shavit had spent most of yesterday and this morning trying to find agents with assets to track the American down.

'Actually, he just left there. He's on a plane bound for Tel Aviv. I'm betting he'll return to Jerusalem.'

Sarah leaned back in her chair and felt her stomach rolling again. Lourds was a traveling storm, full of all kinds of portents, first here, then there. It was most disconcerting. 'He found out something in Vienna that has sent him back to Jerusalem.'

'I believe so.' Melman rested his hands on top of his walking stick and grimaced. 'While he was in Vienna, he incurred the wrath of Klaus Von Volker.'

Sarah was tempted to spit when she heard the name, but she didn't. In her book, evil didn't come much worse than Von Volker. 'He's involved in this?'

'So it would appear. Von Volker is definitely in the Ayatollah's camp.'

That was inarguable.

'As it turns out, Professor Lourds has an interesting history with Von Volker.'

'I wasn't aware that Lourds knew Von Volker. That's something I would have remembered from his file.'

'Actually, the history wasn't with Von Volker.' Melman smiled slightly and shook his head.

In addition to being good at memorizing files, Sarah was good at connecting the dots. 'Von Volker doesn't have a daughter, nor a sister. So it's the wife then?'

Melman nodded. 'Lourds and *Frau* Von Volker were classmates at Vienna, as it turns out, and lovers for a couple of years.'

'How did we miss that?'

'We weren't looking for it. We weren't looking for a connection to Von Volker either.'

'No, but that would explain the German and Austrian mercenaries that turned up dead where Lev Strauss was killed.'

'And the two men Agent Abata killed in Namchee Bazaar.'

Sarah made a note in Lourds's folder to tie him, Von Volker, and *Frau* Von Volker in together. 'Perhaps we should make a history of every woman the professor has been romantically involved with.'

Melman tugged at his white beard and smiled. 'I'm beginning to think that even the vast resources of the Mossad might be taxed to investigate such a thing. Professor Lourds seems to find willing women wherever he goes.'

'We don't know why Lourds is coming back to Israel?'

'No.' Melman shook his head. 'Not yet. But he found something in that book in the bus locker that sent him to Vienna. That much is clear. I'm willing to bet that he found something in Vienna that brought him back here.'

Pulling up the crime scene photos of Lev Strauss's flat, Sarah turned the monitor around so Melman could see. 'There were a number of articles taken from Strauss's flat according to Strauss's neighbor.'

'Mrs. Hirsch, yes, I know. And I was thinking that if Von Volker were behind Strauss's kidnapping, those things might have ended up in Vienna.'

'We have discovered the woman's origins.'

'The one found at Strauss's murder site?'

'Yes. She was from Austria. From her police record, she had a history of selling sexual favors and attaching herself to wealthy men.'

'A mistress?'

'If you want to call it that.'

'Von Volker's mistress?'

'We're investigating that possibility.'

'Can you bring up a picture of *Frau* Von Volker and this mistress side by side on your computer?'

Sarah pulled the images from the files and placed them together on the monitor.

A cold smile thinned Melman's lips. 'Those two women favor each other, don't you think?'

'Yes.' Sarah felt frustrated. That was something she should have caught earlier.

'You weren't looking for the connection.' Melman shifted in his chair. 'You're not perfect, Sarah, but you're closer than anyone I've ever worked with before. Occasionally, everyone misses things.'

'Strauss knew Lourds in Vienna. Lourds knew *Frau* Von Volker in Vienna.' Sarah pursed her lips. 'It's hardly a stretch to believe that Strauss knew *Frau* Von Volker. She could be the reason Strauss left the safe house.'

Melman scratched his beard. 'So the knots are falling neater and neater.'

'Yes.'

'One thing I do detest, *Katsas* Shavit, is Lourds's blatant disregard for our efforts at keeping tabs on him.'

Sarah smiled at the comment. Melman had a very dry sense of humor that was seldom exercised. 'He's hardly aware that we're onto him.'

'Even so. The man's habit of popping here and there is very irritating. I hate playing catch-up on a mission as important as this. So I was thinking we might correct our inability to stay apace with him.'

Interested, Sarah watched him. 'With Miriam Abata?'

Melman smiled broadly. 'You anticipate me so well, Sarah. Between you and my wife, I have no secrets.'

'Agent Abata hasn't fully recovered from her ordeal in Namchee Bazaar.'

'No, I wouldn't expect that she would have yet.' Melman took a breath. 'But you know as well as I do that these things are better dealt with by throwing an agent back out into the field as soon as possible. If she is broken, the sooner we know, the more lives we save. Including her own.'

'I know.' Sarah contemplated the idea. 'She's also exactly the type of young woman that Professor Lourds would allow close to him.'

Melman raised his eyebrows. 'Type? Dear woman, any female that's breathing and vertical appears to be his type.'

'The *vertical* appears to be negotiable. *Horizontal* would be more appealing, I would think.'

Color flushed Melman's cheeks, but he laughed.

'Let me talk to Abata. I'll get back to you.' But the more she thought about the idea, the more Sarah liked it. Also, after what Miriam Abata had been through, maybe tough love was the answer.

34

The Institute of Archaeology
Hebrew University of Jerusalem
Mount Scopus
Jerusalem, the State of Israel
August 9, 2011

Lourds took a taxi up the hill to the college campus in northeast Jerusalem. The land was pretty, falling away in graceful curves equally decorated with dwellings and wilderness.

Mount Scopus peered down on Jerusalem, and it had been the staging point for several efforts to sack the city. The Romans and the Crusaders had gathered there and initiated maneuvers, and the area was hotly contested during the Arab-Israeli War in 1948, then again in 1967 during the Six-Day War. Today, the mountain was zoned within the municipality of Jerusalem.

Looking out over the city, Lourds could pick out all the landmarks that would have been visible to those Roman Centurions in AD 66, and to the French and English Crusaders so many years later. The mind-set of those warriors would not have changed much. Whether armed with a gladius or an assault rifle, those men would have mentally poked and pried at Jerusalem's weakness till the city fell.

Rome had supported Herod as the king of the Jews, and he'd kowtowed to the city's every wish. Under Herod's guidance, though, Jerusalem had prospered and grown, and the Temple Mount area had more than doubled. His descendants had ruled the city till the Great Revolt in AD 66. That was what had brought the Romans to fill the streets with blood. It had taken them four years to break the city's defenses, but eventually they'd done it. Agrippa II, Herod's descendant and the last of the seven Herodian kings, had fled to Galilee with his sister.

General Vespasian had led more than sixty thousand troops into Galilee and crushed the rebellion in the north. From there, he and his son Titus stalled at Jerusalem's walls. The army had dug a trench around the city and set up camp. Citizens caught fleeing the city were crucified and left to rot on crosses on the earthen walls the Romans had built to trap Jerusalem. Historians reported that as many as five hundred crucifixions took place in a single day.

Studying the city now, Lourds could see where the battles had been staged. Gardens and new buildings covered many of the old scars, but they were still there, still ingrained in a culture that would never forget the injustices, the hatred outsiders had poured on them, and the oppression they'd suffered at the hands of foreign invaders.

Some said Jerusalem would never heal until God

Himself descended from the heavens and ministered to the city. But which God? That had been the question for so many ages.

And, as always, predators around the city awaited the moment to strike. Most of those were descendants of those who had gone before, and everything they did was in God's name.

'Professor Lourds.'

Startled, Lourds turned from a group of beautiful coeds sitting in the shade of trees near the entrance to the Botanical Gardens.

A short, well-kept man in his early sixties and a good gray suit approached him. He was hawk-faced, bald, and wore a neat salt-and-pepper goatee.

'I'm Aaron Jacob, president of the university. We talked on the phone this morning.' Jacob offered his hand.

Lourds took the man's hand and shook. Jacob had a strong, practiced grip, but there were no calluses. He'd shaken a lot of hands over the years – as university president that would have been a prerequisite – but he'd pushed pencils more than he'd shifted rock and dirt in the field. 'Just call me Thomas.'

'Of course. Call me Aaron.' Smoothly, Jacob slid his arm around Lourds's shoulders and guided him up the steps toward the main building. 'I'm told this isn't your first visit to our university.'

'No. I've been here a few times, actually. As a visiting professor and as a lecturer.'

'Really? I must have missed those opportunities to hear you. My loss.'

'There are recordings.'

Jacob smiled at that. 'Yes, I'll have to familiarize myself with your work when I have the opportunity. You said this morning you wanted to look around Professor Strauss's office?'

'If I may.'

'The two of you were good friends?'

'Very good friends. We studied in Vienna together, did some fieldwork among the Uighur tribes in the Himalayas, and Lev saved my life in a plane crash a few years ago. That's how he lost the leg.'

'I never did hear that story.'

'Lev didn't like bragging.'

'He seemed like a quiet, intense man.'

'Get a six-pack and a pizza in him, and he could be quite different.'

Jacob grinned. 'I suppose that can be said of most men. Can you tell me what you're looking for?'

'I just want to put Lev's papers in order, perhaps finish some of the work he'd started.' Lourds shrugged. 'It was a drunken promise we made to each other one night. We were young and idealistic. It's one of those foolish promises you make to a dear friend, but while I'm here, I thought I'd see what I could get sorted.'

'You left that marvelous discovery in the Himalayas to come here?'

'Lev sent word to me, asking me to be here. I didn't know we had lost him till I arrived.'

'I'm sorry. That had to have been hard. As for Professor Strauss's office, you could actually help us. We don't know where to get started as far as packing things up.' Jacob looked at Lourds and grimaced. 'Sorry. That came out rather more cold and bureaucratic than I'd intended.'

'At this point, I don't think there's any other way to put it.'

Jacob opened the door and guided Lourds into the air-conditioned building. 'I did put off cleaning the office until we could get someone that knew Professor Strauss well enough to put his work into perspective. The university doesn't want to lose any of his research that needs to be saved.'

Lourds removed his sunglasses and looked at the lobby. History fairly dripped from the walls. Jerusalem was filled with thousands of years of artifacts from cultures all around the world. The Department of Restoration and Conservation specialized in prehistoric, biblical, and classical archaeology. Pictures of digs sat on display.

'A special exhibition of some of the projects the institute has done. To introduce our work to prospective students signing up for fall classes.'

A plastered skull from Kfar Hahoresh sat in a glass case, the closed eyes and straight line of the mouth giving the face the semblance of sleeping. Pottery shards from the Yoqne'am Regional Project were arranged on another shelf. A replica of a mosaic of a Roman archer in armor hung on the wall. Dozens of other pieces, all impressive, occupied more space.

'It should get their attention.'

'It has.' Jacob pointed down a hallway. 'Professor Strauss's office is this way.'

Lev's office looked like a bomb had gone off inside. Lourds would have been surprised to find it any other way. When they'd roomed together in Vienna, they'd both been messy about research and work, and neither had complained about the other. However, each one had known where every scrap of paper he was working with was located.

'I apologize for the mess.' Jacob looked a little embarrassed. 'Perhaps I should have had someone tidy up.'

'No. This is perfect. Lev thought in groups.' Lourds pointed his hat at the organized chaos. 'With everything left untouched, I'll be able to follow Lev's thinking like a bloodhound trails scent.'

'All right. I'm glad you like it.'

Lourds smiled. 'Besides, if people had always cleaned up after themselves, archaeologists would have nothing to discover.'

'I suppose that is one way to think about it.'

'It is.'

Jacob held out a set of keys. 'These will get you into and out of the office. How long do you think this will take?'

'I don't know. A few days at most.'

'All right.' Jacob pulled a business card from his pocket. 'These are my office and home phone numbers. If you should find you need anything, please don't hesitate to contact me.'

'Thank you.'

Jacob nodded. 'There's a university cafeteria within walking distance, and a few places the students like to go. You can even have food delivered from a few nearby restaurants.'

'I'll keep that in mind.' Lourds pocketed the keys and the business card, anxious to get to work.

'A graduate student will be by shortly to assist you.'

Lourds looked at the man. 'Oh?'

'I looked for a volunteer to help you shift Professor Strauss's papers.' Jacob smiled and shook his head. 'That's a lot of work to do by yourself. Plus, she'll know more about the university.'

'All right.' The idea of someone peering over Lourds's shoulder made him slightly uneasy, but there wasn't much he could do to dissuade the university president. He was fortunate they were even letting him onto the premises. He looked around at the office as Jacob said good-bye and walked away.

Of course, the office was a *lot* of work.

For a time while she was walking through the halls of the university, Miriam Abata could believe that she was back in school. Those days were barely behind her. If she could step back, only a few days, the two dead men wouldn't be haunting her.

Every now and again, she thought she saw one of them standing just a short distance away, caught in the corner of her eye, pistol drawn. But every time she looked, no one was there. Nights were the hardest. She played the events over again and again, wondering if there was some other way she could have handled herself.

Let it go. That had been *Katsas* Shavit's advice. *Accept what is, know that you did the best you could to save yourself. That was your job. Save yourself. That is every operative's primary job.*

They had talked for a while, then *Katsas* Shavit had taken her to a piano bar and gotten her drunk. Later, at Miriam's flat, they had cried together. Somehow, *Katsas* Shavit had gotten her into her bed and left.

They'd never talked of the shooting or the drinking since, but Miriam knew the woman would be there for her if she needed her.

She drew a deep breath as she took the final corner toward the office she was looking for. The assignment had come as a surprise because she had expected to be left on her own for weeks. From what she had learned from other agents, that was how things were generally done.

At first, she'd been resentful yesterday when *Katsas* Shavit had laid out the assignment for her. Being involved with Thomas Lourds had already proven detrimental. Then she'd looked at the recent days that she had behind her. For the past week, she had gone to counseling sessions – *I am so sick of those* – worked out in the dojo near her house until she'd barely had the strength to walk to her flat, and drunk entirely too much. She always knew when she drank too much because during those times, she wondered what her father would have thought of her and how her life had turned out.

Would he have been proud?

Or would he have wanted her to be anything other than a Mossad agent?

Most days, Miriam wished she could ask him those questions. She visited his grave regularly, but she hadn't gone there since she'd killed the two men in Namchee Bazaar. Until she made that right in her mind, she knew she'd find no solace at her father's final resting place, and she didn't want to drag that baggage there.

When she reached the office door she was searching for, she took a deep breath. Now was the point of no return. Lourds had been drunk the night he'd seen her, and since then she'd colored her hair black and added an exotic blue-and-white stripe on the right side that drew attention from her features.

He shouldn't be able to recognize her.

She knocked on the closed door and waited, thinking that Lourds would recognize her immediately, and she would be sent back to Tel Aviv. She told herself that would be fine, that she didn't need any part of the man.

Then something crashed on the other side of the door. She gripped the knob, reached for the pistol that should have been at her hip but wasn't, and put her shoulder to the door as she went through.

35

The Institute of Archaeology
Hebrew University of Jerusalem
Mount Scopus
Jerusalem, the State of Israel
August 9, 2011

Lourds lay sprawled on the floor. He looked up at Miriam in stunned surprise.

She stared down at him, then at the pile of books that had toppled from the desk to the floor. *What is it with this man*? 'Are you all right?'

'My ego may be a little bruised.' Gracefully, Lourds pushed himself to his feet. He pointed at the swivel chair behind the desk. One of the wheels lay on its side, crushed, allowing the chair to tilt dangerously. 'The chair gave out.'

'While you were sitting in it?'

'Standing on it, actually.' Lourds picked his hat up from the floor and hung it on the coatrack in the corner of the room. He started picking up books and putting them back on the desk.

'Why were you standing on the chair?' Miriam picked

up books as well. Most of them were heavy and cumbersome.

'To get at a hiding place.'

'What hiding place?'

Lourds looked at her. 'I'm sorry. I just suddenly realized I don't know who you are.'

Relief washed over Miriam as she straightened and offered her hand. 'Miriam Abata.'

'The graduate assistant President Jacob promised?' Lourds took her hand and shook.

'Yes.' That was the cover story *Katsas* Shavit had created for her. Evidently the university was used to doing favors for the Mossad. Miriam had not known that, but it didn't surprise her. The Mossad had resources throughout the country and across the Middle East.

'Did you know Lev?' Lourds picked up a sheaf of papers and set them on the corner of the desk.

'No. I'm sorry. I heard he was a great professor.'

'And a good friend.'

'I'm sorry for your loss.' Miriam squatted and picked up more papers.

'Thank you.' Lourds looked at her. 'Why would President Jacob sent you to help me if you didn't know Lev and his work?'

Katsas Shavit had already thought of that and had briefed Miriam. 'He felt it would be hard on any students who'd worked with Professor Strauss. I'm good with languages and have a minor in archaeology.' Both of those things provided good covers for a spy working in the Middle East and Europe. 'One of my primary fields of study is Farsi, with some work on the Turkic languages of Central Asia.'

'That's a hard field.'

It had been, but Miriam had wanted to be able to speak her father's native language. He had taught her a lot of it as she'd grown up, and majoring in it at college had appealed to her. 'I know.'

'So, are you any good?'

'Oral or written?'

'Both.'

'Yes. Very.' Miriam smiled when she realized how boastful that sounded. 'Sorry. I don't mean to sound immodest.'

'Not at all. I've found it's better to tell people when you're good. Otherwise, they might not notice.' With the last of the papers in hand, Lourds stacked them on the desk and glared at the broken chair. 'I suppose I need to find another one.'

Miriam looked around the ceiling, thinking maybe Lourds had been trying to get something from the top of the bookshelf. 'Perhaps I can get whatever it is you're looking for. I'm light enough to climb the bookcase.' She walked to the bookcase. 'Something from the top?'

'Actually, it's not on the bookcase. It's above the door.'

Miriam turned and looked at the space over the doorway, then immediately thought Lourds was an idiot. 'There's nothing up there.'

'I believe there is. Come here.' Lourds motioned her over behind the desk.

Suspicious of the man, as *Katsas* Shavit had been very thorough regarding Thomas Lourds's predilections toward the opposite sex, Miriam joined him. Despite her superior's stern warnings, Miriam couldn't help noticing how handsome the American professor was. The fading black eye he wore, even though she knew how he got it, made him look like a rough character. He smelled nice, too, some kind of musk she wasn't familiar with.

'Look at the wall now.'

Turning back to the wall, ready to break Lourds's nose if he tried anything, Miriam looked at the area above the doorway. 'I still don't see anything.'

Lourds pushed the office chair up. The crushed wheel shrilled in protest. 'Sit and look again.'

Still uneasy, Miriam sat and looked up at the wall.

Lourds hunkered down beside her and took a small flashlight from his pocket. He switched it on, but Miriam didn't see a beam. However, a glowing yellow symbol appeared on the wall above the doorway.

Miriam forgot about Lourds at her side and stared at the image. 'That's a flying horse.'

'Yes, it is.' Lourds put the flashlight back in his pocket. 'Drawn by Lev Strauss.'

Miriam turned to look at him. *Katsas* Shavit hadn't told her to expect any of this. 'How did you know that was there?'

'Lev left me a message.' Lourds nodded at the wall

and took a Swiss Tinker knife from his pocket. 'If you look more closely, you'll see where a section of that wall was removed.'

Staring more closely at the wall, Miriam realized he was right. There was a section of the wall that looked slightly set apart from the rest of it.

'Think you can get that section out of there if I give you a boost?'

Miriam stared at him and the naked blade he'd opened from the knife. 'You want me to take out that wall section?'

'It's the only way we're going to get at what's behind it.'

'If we're caught, we're going to get into trouble.'

Lourds smiled at her. 'Dear girl, I've been in trouble so often for doing things I shouldn't be doing that the idea doesn't even faze me anymore.'

Remembering how Lourds had crossed the bar – however unsteadily – to rescue her that night in Namchee Bazaar, Miriam could almost believe him. However, he wasn't a trained fighter or survivor. Anyone who didn't know how to do those things and got into bad situations regularly was a fool.

'C'mon.' Lourds's grin widened. 'Remember how much graduate work sucks? Grading papers professors don't want to take the time to grade? Dealing with needy students that aren't willing to spend time with the books so you have to make sure they understand the material? Being taken for granted and never thanked?'

Those things were all true. Miriam remembered all of them too well.

'Time to rebel and get a little payback.' Lourds offered her the knife. 'Let's get you up there and at that wall. You get to stick it to the man.'

His grin was infectious, and when he waggled his eyebrows conspiratorially, Miriam couldn't hold back any longer and smiled back as she took the knife. 'All right, but instead of a boost, help me push the desk over here.'

'The desk?'

'Yes. It's a lot more sturdy than that chair was.'

'Oh. Right.' Lourds looked embarrassed. 'I hadn't thought about it.'

'If you had, maybe you wouldn't have fallen.'

Lourds feigned disapproval. 'Careful there, little missy. Now that I know I have the desk, I may decide that I don't need your help at all.'

Lourds leaned against the desk and pushed. The piles of books and papers shuddered as the desk scooted across the floor, but they didn't turn into an avalanche.

With a lithe motion, her curiosity singing, Miriam stepped up onto the desk. She thought about all the stories she'd recently watched about Lourds's discovery of the temple in the Himalayas. *Katsas* Shavit hadn't told her much about what the American professor was working on, or what Lev Strauss had been involved with, but it had to be archaeological in nature.

When she'd been a little girl, before she'd learned

that both her parents were Mossad spies, she'd dreamed of discovering lost civilizations. Well, not actually historical civilizations. Her interests had been focused more on locating fairy worlds and portals to other dimensions and chasing down impossible magical items in underground labyrinths. Those things now seemed so much safer than what she did currently.

She was all too aware that some young child self she'd thought locked away had come barreling back as she poked and pried at the wall section. Lourds paced the floor like an expectant father in an old cartoon.

'It shouldn't be that hard to get into. Lev wouldn't have wanted to make this difficult. He'd only have wanted to make it a challenge to see. That's what he did, you know. If I hadn't sat in that chair, if I hadn't had the blacklight flashlight, I wouldn't have found that symbol.'

Miriam ignored him and concentrated on the task at hand. Bits of paper, painter's tape, and plaster all scraped free as she dragged the blade along the edge of the section. She blew gently to clear the dust so she could make sure she followed the precut dimensions.

Gradually, the wall section stood framed against the rest of the wall. She drove the blade through the crevice, angled it, and put pressure on the handle. The section popped free of the wall and headed for the floor. Without thinking, she reached down and caught it.

'Good hands, Miriam.' Lourds took the wall section from her and placed it on the desk. 'We'll want to put that back when we're finished.'

'Do you seriously think no one's going to notice that someone cut a hole in this wall?'

'I'm really hoping not to be here when someone does. What's inside?'

Miriam reached into the hole and found a fat book. She brought it out with difficulty because it barely fit in the hiding place. The faint layer of dust on it told her that it hadn't been there long.

The book was an odd shape, about twice the size of a regular hardcover novel, and the paper seemed inordinately white for something that otherwise looked antique. A thick green leather cover bound it, and gold corner pieces protected the corners. Mesmerized, Miriam opened the book and examined the pages.

The paper was pristine and thick. Its rag content was high, and she remembered from her classes that the old paper that had been made hundreds of years ago had been made to last. She'd seen and inspected books that had been made of the same kind of paper.

Instead of type, handwriting filled the pages. Whoever had written the book had possessed a fine, strong hand. The swirls and loops and angles hinted that the language was Arabic, but Miriam couldn't quite fathom what was written.

'May I?' Lourds reached up impatiently.

'Of course. Sorry.' Miriam started to hand him the book, then hauled it back into her arms. 'What are you going to do with it?'

'I don't know. I haven't looked at it yet.'

'Aren't you going to tell President Jacob or the institute about it?'

'Not unless it becomes necessary.'

'This isn't your book.'

'No, it's Lev's, and he left it for me.'

'How do I know that?'

Lourds took the flashlight out of his pocket and waved it meaningfully. 'Other people would have had it by now if they'd been meant to have it. Lev left that book for me to find.'

'Why?'

'Because he couldn't translate it. He thought I could.'

'Can you?'

Lourds frowned at her. 'I'm not a clairvoyant, nor am I a telepath. I'll have to look at it if I'm going to answer that question.'

Irritably, Miriam handed the book to him. She fully expected him to take it and bolt. Instead, he placed the book on the desk and put his hands on her waist to help her down from the desk.

'I could have managed.'

'Probably.' Lourds placed her on the ground, then took up the book. He flipped through pages, then scowled and looked up at her. 'Want to play hooky?'

'What?'

'Ditch school.' Lourds leaned a hip against the desk and slowly showed it back to about where it had been. The broken chair listed sideways behind it. 'I want to get out of here.'

'I was told you just got here.'

'Now I've got what I came for.' Lourds had to shift things in his backpack, but he made room for the book.

'What about Professor Strauss's room? I thought we were supposed to clean it.'

'Later. Right now, we try to figure out the book. And I don't want to do that here.' Lourds picked up his hat and backpack, putting on the former and slipping into the other.

'Then where?'

'A nice, secluded, quiet place that serves beer.'

36

Little Jerusalem Restaurant
Ticho House
9, Harav Kook Street
Jerusalem, the State of Israel
August 9, 2010

When the charming young hostess guided them to their table, Lourds pulled out Miriam Abata's chair. The young graduate student looked at him for a moment, obviously making her mind up about something, then sat.

'Thank you.'

'Sorry if I offended.' Lourds put his backpack on one of the other chairs at the small table in the open-air section of the restaurant. He sat across from Miriam and placed his hat on the back of the chair with his backpack.

'You didn't offend.'

'I pulled your chair out. You hesitated. Obviously, that didn't suit you.'

'I'm suspicious of men who pull my chair out. Generally they have an agenda.'

Gazing at the young woman, taking in her café au lait complexion, striking hazel-green eyes, and smooth jawline, Lourds felt certain a lot of young men had known her and ended up with 'agendas.' The blue-and-white stripe in her black hair really set off her look, and the jeans and blouse revealed that she was athletic. She looked familiar, but he was certain he'd never met her before.

'No agenda. I was merely being polite.'

Miriam took one of the breadsticks from the basket on the table and deliberately snapped it in half before taking a bite. 'That's good.'

'We're just going to have a meal.' Lourds took the thick book from his backpack. 'I'm going to look over this book and Lev's notes.'

'What am I supposed to do?'

'Keep an eye out for me.'

She frowned. 'What?'

'I tend to get involved in my reading. I need you to make sure I'm safe. That we're safe.' Lourds paused and pumped up the gravitas in his voice. 'Whatever this book contains, I believe it's part of the reason Lev was killed. According to the message he sent me, he couldn't read it.'

'Can you?'

'Not yet. But I will.' Lourds wondered why she didn't ask about the potential for danger. That was the part he thought would scare her off.

'You think you're in danger?'

'I think that possibly anyone connected with this book is in danger.'

Miriam took another small bite of her breadstick. 'So who should I look for?'

'Men with rocket launchers. Assault rifles. Grenades.

Guns. Knives. Work your way back from that. Anyone who shows undue interest in us.'

She grinned at him, seemingly delighted in spite of herself. 'You're deliberately being provocative.'

Lourds gave her his full attention. 'Miriam, please believe me: provocative or not, I'm telling you the truth. Do you know what happened to Lev?'

'He was killed by terrorists.'

'Do you believe that story?'

'Why not?'

'Did you know Lev?'

'No.'

Lourds took a deep breath. Talking about Lev hurt. 'For a "terrorist" attack, there was surprisingly little collateral damage. Besides Lev, the only people that apparently got killed were the terrorists themselves. Germans or Europeans, from the pictures I saw and from the media reports. Not Middle Easterners, as you might expect here in Jerusalem.'

Intrigued, Miriam lowered her voice and leaned closer. 'You might try using your *inside* voice.'

Self-consciously, Lourds glanced around. Little Jerusalem Restaurant had inside seating and outside, where they were. The tables sat on flagstones and buffet tables ringed the dining area. A small stage area where live bands performed later in the evening was just outside the main building. Below that, a ridge of flowers – mums, daisies, and others Lourds couldn't identify – showed spectacularly in a long rectangular section.

'I wasn't talking that loud.'

'Your voice carries.'

'Oh.' Lourds shrugged. 'One of the downsides of being a frequent lecturer. As I was saying, Lev's death by terrorist is suspicious. At least to me. In his life, there wasn't much he came in contact with that would have led to him being targeted by someone. He had to have found something of value. For the moment, all I know for sure is that he had this book. He left me messages, one in Jerusalem and the other in Vienna – though he didn't suspect it would be there – that led me to this book.'

Her gaze dropped to the leather-bound volume.

'If this is what people are willing to kill for, and we have it, we're in danger. Do you understand?'

Miriam nodded. 'Why haven't you gone to the police with this?'

Lourds sighed. 'Because the police have rules. They're as bad as college administrations and other forms of bureaucracy. If I tell them what we've got, they're going to want to step in and manage it. The first thing they'll do is take away the book and send it to other *specialists* who know languages.'

'If the book is that important, maybe that's what should happen.'

Lourds scowled at her. 'If Lev couldn't figure out this book, there are precious few other people in the world who could. If he thought I was the only one capable of it, who am I to disagree with his reasoning?'

'I guess there's no ego in that assumption, is there?'

'Of course there is. If I wasn't egotistical to some degree, I wouldn't even try to work with this in the first place.'

Miriam held her hands up in surrender. 'All right. You're the guy who just found a lost temple in the Himalayas. Let's go with the possibility that you're the person for this job.'

'I am.'

'Then why me?'

'Pardon?'

'Why ask me to help you?'

'I thought I just explained that.'

'No. You didn't.'

Lourds held up a finger. 'One, you're not part of the University of Jerusalem hierarchy.' He added another finger. 'Two, you're not a police officer.' And he added another finger. 'Three, you have some experience with Arabic languages, which – if I'm correct about the origins of this book – will come in handy. I don't have that many friends who can do what I'm asking you to do.'

'You don't even know if you can trust me.'

Lourds smiled. 'Dear girl, I don't trust *anyone,* but I have to trust someone.'

'I'd think you'd have a friend to call on.'

'I have called on a friend. She's working on a different angle at the moment.'

'I meant that you could call someone to watch over you.'

'If I did that, the police officers who are already

watching me would have even more reason to keep tabs on my actions. I can't have that.'

'How much trouble can you be in?'

'From whom? The university? They can't touch me because they can't prove this book was theirs. The police? They're looking for a killer. I was in the Himalayas when Lev was murdered.' The word *murder* fit much better to describe what had happened to Lev. 'The only people I have to worry about right now are the ones looking for this book.'

'Maybe they gave up after your friend was killed.'

'No.'

'How do you know that?'

'Because a Viennese Austrian People's Party member named Klaus Von Volker had men kidnap me in Vienna. They were going to kill me. I escaped and came here.'

Miriam just stared at him.

'Look.' Lourds felt guilty. 'I need someone to act as an extra set of eyes and ears right now. But if you feel this is too dangerous, I'll totally understand.'

She still didn't speak.

For a moment, Lourds thought she might get up and walk out on him. But he'd been telling her the truth about needing someone, and his reasons for not calling in someone else. He didn't know anyone trained well enough to act as a bodyguard in the places he was certain he would have to go.

'Miriam, I know this is a lot to take in, but I'm going to offer you something that could be valuable. I don't know where your dreams lie with regards to your education and career, but if you work with me, nothing dangerous, just act as a lookout, I'll give you partial credit for whatever we discover. I promise, if this turns out as big as Lev thought it was, it's something that could make your career.'

She blinked at him.

'So?' Lourds took a deep breath. 'What do you say?'

For the next three hours, Miriam watched Lourds struggle with the mysterious book she'd helped him get from the university. Thankfully, he'd had a couple of paperbacks in his backpack that she could read while she performed lookout duty. Both of the books turned out to be spy novels, though, about big, violent men who killed indiscriminately. That wasn't how spies killed. At least, it wasn't how she killed.

Part of her still resented Lourds for his part in the shootings. Then she relented a little when she realized he'd gotten caught up in the scramble for whatever it was they were looking for just as much as she had. Lourds hadn't asked his friend to call him up and drop him into the middle of this.

And God knew Lev Strauss hadn't intentionally gotten himself killed either.

Working through that actually seemed to help her with her own guilt regarding the two dead men. She had gotten caught up in the web of lies and deceit while trying to help Lourds, just as he had gotten caught up.

Instead of running away or dumping the problem in someone else's lap, he'd stuck with it.

Of course, part of that reason was that incredible ego of his. No one else, in his mind, could do quite the job he could of sorting things out.

In the end, in spite of the ego, Miriam found herself liking and respecting Lourds more than she'd thought she would when *Katsas* Shavit had asked her to take the assignment. It was, to say the least, startling and mystifying. Instead of remembering how Lourds had gotten knocked out with one punch, she seemed focused on the fact that he'd gotten up in the first place – knowing that he wasn't at his best and probably would have been outmatched even if he were – and tried to help her.

That was both innocent and foolish.

She suddenly realized Lourds was looking at her. 'Sorry?'

'I said, is that book not holding your interest?'

'It's fine.'

'You haven't turned a page in twenty minutes that I know of.'

'I was watching for men with rocket launchers.'

Lourds grinned, and the genuine humor was infectious. The overall effect was blunted by the fact that it was true. Miriam had been watching for suspicious people.

'I was also thinking that maybe we are sitting in the open, making it too easy to be attacked. If it should come to that.'

'I like to think of it as hiding in plain sight.' Lourds

shrugged and took another bite of the sweet cheese blintz he'd ordered for dessert.

As she'd watched him eat, Miriam hadn't been able to understand how he could put away as much food as he did and be as trim as he was.

'People are killed in plain sight, too.'

'We're still alive.'

'I'm beginning to think the waitress wishes we were dead.' Miriam took another sip of her Turkish coffee. Lourds had stuck with muscat dessert wine, but he drank it slowly.

'I tip big.'

'How are you coming with the book?'

'I don't think the language is natural.'

'What do you mean?'

Lourds put the book in his backpack, stretched, and yawned. 'Pardon me. The last few days – weeks, actually – have been filled to the brim.' He assembled his thoughts. 'I can translate bits and pieces of the narrative here and there, just enough to give me a glimpse of what's actually being written about, but I think there's a subtext as well.'

'What do you mean?'

'The book contains a narrative by a man who claims to have known Mohammad ibn Abdullah.'

'The Prophet.' That surprised Miriam. *Katsas* Shavit had told her that the Iranians might be involved in the mission, but she hadn't expected this.

'Yes.' Lourds picked up his journal. It was covered

with Post-its he'd removed from the book. 'According to Lev's notes, he'd had the book carbon-dated. It's fourteen hundred years old.'

Miriam looked at the backpack. 'How much is it worth?'

'It's not a scientific study by any recognized scholar, doesn't cover anything concrete about scientific thinking or verifiable history, and focuses on a tale that can't be verified.' Lourds stopped himself. 'At least, the story can't be verified at this moment. I suspect some of it will become quite real.' He frowned. 'And that might be unfortunate for many of us.'

'What are you talking about?'

Instead of answering, Lourds looked back over the notes stuck to his journal. He tapped one of them. 'Lev was talking to an Iranian professor named Hashem Nabi Namati. He's a professor at the Central Library of Astan Quds Razavi. Are you familiar with it?'

Miriam thought for a moment, then placed the university. 'They handle old and rare manuscripts.'

'Exactly. The university was first established prior to 1457 and holds over a million books focusing on Islamic research. They've got over seventy thousand documents in the antiquities section, nearly twenty thousand of those handwritten documents. Much of the collection is over a thousand years old.'

'What does that have to do with the book Professor Strauss had?'

'Before his death, Lev was doing a lot of communication with Professor Namati. Letters, e-mail. I saw the name several times on documents at Lev's office and on his computer.'

'Maybe they're just friends.'

'Possibly. Except for this.' Lourds pulled out a Post-it and passed it over to Miriam.

Namati code cipher?

Miriam pushed the piece of paper back across the table. 'What does that mean?'

'You know what a code cipher is, don't you?'

'It's a master key to a code.'

'Exactly.'

'I don't understand.'

Lourds grinned. 'If I'm right, and I think that I am, that book Lev was working so hard to translate is written in code as well. Merely cracking the language to provide a translation isn't going to be enough to solve all the mysteries associated with the book. Something else is hidden in its pages, and I'm sure Lev suspected that.'

'Does Professor Namati know he has the code cipher?'

'I doubt it. But in order to ascertain that, we'll have to talk to him.'

'"We"?'

Lourds nodded. 'If you're up to it.'

'We're going to Iran?' The thought made Miriam's guts churn. Her father had escaped that country once, then died there trying to close a case for the Mossad.

'Yes.'

'Just like that?' Miriam didn't have to fake incredulity. She was feeling it.

'Well, I'll have to talk to the US State Department first, but it shouldn't be a problem. I can trade on the fact that I'm a scholar. I've spoken in Iran before, though it's certainly been a while. But it shouldn't be a problem. If you're up to a little adventure, I think I can fold you under the umbrella as my graduate assistant. I'll pay your expenses and will add a stipend at the end of this.'

Miriam thought about that, and her throat turned dry. With Iran in its current situation under the Ayatollah, with a populace striking back to get their voices heard in elections, she felt like she'd be surrounded by enemies. She swallowed hard. 'Okay.'

She could only imagine what *Katsas* Shavit would say when she learned of the plan.

37

Security Checkpoint
Ben Gurion International Airport
Outside Lod, the State of Israel
August 11, 2011

Tense and anxious, Miriam sat in the taxi's backseat and watched the line of cars approaching the Israeli airport checkpoint.

'Shouldn't be much longer.' The heavy-set driver cranked down his window, filling the car interior with the smell of exhaust along with his sharp cologne, and picked up his papers. 'Some days you get through quickly. Other days, like today, not so quickly. That's why it's always better to arrive early. Have your passports ready.'

Miriam dug hers out from her purse. Next to her, Lourds was lost in Lev Strauss's mysterious book. He had it open on one knee and was making notes in his journal.

They'd had breakfast together that morning, but only after she'd beaten on his door to wake him. Lourds hadn't been a scintillating conversationalist. It had taken him most of yesterday to get tickets for her and himself, and he'd gotten frustrated. Miriam had finally taken it upon herself to spend time on the phone talking to travel agents, and even had to have *Katsas* Shavit intercede – quietly – to make the trip happen. Travel at the time was exceptionally high.

Part of his frustration, she felt, was related to his inability to make sense of the journal. He seemed to be translating it quickly, and she was impressed by that because she'd worked at translating some of the pages herself and found it almost beyond her grasp. She'd even copied some of the pictures with the specially encrypted phone the Mossad had provided for her and sent it off to the intelligence division. The encryption staff there had only marginally improved on what she'd been able to do.

Katsas Shavit had admitted that the book was beyond what the intelligence division could do – and many of them were linguistics professors. She'd also learned that Professor Thomas Lourds was a frequent translation go-to person for the Mossad, CIA, and other international intelligence agencies.

That impressed Miriam even more because Lourds had never mentioned it. She didn't know if he was merely being secretive or if he really didn't think that much of the work he'd done for those agencies. In some ways, he was different than she'd thought he would be. Arrogant and egotistical, definitely, but he was also putting his life on the line to find out who had killed his friend.

She nudged his knee, then had to do it again, almost hard enough to dislodge the book. 'Hey, Professor.'

He looked up at her and, for an instant, looked like a

small child who had just woken up in a strange place. He glanced around, then took a deep breath and stretched. 'What?'

'Passport.' Miriam brandished hers.

Turning to his backpack between them, Lourds withdrew his passport and handed it to her. She was amazed at how thick it was. He returned his attention to the book and his work.

'Have you been to Istanbul?'

She nodded, then realized he wasn't watching her. 'Yes.'

'Beautiful city.'

'One of my favorites.'

'When did you go there?'

'My father took me when I was a little girl.'

Lourds looked up at her then and smiled. 'Your father traveled a lot?'

'Some. He repped some art-acquisition galleries.'

Before Lourds could respond, a bullet cored through the back window behind them and spread their driver's brains over the windshield in a crimson splash.

Behesht-Zahra (The Paradise of Zahara)
Tehran
The Islamic Republic of Iran
August 11, 2011

Colonel Davari cursed and reached for the microphone headset's transmit controls. 'Watch what you're doing, you imbecile! You almost hit Lourds. Do not kill him! We need him alive!'

The images on the computer monitors jerked and heaved now that the attackers were in motion. The wireless cameras attached to their headsets connected to a nearby van loaded with equipment that relayed the signal to the Ayatollah's palace.

The man himself stood nearby, watching the scene much more calmly than Davari.

Putting the whole picture together in his head from the six camera views was difficult. Even though he'd planned the attack with the Hezbollah operatives he'd briefed on the task, the action was proving distracting. Attacking at the checkpoint was risky, but it was the only place Davari knew for certain they'd get a chance to take Lourds.

With the driver dead at the wheel, the taxi lurched forward and slammed into the car ahead of it. Only two vehicles were in front of the taxi. They were enough to hold up progress, but they allowed the taxi to get blocked in by other cars when they tried to scatter amid the gunfire.

'I've got the van camera online, Supreme Leader,' said one of the men at the computers in front of the Ayatollah. Davari looked up at the screen before him as it filled with images.

The van had a mounted camera that telescoped up from the top to give an overview of the attack site. It hadn't been deployed until the attack and kidnap attempt had been initiated.

Almost immediately, the scene at the airport's security checkpoint became much clearer. The Israeli security people responded to the attack, but it was too late to hope to control anything. Drivers behind the taxi steered wildly in an effort to get out of harm's way and only ended up miring themselves in the resulting confusion. Vehicles slammed into each other, effectively choking off escape routes.

One of the Hezbollah attackers stopped and brought up a rocket launcher. No sooner did the long weapon rest on his shoulder than he fired. The warhead slammed into one of the outside cars broadside, flipping the vehicle into the air. It crashed down roof-first onto the car beside it with a spray of glass and shriek of overstressed metal. Flames roared from it, and the passengers scrambled out and away to escape the pyre.

By then the snipers were in place. Sharp cracks carried over the streaming audio. The synchronization between the audio and video wasn't complete, and there was at least a two-second lag between them, giving the events a surreal feel that Davari found irritating. The uniformed security guards dropped and spun, helpless before the Hezbollah snipers.

Davari smiled in anticipation. Now that they were certain Lourds had the book, they could take him and force him to help find Mohammad's Koran and the Scroll.

Nothing could prevent that.

Security Checkpoint
Ben Gurion International Airport
Outside Lod, the State of Israel
August 11, 2011

As soon as he realized the driver had been shot, Lourds dove for Miriam. She was already in motion, though, opening her door and throwing herself outside.

At first he thought she was running for cover, and he was vaguely disappointed. He'd thought she was made of sterner stuff, or maybe he'd only wished she was because of the journey they were undertaking. She hadn't flinched at all when he'd told her they were going to Iran.

Instead of running, though, she stayed low as one of the vehicles behind them suddenly exploded and flew into the air. Shrapnel slapped against the taxi like popcorn popping, and tongues of fire flashed across the back glass, coming in through the hole left by the rifle bullet for just a moment before dying.

Miriam opened the car door and yanked at the dead driver. Despite her desperate efforts, she couldn't move the bulky corpse. She glanced back at Lourds. 'Help me!'

Galvanized into action, Lourds got out of the taxi on his side, crept up to the passenger door, and threw it open. He hesitated for just a moment at all the blood, then put both hands on the dead man and shoved as Miriam pulled.

The driver toppled out of the car as at least one round shattered the passenger-door window and rained broken pieces down over Lourds's back. Thomas stayed low across the front seats. Miriam put her hand in the middle of his face, mashing his sore nose hard and causing him to yelp in protest as she shoved him into the passenger seat.

Behind the wheel, she shoved the transmission into reverse and backed swiftly toward the burning car atop the other vehicle.

Lourds pointed. 'The car.'

'I see it.' Miriam stomped on the brake, and rubber shrieked as the tires locked up on the pavement. The taxi's rear butted up against the bottom car, and the burning wreckage above slowly started to topple – and was heading straight for their battered taxi.

'The *car*!'

'I *see* it!' Miriam changed gears and pressed the accelerator to the floor. The taxi's engine screamed like a tortured animal, but the tires caught and propelled them forward. 'Hang on.'

Lourds braced himself with his hands and feet as Miriam crashed into the rear of the car ahead of them. Metal crumpled, and the front windshield shattered, spraying bloody glass fragments into his lap.

Miriam shoved the transmission into reverse and backed again at a sharper angle. Lourds reached for the open passenger door, intending to close it, but one of the security posts took it off in a wrenching rasp.

This time when the taxi backed up, it hit the burning car. Flames spread across the back of the vehicle and stayed with them as Miriam sped forward again.

38

Tactical Room
Covert Operations
Institute for Intelligence and Special Operations (Mossad)
Tel Aviv, the State of Israel
August 11, 2011

'Orchid, be advised that we have a team en route.' Tense and frustrated, Sarah Shavit watched the wallscreen in the tactical room.

Miriam Abata was showing considerable resilience despite the odds against her and the element of surprise her enemies had wielded. She had seized control of the taxi and almost fought free. Unfortunately, it looked as though the burning vehicle had spread a pool of flaming liquid across the taxi's rear.

'Affirmative, Gardener.' Miriam's voice splintered as she responded. The noise of the gunfire and her unwillingness to reveal her true identity to Lourds made her hard to understand. She wore an earpiece that picked up vibrations along her jawbone and transmitted them.

Covering her mouthpiece, Sarah turned to the computer operator beside her. 'Have you reached the airport's security chief?'

'Not yet, ma'am. I'm still trying.'

'Let me know as soon as you do.'

'Of course.'

No longer able simply to watch, Sarah paced back and forth in front of the wallscreen. The attackers moved efficiently, mowing through the airport's security people, predators stalking game. They wore bulletproof armor and weren't afraid to die for their cause, and that was a terrible combination for anyone to face.

The door opened and Isser Melman walked into the room, leaning heavily on his cane. 'I hear we have a situation.' His stony face revealed nothing of his thoughts. 'What happened?'

'Orchid and her package were attacked on-site.' No names were used inside the tactical room.

'Do we know if they're targeting Orchid and her package?'

'Yes. Orchid is in the taxi. The shooters are converging on the vehicle now.'

On-screen, the taxi rammed the car in front of it again, creating more space. This time it kept surging against the other car till it fought free.

'Who's driving the taxi?'

'Orchid. The first round took out the driver. The attackers have snipers on the scene who dropped the driver and the airport security team.'

Melman's face creased into a grim smile. 'She's a very determined young woman.'

'She is.' Sarah knew she should take pride in Melman's

recognition of Miriam's abilities and drive, and later she would. But for the moment, her heart went out to the young woman whose life could be snuffed out at any second.

The taxi finally bulled through the bottleneck created by the stalled vehicles. Fenders and bodywork dropped along the pavement behind her.

'And a very lucky one.'

'She makes her own luck.'

'Do we have a team covering them?'

'Yes. They're moving into position now.'

On-screen, armored attack vehicles were being deployed. Mossad agents dressed in Israeli army fatigues boiled out the doors and took up positions.

'Sniper Team Alpha in position.'

'Sniper Team Bravo in position.'

Sarah clicked back into the frequency. 'All sniper teams, acquire targets and take them down. Be advised your targets are armored.'

The sniper teams opened fire immediately. A handful of attackers dropped before they realized they had aggressors targeting them. Reacting quickly, they took up positions behind the stalled cars. As Sarah watched helplessly, the attackers ruthlessly killed the citizens inside the cars.

Melman's voice was hard when he spoke. 'Tell your teams there are to be no survivors. We already have an idea who sent these men.'

Without any remorse, Sarah relayed the command.

'*Katsas*.'

Sarah turned to the computer tech at her side. 'Yes?'

'I have the security chief.'

'Patch him through.' Sarah heard the click. 'This is Mossad Intelligence Division Officer Sarah Shavit. With whom am I speaking?'

The man sounded out of breath, and gunfire could be plainly heard around him. Evidently he'd gotten into the action quickly. 'Captain David Lavi. I'm in the middle of a situation.'

'We're there as well, Captain. I've got agents taking out your attackers as we speak.'

'Did you bring your baggage into our airport?'

Sarah ignored the angry accusation in the man's voice. Mossad wasn't thought well of by everyone. 'No. We were providing a loose backup to a probable situation when this erupted.'

'Why wasn't my office notified?'

'If we had known this would happen, we would have notified your office.' Sarah hardened her tone. 'There is a taxi that has just gotten past your checkpoint.'

'I see it.'

'I don't want the occupants harmed. They are not part of this.'

'If they don't stop, they're going to be shot. I can't allow them to gain access to the planes or the buildings.'

'Understood. I will get them to stop and surrender themselves.'

'Do it now.'

Sarah clicked out of the channel and back into the one with Miriam Abata. 'Orchid, local security has been notified of your situation, but not your identities. Stand down before you are shot.'

'We're not clear.'

'You don't have a choice. Do it before the airport's security people take you out.'

On-screen, the taxi screeched to a halt. Coolly and calmly as she could, Sarah continued to watch.

Behesht-Zahra (The Paradise of Zahara)
Tehran
The Islamic Republic of Iran
August 11, 2011

In disbelief, Davari watched as his well-made attack plan fell to pieces. He cursed and wished he were there, feeling that somehow he could have saved things, but knowing in his heart that was a foolish thought, and that he would have only died with the attackers.

'Our comrades among the Hezbollah will count this as a victory though we do not.' The Ayatollah spoke quietly, but his rage was evident in every clipped word.

'I apologize for this, Supreme Leader.' Standing there, the colonel realized that his life was forfeit if the Ayatollah chose to view the situation as his fault. Mohammad Khamenei was not known as a forgiving man.

The Ayatollah shook his head. 'This is not a bad

thing, Colonel. Think of this as a feint. Perhaps we have not secured our prize yet – and we will – but we have managed to draw out our true enemies in this endeavor.'

Watching the organized warriors spill out across the scenes, taking out the Hezbollah gunners one by one and securing the area behind them, Davari nodded. 'The Mossad.'

'Exactly. Now we know for certain that the infidels and nonbelievers are warring against us.' The Ayatollah took a deep breath. 'This is proof that our war is for God. Otherwise, Shaitan would not have arrayed so many of our enemies against us.' He smiled grimly. 'And we will have opportunities to kill them as we search for our goal.'

On-screen, Davari saw the bodies of two Mossad agents lying on the paved road leading up to the security checkpoint. Their efforts had been costly as well.

'Do we know where Lourds is going?'

'Yes, Supreme Leader. Tehran.'

The Ayatollah looked at Davari. 'He's coming here?'

'Yes. We confirmed his plane tickets. There is a layover in Istanbul. We could arrange an abduction there.'

'No. The benefit of taking Lourds on Israeli soil was to give us deniability in his disappearance, and a chance to bloody Israel's nose. If Lourds is coming here, let him come. We will make him vanish here if necessary. If he's coming here, I believe everything we need to know to find Mohammad's Koran and the Scroll is here. God has put our salvation in our own backyard.'

'What if the Mossad chooses to stop Lourds from coming here?'

'They would have already done it. And now they have no choice in the matter.' The Ayatollah smiled. 'Now they know that we know what is being searched for. With Mohammad's Koran and Scroll here, they have to allow Lourds to look for it. They will also have a harder time keeping watch over him in our country. We will make that work for us as well.'

On-screen, a dark-haired black woman opened the taxi door and got out.

'Who is the woman?'

'According to our intelligence, she is a graduate student.'

'Lourds has a weakness for women. When they get here, exploit that. Take that woman into custody and find out what she knows. Use her against the American infidel.'

'It will be done, Supreme Leader.'

The Ayatollah started to walk away, then turned back. 'Has Von Volker arrived?'

'Yes. I have placed him in guest quarters.'

'Good. I will talk to him soon.'

'He won't be able to help us with Lourds. His own wife turned against him and helped Lourds escape. He's wanted for questioning in his own country.'

'An embarrassing moment, perhaps, but all that can be made to go away. Politics allows convenient forgetfulness. Von Volker is still a powerful man in the

Austrian People's Party. As such, he is a friend to our country and our God. We can use him.'

Davari nodded. Then he turned back to the screens and watched the slaughter of the Hezbollah continue as the Mossad agents walked among their wounded enemies and executed them.

Security Checkpoint
Ben Gurion International Airport
Outside Lod, the State of Israel
August 11, 2011

'Why are you stopping?'

Scared and angry, Miriam put the taxi's transmission in park and looked at Lourds staring at her in disbelief.

'Keep going.'

'If I do, the security people will shoot us.'

'Why?'

'They'll think we're carrying explosives. Get out of the car.' Miriam opened her door and got out. A hail of bullets took out the front-passenger side tire, and the taxi settled heavily on the ground, like an old dog lying down. She reached back into the vehicle, captured Lourds's arm, and yanked. 'Get *out* of the car now!'

Temporarily overpowered, Lourds flailed, then slid across the bloody seat on top of Miriam, pinning her to the ground under him.

'Sorry.'

Before Miriam could reply, the professor pushed up off of her, got to his feet but remained hunkered down, and opened the rear passenger door. Bullets sprayed the flaming rear of the taxi. Instead of going away, the flames had spread, taking hold of the vehicle. As Lourds reached into the backseat, the fire spread to the rear tire, burning through the wall to let the air out, and the vehicle sagged again.

Miriam got to her feet. 'What are you doing?'

Lourds pulled back from the taxi. He slung his backpack over one shoulder, held the thick book, their passports, and his journal in one hand, and clapped his hat on his head with the other.

Miriam silently cursed. In her efforts to save them, she'd forgotten about the book. But Lourds hadn't. She reached out and took his hand, yanking him into motion as they ran away from the burning car. More bullets smacked into the taxi as they ran, and a moment later either the fire got to the gas tank or the bullets did.

The taxi exploded and leaped into the air, then came crashing straight back down. The concussive wave knocked Miriam and Lourds flat on the pavement.

Briefly stunned, Miriam gathered her whirling senses and struggled to get to her feet. Before she could stand, someone planted a hand in the middle of her back and shoved her back down again. She rolled over and the sun shone into her eyes, turning the men standing over her into painful silhouettes. Behind them, black smoke coiled up from the burning taxi and other vehicles, staining the blue sky.

She moved her head slightly and brought the man into view. She recognized the airport security uniform at once and felt relieved.

Beside her, Lourds sighed. 'Thank God that's over.'

39

First Class
Turkish Airlines
34,000 Feet
Leaving Istanbul, the Republic of Turkey
August 12, 2011

Lourds sat in the quiet gloom of the first-class cabin and blinked blearily. He hadn't known he'd gone to sleep. The first thing he did was to make certain Lev's book was still in his backpack at his feet. It was. Then he noticed that someone had covered him with a blanket.

At his side, Miriam Abata kept sleeping. She had turned sideways facing him, one arm tucked up uncomfortably under her chin like a child. He didn't know how she could sleep like that. If he had, he'd have awoken stiff and hurting.

Glancing around, he found a bottle of water in the armrest, uncapped it, and took a sip. Then he leaned down, took the book from his backpack, took out his journal, and settled back to work. He felt eyes on him. When he looked back at Miriam, she had her eyes open.

'Sorry. Didn't mean to wake you.'

'It's okay. I didn't mean to fall asleep.' She sat up

and rubbed her eyes. 'Guess I'm not a very good lookout.'

'On the contrary, I think you did an exemplary job yesterday. But I'm beginning to think we should have restructured our trip to Tehran. Neither one of us is going to be much use for this morning's meeting.'

'Speak for yourself.'

Lourds smiled at her. 'Actually, I'm not sure if we should stick to our schedule at all.'

Miriam suddenly looked more alert. 'Why?'

'I've been thinking about the attack at the airport.'

'What about it?'

'I don't think that was a typical terrorist attack.'

'Is there such a thing as a *typical* terrorist attack?'

Lourds shook his head and grinned wryly. 'Of course not. But I'm thinking maybe the attack was aimed at us.'

'Believe it or not, Professor, not everything is about you.'

'I know. But I saw the media footage of the attack while we were in Istanbul. It's already on YouTube. From what I saw, those men were coming straight for us.'

'We were the only ones there in a taxi. Perhaps that marked us as a target of opportunity. Outsiders. Tourists. Killing Americans always makes a big international news splash. That's what terrorists want.'

Lourds couldn't argue that point. The media was already erupting with news of the attack. It was currently in the top ten on Twitter. 'I'd think someone in a limousine would have made a better target.'

'People in limousines tend to have more defensible vehicles and security guards.'

'True.' Lourds scratched his goatee. 'We were fortunate the Israeli army was arriving. Otherwise, there would have been no help at all.'

'Then we should count our blessings.' Miriam's gaze dropped to the book in his lap. 'How are you coming on with the translation?'

Lourds shrugged and opened his journal. 'If you just read the text, you don't see anything eventful.' He cleared his voice and started to read. "The prophet of God said: 'While I was sleeping within the wall of the Ka'ba, Gabriel came to see me and kicked me with his foot, so I sat up, but not seeing anything, I lay again on my bed. He kicked me then once more, and I sat up and did not see a thing, so I lay back on my bed. He then kicked me a third time, and I sat up, whereupon he pulled me by the arm, and I rose, and went to the door of the temple. There was standing a white beast, between a mule and an ass in size, with two wings on its thighs, digging its hind legs in and placing its forelegs as far as it can see. Gabriel carried me on the beast, and we went together at the same speed.' So the Prophet of God journeyed, and with him also Gabriel, until they reached the temple in Jerusalem. He found there Abraham, Moses, and Jesus, among other prophets, and he led them in prayers. Then he was given two vessels, one filled with wine and the other with milk, so the prophet of God took the vessel with milk and drank it, leaving the vessel of wine. Seeing that, Gabriel said to him: 'You were guided to the true religion [Islam] and so was your nation, for wine is forbidden unto you." This is all pretty much relayed in any version of the Koran you'd care to peruse.'

'You have a wonderful reading voice.'

Startled, Lourds looked at the young woman. 'Thank you.'

'Sorry. I didn't mean to distract you.' Miriam looked embarrassed. 'But we already knew the surface reading wasn't extremely helpful.'

'I know. It's just frustrating because I know the answers Lev was looking for are somewhere in these pages. I just can't seem to find them.'

'Yet. Remember, Professor Strauss also believed Professor Namati has a cipher key that will unlock this book.'

'Perhaps.'

'You said the man who wrote this book was Yazid Ibn Salam.'

'Right.'

'All I can remember about him was that he had something to do with the Dome of the Rock.'

Lourds smiled. 'Dear girl, not just *something* to do with that building. He was involved in the engineering of the Dome of the Rock, and he certainly cocontrolled the purse strings with Rajah ibn Haywah.'

'What do we know about Salam?'

'Not much. He's almost a shadowy figure in history.'

'Sounds suspicious already.'

'Yes.' Lourds chuckled. 'What historians are fairly

sure of is that Salam was born into a local Jerusalem family. Haywah was deeply enmeshed with the political doings in Palestine.'

'It's a wonder they got along.'

'I think it was probably the idea of creating something lasting and unique that drew them together. Jerusalem had been conquered by the Rashidun Caliphate army at the time the Muslims overran Syria. Rome had already been battling the Persians during that time. That was in AD 637, shortly after Mohammad's death in AD 632. The Dome of the Rock, Masjid Qubbat As-Sakhrah, was intended to be a shrine for pilgrims, not a mosque.'

'I didn't know that.'

'An education is a wonderful thing. The Umayyad caliph, Abd al-Malik ibn Marwan, assigned Salam and Haywah to build the Dome over the Foundation Stone. You're familiar with that?'

'In Hebrew, it's called *Even haShetiya*. And it's also called the Pierced Stone.'

'Because of the small hole in it that enters a cavern beneath the rock.'

'They call that the Well of Souls.'

'Correct. According to Muslim beliefs, during the end of days, the Foundation Stone will join with *al-Hajaru-l-Aswad*, the black stone of Mecca that lies in the Kaaba, which is supposed to have come from the time of Adam and Eve.'

Miriam looked at him quietly. 'Have you given much thought to the end of the world?'

'Not much. If you ask me, dwelling on that is both wasteful and depressing.'

'Why?'

'The end of the world? Most depressing thing ever, don't you think?' He smiled.

She laughed, a pleasant sound in the nearly silent first-class compartment. 'All right, I'll give you that, but why do you think trying to figure anything out about the end of the world is wasteful?'

'We're talking about the will of God here. Figuring it out isn't going to give you the power to change it. And most religions agree that the end isn't something meant to be realized by mortal men until such time is upon them.'

Shifting in the chair, Miriam thought for a moment. 'So, as a record of Yazid ibn Salam, this book is unique because so little is known about him.'

'The fact that so little is known about him also works against us.'

'How?'

'Verifying the authenticity of the authorship of this book is going to be next to impossible.'

'So we have to take it on faith.'

'Amazing how much of that is involved in our little adventure, isn't it?' Lourds shook his head. 'Lev believed he was onto something important. I believe in Lev. And we all have to believe in this book.' He brushed at the cover and ran his fingers over the brass corner pieces. 'I have to admit, I do like the way it's constructed.'

'Read some more of it.'

Glancing at her and seeing she was once more curled up in the chair and looking sleepy, Lourds smiled. 'Bedtime story?'

'Something like that.'

'All right.' Lourds paged through the book and made a selection. 'It is said: "The Caliph in Jerusalem sought to build for the Muslims a *masjid* that should be unique and a wonder to the world. And in like manner, is it not evident that Caliph Abd al-Malik, seeing the greatness of the martyrdom of the Church of the Holy Sepulcher and its magnificence, was moved lest it should dazzle the minds of Muslims and hence erected above the Rock the dome which is now seen there."'

He kept reading, absorbed in the story and searching for clues amid the complexity of the language. He didn't know Miriam had gone back to sleep until he felt her head sag onto his shoulder. Then he covered her with his blanket, left the book in his lap, and closed his eyes. Sleep came for him in a rush, and he dreamed of the many times he'd visited the Temple Mount, never once suspecting that he would be drawn into a mystery that involved it.

In the back of the plane, Mufarrij sat quietly and thought about entering the land of his enemies. When he had seen the attack at the checkpoint while waiting for the flight at Ben Gurion International Airport, he'd worried that Lourds might be killed and the trail all but washed away. Then, when he'd discovered the American professor had survived, he'd worried that Lourds might cancel his trip altogether.

Mufarrij had stood back in the waiting area until Lourds had booked a later flight, then bought a ticket for that same flight. The police and security people had held Lourds for a while, but eventually they'd released him, as they'd released all the other people who'd been present during the attack.

If some of the travelers to Istanbul and to Tehran hadn't been killed in the attack, seats would not have been available for Lourds and his companion, or for Mufarrij.

God provides, Mufarrij reminded himself as he watched the first-class-section doorway. From his position, he could see the woman's arm on her chair. He kept focused on that and bided his time.

While in Tehran, he would be in constant danger because of the price on his head, but he had gotten adept at slipping into and out of that country over the years. The Iranian Revolutionary Guard knew him by reputation, by the long line of dead men he'd left in his wake, but almost no one had seen him in the flesh. Any pictures they had of him were years out of date.

Under the circumstances, he knew he couldn't feel any safer than he did at the moment.

Things would change in Tehran. He felt that in his bones.

40

Imam Khomeini International Airport
Tehran, the Islamic Republic of Iran
August 12, 2011

'This is the captain. Please be advised that we'll be landing in approximately twenty minutes. Put your seats in the upright position and return the trays. Temperature on the ground is twenty-two degrees Celsius. The local time is six fifteen. On behalf of Tehran, I bid you welcome.'

Lourds struggled to wakefulness, wiped at his eyes, yawned, and checked his satphone to make sure it had made the time change. He glanced at Miriam. 'Want to grab breakfast at the hotel? Or get something in the airport?'

'I can wait till we reach the hotel if you can. Things will be less stressful there.'

Before Lourds could ask her what she meant, she pushed up from the seat.

'I'll be right back.' She walked down the aisle to the bathroom with her toiletry bag.

A few minutes later, she returned wearing a black *hijab* and *burqa*. Lourds stared at her.

'What?' She smoothed the *burqa* as she sat.

'You're Muslim?'

'No.' Miriam scowled. 'And if I was, I wouldn't buy into any part of religion that oppressed women.'

'Then why are you wearing all that?'

'Camouflage. And it's worn under protest. If we're going to meet with Professor Namati, there's a good chance that he believes the *modesty* of women should be protected. If he's a progressive thinker, we're still meeting him at the university, and his peers might not feel so progressive. Then I'll be protecting him as well as myself. And you.'

'Oh.' Lourds felt uncomfortable. 'I'm sorry.'

'For what?' Miriam tucked the ends of the headdress, so the garment wouldn't easily fly away.

'I didn't think about the pressures you would be under in this country when I asked you to come.'

Miriam focused on him, giving him a serious look. 'Does that mean I get top billing on any paper we do on this?'

Surprised, Lourds laughed. She joined him.

'No.'

'So maybe I should think I'm wearing the *hijab* for you as well? Since you're going to repress my valuable contributions to this?'

'Ouch.'

As they deplaned, Lourds headed for the ground car pickups. 'I suppose there is an advantage to having your luggage burn up in the back of a taxi. You don't have to wait for your bags.'

'We're still going to need to do some shopping.'

'Looking forward to it, are we?'

'Yeah, I can't wait to see how many colors and styles *hijabs* and *burqas* come in.'

'I think you can get away with just wearing the *hijab*.'

'Yes, but jeans mark me as a probable American or European immediately.'

'I'm not taking off this hat, and I know it makes me stand out as well.'

'Shopping. Soon. Before we meet with Professor Namati. The stores should open at ten, and there should be some close to the hotel.'

'Your clothes burned up in the taxi, so maybe we can look at that as my responsibility. I'd be happy to buy you some new ones.'

Miriam didn't hesitate. 'I'll take you up on that, Professor Lourds.'

'Within reason.' Lourds shifted his backpack on his shoulder. 'I'll get you some money at the hotel.'

'You're not coming with me?'

'Do you want company?'

'You're allowing me an hour of shopping, to get a whole outfit, in a foreign country, to represent myself in a nice way and still be true to myself, before we meet Professor Namati. Surely you can cut your sleep short enough to do that.'

The idea of watching the young woman try on

clothes did sound fascinating to Lourds. He smiled. 'All right. Just let me know when you're ready.'

'I'm ready now. I rolled on the pavement yesterday in these clothes, and I just got up from sleeping in them.'

'I don't think sleeping on the plane counts.'

'Maybe not to you. I'm also ready for a bath.'

'*Professor Lourds!*'

Miriam caught Lourds's wrist in her hand and squeezed, already putting pressure on his arm to pull him along wherever she bolted. Lourds thought that was overreacting, but the day before had hardly been an average one.

A young man with an earnest expression stood a few yards away, holding a sign in English over his head: professor thomas lourds.

'Ah.' Lourds took Miriam by the elbow and guided her through the crowd departing the airport. 'That must be the young college student Professor Namati assigned to drive us around. The government uses students to escort American and European scholars.'

'New slave labor for graduate assistants?'

'Actually, no. They're more like a built-in spy network for the Revolutionary Guard.'

'You're serious.'

'Very.'

'Then why are we going with this guy?'

'Because not going with him would be considered very suspicious.' Lourds crossed the last few feet and offered his hand. 'I'm Thomas Lourds.'

The young man dropped the sign he was holding to his side and took Lourds's hand. He was small in stature, slender, with intelligent brown eyes and a sparse beard. He wore a striped pullover and khakis. 'I am Reza al-Shahul. Professor Namati asked me to be your guide while you are here.'

'Pleasure to meet you, Mr. al-Shahul.'

The young man smiled with polite amusement. 'Please. Call me Reza. Everyone who knows me calls me Reza.'

'All right, Reza.' Lourds introduced Miriam.

She returned Reza's greeting in flawless Farsi.

Lourds felt a twinge of envy. No matter how hard he'd worked, he still maintained something of an accent in Farsi. Many people said they couldn't hear it, but he could. Miriam had no detectable accent of any kind.

Reza was obviously delighted and smiled hugely. 'You are from this country?'

'For a time. My father lived here. I learned the language from him. We visited several times before I lost him.'

'I am sorry for your loss. A father is very important.'

'I agree. Thank you. I don't want to trouble you, Reza, but there is a favor I would like to ask.'

Reza's smile didn't falter. 'Anything.'

'Professor Lourds and I lost our baggage prior to boarding the plane.'

A scowl darkened Reza's face. 'I saw the incident on YouTube. A very terrible thing. I did not know the two of you were caught up in it.'

Lourds thought about that with interest. Many American influences, such as Internet sites and popular culture, were banned from Iran at the Ayatollah's command.

'I would like to go shopping briefly before Professor Lourds and I meet with Professor Namati.'

'Of course. Just let me know when you would like me to pick you up.'

'It's six forty-five now. Would ten thirty be a problem?'

'Not at all. If you'll just follow me this way to the car, I'll get you to the hotel.'

Lourds followed after the two of them, listening to them conversing in rapid-fire Farsi. He couldn't help thinking that Reza didn't look like a spy, but then spies rarely did.

Ferdowsi Grand Hotel
Ferdowsi Avenue
Tehran, the Islamic Republic of Iran
August 12, 2011

'You'll meet me in the lobby at ten thirty.'

Lourds wanted to groan. It was already almost eight. They'd stopped for a quick breakfast in the French restaurant downstairs. Reza had hesitantly agreed to join them, then had chatted incessantly about popular American movies he'd seen and books he'd read. He was evidently a big fan of Japanese manga as well, something that he shared with Miriam, which had also stunned Lourds.

'Yes.'

Miriam didn't appear happy with the lackluster answer he'd given. 'Maybe it would be better if I came to get you, and we went down together.'

'I really think Reza would be happy taking you shopping by yourself.'

She frowned at him. 'That would mean Reza would have to return to the hotel to pick you up.'

'I'm sure he wouldn't mind.'

'In order to do that, I'd have less time for shopping.'

Lourds held up his hands in surrender. 'Come by the room if you want. You're right next door.'

'Okay. Thanks.'

Tiredly, Lourds slotted the hotel key, watched the lights flash green to admit access, then twisted the handle and walked into his room. He could barely keep his eyes open. His body ached from all that it had been through the day before, and from traveling most of the night.

He gazed around the room. No matter where he went, no matter what country, walking into a hotel room was most nearly always the same. The layout had to be the most homogenous thing of the twenty-first century.

He dropped his backpack onto the bed and fished out the book Lev had given his life for. Taking his boots off, he stepped up onto the bed, pulled his Swiss Army Tinker knife from his pocket, and selected the Phillips screwdriver. He removed the screws from the air-duct grille, made certain it was relatively dust-free, then wrapped the book in the plastic bag from the trash can and put it inside.

It wasn't unusual for the hotel maids to go through guests' belongings in Tehran – especially when they were visiting scholars. Other professors that Lourds knew had had their things searched while they were out of the room. The book, with its strange markings and language, might be enough to prompt petty theft.

He replaced the vent cover, undressed, and showered. Still naked, mostly dry, he toppled into the bed and was almost instantly asleep.

College of Social Sciences
University of Tehran
Tehran, the Islamic Republic of Iran
August 12, 2011

At the university, Reza led Lourds and Miriam to a modest office at the back of the building. Miriam wore her new clothes under the *burqa* and had opted for business casual rather than jeans. Lourds regretted the shapeless shift because it masked the slender, hard-muscled curves he'd noticed while she was trying on clothing. He'd resolved to take her shopping once more before they left the country, in order to properly resupply what she'd lost, of course, and take more time to enjoy the experience.

He'd gotten new clothing as well, but went with olive cargo pants and a dark red Oxford shirt that felt incredibly soft. He carried his backpack over his shoulder, lighter now that the book wasn't inside it.

Reza knocked lightly at the door. 'Professor Namati? Professor Lourds and his graduate assistant, Miriam Abata, are here.'

Behind the modest desk, Professor Hashem Nabi Namati glanced up from the yellow legal pad he was writing on. He was a short, square man dressed in a suit and sweater. His head was covered and his black beard was laced with gray. He removed his reading glasses and stood with a smile.

'Welcome. Come in, come in.'

Lourds entered the office and took the man's hand, at the same time taking in all the books and the artifacts on the shelves. One of the most outstanding was a statue of al-Buraq rearing proudly, his mighty wings spread. Several pictures on the wall showed Namati standing in a *dhow*, a lateen-rigged sailing vessel. In some of them, as an older man, he was with a little girl who smiled with excitement.

'You sail?'

'When the chance presents itself. Sadly, those chances come fewer and fewer these days.' Namati smiled. 'Not all of us get to travel the world locating sunken continents and lost temples.'

'Well, Professor, all I can say is you're not getting out of academia often enough. Those things are out there for the discovering. They're not just waiting for me.'

'From where I sit, it seems as though they are awaiting your attentions. I'm sure a lot of the world would agree with me. As for getting out of academia, I appear to be shackled here more often than not.' Namati gestured to chairs in front of his desk. 'Please, sit.'

Miriam sat in one of the chairs. Lourds took the other.

'Reza, you should be able to find a chair in one of the other offices that isn't being used.'

'Professor Namati, if I may?'

'Yes.'

Lourds glanced at Reza and felt slightly guilty, but he knew the likelihood of the young man's being a spy to be a fairly good one. 'I'd like to keep this private for a little while. If that's all right.'

If Reza was put off by the dismissal, he didn't show it. 'Of course. I'll just be down the hall when you're ready to go.' He left.

'Would you like anything to drink?' Namati spread his hands in invitation.

'I think we're good for the moment. I would like to take you to lunch later, if you can escape academia for that long.'

Namati laughed. 'I cleared my schedule for you today. Lunch would be wonderful.' He sat. 'I have to admit, after what the two of you went through yesterday, I'm really surprised that you still showed up today.'

'Our visit here is important.'

Namati nodded. 'This is about that book Lev found, isn't it?'

41

College of Social Sciences
University of Tehran
Tehran, the Islamic Republic of Iran
August 12, 2011

'We didn't discuss any of the particulars of our visit on the phone. What would make you ask that?' Lourds regarded Professor Namati with increased interest.

'Because if you actually have that book, your lives are in danger. You should have gathered that much from yesterday's events.' Namati studied them. 'Though I suppose you already knew that.'

'What makes you think that what happened yesterday had anything to do with a book Lev might have found?'

Namati shrugged. 'Perhaps it didn't. But the last time I talked to Lev, he'd mentioned bringing you in to look at the book. He was convinced that he'd gone as far as he could on it.'

'Have you seen the book?'

'Sadly, no. I was curious, but Lev felt the last place it should be was in Iran. There are people here that desperately want that book. Outside interest in what he was doing here caused Lev to leave before he'd finished his research.'

Miriam shifted slightly in her chair. 'Why do you say the book is dangerous?'

Namati stared at her for a moment, then scratched his chin. He shifted his attention to Lourds. 'Why is she here?' He glanced at Miriam. 'I mean no disrespect.'

Miriam stiffened slightly, and Lourds knew she was miffed, but to her credit she didn't say anything.

'I asked her to accompany me. Her Farsi is much better than mine.'

'Really?' Bright suspicion dawned in Namati's eyes as he focused on Miriam. 'How is it you speak Farsi so well?'

'My father was born in Tehran,' Miriam replied effortlessly in Farsi. 'He spent most of his adolescence here, then went away to university and met my mother. He told me on many occasions, before I lost him, that love has a way of transporting a seed to new and fertile ground where it springs anew.'

Namati smiled, and his eyebrows raised in surprise. 'You *do* speak Farsi well.'

'Thank you. My father taught me the language and refused to let go of his heritage. My mother learned Farsi as well, and we spoke it often in our home.'

'Have you been to Tehran before?'

'Several times. My father traveled here every time he could. He brought me when he was able.'

'How long has it been since you were last here?'

'Years. I lost my father and have not been back till today.'

'I am sorry for your loss. And, time permitting with Professor Lourds's good grace, I can take the two of you around and show you some of the changes that have taken place in the city.'

'I would love that.'

Namati leaned back in his chair and rubbed his hands together. He switched back to English. 'As far as why that book is dangerous, have you read the story in it?'

'I've translated some of it.' Lourds shrugged. 'It seems to be a retelling of the Prophet's early days. Nothing overly interesting. Other than the fact it's supposed to be written by Yazid ibn Salam. I haven't had it carbon-dated, but Lev's notes indicated he had.'

'The book was carbon-dated. I've seen those reports. Lev sent me part of the translation, and I'd have to agree that on the surface the story isn't anything that scholars haven't already seen. Except for one thing: Lev mentioned there was a legend of Mohammad's own Koran, written in his own hand as God told it to him. And the Scroll that foretells the future of Islam.' Namati's voice lowered. 'That alone can get you killed by devout Muslims.'

'For the book?'

'Or over it. If the story is true, and among some of my peers, that statement would be considered sacrilege, there are some who would kill to possess the book if you were not Muslim. They feel the book must be recovered and Mohammad's lost Koran and Scroll found.'

Lourds resisted the urge to point out that he knew the Ayatollah was one of those 'peers' who would do that. Klaus Von Volker's involvement proved that.

'And if the story is a lie, there are other Muslims who would see that book destroyed as an abomination. No matter if it is of historic significance.' Namati took a breath. 'When Lev was here, asking around about the book and this new legend of Mohammad, he had to be very careful. He thought some of the fundamentalists had already sniffed him out and were on his trail.'

'Were they?' Miriam sounded tense.

'Perhaps. I don't know. When I first heard Lev had been killed, I thought the fundamentalists were behind his murder. As it turned out, the men who killed him were German mercenaries.'

'What do you think about the legend?'

'You mean, do I believe it?' Namati shrugged. 'I am a Muslim. I believe in the teachings of God, but I don't believe that God wants genocide for the rest of the world. I believe the Scroll could exist, and that it might foretell the future of the Muslim world. But many believe the Scroll would give the Muslim faith power over the rest of the world. That God's wrath is somchow writ on that Scroll and any Muslim who possesses it and wants to can bring down furious punishment on nonbelievers.' He paused. 'Have you heard of Winston Cardwell?'

'The British historian who's written extensively on

the Muslim world?' Lourds not only had heard of the man, he'd recently met Cardwell at a large signing in London while promoting his latest book.

'Yes.'

'Lev had talked to Cardwell about the book, hoping for some direction on his research. Cardwell didn't have any information that Lev didn't already have, but he evidently began searching for the truth of the tale. Somewhere along the line, he asked the wrong people. Two days ago, he was found murdered in a terrorist safe house in London. Someone had beheaded him.'

Lourds winced. Winston Cardwell had been a good man, overly ambitious, perhaps, and certainly pushy. But he hadn't deserved such a fate. 'That's horrible.'

'So you can understand why I might suspect your investigation into this book could have prompted an attack such as the one you faced yesterday.'

'I do.' Lourds took a breath. 'I haven't found any mention of what happened to the Koran and Scroll after Mohammad lost them. Do the legends say anything about that?'

'They do. According to legend, a religious man among the workers constructing the Dome of the Rock found the Koran and the Scroll. He was moved by God to hide those things within the building.'

Lourds's blood sang in his veins. At last they had a potential final resting place for the objects Lev had been looking for. No wonder his friend had been in Jerusalem. Lev must certainly have felt he was sitting on top of the find of his life. 'No one knows where he put those things?'

'If anyone knew, they would have been found long ago.' Namati clasped his hands. 'Scholars have searched for the Koran and Scroll for generations.'

'But they didn't have the book Lev found in Cairo.'

Namati nodded. 'It is as you say. Lev was also convinced he'd found a map that led to the Koran and the Scroll. Was there any mention of that in his notes?'

'No.' Another wave of excitement surged through Lourds. There had been no mention of a map, but maybe Lev hadn't written about that on purpose, afraid of his notes falling into unfriendly hands. Or maybe there was another hidden message Lourds hadn't found yet.

'Well, he was convinced he'd found the map, but there was no way to decode it.'

'Did Lev say where he found the map?'

'He told me it was part of the book, that he found it by accident. That was only a day or so before he was killed. It was a recent discovery.'

'"Part of the book"?'

'That's what he said, yes.'

Lourds nodded at the clock on the wall. 'Maybe I could take you to lunch now.'

Namati smiled. 'That would be wonderful. Would you care for the local cuisine?'

'I would love the local cuisine.'

Namati turned his attention to Miriam. 'And you, Miss Abata?'

'I haven't had genuine Persian food in many years. I'd love it.'

'Then we will go in memory of your father.'

Alborz Restaurant
Sohrevardi Shomali Avenue
North Sohrevardi District
Tehran, the Islamic Republic of Iran
August 12, 2011

Named after the Alborz Mountains, which jutted up so proudly in northern Iran, the Alborz Restaurant occupied a comfortable space in the neighborhood. Tehran splashed into the foothills, and the mountains towered above even the Milad Tower, the tallest structure in Iran, and the four largest telecommunication towers in the world.

Lourds took in the white-capped mountains as he walked from the car to the restaurant. Even though Tehran was brimming with things from the modern world, the overpowering shadow of the nearby mountains still made it seem Old World, tucked into the security of a natural barrier against enemies.

Namati quickly negotiated a table for them, and they were led past diners facing heavily laden plates of *chelo kebabs* loaded with steak, chicken, lamb, and salmon. The amount of food looked daunting, but Lourds felt capable of meeting the task. The French breakfast hadn't stayed with him as long as he'd expected.

The server showed them to a table.

Reza remained standing while everyone else sat. 'If you'll excuse me, Professor Namati, I've got some work I can be doing while you eat.'

'Nonsense.' Lourds gestured to a chair. 'I'm treating.'

'I appreciate the offer, Professor Lourds, but I am experiencing some indigestion. Please. Enjoy your meal. I will be up front when you need me.' Reza turned and walked away.

Lourds felt bad for the young man. 'Did I hurt his feelings earlier when I excused him from our meeting?'

'Reza isn't so vulnerable. I wouldn't worry about it.' Namati reached for the hummus and smeared it onto a slab of homemade bread.

'A college student turning down a free meal?' Lourds shook his head. 'That just sounds wrong.'

Namati chuckled. 'Some of the students are still embarrassed about eating in front of strangers.'

'That only means you go hungry a lot when you get out into the world.' Lourds spread hummus over a chunk of bread after Miriam had helped herself. The aroma of the tahini, garbanzo beans, garlic, lemon juice, and olive oil was intoxicating and tasted even better.

They ordered the *chelo kebabs*, lamb for Miriam and Namati, and Lourds selected steak.

'I feel I must point out another possibility for Lev's death.' Namati took a short breath. 'I don't mean to undermine your interest in this book, but legends are sometimes that: beautiful or terrifying stories. Both, in this case. I know the Eastern and Western worlds would view the existence of Mohammad's Koran and the Scroll in much different lights.'

Lourds slathered another piece of bread with hummus and waited.

'Lev Strauss was my friend, and he was a very progressive thinking man. I don't know if he talked much to you about his views of Islam and Judaism.'

'Somewhat. I've always been more interested in forgotten history than in fixing the world's views of God.'

'Yet, in this case at least, both of those goals appear attainable.'

'Perhaps.'

Namati brushed that away. 'If that Koran and Scroll exist, you will be in a position to shed some light for the world. If you find them. But I digress. As I was saying, Lev had remarkable mien. He believed that the Jews and the Muslims could find a way to live together. He believed in the peace process. He actively tried to reach out to the Islamic world, and I was one of his chief supporters. The far right in his own country hated him.'

Lourds knew that was true. Lev had always been a man to follow his own course through the world, and his loss was going to make the world poorer for it.

'It's very possible that his own people murdered him.'

'With Austrian mercenaries?' Miriam's rancor with that statement echoed in her words.

'Is it any easier to believe that someone in Iran hired those mercenaries?'

Before Miriam could respond, Lourds lightly kicked her foot under the table. She ducked her head and returned her attention to her plate.

Namati focused on Lourds. 'You remember Yitzhak Rabin?'

'Of course.' The Israeli politician and military general had been assassinated while serving as prime minister in his country. Yigal Amir, a right-wing Israeli radical, killed Rabin for signing the Oslo Accords, which had come out of the first face-to-face arrangement between Israel and the Palestine Liberation Organization.

'He was, perhaps, a message for our time.'

'What message?'

'That the Jewish and Islamic worlds are not yet ready to come to an arrangement that will leave both happy.' Namati shrugged. 'Lev was still a believer, and I loved him for it, but I also feared for him.'

'I hope that's not true.'

'Would it be better if the men behind his murder were Islamic extremists?'

For a moment, Lourds was tempted to tell the man they had proof that Lev's death had come through orders of the Ayatollah. The anger over his friend's death burned harshly in him. But he curbed it, knowing saying that to anyone who might be connected to the Revolutionary Guard could get him killed.

'No. It wouldn't be better.' Lourds glanced at the front of the restaurant as their *chelo kebabs* arrived.

Reza sat in the foyer and talked on a cell phone. As

Lourds inhaled the aroma of the flame-broiled beef on a bed of basmati rice, he glanced through one of the restaurant windows and spotted a black car with two men in it parked across the street.

He tried to remember if they'd been there before and couldn't. However, it was unusual for two men to sit inside a vehicle in the heat. The temperature had almost reached a hundred degrees. He glanced at Miriam and saw she had noticed the men as well.

42

Ferdowsi Grand Hotel
Ferdowsi Avenue
Tehran, the Islamic Republic of Iran
August 13, 2011

Alice called while Lourds was at his desk in the hotel room, poring over the mysterious book. The fact that the answer – and a map – lurked somewhere within its pages felt unnerving. Everything was within his grasp, yet he couldn't close his hand around any of it.

He welcomed the distraction of the phone call. 'How have you been?'

'Well enough.' Alice sounded exhausted.

Lourds stood and paced as he talked. Concentrating on tomes and scrolls was backbreaking labor, made even harder when the frustration levels peaked.

'You're safe?' He lifted the curtain and looked outside, surprised at how dark it was. He'd spent the afternoon with Namati, Miriam, and Reza, taking in the sights of Tehran as the professor pointed them out. Then he'd returned with Miriam to the hotel and taken a nap. He'd been working on the book ever since.

'I am. I absconded with several million euros and

hired a private security company out of Britain. All ex-SAS soldiers who don't think highly of Klaus's pro-Iran position. I'm thinking of the money as my early divorce settlement.'

Lourds chuckled. 'Just remember that Von Volker is a dangerous man.'

'I'm safe, but I worry about you, Thomas. You're the one sticking your head in the lion's mouth. I saw what happened at Ben Gurion.'

'We came through it all right.'

'I didn't see much of the young lady accompanying you, but she looks very pretty.'

'I hadn't noticed.'

Alice laughed. 'For a world-renowned linguist, you lie pathetically.'

Feeling a little uncomfortable, Lourds chuckled. 'All right. Perhaps I have noticed. She took me shopping today.'

'Seductress.'

'Actually, our clothes burned up in the taxi, and we were pressed for time.'

'A woman only takes a man shopping for one reason. To have him watch her dress.'

'I believe there are two reasons. I offered to pick up the tab since she's a college student, and replacing the clothing would have been a hardship for her.'

'How very gallant of you. I suppose you insisted on going along to see how your money was being spent.'

'Nope. I tried to stay at the hotel and squeeze in

another couple hours of sleep. She insisted I go along to save time. Or to give her more time.'

'Then I return to my initial supposition. You were getting vamped.'

'I didn't feel as though I was getting vamped. I usually know these things.'

'I beg to differ. As I recall, even with the history between us, I had to make the first moves and even flag them for your attention.'

Lourds sighed. 'Okay, okay, stop. I'm tired, and I'm not at my best for wordplay. I'm still trying to wrap my head around this book Lev found, and I'm getting my butt kicked.'

'No help in Tehran?'

'Not really. Maybe I should say, not so far. Lev left a note that made him sound like he was convinced the professor I've been in contact with here knew something or had something.'

'Then maybe I can help brighten your day.'

Smiling, Lourds paced a little more energetically. 'You found something?'

'Perhaps. I went through the Islamic artifacts as you suggested. As it turned out, Lev had collected seven figurines of al-Buraq.'

'Special fascination?'

'According to his records, which Klaus also arranged to get, five of these figurines were recent purchases. Do you have a timeline on when Lev found the book you're translating?'

Lourds checked the notes in his journal. 'Lev acquired the book in Cairo in January of this year.'

'Five of these figurines were collected from the month of May. The most recent acquisition was in July.'

'Why the interest in al-Buraq?'

'He was the winged horse that took Mohammad to the Al-Aqsa Mosque.'

'But that's not enough – '

'A further detail of interest: all five of these figurines are supposedly modeled on an artifact sculpted by one of the builders who worked on the Dome of the Rock. A man named . . . Sahih al-Maliki.'

'I saw that name mentioned in the book, but I haven't had time to research him. He was just listed as one of the men who helped build the Dome of the Rock.'

'I researched al-Maliki.'

'Good woman.'

'There's not much information on him. In addition to helping build the Dome of the Rock, he left behind a few sculptures.'

'More flying horses?'

'Al-Maliki only made the one al-Buraq. Want to guess who owns it?'

Lourds sat in his chair and felt as though a lightning bolt had zinged through him when the pieces started dropping into place in his mind. 'Professor Hashem Nabi Namati.'

Alice sounded surprised. 'You already knew that? Lev spent seven weeks tracking the manifest on that piece.'

'I didn't know that, but I saw a statue of al-Buraq on one of the shelves in Namati's office only a few hours ago. I suspect Lev saw it too, and that's why he verified the authenticity of the piece. Is there any mention of why Lev went to such trouble?'

'No, but there is something odd in Lev's notes. He took rubbings of all seven al-Buraqs in his possession. There are also rubbings of other flying horses as well. Lev was searching for something.'

'Yes.' Lourds sat at the desk and pondered the pages of the book, imagining how the statue of al-Buraq in Namati's office would look across the pages. From his estimation, the statue would fit from top to bottom.

'You're quiet all of a sudden.'

'I'm thinking.'

'Care to share?'

Lourds took a deep breath and let it out. 'I think I know how this book was coded, and I think Lev had figured it out, too. In order to confirm it, however, I'm going to have to get Professor Namati's statue.'

Miriam didn't know what woke her, but she came up from the bed with her fist curled around the Chinese Type 54 pistol she'd gotten from her Mossad contact in Tehran. She'd gotten it from the man when she'd been out shopping with Lourds.

The pistol was modeled on the Russian Tokarev T-33. Chambered in the 7.62x25mm round, the weapon was the equivalent of a 9mm pistol. It came with an eight-round magazine, but the Mossad agent had provided two fourteen-round magazines as well. They were his 'special gift' for her, and he wished her well when he left.

In other words, if she had to use the pistol, things would be particularly nasty, and she'd need the extra firepower.

The room was still and silent except for the air-conditioning.

'You're imagining things.' With a sigh, she flipped the safety back on the pistol and tucked it under her pillow once more. She lay there for a moment more, thinking of how the faces of the two men continued to haunt her sleep.

The night wasn't as bad as others had been. But she still had a lot of it to go. According to the clock on the bedside table, it was only a few minutes after one. She lay there a moment longer, then got up for a drink of water.

While in the bathroom, wood shrieked as screws were pulled loose as the door burst open. Miriam dashed from the bathroom and streaked back to the bed, reaching for the pistol.

A man threw himself at her and wrapped an arm around her ankles. Unable to take another step, she tripped and fell. Catching herself on her hands, she flipped over, freed a leg, and drove it into the face of her captor. The man's head snapped back, and she slithered free.

In that instant, she recognized him as one of the two men who had followed Lourds and her around much of the day. She got to her feet and leaped toward the bed, then the second man – standing in the broken doorway – lifted a pistol and shot her twice.

Pain pierced her abdomen. Looking down, she saw two hypodermic darts jutting out of her stomach. Before she had a chance to fully realize she'd been drugged, not mortally injured, the drugs whispered through her system and shut her down.

After telling Alice good night, and to get to Jerusalem where he'd be meeting her in the next couple of days if everything went well, Lourds pulled on his khakis and the Oxford shirt he'd worn earlier that day, stepped into his boots, and pulled on his hat. He shoved the book back into its hiding place in the air duct, then headed for Miriam's room.

He was too excited to sleep, and he wanted her thoughts on how they could steal the al-Buraq statue from Namati's office. There was no way Lourds intended to give Namati a clue about what he potentially held.

Lourds knew that he – and Lev – could still be wrong about the statue. But he only needed it in his hands for a few minutes to know for certain.

When he stepped out into the hallway, Lourds saw two maintenance men working on the door to Miriam's room. From the looks of things, the door had been ripped from its hinges.

‘What happened?’

One of the maintenance men looked at Lourds. ‘No English.’

Lourds shifted to Farsi and repeated the question.

‘The door is broken. We are repairing it. You go now.’

Concern for Miriam drove Lourds through the door. The workers tried to stop him, but he was stronger than they were and got through despite their efforts.

Miriam’s room was empty, like she’d never been there.

Lourds wheeled on the men, grabbing the nearest one by the shoulders. ‘Where is the girl?’

‘There was no girl. This room was empty. It had a broken door. We are repairing the door.’

Knowing the man would only keep lying to him, Lourds returned to his room and called the desk.

‘Good evening.’

‘This is Professor Thomas Lourds. I want to know where my companion is.’

‘What companion is that, Professor Lourds?’

‘The young woman I checked in with yesterday morning. Miriam Abata.’

‘Let me check.’ The clerk was silent for a moment before returning. ‘According to our records, Professor Lourds, you checked in alone.’

‘I didn’t check in alone.’

‘I’m afraid I can’t help you any further.’

The phone clicked dead in Lourds’s ear. Panicked now, he started to get the book from the air duct, then realized that if he was picked up, he didn't want it found on him.

He left the book where it was, but he grabbed his backpack and slung it over his shoulders. Then he went out, knowing enemy eyes were probably watching his every move.

43

Evin Prison
Evin District
Tehran, the Islamic Republic of Iran
August 13, 2011

Miriam woke cold and alone in a dark concrete room. Shackles bruised her wrists and she hung on a chain from a thick metal ring mounted on the ceiling. She could barely touch the concrete floor with her toes, but if she didn't, her weight made it feel like her arms were slowly being torn from her shoulders. She muffled a cry of agony, not wanting to give her captors the satisfaction of hearing her in pain.

A shadow moved against the wall. She barely made out a man's form as he knocked on a metal door.

A metal plate slid across an opening, allowing a square foot of hard white light to filter into the room.

'What?'

'Tell Colonel Davari the woman is awake.' Light glinted off the machine pistol slung at the shadow man's shoulder. Both men spoke Farsi.

Miriam knew she'd been taken by members of the

Revolutionary Guard – the language and her surroundings removed any doubt.

She was cut off from *Katsas* Shavit and the Mossad. All alone in enemy hands. The worst enemy hands, because even more damaging than being a spy, she was a woman.

For long minutes, Miriam hung there with the chains biting into her numbed wrists, her calves and toes ached and cramped from standing on her toes, no relief in sight.

Finally, dead bolts clanked on the door, and it slid out of the way. The sudden blaze of light was so powerful it felt scalding on her eyes. Heart pumping wildly, adrenaline spiking her system and temporarily lessening some of the pain, she watched as the grim-faced man in a Revolutionary Guard uniform strode into the room and stop in front of her. His insignia identified him as a colonel.

'Miriam Abata, you are in Iran as a spy.'

'No.' Miriam wanted to be more articulate, but the frightened animal lurking in the back of her mind exploded out of the darkness and took control. She didn't want to die. She didn't want to be tortured. 'I am a student. I am here to study. I am not a spy.'

The colonel put his hands behind his back and gazed down at her. 'You are lying, spy.'

'I am a visiting scholar. Check my passport.'

With insane speed, the colonel backhanded her across the face.

Pain spiked through Miriam's brain as her head snapped back. She sagged at the ends of the chains and felt the raw fire of the links biting into her wrists. She tried to get her feet under her again as the salty taste of blood filled her mouth.

'Your passport is as full of lies as you are.'

'No. I am an Israeli citizen. You must let me go.'

'We execute spies in Iran. I'm sure your minders told you that before you accepted this mission.'

'I am a visiting scholar.' Miriam swallowed blood and felt two of her teeth loosened by the impact. Her face was already swelling, her right eye closing a little. The man hit very hard.

'Where is the book? We know Lourds found it.'

'The American professor brought many books. Which book are you – '

Colonel Davari didn't move as fast this time. He slowed himself intentionally, letting her see it coming. Miriam ducked her head into her shoulder, but in the end, it did no good. He punched her in the stomach hard enough to drive the air from her lungs and make her vomit. The stinking mess ran down her clothes.

Davari gestured to two of his men. 'Get that off her.'

At first, Miriam thought they were just going to remove the vomit. Instead, they both drew knives. The blades flashed as they yanked at her clothing. Each movement was excruciating to her wrists and calves. Her stomach throbbed from Davari's punch. They didn't work carefully. As they cut her clothing from her, various nicks and cuts tracked her body.

They dropped her blouse and pants at her feet in rags. One of them slid his knife between the cups of her bra and pulled. The lacy material parted, and her bra fell to the floor as well, leaving her naked and unprotected except for the gauzy red panties that barely kept her modest.

Another man unwound a water hose from a wheel on the wall. He turned the water on and used the spray attachment to hose her down. The cold deluge felt near freezing and took Miriam's breath away. She cried unashamedly then and screamed in pain and fear and helplessness. The man directed the stream at her face and forced her to shut up or drown.

Finally, the colonel raised his hand, and the man turned the water off.

Sodden, shaking, her teeth bloody and chattering, Miriam hung at the ends of the chains and hoped the fiery pain in her arms and legs would cause her to black out. Unconsciousness eluded her, however.

Davari stepped back into her face again. 'Where is the book?'

'Lourds has it.'

'Where?'

'I don't know.'

'You know which book I'm talking about?'

'The professor brought many books with him. If the book you're looking for is one of those – '

Davari hit her again. This time blood trickled from her nose. 'Where is the book?'

'I don't know.'

'You're being a very foolish girl.'

'I am a visiting scholar. Not a spy.'

'You are a spy, and you don't know enough to save your own life. The Mossad will wipe their hands of you.'

Miriam knew that was true. Before she had left Jerusalem, *Katsas* Shavit had told her that the Mossad could not risk much finding her if she was taken. Miriam had never thought she would be captured. They weren't doing anything dangerous, nothing that would make them stand out.

Then she realized that Lourds had been right. The men at the airport had been coming for them. Colonel Davari and the Revolutionary Guard had known she and Lourds were coming, and they'd lain in wait. She wondered if they had Lourds, but she didn't dare ask.

No one would be coming for her. She could only hope that she died soon, and with as little pain as possible.

Davari leveraged a callused finger under her chin and lifted her battered face up to his. 'You know this is true, don't you, girl? You know not to cling foolishly to the hope that you will be rescued by your compatriots.'

Miriam didn't say anything. She knew anything she said to demean him would only be used against her. And it was futile. Mostly she was afraid he would be encouraged to hurt her some more.

'Do you know how I know you were a Mossad agent?'

She didn't rise to the bait.

'Because I know your father was a Mossad agent. He told me so in the final minutes before I killed him.'

A scream erupted from Miriam and carried with it a strength she didn't know she possessed. Hauling herself up on the chains, she lashed out with a foot, delivering a kick to Davari's face.

The colonel staggered back, blood trickling from his split lip. Then he clenched a fist and lunged forward, driving it into her face, finally delivering the blessed unconsciousness she was seeking.

Imam Khomeini Metro Station
Imam Khomeini Square
Tehran, the Islamic Republic of Iran
August 13

Lourds got off the rapid-transit metro with the rush of morning workers. He was frazzled and worn, sick with worry, and still didn't have a concrete plan for finding Miriam Abata, getting Namati's al-Buraq, or getting out of Tehran. At the moment, all of those tasks seemed impossible.

The Imam Khomeini Metro Station was located at the junction of Line 1 and Line 2. He skipped the elevator because it was filled with Muslim women who wouldn't allow a man to ride with them. He'd almost made the mistake of trying to enter the last car on the train earlier. The first and last cars of every train were set aside for women who didn't want to ride with men.

He took the stairs up the sixty feet to the surface and stepped out into the station's main area. With all the *burqas* and *hajibs* swirling around him, Lourds felt alienated, an obvious outsider in a foreign – and definitely hostile – land.

Hitching his backpack over his shoulder, Lourds crossed the polished floor laid out in a pattern of brown tiles in the midst of white toward the entrance, bypassing the phone banks and cash machines. Even the beautiful Persian artwork on permanent display couldn't distract him.

He'd spent the night away from the hotel, hanging in cybercafés that didn't deserve the name because they had limited access to the world. He'd searched for any news of Miriam, but there was none. Nor was there any mention of an Israeli grad student disappearing from the Ferdowsi Grand Hotel.

While thinking desperately, Lourds had considered calling the Tehran police, but they were essentially the Revolutionary Guard, the same people who had 'disappeared' Miriam. The United States didn't have an embassy in Tehran. Neither did Israel. The Canadians maintained ambassadorial relations, but Lourds knew they wouldn't want to get involved in his current predicament.

He was on his own, and he was hardly an army of one.

Outside, Lourds took a deep breath and gazed out

over the square. In the past, the neighborhood had been called the Shah Square. For a time it had been known as Toopkhaneh Square, literally translating into cannon house. Dar al-Funun, Iran's first modern college, had found a home there during the nineteenth century, and it had been a place where regal state ceremonies had been conducted.

Those glory days were basically over. Protestors often gathered there to rebuke the Ayatollah and suffer the harsh wrath of the Revolutionary Guard and the *Basij* militiamen. Those brave Iranians standing up for self-government had paid for their courage with blood. Protestors had been maimed, terribly injured, or died there.

The telecommunications building on the south side of the square didn't even pretend to mimic Muslim influence. It was serviceable and massive, a gray wall that shadowed the square. On the other three sides of the square, small shops and boardinghouses fought for space where the poorer families in Tehran lived.

Lourds felt the heavy despair that filled the neighborhood. He also drew several curious stares from passersby.

In the end, he knew what he had to do. Just as with Miriam, he had to trust someone, and there were precious few in Tehran to trust. But something had to be done. He took his satphone from his pocket and called Reza.

*

'Miss Abata was taken from the hotel?'

Across the small café table from Reza, Lourds tried to maintain his calm. 'Yes.'

'By whom?'

'I have to assume it was the Revolutionary Guard.'

For a moment, Reza looked panicked. The reaction made Lourds feel a little better. Anyone who felt threatened by the mere mention of the Ayatollah's bullies had to be close to being on his side.

'I shouldn't be here.' Reza started to rise from his chair.

Lourds leaned forward and put a restraining hand on the young man's forearm. 'Reza. Please. If something isn't done, I'm certain those people are going to kill Miriam. I need help.'

Reza stood a moment longer, halfway between rising and sitting. Finally, he blew out a breath and sat back down. 'What have you done that would call the Revolutionary Guard down on you?'

'Have you heard of Lev Strauss?'

'Of course. I've read many of his proposed peace agreements regarding the Middle East.'

'You know about his death?'

'Yes.'

'I have reason to believe he was killed by the Ayatollah's death squads because of something he was working on. Now I'm working on it.'

'This is what you were talking to Professor Namati about yesterday?'

'Yes. I excluded you because I know that many of the students are spies for the Revolutionary Guards.'

'And if I am such a spy?'

Lourds shook his head. 'Then I'm caught, and there's nothing I can do.'

Reza regarded him in stony silence. 'Trusting you with my secrets is equally dangerous, Professor Lourds.'

A tremendous weight seemed to drop off Lourds's shoulders, and he felt like he was in free fall.

'If you want passage out of Iran, I can take you through the Kurd lands. The way will be harsh, but staying here may well mean your death.'

'I don't want passage out of Iran yet.'

'Then you're a fool.'

'I can't leave Miriam behind if there's any chance to save her. I got her into this mess, and I need to get her out.'

Reza grinned mirthlessly. 'You can't even get yourself out of the city.'

'I don't know that yet. What I do know is that I don't have a prayer of finding Miriam if I'm constantly having to stay out of sight.'

'I understand. Professor Lourds, there are many of us in Iran who love democracy, but we haven't yet had the chance to embrace it. We yearn for it. We die for it.' His face crumpled a little, and his voice turned hoarse. 'Less than a month ago, my girlfriend Liora was killed by the *Basij* during a peaceful demonstration. She was an innocent, barely eighteen years old.'

'I'm sorry for your loss.'

'As am I.' Reza's eyes gleamed wetly. 'Liora's death wasn't for nothing. I won't let it be for nothing. More and more of us, not just the students, but adults as well, who were once afraid to show their distrust and dislike of the Ayatollah, are standing together. We know we must act against the tyranny of the theocracy in Iran, but at the same time we cannot forget the importance of being good Muslims and being faithful to God.'

'I understand.'

'After all these deaths, there are some in the Revolutionary Guard who are beginning to disagree with the Ayatollah. They do so secretly, but we are able to work through them. We can get more information these days. They know change is coming for our people, and they want to be on the right side of history.' Reza leaned back. 'If it is not too late, we will help you find Miss Abata. Then we will see about getting you out of Iran.'

'Thank you.'

'Just promise me one thing.'

'If I can.'

'Whatever it is you are working on, if it will help undermine the Ayatollah's regime, get it done.'

Thinking of Lev's murder and now Miriam's abduction, Lourds nodded grimly. 'You've got my word on that.'

44

Professor Namati's Residence
Qeytariyeh District
Tehran, the Islamic Republic of Iran
August 13, 2011

One of Reza's student friends drove Lourds to Professor Namati's home. It was Saturday, and the professor should have been there. Lourds didn't get Namati's home phone number. The house was a modest single-story with a nice garden out front.

Lourds walked up to the front door, took off his hat, and knocked politely.

A young woman answered the door and looked frightened. She was an older version of the young girl Namati had pictures of in the *dhow*. Her red eyes gave away the fact that she'd been crying.

'May I help you?' The young woman stood her ground behind the door.

'I hope I'm not coming at a bad time.' Lourds felt uncomfortable, but he wasn't leaving without speaking to Namati.

'My father isn't here.' Her voice broke.

'I'm Thomas Lourds.'

'I know who you are, Professor Lourds.' Her eyes hardened. 'You are part of the reason they took my father.'

'Who took your father?'

'The Revolutionary Guard. They came this morning and took him away. They said it was just for routine questioning, but my father knew it was a lie. He did not want to go with them. They told him they would kill me if he did not. So he left. They wanted to know if he had seen you.'

Stunned, Lourds stood there for a moment and didn't know what to say. 'Do you know where they took your father?'

'Where does the Revolutionary Guard take any intellectual they view as a threat to them? To Evin Prison.'

For the first time, Lourds realized where Miriam had probably been taken, and the knowledge left him terrified. Horrible things happened at that prison. Although the regime denied it, reports came out of Iran frequently about the serial rapes and other brutal torment that went on inside that prison.

He concentrated on the young woman. 'What's your name?'

She hesitated, but she finally spoke. 'Shirin.'

'Shirin, if there is a way to do it, please understand that I'm going to help your father. I promise you that.'

She only looked at him until finally he couldn't bear it any longer and returned to the waiting car. As he got in, he watched Shirin close the door and lift the window curtain. He didn't know if she was calling the Revolutionary

Guard to let them know that he'd been there or if she was trying to convince herself to believe him.

The student put the car into gear and pulled into the street.

Lourds dialed Reza's number and waited as the call connected.

Evin District
Tehran, the Islamic Republic of Iran
August 13, 2011

In the shade of the teahouse beside the prison, Mufarrij sat and watched the installation. He'd reconnoitered Evin Prison before, but he'd never been assigned to break into the penitentiary. Now his orders were to do whatever it took to free the Israeli woman who had been with Thomas Lourds.

'You are sure this man will come here?' Haytham sat across the table from Mufarrij. His name translated into young hawk, and he resembled the predatory bird in his hooked nose and sharp, flashing eyes. He was in his early twenties, but was a stone killer and had slit his first throat – that of a Revolutionary Guardsman who had tried to rape his sister – when he was twelve.

'Yes. The American is predictable. Once he finds out the woman is here, he will come. He won't be able to help himself.'

'I have seen this man's files. He is no warrior.'

Mufarrij smiled at that. 'It is even worse than that. The American is a romantic. He believes that good will triumph over evil.'

Haytham snorted in derision. 'And, of course, America is good.'

'Of course.'

'I suppose he is going to raise an army to allow him to break in?'

'I do not know. That is why we must be ready.' That was also why the king had allotted Mufarrij the twenty men he now commanded. The Saudi spy network had integrated with the Iranian security measures seamlessly. These days the Revolutionary Guard didn't know the Saudi spies were among them till it was far too late.

As it would be at Evin Prison.

'Do you know where the woman is being held?'

'Yes.' Mufarrij reached into his jacket and took out a sheaf of papers. 'I have drawn a map of the woman's location. She is in one of the back units. We can blow the wall in that area and reach her within seconds. However, I want it to look like we are attacking from the front of the prison.'

'To draw their security teams there?'

'Yes, but also to make the Revolutionary Guardsmen think the attack is merely that of dissidents. I don't want them to know true warriors are among them till we have blown that wall and have entered.'

'Of course. How did you come by the information?'

'The Revolutionary Guardsmen aren't the only people inside that prison. There are prisoners as well, and sometimes they are allowed to speak with their families. I spread money among some of those families this morning when they went in to visit their loved ones.' Mufarrij shrugged. 'They needed the money. I needed the information. Also, as a bonus, I am certain they knew I meant no goodwill with the knowledge I received.'

Haytham smiled. 'This is most assuredly so, my brother. But why do you not seek out this American and cast our lot in with his?'

'Because at the first opportunity the American got, he would separate from us. Once he returns to Jerusalem, and I am sure that he must because the Dome of the Rock is there, and so is the secret that we all search for, it would be far too easy for him to escape us.'

'However, if he never knows we are on his trail, we can seize the book.'

Mufarrij nodded. 'Our goals are not his goals. I do not know what he intends to do with Mohammad's Koran and the fabled Scroll when he finds them other than to make sure the Ayatollah doesn't get it. But we must have it.'

Haytham scowled. 'Is it as dangerous as I have heard?'

Taking a moment to think, Mufarrij sipped his tea. 'From what I have been told about the legend of Mohammad's lost Koran and Scroll, that Scroll outlines a worldwide *jihad*. We know that the Ayatollah has been stockpiling nuclear weapons he has received from Klaus

Von Volker. If the Ayatollah can construe the Scroll to call for the destruction of the West and all nonbelievers, he can convince his followers to use those weapons. Even if he can't control God's vengeance to smite his enemies as he wishes, the Ayatollah can unleash enough destruction to change the face of the world forever.'

Haytham grimaced. 'Then we have a most urgent mission upon us.'

'Now you see.' Mufarrij turned his gaze back to Evin Prison. 'First we make sure the American and the Israeli woman are free to pursue their objective, then we kill any of the Ayatollah's dogs who stand in our way as we take the Book and the Scroll.'

'The American might not part with those things when he finds them. What do we do then?'

Mufarrij shrugged. 'We kill him if we must. We were not assigned to this to fail.'

Evin Prison
Evin District
Tehran, the Islamic Republic of Iran
August 13, 2011

Screams from a man in horrible pain woke Miriam. She sat huddled in a corner of the cell, no longer shackled to the ceiling. Her relocation wasn't a kindness on part of the Revolutionary Guard. Her body could only take so much pain before rendering her unconscious. She had reached her limits and passed out routinely within moments of being hung from the ceiling.

That had been frustrating for her torturers. She didn't think of them as jailers. That wasn't what they were doing in Evin Prison. She tried not to think of all the horror stories she'd heard about the place, but she couldn't keep the tales from her mind.

Now she sat only in her soaked panties, the floor still wet from the last round with the hose.

The man screamed again, hoarsely. Then someone shouted questions. 'Where is the book, Professor Namati?'

There was a mumbled reply, then the man yelled again.

'You will tell me what I wish to know, dog. If you lie to me again, we will cut off another toe.'

Cringing, Miriam pulled her knees up to her chin and wrapped her arms around her legs for warmth and protection. She imagined Namati as he had been the previous day, as arrogant and swaggering as Lourds was in his own way. Maybe even more so, because Lourds wasn't as consciously aware of it.

'Where is Professor Lourds?'

'I don't know.' The hoarse answer echoed through the hallways and prison cells. 'Please . . . please don't hurt me anymore.'

Hearing the man beg for his life was horrible. Miriam could close her eyes and block out the sight of the cell, but she couldn't close her ears.

'You were in contact with Lev Strauss.'

'Strauss was a friend. Nothing more.'

'He told you about the book containing information about Mohammad's sacred Koran and Scroll.'

'That's only a story, a legend.'

'So now you contradict your God?'

'That's not what I meant.'

'Then you contradict the Prophet?'

'No!'

'But you refuse to admit that the Ayatollah is next to God.'

'No!'

'Then tell me where the book is.'

Namati moaned and cried. Panic and pain twisted his voice, twisting it into something inhuman.

'Take another toe. We will have the truth from this dog or we will have him dead.'

'No! No! Please!'

A crunching sound pealed through the hallways, punctuated by a strangled cry of pain that ended abruptly.

'Is he dead?'

'No, Colonel. Only passed out.'

'Rouse him. When he's awake, cut off another toe for passing out.'

'Yes, sir.'

Miriam retreated inside her head, summoning up memories of her father, something solid and reassuring to cling to. The two men she'd killed in the Himalayas no longer haunted her, and she accepted that some men had to be killed. If she had the opportunity to kill Davari, she knew she wouldn't hesitate.

Footsteps scraped the wet floor, and she knew that the colonel had reentered the room even before he spoke. 'Well, spy? Are you ready to talk now?'

Miriam forced herself to open her eyes and look at him. 'I've said everything you want me to say.'

'You have not told me where the book is.'

'I don't know.'

'You have not told me where Lourds is.'

'Again, I don't know.'

Davari grinned. 'You have not admitted that you're a spy.'

'I'm a scholar. I'm here to learn about archaeological history.' Miriam didn't know why she clung so fiercely to that lie. Some part of her hung on to her anger just to spite him, and she couldn't believe her fear hadn't outweighed that yet.

Or maybe, if she admitted that, she would be less in her own eyes.

'I am not being gentle with the professor.'

'Hurting him isn't doing any good. If he knew anything, he would have told you.'

Davari shrugged. 'Probably. It does not matter. I am going to kill him anyway. In the meantime, his misery can work to further torture you. That is enough.'

'Colonel?'

'Yes.'

'The prisoner is awake again.'

Davari stared at Miriam. 'I will be back. Then I will ask these questions once more. It will not be pleasant.'

45

Evin Prison
Evin District
Tehran, the Islamic Republic of Iran
August 13, 2011

Lourds hated the handcuffs pinning his hands behind his back. He tried to find a comfortable position for them and couldn't. The fact that he couldn't see through the blindfold bothered him tremendously as well. 'I think the handcuffs are too tight. My hands are going numb.'

The two men in the front seats and the two men beside him in the back of the car didn't say anything.

'Did you hear me?'

'Professor Lourds, you must be patient. If this ruse is to work, you must play your part.'

Lourds tried to focus on that. He was playing a part. He wasn't really a prisoner. They were just faking it. But that fact kept rattling around in his head and wouldn't leave him alone either.

'How are you going to fake your way around the guards at the prison? They know the personnel there. There are checkpoints. Identifications.'

'Let us worry about that.'

That was easy to say. Those men weren't sitting in the backseat handcuffed and blindfolded. 'No matter how good your forgeries are, they won't be good enough.'

'I think we should have gagged him as well.' That was from the driver, but the other two men joined him in laughing.

The laughter didn't sound quite right, though. It was thin and strained. Lourds thought back to all the James Bond films he'd seen. Every time 007 penetrated a villain's secret base under false pretenses, he was always caught. Bond was a lethal secret agent, though, and the script was always written in his favor. Lourds's blood felt like it was about to congeal in his veins.

'Reza really didn't have time to tell me much about you people when he introduced us. Shortly after that, you put me in handcuffs and the blindfold, and told me we were going to the prison.'

The car slowed.

'Please be silent, Professor Lourds. You are supposed to be a prisoner. Prisoners are either scared silent or they whine incessantly about their innocence.'

'I do not care for whining.' That was the driver again.

The passenger snorted with laughter.

Lourds lifted an eyebrow and tried to peer under the blindfold. All he could make out was the car window, the darkness beyond, and the pool of light ahead.

A moment later, the car rolled to a gentle stop. Footsteps crunched on gravel, and the driver rolled his window down.

'Sediq, back again?' The greeting came from outside the car.

'I am, Hamid. God was watching over us tonight. We found the professor Colonel Davari is searching for.' That came from the driver.

A flashlight beam shone in Lourds's face, and it was bright enough to hurt his blindfolded eyes. He closed them and felt all hope leaving his body. Reza had tricked him. Something must have happened, for Lourds had believed the young man about his lost love.

'So this is the famous Professor Lourds.'

'Yes.'

'The colonel will be very glad to see him. You will probably get a bonus for this.'

'I hope so.'

'How did you find him?'

'We were having dinner at a restaurant. This fool walked in tired and hungry and scared.'

'Did you let him eat?'

'No.'

'Too bad. A condemned man should have a last meal.'

Lourds tried to swallow, but his mouth was dry. He'd been such a fool for trusting Reza. Then again, he couldn't really blame the young man. He hadn't asked for Lourds to dump the story on him. He'd only been protecting his best interests. If the roles had been reversed, Lourds didn't know if he would have risked his neck to save someone viewed as a criminal in his country.

'Proceed, Sediq, and if the colonel sees fit to bless you with a bonus, remember who your friends are.'

'Always, Hamid.'

Metal shrieked, and Lourds imagined the big metal gates parting in front of the car. Then they drove through.

In the darkness beyond the security lights surrounding Evin Prison, Mufarrij lay on his stomach and watched the car entering the security gates. He trained his night-vision binoculars on the car's occupants, missing Lourds in the backseat the first time because of the blindfold and the fact that the man wasn't wearing his ugly hat.

But there was no doubt that it was the American professor.

Mufarrij tapped the radio's transmit button on his bulletproof vest. 'Be advised, the American is inside the prison. We will give them twenty minutes to put him away. Then we're going in.'

His teams quickly checked in and confirmed the order.

Moving as gracefully as a leopard, Mufarrij rose to his feet. Staying hunkered over, he trotted to the back of the prison and joined the team at the rear corner. They'd taken out the perimeter guards to climb the outer wall, but that wouldn't go unnoticed for long. Thankfully, it didn't have to. God willing, Davari would detain Lourds in the same area as the woman.

He ran his hands over the AK-47 he carried, trailed

them over the pistols he had belted at his waist and chest, and checked his watch once more.

The countdown was ticking down. He felt loose and ready, and he was going to kill as many of his enemies as he could.

Tonight, there would be no mercy.

'Okay, time to go.' The man to Lourds's right caught his elbow and tugged.

Awkwardly, Lourds got out of the car and stood awaiting other orders. His mind raced, and he wondered what he was going to do. Living to see the morning seemed suddenly optimistic.

Then the man holding him removed the handcuffs. 'I need you to keep playing the game, Professor. Do you understand?'

'Yes.'

'Do not talk. Just listen.'

'You people are really guards here, aren't you?'

The man slapped the back of Lourds's head. 'Shut up, or you will get us all killed. As for who we are, we are men who believe democracy is the only way for our country. We must get rid of the Ayatollah. Tonight, we are risking our lives because Reza tells us you can help make that happen.'

'I will. Are you going to take off the blindfold, too?'

'Shut up. The blindfold stays in place. You are supposed to be a prisoner. We are not supposed to be nice to you.'

'Okay.'

The man sighed.

'Sorry.'

'I am putting a pistol in your waistband. Do you know how to use a pistol?'

'I'm not really a gun guy.'

'Would you prefer a knife?'

'Not a knife guy either.'

'Then what?'

'Pick a language. I'll conjugate any verb you want so fast it will make your head spin.'

'You must be fun at parties.'

'Ones where munitions aren't involved? You bet.'

Something cold and hard and heavy slid into the back of Lourds's pants. It was a decidedly uncomfortable feeling.

'All right. We are taking you inside. We should be able to get you back to where your friend is.'

Lourds nodded.

'Start walking.'

As he moved in step with the man, guided by the hand on his elbow, Lourds tried not to think of what these men had probably done while they'd been guards at the prison. They were Reza's friends. They were helping him save Miriam.

Please let her still be alive and whole.

Lourds walked, sensing as the lights changed around him. He remained silent as his 'captors' filled out the necessary forms and passed through the checkpoints.

He still didn't know how the men hoped to get him and Miriam back out of the prison even though they were guards there. Doubtless Miriam was under lock and key, and Lourds would be as well.

He only hoped Lev's book was still in the air duct at the hotel. Surely, the Revolutionary Guards would have sent someone to search the room after he'd left.

And he still had to get Namati's al-Buraq figurine.

One thing at a time. Just stay alive, and you'll figure out a way.

Only a short distance farther on, after passing though after a half dozen turns and two more electronic gates, the man next to Lourds removed the blindfold.

'Be ready. And when you must, shoot to kill.'

'*When*? Not *if*?'

The man didn't reply. He took out his sidearm and drew back the action. Then he freed a knife with a curved blade.

Walking a bit farther, they paused at an office. One of the other men unfolded a sheaf of papers and handed them to a guard sitting at a desk, watching security monitors. 'Your lucky night, I see. The colonel will be happy to see your prisoner, Foad.' The man flipped one of the pages as Foad stepped behind him. A knife flashed briefly in Foad's hand as he slit the security man's throat.

Lourds stood there frozen, not believing the cold-blooded killing he'd just witnessed.

Foad grabbed the dying man's hair and shoved his face into the desk, preventing him from standing and fighting in the small room. Crimson sprayed over the desk and the monitors.

'Go, Adan!'

'God be with you, Foad.' The man holding Lourds's arm tugged him into motion. They rounded another corner. A uniformed guard stood in front of a door. He looked over at them and yawned, then smiled and waved.

Without a word, Adan left Lourds and took a step toward the man and drove his knife up under the guard's jaw. The blade slid through the soft palate and into the man's brain. He died as he was falling.

Horrified, Lourds watched as Adan grabbed the dead man's radio earbud and an electronic key from the dead man's pocket. Adan shoved the key into the door's reader and waited for the light to turn green before slipping the dead bolts free. He pushed the door open and motioned Lourds inside.

Heart beating rapidly, Lourds entered the room and spotted Miriam huddled in the corner. At first he thought she was dead. Then she stood and tried to approach him. Chains mounted on the wall kept her from taking more than a few steps.

'Thomas . . .' Her voice was hoarse and ragged. Bruises marred her face, and all she wore was a pair of red panties.

Lourds went to her, not knowing what to say or do. Instantly, she wrapped her arms around him and pressed her cold body up against his. Warm tears trickled down her swollen face. Anger and sadness swelled in a knot at the back of Lourds's throat. He turned to the two men with him. 'Can someone get these chains off her?'

Adan dragged his kill into the dark prison cell. The other man produced a picklock set, crossed to Miriam, and got to work on her cuffs.

In a few seconds, Miriam was free. 'You came for me.'

'I did.'

'I knew if anyone did, it would be you.'

Before he could reply, the dull roars of several explosions filled the prison cell.

46

Evin Prison
Evin District
Tehran, the Islamic Republic of Iran
August 13, 2011

The shaped charges at the back of the prison building worked perfectly, creating a smoke-filled crater Mufarrij could have driven a tank through. The shattered wall burst apart in broken chunks.

Mufarrij pulled a scarf over his lower face to block the dust, then stepped into the prison, his AK-47 leading the way.

A man coughed to the left, and Mufarrij turned with his finger on the trigger. The emaciated body and dulled eyes belonged to a prisoner, though. The man lay unmoving on a thin mattress on the floor and watched with little interest. He lifted one sticklike arm.

'Water. Please. Water.'

Mufarrij ignored the man and pressed on. The blast was supposed to allow them entrance to a hallway. Instead, he stood in a prison cell. Their intel had been off. That would cause complications, which he hoped wouldn't snowball.

On the other side of the bars, two dazed guards started to pick themselves up. Seeing him, their hands fumbled for their dropped weapons.

Mufarrij shot them, hitting both men with short, controlled bursts that drove them back and burst their hearts and lungs. Some of the rounds danced between the steel bars, striking sparks. One of the ricochets flattened further against Mufarrij's body armor.

At the door, he pulled out a shaped charge, slapped it onto the locked door, and activated the three-second timer. When he stepped back, the six men following him stepped back as well. They worked as a unit, as he had trained them.

The charge exploded, blowing the locking mechanism to bits. The door swung open, clanging against the far wall.

Mufarrij went through, holding the assault rifle close to his body. At the corner ahead of them, a guard peered around and pointed a pistol at the advancing Saudi strike team.

Never breaking stride, Mufarrij stitched a short burst at the man. One of the rounds struck the wall, and the next two smashed the Guardsman's face into pieces and pitched the corpse into the hallway. Mufarrij stepped over the dead man and took a quick look into the hall beyond.

Three Guardsmen held the corridor. Their rifle rounds smacked into the walls, ceiling, and floor, one bullet nicking Mufarrij's right ear. He pulled back, warm blood spilling down his neck, and motioned to the squad member who carried an AK-47 outfitted with a GP-30 Obuvka.

The man nodded, readied the underbarrel grenade launcher, and pointed it out into the hallway. He fired immediately and ducked back to cover.

When the grenade exploded, filling the hallway with a deafening *BOOM!*, Mufarrij wheeled around the corner with the assault rifle snugged tight against his shoulder. One of the three men staggered out from the wall and lifted his weapon. Mufarrij put a short burst into him, dropping the guard where he stood, and kept going.

Waking up from his rest in one of the unoccupied cells – which were growing fewer every day – Colonel Davari ran to the main prison security network headquarters. He carried a rifle he'd taken from one of the Guardsmen along the way.

'What is going on?'

The three Guardsmen manning the security cameras talked rapidly into their microphones, trying to organize the security details. They sat tensely at their workstations, juggling between the different cameras with their keyboards and joysticks.

Davari crossed to the officer in charge, a hard-faced man who had served the prison for a dozen years. 'Wafaei, what is happening?'

'The prison has been attacked.'

'I can see that!' Davari's gaze raked the monitors.

A full-scale offensive lit up the front of the prison. Heavy weapons fired on the tall security wall, knocking down sections, shorting out electricity. On one of the screens, a Guardsman returning fire was standing beneath one of the wall sections as it came down. One moment he was there, the next he was gone, buried under hundreds of pounds of rock and concrete rubble. 'Who's attacking us?'

'We do not know.'

'Have you seen them?'

Wafaei crossed to one of the workstations and took over the keyboard. He tapped keys, and the image blanked. 'This is all we have seen.'

A new window opened on the computer monitor. Three men caught by the security cameras as they crept close to the wall. They wore *thobes*, but those served only to disguise the weapons they carried. When they were challenged by a Guardsman walking his post, the men reacted immediately. One shot the Guardsmen while the other two pulled out rocket launchers, took aim at the guard posts at either end of the wall, and fired. They were already pulling back before the rockets struck their targets.

'They took out the sniper teams in the front.' Wafaei wiped sweat from his face.

'I have eyes. I can see for myself.'

The image closed and returned to real time as another wave of rockets smashed into the front of the main building.

'These men are too well trained, too well equipped to simply be rebels.' Davari thought furiously. 'They have specific goals in mind.' He gestured toward the computer. 'Bring up the security camera in Miriam Abata's cell.'

Wafaei checked a printout from his uniform blouse and spoke to the computer tech. 'Cell Ten.'

A window opened on the computer, but it remained blank and gray.

The tech entered the command sequence again, but got the same result. 'The camera is offline.'

Another tech whirled around in his chair. 'The rear of the prison has just been breached, Colonel. There are reports of casualties and an invading force.'

Cursing, Davari took one of the walkie-talkies from a nearby table, hooked it to a bulletproof vest, and pulled the vest on. He shoved the earpiece into his ear. 'Keep me in the loop, Wafaei.'

'I will.'

Davari returned to the hallway and called to a half dozen Guardsmen who looked like they'd just gotten out of bed. 'You men, come with me.'

They turned toward him.

'There are armed men at the rear of the prison. We are going to find them and kill them.' Davari turned and ran through the hallway, heading for the confrontation.

Adan turned to Lourds, his face pensive. He'd been listening to the prison frequency on a headset. 'Someone else has broken into the prison – it is also under attack from an outside force.'

'Gonna be a busy night.' Lourds looked around the cell for Miriam's clothing, but couldn't find it. He took off his Oxford and handed it to her. 'I'm sorry. It's the best I can do.'

Gratefully, Miriam took his shirt and pulled it on. It was far too big, but the tails dropped to just above her knees and preserved some of her modesty.

Meanwhile, Adan had been stripping one of the dead guards of his boots. When he had them off, he tossed the pair to Miriam. 'Put those on.'

Miriam laced the boots on, looking like a very frightened orphan.

Adan waved to Lourds. 'Follow me. We will go very quickly now. If we do not hurry, we will be caught between the two forces.'

'We need to find Professor Namati.'

Miriam shivered. 'He's down the hall. They've been torturing him.'

Adan glanced at the other man. 'Shahram, go see.'

The other man went, and Lourds was at Shahram's heels. If the Guardsmen had been torturing Namati, the professor probably wouldn't be able to walk unassisted.

When he saw Namati limply hanging from the chains attached to the ring in the ceiling, the light glazing his dead eyes white, Lourds knew they were too late to save the man.

Namati was slack-jawed in death. Burns showed black across his naked body. Someone had cut off all his toes, which lay scattered around the floor. Cables from a car battery were clipped to the mutilated stumps as he hung inches above the floor.

'Oh my God.'

Hearing Miriam's voice right behind him, Lourds wheeled around and grabbed her by the shoulders, hustling her back out of the cell and the horror that hung there.

Unable to control herself, Miriam shook. Lourds tried to help her, but she just pushed him away. 'I can do this.' She wiped tears from her bruised face. 'Let's go.'

Lourds nodded to Adan, and they headed out. Miriam knelt beside the dead man whose boots she wore. She stripped his pistol from his holster, checked it with amazing proficiency for a graduate student, then plucked two spare magazines from the dead man's pockets. When she stood again, the tears were gone, and a cold fury had settled over her features.

Adan stared at her for a moment, then nodded and spoke in Farsi. 'You have the heart of a lioness.'

'This lioness is pissed now.' Miriam stepped in front of Lourds, took a position to Adan's right and a two-handed grip on the pistol, and trotted after the guard in her too-big boots.

Remembering the pistol tucked into his waistband, Lourds drew the weapon and felt immediately foolish. He had never shot anyone and wasn't planning on starting today. When they paused at an intersection, he leaned close to Miriam. 'Can you use another pistol?'

She looked at the gun in his hand, then at his face. 'Won't you need that?'

'I don't shoot people.'

She took the pistol and flicked off the safety. 'After everything I've been through last night and today, after seeing Professor Namati, I know there are people that need to be shot in here.'

Lourds didn't know what to say. That certainly wasn't the attitude he got from most graduate students he'd known. But he didn't doubt her words for a moment.

They crept forward again. The hardest thing for Lourds was leaving behind all the poor souls trapped in the steel cages. Most of them looked to be at death's door, miserable and suffering from malnutrition, many carrying horrible scars. The worst of the lot were those that simply lay in bed or sat on the floor and acted like nothing was going on, devoid of all hope.

Adan listened intently on the headset, waiting for a moment at the next intersection, then glanced down the hallway to the left. 'Foad is joining us. We have to find another way out of the building.'

In the next instant, Foad rounded the far corner at a dead run. 'They're coming!'

Adan lifted his rifle to fire, but hesitated an instant too long when four men rounded the corner in pursuit of Foad. One of them fired, and he fell.

Lourds reached for Miriam, intending to pull her

back to safety. She eluded him and thrust both pistols forward, standing over Adan. 'Get down!'

Foad dove to the floor. As soon as he was clear, Miriam opened fire. The pistols bucked and thundered in her fists, sounding as rapid as a machine gun. Both weapons locked back empty at the same time. Calmly, she tucked one under her arm and reloaded the pistol in her hand, chambering a round. Then she loaded and readied the other one as Adan and Foad climbed to their feet.

At the other end of the hall, the four Guardsmen lay dead. At least three of the four were down with multiple headshots.

'I thought I was dead.' Foad looked shaken as he picked his rifle up from the floor.

'I've never seen anything like that.' Adan tentatively tested his bloody shoulder with a wince. Evidently the wound was messy but not debilitating, because his movement wasn't restricted.

Lourds stared at the young woman.

'Hours and hours of xBox 360.' Miriam turned to Adan. 'We need to get out of here.'

Adan took the lead again, with Miriam running by his side. Shaking his head, Lourds followed, while Foad and Shahram watched their rear.

47

Evin Prison
Evin District
Tehran, the Islamic Republic of Iran
August 13, 2011

'I've hacked into the prison's closed-circuit TV.'

Mufarrij ducked as men inside an office area fired at him. Squatting, he took shelter behind a low wall. Unclipping a grenade from his Kevlar vest, he pulled the pin, released the spoon, counted off two seconds, and heaved it over the heads of the men firing at him.

The grenade went off, and shrapnel spun out in razor-sharp pieces that dotted the walls and turned the Revolutionary Guards into bloody rags.

'Find Lourds.' Mufarrij stood and ran into the office, killing the survivors before they could do anything to save themselves.

'I'm tracking people now. The inside of the building is very confusing. I am having to make up a legend so I know which camera is which.'

'You are talking far too much.'

'I have you now. There is an ambush ahead of you. Is that talking too much?'

Mufarrij grinned despite the dangerous circumstances. Death and he were old acquaintances. There was no fear of dying in him any more. That had been worn away on far more battlefields than he could remember. Only the fear of failure remained now.

He pulled up short at the next doorway and waved the men following him into position. He freed another grenade. 'Is the ambush to the left or right?'

'Left. About eight meters down.'

'Find Lourds.' Mufarrij leaned around the doorway and threw the grenade, bouncing it off the far wall.

After the deafening blast, wounded men cried out in fear and pain.

Mufarrij swung around the doorway and opened fire, blazing through one magazine, then pulling back to reload. As he did, Haytham slid out into the hallway and emptied his magazine as well.

There were no survivors after that.

Striding out into the hallway slick with blood and body parts, Mufarrij kept going.

'I have Lourds. He and the men – and woman – with him have reached an emergency exit area. They're meeting heavy resistance.'

'Where?'

'I will guide you. Continue down the hallway you are in now.'

Mufarrij increased his pace to a jog. Lourds needed to go free. The Ayatollah's butchers would not be allowed to get him. He followed the intel officer's directions, turning again and again, making his way through rows of pitiful wrecks who had once been human.

When Mufarrij rounded the final turn, he arrived at the intersection at the same time as a group of Revolutionary Guardsmen. Recognizing their leader as an old enemy, he brought up his rifle.

Just as triumph seemed imminent, Davari's good feelings vanished when he saw a hated face appear in front of him. The security people had tracked Lourds, the woman, and the traitors to the emergency exit leading to the prison hospital. A separate entrance was used there to keep the prison populace under guard at all times. A narrow, barred walkway crossed to the hospital.

Just as Davari was about to close the trap and seize the American, Rayan Mufarrij appeared as if dropped there by Shaitan himself. Davari recognized the Saudi even though a scarf covered the lower half of the face.

It was the vilest of tricks. Mufarrij had killed two of Davari's brothers and many friends over the years of the war between the Sunni and Shiite Muslims. In the intervening years, the man had been a ghost, appearing to strike against Iran many times, then vanishing like he'd never existed.

Davari dodged to the side, and the bullets Mufarrij had intended for him pulped the face of the Guardsman standing behind him. Bringing up his weapon even while falling, he fired and watched in satisfaction as his line of bullets stitched up Mufarrij's chest, and his head snapped backwards in a rush of crimson.

'Die, Mufarrij!' Davari rolled to cover, then got up and ran as one of the Saudis threw a grenade into the area.

Instead of shrapnel, though, the grenade spewed dark red tear gas. The choking haze filled the hallway, searing Mufarrij's lungs, nose, and eyes. Through his tears, he glanced back at the hallway, but could no longer see Lourds and the traitors.

'Wafaei!' Davari hacked and choked as the tear gas burned him. 'Wafaei!'

'I am here, Colonel.'

'I have lost the American. Where is he?' Davari roped an arm over his lower face in an effort to cut down the effects of the tear gas. That didn't help his eyes, and they watered incessantly.

'I have locked the emergency door. They cannot escape.'

'Good. Make sure the men know I want the American alive.' Davari put a fresh magazine into his assault rifle as Wafaei broadcast the instructions. Then the colonel readied himself for when the cursed smoke thinned enough to proceed.

Adan threw himself against the emergency door, but only bounced off.

Lourds bulled up against the door with the man, intending to use his greater bulk to power through the door. He set himself. 'Again. Together. On three.' The tear gas was leaching the oxygen from his lungs and blurring his vision. He coughed through one and two, then they hit the door with their shoulders at the same time.

The door didn't move.

'They've locked it.'

Wincing, Lourds drew back and looked at the door. A small mesh-screened window was inset high on the door, not large enough to crawl through.

'We're trapped.' Adan turned back toward the hallway, where two groups were momentarily held at bay.

Lourds had been surprised when the two groups had started firing at each other. That had been a bit of luck, but it hadn't been enough to get them to freedom.

Foad talked into one of the walkie-talkies. When he finished, he looked at Adan. 'Sediq is still with the car. No one has bothered him.' He coughed and wiped tears away.

'Get him over here.'

Foad spoke into the walkie-talkie again, then shook his head. 'If we can't get out, having him over here won't do any good.'

'Thomas Lourds!'

Startled by hearing his name on a stranger's lips, Lourds whirled around and spotted a barely-visible man with a bloody face, wild hair and beard, and an assault rifle leaning against the wall.

Adan jerked his weapon up and fired. Miriam held her fire, but she was ready as well.

The bullets thudded into the wall where the man's head had been a moment earlier. Out of view, his voice carried to them. 'When the lights go out, the door will open. You must go before the generators come online. We will cover your exit. Do you understand?'

'Yes.' Tensely, Lourds waited, one shoulder still pushing against the door.

Head throbbing in agony, Mufarrij gave the command over his headset. 'Blow the generators.' He gripped his assault rifle, willing himself to stand despite the dizziness that swept over him. Davari's bullet had glanced off his skull and left a deep, bleeding gouge behind.

A huge, dulled *thump* sounded outside, then the lights inside the prison dimmed, then went out. It was pitch-black for a moment, then the battery-powered security lights came on.

Mufarrij knew it would only be a few seconds before the prison's power came back on. He heaved a pair of grenades into the hallway where he'd seen Davari. As the explosions blasted the dimness with bright light, Mufarrij saw Lourds and his group running out the security door.

Mufarrij fired into the hallway, but a barrage of return fire zipped through the air. He'd considered trying to get out the same way as the American, but couldn't get there without being shot by Davari or perhaps even Lourds's companions. Mufarrij resolved to extricate himself and try to catch Lourds again. There were only so many ways out of the country for a man the Ayatollah's butchers were searching for. He knew them all.

Frustrated, Davari pulled back from the hallway as the Saudis hammered the area with grenades and bullets. He'd had Lourds within his grasp. Then, when the power had gone off, the security door had unlocked. And just that quick, the American had escaped from the building.

But not necessarily the grounds.

Davari ran back toward the security point. 'Wafaei! Get troops to the hospital entrance! The fugitives have escaped that way! Hurry!'

When the door opened as the lights went out, Lourds pushed through in a rush and almost stumbled. He got his balance back and whirled around to grab the door and keep it open. As he caught it, the security lights inside the building flashed on. He expected a bullet to cut him down at any moment, especially when more gunfire erupted and what sounded like grenades exploded in the hallway opposite the bearded, wounded man.

Adan came through next, followed by Miriam, Foad, and Sediq. Lourds held the door open a moment longer, thinking the bearded man might try to follow them, but the gunfire was loud and dangerous. When bullets started whining off the open door, he realized the Revolutionary Guardsmen were shooting at them. He pushed the door closed and heard the electronic locks click back into place.

'Come on.' Adan grabbed Lourds and pulled him into motion.

Lourds caught up to Miriam and ran beside her, ready to help in case she tripped in the too-big boots.

Near the front of the prison, a car with one headlight roared through a downed section of the wall. It skidded to a stop on the rough terrain, drifting well past the fugitives.

Adan opened the rear passenger door. 'Get in.'

Foad ran around to the other side and opened that door. Lourds loaded Miriam into the backseat, then slid in beside her. Shahram jumped into the front seat, joined by Adan, and Sediq tromped on the accelerator. The car hesitated just a moment, then roared forward.

Turning the wheel sharply, Sediq pointed the vehicle back toward the impromptu entrance.

'Someone is coming!' Adan peered behind them, his face tightened by fear.

Glancing back, Lourds spotted a military vehicle gaining quickly on them. Bright flashes came from the windows, right before the first bullets rattled the escape car's body and shattered the back window.

In the next instant, the Revolutionary Guards' vehicle blew up and overturned. It flipped three times, throwing flaming bodies in all directions, and finally came to a stop on its side as Sediq drove them back across the downed prison wall.

Adan looked at Lourds. 'Who was that man that called your name?'

Lourds shook his head. 'I don't know. A fan? Those people turn up in the oddest places.'

A white grin split Adan's smoke-smeared face. 'You are crazy.'

'After tonight, I wouldn't doubt it.' Lourds looked behind them to see if anyone else was pursuing them.

No one did.

'Whoever that man is, he knows you, Professor Lourds. I do not know if he means you good or evil, but I do not think you have seen the last of him.'

Lourds assumed that as well. He'd seen the maniacal look in the man's eyes.

Head pounding, senses swimming, Mufarrij jogged from the prison as fast as he could move. As soon as he exited the hole in the back wall, four vehicles sped in from the front of the prison. No Revolutionary Guardsmen left alive inside the prison came out to challenge them.

His men got in, carrying their dead with them. They had lost six of their brothers in arms. It was a high price to pay.

'Where do we go now?' Haytham sat beside Mufarrij in the rear seat of the car.

'There is only one place the American can go if he wishes to escape Tehran and the wrath of the Ayatollah.'

'The Kurd lands.'

'Yes. We will follow.' Mufarrij mopped blood from his face with his sleeve.

'And when we find him?'

'We keep him safe. Davari is involved in this.'

'I know that name. He is a colonel among the Guardsmen.'

Mufarrij nodded and instantly regretted the action, as his head pounded. 'Davari is a very dedicated warrior who serves the Ayatollah. Also a very dangerous man.'

'So I have been told.'

'Evidently he has been assigned to find the American and bring him before the Ayatollah. Davari will not quit until he has Lourds or he himself is dead.'

Haytham smiled coldly. 'There is no reason we cannot arrange the latter. It will only be a matter of timing, my friend.'

48

Young Revolutionaries' Safe House
Tehran, the Islamic Republic of Iran
August 15, 2011

When Miriam woke, she saw Lourds sitting at the small desk in the corner of the basement room they were hiding in. Reza and his friends were working out the details of the rescue effort to get Lourds and her out of the country. One of Reza's people had already retrieved the book hidden in Lourds's former hotel room.

The story about the prison break-in – touted as an attack by US- and Israeli-backed terrorists in the Iranian papers and media – was all over the news. They also declared the Revolutionary Guardsmen had provided a good accounting of themselves, killing upward of a hundred of their attackers.

The tale had been concocted to account for the damage that had been done, to make the Guardsmen look better, to refute the idea that a small force could have reduced the place to shambles, and to explain all of the bodies coming out. Whoever the other team was, they had been lethally efficient.

Fully dressed under the blanket in case she had to get

up and bolt at a moment's notice, Miriam watched Lourds working. She didn't know if he'd slept on the thin pallet Reza had provided beside the small bed she slept in.

Fresh scrapes and bruises showed on his face and arms. Every now and again, he touched his face and jerked as pain sliced through him. It reminded her that he wasn't a soldier – or a Mossad agent – used to hardship and injury.

He leaned back in the chair and stretched, and she wondered at how he could put in such inhuman hours. After Reza had gotten Professor Namati's statue of al-Buraq from his office, Lourds had been extremely excited, and had even told her that he'd figured out how to break the code in the book.

But, as the hours had stretched on, he'd become more dispirited and morose. The solution hadn't come as easily as he'd expected.

He leaned back now, putting his hands on his forehead and staring up at the featureless ceiling. He was lost, she knew, tangled somewhere in all the evaluations and permutations of his thoughts. She felt sorry for him.

She could only guess how afraid he'd been to go along with the risky plan the former Revolutionary Guardsmen had come up with to break into the prison and get her out.

But, in the end, he'd been there.

It said a lot about him.

'Stuck?'

Startled out of his reverie, he turned and looked at her. 'Good morning.'

'Is it?'

'Beg pardon?'

'Morning. I've lost all track of time.'

'It is.' Lourds looked at his satphone. 'No. I'm wrong. It's two in the afternoon.'

'Have you slept?'

'Yes.'

'Much?'

'Not really.' Lourds gestured at the book and the statue. 'I don't like being stymied. It's always part of the process, but I've never gotten used to it.'

Miriam threw the blanket back and swung her legs over the side of the bed. 'Would you explain what you were talking about with the flying horse again? I can barely remember yesterday.' She'd slept most of yesterday, with her pistols under her pillow and Lourds in the room with her.

'Why don't I go get us something to eat, and we can talk over lunch. You haven't eaten very much, and I'm famished.'

'You're always famished.'

Lourds showed her a mock scowl, then headed for the corner of the room where the ladder led up to the house above them. He knocked, was allowed to exit, and went up.

Miriam lay back on the bed and stared at the winged horse.

*

She awoke again when Lourds sat on the bed. Her hand curled on the butt of one of the pistols almost before she realized it.

Lourds grimaced, knowing what had happened. 'I've never had a graduate student quite like you.'

Feeling slightly embarrassed, not sure if Lourds's naïveté was genuine or not, Miriam left the pistol under the pillow and sat up.

He held a plate loaded with food. 'I thought we could share.' He handed it to Miriam, who balanced it on her crossed legs.

Lourds got up and returned with the statue and the book. 'Lev caught onto the secret behind the code before I did. Maybe it was something he saw or something he read. Maybe he read Sahih al-Maliki's name and realized that the man had made the statue of al-Buraq that Professor Namadi had, I don't know. Perhaps he learned we're starting with different theories in our translations.' He held up the winged horse. 'The code is with the horse.'

Leaving the food alone for the moment, Miriam took the horse and examined it. It felt heavy and solid, just as she remembered it had from the previous day. 'There are no hiding places in the statue.' She hesitated. 'I think you said the secret wasn't what was *inside* the horse, but what was on the *outside*.'

'Exactly.' He captured one of her hands in his and held her fingers flat as he stroked the horse's side. At first, she felt nothing, then she noticed the small nubs, irregularities. 'Do you feel those?'

'Yes.'

'We were very fortunate. Those could have been worn away over the years. I don't think the secret of the horse and the book were supposed to be separated. They were meant to stay together. Maybe only one or two people each generation knew their secret as they were handed down. A death robbed the world of this treasure for hundreds of years or even more than a thousand. The important thing is that they're meant to be used together.'

'How?'

Lourds opened the book and laid the statue on one of the pages. He squared the horse up so it was facing toward the center of the book and the foundation matched the line drawn across the bottom of the page. 'I used a light dusting of charcoal to mark the contact points and pick out the symbols.'

When he removed the horse, six of the Farsi words on the page were marked.

Stunned, Miriam gazed at the words. 'These words are part of a hidden message?'

'Yes.'

'What's the message?'

'It's dire, I'm afraid.' Lourds cleared his throat. '"I have held the Holy Koran of the great Mohammad in my hands. I have held the scroll that is our future. A worker found them both in a secret chamber dug under the holy rock from which Mohammad ascended to the heavens. I ordered the worker killed so no word of the Great One's texts would ever be known. No man's eyes should rest upon the sacred scroll because the Great One foresees the coming of the last religious campaign to turn the world into believers. The sky will burn with great fire and explosions that will destroy cities and states. The fire will rise high into the sky and reach the heavens. The explosions will shake the earth and be heard around the world. Islam will lay waste to the armies of the nonbelievers across the world. The Scroll orders in the future a great *jihad* against all infidels using this great fire and explosion which Islam has acquired until all finally yield to the power of Islam and convert. The Christian Kingdoms shall fall first before the devastation." The author adds, "Look for the Winged Beast, and the texts of the Great One will be found."'

Miriam was surprised at how afraid the passage made her feel. 'That sounds suspiciously like nuclear weapons.'

'I know. There's another message that's repeated over and over, but I can't make sense of it. It says that the key lies in the four corners of the world.'

'Maybe it's referencing a map in the text. Isn't there a map in the book?'

'Several in fact.' Lourds flipped through the book and showed her the beautifully hand-drawn maps of Jerusalem, Mecca, Abyssinia, Yathrib – Medina, and other countries of the Arabian Peninsula. 'There's even blueprints of the Dome of the Rock.' He turned to that page, located in the center of the book, and the pages fell open evenly.

Miriam stared at the diagram of the Dome and was again taken by its beauty. The blueprint was done with a sure and steady hand, and there were even engineers drawn into it as they worked on various facets of the Dome.

'Maybe . . . maybe I translated it wrong.' Lourds's voice was hushed as he studied the drawing. 'Maybe it wasn't the four corners of the world. I was thinking world, but maybe al-Maliki was referring to the book.' He reached for one of the hinged brass corner pieces of the book.

Excitement thrilled through Miriam as she watched him work. He took out the small knife he carried and opened one of the specialty blades. Working the tip between the leather and metal, the corner piece popped off into his palm. When he opened it, forming an hourglass shape, scratches marred the smooth finish inside.

Symbols marked three of one of the piece's sides and two sides on the other. The two pieces both shared one of the symbols, and Lourds unhinged both pieces and refitted them together, matching the symbol on the first piece to its mate on the second. Delicate burrs on the sides of the pieces allowed them to fit together exactly. Engraved lines met perfectly.

'This is it.' Lourds's voice was a hoarse whisper. With meticulous care, he took apart the other three corners and opened them.

Together, they matched the symbols and fit the pieces together till they had a brass map assembled of the eight pieces. It wasn't square as Miriam had at first thought it would be, but a stair-stepped construction instead.

'Is that a cavern system?' Miriam traced the markings.

'That's what it looks like.' Lourds peered more closely at it. 'There's writing here.' He went to his backpack and drew out a magnifying glass. He turned the map to better catch the light. Then he gave the map to Miriam. 'See if you can read that.'

Miriam took the map and the magnifying glass. She struggled with the symbols, and Lourds helped her in several places. '"Where do the Souls gather in the Well and where does Mohammad see heaven?"' She looked up at Lourds in disbelief. 'You think this refers to the Well of Souls in the Dome of the Rock?'

He stared back at her. 'Don't you?'

Miriam couldn't answer. It was too fantastic. And yet, just like the corner pieces of the book, it all fit. 'There's a cavern under the Dome of the Rock?'

'According to that map, there's more than one. Mohammad's Koran and the Scroll are hidden somewhere in that cave system. If we can find the right starting point, if we can find these caves – '

'If you can get into that place without being killed.'

'If *we* can. Then we can find out if this legend is true.' Lourds looked at her. 'There may not be anything there. This might all still be just a story, you know.'

'But you don't think it is.'

'No.'

'Neither do I. Keep that thought. I've got to go. I'll be back as soon as I can.' She reached under the pillow for her pistols, tucked them into her waistband, pulled on the hated *burqa* that now served to disguise her armament, and left him standing there looking like he'd been hit with a baseball bat.

49

Covert Operations
Institute for Intelligence and Special Operations (Mossad)
Tel Aviv, Republic of Israel
August 15, 2011

The phone rang, and Sarah Shavit picked up the handset. 'Hello.'

'*Ketsas* Shavit, I have a phone call from Orchid.'

Sarah let out a sigh of relief. She had worried for the past two days, ever since Miriam Abata had abruptly gone missing. Despite years of experience as a *ketsas,* the job still took its toll because there was no way to completely divorce herself from the fears that arose on a daily basis.

'Put her through.'

Connections clicked, then Miriam was there.

'Hello, Auntie.' Miriam sounded worn, but she also sounded like she was handling herself.

'Hello. I haven't heard from you lately.'

'It's been busy here. I think you saw the troubles in the news.'

Meaning the prison attack? 'There has been some mention of local discontent.'

'I was in the middle of it.'

Sarah's stomach filled with cold lead. She'd heard the stories that came out of Evin Prison. The place was a pit of blackest evil. 'Are you all right?'

'My professor saw me through.'

'Really?' Sarah couldn't believe Lourds would have had the wherewithal to manage something like the assault on the prison.

'He's met some really good friends here. They're going to take us to our next destination.'

'The northwest section?' Meaning the Kurds.

'Yes. We thought we'd visit Turkey before we returned home.'

'I will let your uncle know to expect you.'

'Good. The professor's friends will be helpful, but I'd like to know that family is looking out for us as well.'

'They will be there.' Sarah made a quick notation of the Mossad teams she would put into the area. 'I want to send you a care package.'

'I would love something from home.'

Sarah wrote a quick e-mail to get one of the local Mossad spies to deliver an encrypted phone to Miriam. 'It will be there soon. The same place?'

'That would be fantastic.'

'What about your professor? Did he get the chance to finish his work?'

'He did, although he still needs to explore the matter further.'

'He's returning as well?'

'Yes. We hope to see you soon.'

Young Revolutionaries' Safe House
Tehran, the Islamic Republic of Iran
August 15, 2011

Despite the relative safety of his hiding place, Lourds's stomach still tightened when the trapdoor opened. He was relieved and confused when he saw Miriam descending the ladder with a bag in one hand. She'd been gone almost two hours, and he'd begun worrying about her.

'Where have you been?'

'Shopping.' Miriam dropped the *burqa* to the floor and stood there in a new blouse and business slacks. The shoes were new, too. 'I seem to lose more clothes in this country.' Without another word, she divested herself of the blouse and slacks as well, hanging those carefully over the back of a nearby chair.

She stood there in lime green bra and panties.

'I can see how you'd have a problem losing clothes.'

'Get over here, and you can help me lose these.'

Lourds got up and went to her. He kissed her deeply as he slid his arms around her. Her small, hard body pressed into his, and he felt her hunger. They kissed passionately for a time, then she started stripping him as he stood there. As she unbuttoned and unzipped his clothing, he stroked her breasts and hips, making her breath quicken in anticipation.

Then, when he was nude, she pulled him toward the bed.

'I do hope you locked the trapdoor.'

She grinned at him as she backed onto the bed. 'I told them to leave us alone unless the Revolutionary Guard comes calling.'

'I certainly hope they don't.' Lourds kissed her deeply again. 'For several reasons.' He removed her bra with a deft twist of his fingers that made her giggle in delight. Then he slid her panties off.

When he went to her, she was warm, wet, and ready. He sheathed himself and rode her tenderly, bringing her to a surprisingly quick climax that ended in tears.

'I'm sorry.' Lourds tried to back away.

She caught him and held him, smiling. 'Don't you go anywhere. I'm not done with you.' She looked up at him. 'Three days ago, I thought I was going to die. Now I want to celebrate the fact that I didn't. This . . . this is a big part of the celebration.' She grinned at him impishly. 'Bigger than I'd anticipated, actually.'

Lourds leaned down and started kissing her again, then started moving, finding her more and more accepting, till the mutual rush of pleasure swept them away.

Kurd Village
Three Miles East of Turkish Border
Oshnaviyeh (Shino), West Azarbaijan Province
The Islamic Republic of Iran
August 16, 2011

Davari stood on a craggy rock shelf and looked down at the treacherous mountain terrain. Even though the trail was used often enough to be clear, it would be hard to follow at night. But the people he sought were desperate. The American professor and the woman had been largely undetectable until a few hours ago, when one of his Kurd spies had called the Revolutionary Guards from a short-wave radio.

There had been a chance that Lourds and the traitors that helped him would get through, but Davari had spread the word – and the Ayatollah's wealth – to arrange a spotting network. The Kurds were their own people, as hard and as unforgiving as the mountains they lived in. They knew no masters and very few friends, but they appreciated the weapons Davari had offered in exchange for information.

The expedition had set out on horseback nearly eight hours ago and obviously intended to keep riding till they crossed over into Turkey a few kilometers farther north.

'Is that them?'

Davari looked back over his shoulder.

Klaus Von Volker stood in the cold, looking decidedly unhappy. He'd been a reluctant guest in the Ayatollah's palace since he still hadn't dealt with the investigation awaiting him in Austria for the attempted murder of Thomas Lourds.

'Yes.' Davari identified Lourds's hat. The American's conceit was going to be the death of him one day. The colonel waved to his men, and they took up their positions along the mountain ridge. He lifted the assault rifle and peered down at the line of horses, curling his finger around the trigger and waiting for the right moment to spring his ambush.

Hunkered down in the mountains only a few hundred meters away, Mufarrij removed the blanket he'd had covering the Dragunov SVDK sniper rifle. The weapon was a favorite of his, an upgrade from the SVD. The SVDK chambered a 9.63x64mm round capable of punching through vehicles and heavy body armor up to ten millimeters thick.

It had taken his men and him an hour to creep this close to Davari, then Mufarrij had waited till the Revolutionary Guardsmen had deployed from their vehicles and taken up positions. Mufarrij didn't want to leave any of them alive behind him to organize any kind of pursuit.

He knew he wasn't at his best. The day after the attack on Evin Prison, he didn't think he was going to survive. During the last three days, he'd been living on pain pills and antibiotics to combat the fever from his wounds. The injuries on his skull and the side of his face still looked horrible and would leave him disfigured. If it weren't for his *keffiyeh,* which he used to cover his face, he couldn't have walked around without drawing intense scrutiny.

The riders kept coming closer, unaware of the death waiting above them.

Mufarrij was frustrated that he couldn't get a clear shot at Davari. The Revolutionary Guards colonel was concealed in the rocks too well to make a good target. Mufarrij faulted himself for not taking the shot sooner, but he also wanted the chance to intercept Lourds. If he fired too soon, there'd be no chance of capturing the American at all.

But the time to act was now, before Davari and his dogs could attack.

Mufarrij put the sniper reticule over one of the Revolutionary Guardsmen and squeezed the trigger. The massive rifle recoiled against his shoulder, and the thunder of the shot echoed off the nearby mountains.

Three hundred and sixty-seven meters away, the Revolutionary Guardsman's head exploded like a smashed pumpkin. The shot initiated a barrage of fire that chopped into the riders below. A few dropped, but Lourds and the woman remained alive. Davari had surely ordered that they be left unharmed.

The riders bolted to the right, heading for shelter behind a ridgeline. A horse went down before it reached safety, but the rider ran into the rocks.

The second wave of Mufarrij's offensive lit up the night as his team fired flares into the midst of Davari's people. The Revolutionary Guards drastically outnumbered the Saudis. The flares robbed the Ayatollah's butchers of their night vision, preventing them from locating their enemies. It also kept the Guardsmen from firing on the American and the people with him.

Mufarrij searched among the bright landscape and shadows for his next target, found it, and fired again.

Lourds squatted behind a tall stand of rocks, holding the bridles of Miriam's and his mount. Both the horses were mountain-bred Kurd stock, used to warriors and weapons. They shivered in the cold night air, but didn't bolt when the gunfire began. For that, Lourds was thankful. If he didn't end up shot dead in the next few minutes, he didn't look forward to being dragged to death over the rocky terrain.

Adan dragged Foad to safety. Blood streamed from Foad's leg, and he couldn't put any weight on it.

Farther up the mountain, Miriam stood with both pistols in her fists, totally unlike any graduate assistant Lourds had ever seen. She also seemed to be talking to herself. Or maybe she was praying. That would have been the more understandable alternative.

Lourds didn't know who had shot at them from the top of the mountain, but it now seemed that the two groups were battling it out. One group was limned by flares that burned their shadows out of harsh yellow-white light.

Suddenly, the sound of far-away bumblebees filled the air. Curious, Lourds glanced up and saw aerodynamic shapes zoom across the skies. For a moment he thought he was looking at something out of science-fiction movies because what was coming at them were scaled-down, futuristic flying machines.

In the next second, however, the machines did a lot more than just fly overhead. Flashes from machine guns and rockets lit up the sky. Bullets sprayed into the rocks along the ridgeline, smashing everything they touched, flesh and blood as well as stone. Missiles dug craters in the ground and blew bodies into the air.

Drones. Lourds recognized their handiwork now. Though he'd never seen them close-up before, he'd seen documentaries and read magazine articles on the next generation of aerial weaponry.

The advantage in the battle along the ridgeline shifted dramatically. The unmanned weapons slew mercilessly, like vicious monsters out of legend whose thirst for blood would not be slaked.

Davari ran for his life. He knew the drones were from the United States or the Israelis. No one else had that kind of technology. Instead of laying a trap, he'd been lying in one. In two, actually, because he suspected the people who'd fired on his men had been the Saudis. He didn't think Mufarrij still lived – didn't know how the man could have survived being shot in the head – but someone must have taken over his unit and come after Lourds.

Scrambling along the ridge, Davari headed for one of the armored vehicles, hoping he could get away. He reached the passenger door of one as it started rolling forward, and tugged on the handle, but it was locked.

Looking inside, Davari saw Von Volker at the wheel. The Austrian glanced over at him and laughed. Davari raised his pistol, wiping the smile from Von Volker's face. The colonel fired, but the bullet only fractured the bullet-resistant glass and ricocheted away.

Laughing harder, Von Volker accelerated and drove away. Unable to keep up, Davari tripped and fell face forward just as he saw a drone fire a missile at the car. In an eye-searing instant, Von Volker died in the fiery hell unleashed by the remote-controlled weapon.

'Who has the last laugh now?' Davari lay in the shadows as the battle raged around him. There was nothing he could do to stop Lourds. They would already be making their way around the ridgeline on horseback. Even if Davari could get a car, he wouldn't be able to trail them. They could make it into Turkey on horses now.

But Davari knew where they were heading. Lourds was going back to Jerusalem – and if he had solved the mystery of Mohammad's Koran and the Scroll – the professor would only be going to one place – the Dome of the Rock.

Davari would be there waiting for him.

50

Dome of the Rock
Temple Mount
Jerusalem, the State of Israel
August 18, 2011

Lourds sat in the passenger seat of the rental car with his backpack at his feet. The morning heat was sweltering, and he felt sweat trickling under his shirt. The *thobe*, *bisht*, and *keffiyeh* he wore made the heat even more oppressive. Part of that was nerves, though.

Although he'd chafed to return to Jerusalem for the day and a half it had taken Miriam and him to get back there, now he was extremely nervous.

'Having second thoughts?' Alice sat behind the wheel. She was elegantly dressed, as befitting a happy widow.

Klaus Von Volker's death was currently the subject of an ongoing investigation that investigators felt would tie back to his proclivities for black market weapons. The consensus was that one of Von Volker's unhappy customers had blown him to smithereens – though enough of him was left over for identification. As a result, Alice wasn't just getting what she'd absconded with. She was getting it all. And widowhood seemed to agree with her.

'Oh, I'm well past second thoughts and into near panic.'

Alice reached over and took his hand. The dark sunglasses hid her eyes, but worry tightened her lips into a near frown. 'You could let someone else do this.'

Lourds saw Miriam tense up in the backseat. He wasn't sure if it was because of Alice's suggestion or the casual familiarity the older woman showed with him. Lourds suspected it might be a combination of the two and knew he might have some explaining to do later.

Provided he survived the trip into the Dome of the Rock.

'Who would I let do this?' Lourds shook his head. 'If I told the Israelis about this, and they got caught, it would turn into – at the very least – an international incident, if not a war. And I'm not interested in telling the Ayatollah that he might have the very objects that he killed Lev to obtain at his fingertips. That's not going to happen.'

'If you're caught, they may kill you.'

'If I'm caught, they'll be killing a curious American professor of linguistics who wandered into a place he shouldn't have been. That's not an international incident.' Lourds couldn't believe he was talking so casually about his own death. He told himself he was worrying needlessly, that he wasn't going to get caught.

After all, no one even knew to look for him – or Mohammad's Koran and Scroll – there.

'And if that should happen, you go to the United States embassy and give someone in the State Department all the information I've given you.' Lourds had made copies of Lev's journal and all the translations he'd rendered, including the map from the corner pieces.

'I will. But I'd much rather you come back safe and sound, whether you find anything there or not.'

Lourds gazed out at the Dome of the Rock. The octagon-shaped building looked beautiful and benign in the morning sunlight. Built in the shape of a Byzantine martyrium designed to hold saintly relics, the Dome was covered with mid-Byzantine art. The colorful mosaics included blue, white, orange, yellow, and green Iznik tiles in ornate shapes, giving the building its unique, glassy appearance.

At one point it was said that one hundred thousand dinars had been reforged into the Dome's exterior. Originally, its construction had taken seven years, but considerable effort had gone into the maintenance, too. In 1960, the Dome had required additional protection, and the distinctive aluminum and bronze alloy had been added. Cast in Italy, the metal covering shone in the bright sunlight.

'Me too.' Lourds smiled. 'I'm all about being safe and sound. It's the situations and circumstances that keep disagreeing with me. If these things were hidden in safe places, however, everyone would find them.' He opened the door and prepared to get out.

Alice caught him behind the head and pulled him to her in a passionate kiss. That surprised Lourds, as well as complicating the situation with Miriam, but it didn't stop him from kissing her back.

She drew back. 'I'll see you soon.'

'Yes.' Lourds slid out of the car, regretting that he couldn't take his backpack and hoping he'd brought everything he needed in his cargo pants. He also hoped the flashlight, pry bar, and other tools wouldn't clank when he walked.

He pulled the *keffiyeh* into place to better shadow his face and turned to face Miriam as she got out of the car. Like him, she wore Muslim dress. They started walking toward the Dome.

'Kissing in public?' The note of disapproval in her tone was unmistakable, and it seemed to be even sharper because she spoke in Farsi. 'That hardly suits a Muslim man.'

'I don't think anyone noticed.'

'You don't know that.'

'And there are several Muslim men who have American and European girlfriends. Even when they have several wives.'

'Whatever.'

Whatever? Lourds knew he was on dangerous ground. Not just from whatever waited on him in the Dome.

'You know, Professor Lourds, I'm putting my ass on

the line for you here, hoping you can hold up your end.'

'I know.'

'This is hardly the kind of thing that you should have brought your girlfriend to.'

'She's not my girlfriend. She's just a . . . good friend.'

'A *good* friend? That's what you call it?'

'Yes.'

'Does she know she's a *good* friend?'

'Of course.'

'And that you have other *good* friends?'

'Yes.'

'Are you going to be *good* friends again anytime soon?'

'I don't know. I'm working hard on just surviving the next few minutes.'

'That's exactly why I want you to stay focused.'

Lourds stopped in the street and faced the young woman. 'If I have hurt you in any way, Miriam, I'm sorry. That was not my intention.'

She stared at him for a moment, then let out a breath. 'I know. Getting involved with you was my idea.'

'Maybe I should have said no.'

Her eyes flared open wider. 'You could have told me *no*?'

Lourds desperately backtracked in his mind. This was what he hated about trying to maintain a relationship that lasted more than a few days or weeks. There were just too many things to pay attention to and revisionist history regarding events and motivations shifted as suddenly and dangerously as quicksand. Translating dead and forgotten languages was much safer. 'Of course I couldn't have told you no.'

'Your problem is that you can't tell *anyone* no.'

Lourds felt like he'd walked out into the middle of a minefield. There were no right answers. He hated that. At least working translations, there were right answers.

'Did you tell her about us?'

'No. Why would I do that? I didn't tell you about Alice and me.'

Miriam frowned.

Lourds sighed. 'Might I suggest there's a better time and place to work this out? We're all consenting adults.'

Obviously not happy about the situation, Miriam turned and continued walking toward the Dome.

Lourds hurried after her. 'Hey. As a proper Muslim woman, you're supposed to walk behind me.'

Miriam turned and glared daggers at him, but waited until he passed her and trailed behind him. Somehow, that didn't make Lourds feel any safer at all.

As with every other time he'd visited the Islamic shrine, Lourds found his breath taken from him when he stepped inside the wooden walkway adjacent to the entrance to the Wailing Wall. Already he could hear prayers at the Wall. Jews were not permitted inside the Dome to pray.

Muslim security guards from the Ministry of Awqaf checked all the visitors.

The huge rock face in the center of the Dome, surrounded by gorgeous pillars, was steeped in the emotional history of the Bible, the Koran, and the Talmud.

It was here that Abraham had come to sacrifice his son, Isaac, as commanded by God, and it was from this Rock that God had created the world. It was here that Mohammad had arrived on the winged beast, al-Buraq, and – some believed – his footprint was still upon the rock. It was here that the Ark of the Covenant was delivered to the First Temple, which was built by King Solomon after his father, King David, was denied the task by God. That temple had been destroyed by the Babylonians and rebuilt, renamed Herod's Temple, and was destroyed by the Romans in AD 70.

Lourds's chest swelled at the sight of the Rock. Even though he knew the location was argued over by the different theologies, and they even disagreed if this was *the* Rock, he knew there was something hugely significant about it. He could feel it. That bothered him because he preferred his feelings based in history and fact.

This, though, was pure faith.

And he'd come to plunder this holy place. Thinking that wasn't a most auspicious beginning, especially since Lourds was immediately reminded of the penalty he faced if he got caught. But he put one foot in front of the other and got to it.

Men and women were allowed to enter through different doors, and had to occupy different parts of the

Dome. Neither Miriam nor Lourds was certain where the entrance to the underground labyrinth – if it even existed – was.

Lourds walked in a semicircle around the Rock, watching carefully through the ornate pillars. He followed the small morning crowd of Muslims and tourists through the tour, ending up in the Well of Souls. The cave was located below the Foundation Stone.

He peered through the small hole that showed the interior of the cave, then continued to the entrance on the southern side, where the stairs were. The stairway was lined in brown-and-white carpet, but the hard stone underneath was evident. At the bottom, he walked through the gap between the Stone and the rock wall.

In wonder and frustration, he surreptitiously searched the room. If there was a clue to the location of Mohammad's Book and Scroll, he didn't see it. A steady resonance filled the room, and Lourds was reminded again of the sound of the sea. Many people believed the phenomenon was created by the enclosed space and the presence of so many people above and around the Well of Souls.

'You see, my son, this is where the souls of the dead come to await Judgment Day.' A man in American clothing stood holding the hand of his small son.

'When I die, I'm going to come here?'

'Some say that.'

The boy looked at the cave thoughtfully. 'Seems small. And there's no bathroom.'

Lourds chuckled, then masked the sound with a small coughing fit. Frustrated, knowing Miriam would be worried, he turned to go back up the stairs. Then the feeling he'd first gotten when he'd entered the Dome slammed into him again. This time he thought he was going to fall.

Several people around him got excited and nervous.

'That was a tremor!'

'The ground moved! Did you feel it?'

'Was that an earthquake?'

All the voices spoke different languages, but Lourds understood them all. What he didn't understand was the tremor. He'd never experienced one inside the Dome before though he knew the earth shifted and moved constantly, and that this region was overdue for a major earthquake.

At the bottom of the stairs, behind the stairwell, Lourds spotted a crack in the wall that he was pretty certain hadn't been there before. As he stared at it again, another tremor surged through the cave, and the crack grew wider. He walked closer and saw that the crack actually outlined a section of the wall. Standing next to it, he felt a stone at his feet shift.

Looking down, he saw that the carpet had shifted slightly to reveal a winged horselike beast. 'Al-Buraq.' His heard his own whisper though he couldn't remember speaking.

The cavern shifted again, and this time a new exodus began, this one involving panicked flight from the Well of Souls. Hasty feet and frightened voices echoed up out of the cave.

Lourds stood his ground, hiked up his *thobe,* and took out his pry bar. Inserting the hardened tip into the crack, he pushed hard.

The wall section slid open to reveal a small crawl space beyond. On the lip of the entrance, another image of al-Buraq was cut into the stone.

Lourds took a flashlight from his pocket, turned it on, and crawled inside. He paused long enough to push the wall section back into place, then started crawling forward into the darkness.

51

Dome of the Rock
Temple Mount
Jerusalem, the State of Israel
August 18, 2011

Keeping her head down, trying not to make eye contact with anyone, Miriam circulated through the Dome of the Rock. She tried to concentrate on finding Mohammad's Koran and the Scroll, but her thoughts kept returning to Thomas Lourds. Even though she'd held no illusions about the intimacy they'd shared turning into something lasting, seeing Alice Von Volker's obvious familiarity with him had been a bit much.

Even worse, Lourds didn't even seem that upset by what had happened. He'd stayed focused – eyes on the prize. That was enough to undermine a woman's confidence.

Get your head together. Concentrate on doing what you came here to do. If you do anything less, you're going to be dead soon.

'Orchid, do you have the package in sight?' That was *Katsas* Shavit over the earpiece Miriam wore. The Muslim security people hadn't caught that.

'No. We're still separated.'

'You need to find him.'

Miriam glanced at her watch and realized that more time had passed than she had realized. She'd gotten lost in her thoughts. Getting back from Turkey had been a nightmare, and they'd been on the move almost constantly.

Almost.

They'd managed to find a hotel room last night before meeting with Alice Von Volker this morning. Miriam hadn't been happy about Lourds's choosing to share information with the woman, but she hadn't been able to do anything about it without blowing her cover. Such as it was.

Though Lourds hadn't said anything, she was fairly sure he wasn't buying the 'graduate assistant' story anymore.

'I'm looking for the package now.'

'Where would it have gone?'

Miriam wanted to point out that the 'package' had the distraction level of a two-year-old and could forget it was in danger. 'It was en route to the Well of Souls.'

'Can you get there?'

'Yes. I'm on my way.' Miriam turned and headed for the Well of Souls.

'Hold your position.'

Casually, Miriam stopped and adjusted her *hijab.* One of the buttons on her *burqa* had been replaced with a minicam. Signal boosters for the earpiece and the camera had been built into her shoes. Getting through security had been nerve-wracking, but she'd worked with the hardware before and trusted that the modifications were undetectable.

'Do you see the man at your three o'clock?'

Looking forward, Miriam used her peripheral vision to look at the man *Katsis* Shavit had pointed out.

He was lean and bearded, with a haughty demeanor. A scar from a knife wound bisected his nose and scored his left cheek. Miriam was certain she'd never seen him before, and just as certain that she would remember him.

'That is Bozorg Alavi, a member of the Revolutionary Guards. He's an associate of Colonel Imad Davari.'

Miriam's stomach churned a little at the man's name. Those hours she'd spent in Evin Prison were still too close. They haunted her dreams, and only lying next to Lourds had prevented them from overwhelming her.

She felt a flush of guilt then as she realized why she'd been drawn to him. She'd been using Lourds as a security blanket. That was *not* what she wanted in a man.

'Then Davari is here.'

'We couldn't confirm him as a casualty during the skirmish at the Turkish border.'

Miriam took a deep breath. 'I've got to get to the package.' She headed toward the Well of Souls, hoping she would be in time. At that moment, another of the strange tremors that had manifested only moments ago shook the Dome.

At the stairwell, a crowd of people emerged from

below, and the wailing noise inside the cave intensified. An electric pang of fear passed through Miriam.

Bozorg Alavi had headed for the Well of Souls, too.

Colonel Davari paused at the top of the staircase and peered down as the crowd of people fled up the steps. He despised them, knowing they'd gone down into the cave and frightened themselves over the small tremors. Those were nothing.

At the bottom of the stairs, Lourds paused at the wall. Something long and metal glinted in his hand as he worked on the wall. In the next moment, Davari watched in astonishment as the American professor pulled out a section of the wall, crawled inside, and pushed the section back into place behind him as though it had never been disturbed.

All the frightened idiots fleeing up the stairs didn't notice the professor's disappearance.

Davari called to his men over the earpiece he wore, summoning them as he descended into the Well of Souls.

Pausing for a moment, still on his hands and knees, Lourds shined his flashlight around and saw the surrounding stone was worn smooth. Obviously, the tunnel had been used frequently in the past, but had sealed over and been forgotten long ago.

Pointing the flashlight forward again, he kept crawling. After a couple of turns, he came to a large cavern. He slid out of the tunnel headfirst, landing on his hands, losing the flashlight for a moment, then rolling to his feet.

The light didn't span the distance across the dark cavern, and his footsteps echoed in the emptiness, but he also heard the sound of running water. The water was a constant flow, but it wasn't a rush.

Something snapped underfoot. When he shined the flashlight down, he discovered he'd stepped on a rat skeleton, snapping the rib cage like small firecrackers.

Realizing he was walking out into the darkness with no point of reference, he turned back around. He felt panicked for just a moment when he discovered he'd walked farther than he'd thought. Gratefully, he reached the cave wall again, then lifted the flashlight to peer into the tunnel.

His light struck the eyes of the man hiding within the tunnel. Before Lourds could back away, the man leaped at him and knocked him backwards. Lourds tried to stay on his feet, but the man's speed and strength overwhelmed him and drove him farther back and back, until he finally tripped and went down.

The man crashed on top of him, forearm pushed up under his chin and so heavy on his throat that he couldn't breathe. Lourds swung his flashlight at the man's head, but the man simply shifted his forearm and smashed it into Lourds's face.

The blow on his still-sore nose brought tears to his eyes as his head rebounded from the cavern floor hard enough to fill his vision with spots and make blood roar in his ears. Lourds gasped for breath, and the man shoved the snout of a vicious-looking pistol into the professor's mouth.

'Professor Lourds, my name is Colonel Imad Davari. I have traveled very far to find you, and what you seek. I will not be denied. If I have to, I will shoot you. I will not kill you, but I have learned from great personal experience that you can shoot a healthy man a number of times without any of those wounds being lethal. To do what I need you to do, you don't need to be able to walk or to move your arms. Therefore, I will shoot out your knees and your elbows to begin with.'

Lourds focused on the man. Miriam had mentioned the colonel in her description of the events that had happened in Evin Prison. There was no doubt that the man would do exactly what he said.

'Do we have an understanding?'

It was hard speaking around the gun barrel in his mouth, but Lourds was a trained orator, used to making himself understood in many languages. 'Yeth.'

Davari smiled. 'Good.' He patted Lourds's cheek with his free hand, then pushed himself to his feet. 'Get up.'

As Lourds stood, he noticed the other five men standing behind Davari. All of them wore *thobes* and *keffiyehs*. His heart sank.

The Revolutionary Guards colonel shined his flashlight around the cavern. 'What is this place?'

'Before the Dome was built, this was the site of the First and Second Temples.' Despite his fear, Lourds studied the walls. Some of Davari's men carried high-powered lanterns. 'The Temples were carved out of the mountain, taking advantage of natural caverns here. This one was evidently forgotten.'

'Where are Mohammad's Koran and the Scroll?'

'I don't know.'

Davari grinned at him. 'Then perhaps we need to explore a little further.' He waved Lourds forward with his pistol.

The colonel needn't have bothered with the weapon threat. Lourds picked up his flashlight and went willingly. He didn't know what he was going to do if there was no Koran and no Scroll.

Except die. Only he felt pretty sure that was going to happen no matter what.

Mufarrij watched as the last of Davari's men clambered into the hole in the wall beside the stairs. Two other Revolutionary Guards remained on the main floor, keeping an eye on the exiting tourists. They had talked briefly before most of them had split off to follow Davari into the Well of Souls.

Moving swiftly and fearlessly, his wounded face still throbbing, Mufarrij threw himself over the side of the stairs and dropped. When he landed on his feet, his injuries filled his head with such screaming pain that he almost dropped to his knees. He forced himself to move through the agony, reaching out and yanking the stone section back before it completely closed.

The action caught the man in the tunnel off guard. Still holding the wall section, he got dragged forward. His hand flashed to the pistol holstered on his hip, but the *thobe* got in the way.

Grabbing the man's neck, Mufarrij twisted violently, shattering his spine like a rotten stick. The body fell to Mufarrij's feet, and he knelt beside it, searching him. Beneath the loose folds of the *thobe,* the man carried a silenced 9mm pistol and a machine pistol, an ammo belt around his waist holding extra magazines for both weapons, and a boot knife.

Evidently Davari had an agreement with the Ministry of Awqaf that most visitors didn't enjoy.

With the ammo belt around his own waist, the pistol in his hand, and the machine pistol looped over his shoulder, Mufarrij climbed into the tunnel. He was doing God's work now, and he intended to see that Mohammad's Book and the Scroll did not fall into the Ayatollah's bloodthirsty hands.

Only a short distance away, Lourds discovered the source of the water noise. A short flight of steps led down into a cistern filled halfway with water. He supposed it had been built during the time of the First or Second Temple and used to supply the people that had lived there. Or, since the Muslim builders of the Dome had lived there as well, perhaps it had been used by them as well.

'Where are Mohammad's Koran and the Scroll, Professor Lourds?' Davari glared at him.

'I don't know.'

'This is a trick.'

Lourds glared back at the man in disbelief. 'How can it be a trick? I've never been here before. I've never seen this place. The first time I got here is the first time you got here.'

For a second he thought Davari might shoot him just on general principles. Then a thought occurred to him.

He cocked his head. 'I hear running water.'

'What does that have to do with anything?'

'Running water has to go somewhere.' Ignoring the pistol in the man's hand, drawn by his own curiosity, Lourds tracked the noise. 'Water is a notorious destroyer. Give it the tiniest little crack, and it will cut a chasm through the earth if there is an endless supply. It destroys things more completely than a fire, because you can reconstitute something from ash, but once water has its way with something, there's usually nothing left.'

Lourds walked to the end of the cistern area, tracking the noise. Directing his light down, he discovered that the cistern had been built in sections. He thought perhaps it might be for rotating the water supply and keeping it fresh.

Set into the center of the last chamber was a block of stone. Water seeped around and under it. Lourds knelt and shined his light into the center of the cistern chamber.

'What is that?' Davari was at his side, adding his light to Lourds's.

'That is a drain that has evidently worn down over time.'

'A drain?'

'Possibly to keep the water fresh, or to get rid of any that was contaminated.' Lourds shined his flashlight across the tops of the section walls. 'See there? Those are built like dams.' He played the light over the sections. 'Open them up, and the water in that section drains into the one next to it.'

'Where are the things we came in search of?'

Lourds paced back along the cistern, puzzling it out for himself. Then, in the next-to-last section, he spotted the image of a flying beast lightly chiseled into the stone. Leaning low over the murky water, he directed his beam at the bottom of the cistern.

Unfortunately, it wasn't strong enough to penetrate the murk. He looked up at Davari and held out a hand. 'I need your flashlight.'

Davari hesitated a moment, then handed it over. 'What do you see?'

'Nothing yet, but that carving wasn't done for no reason.' Even though Davari and the Revolutionary Guardsmen were all around him, Lourds couldn't draw back from the puzzle before him. He leaned down, his face only inches from the still water.

The more powerful beam barely penetrated the water, but there at the bottom of the cistern chamber, a bronze disk nearly a yard across gleamed dully in the light.

52

Dome of the Rock
Temple Mount
Jerusalem, the State of Israel
August 18, 2011

'Quickly! Drain the far chamber!' Evidently Davari had seen and figured out the significance of the bronze disk as well.

Lourds silently cursed himself for being so drawn into the mystery. But in his heart, he knew he hadn't had a choice. If Davari was going to kill him, if he was going to die, Lourds couldn't resist solving the puzzle first.

And his hubris might have damned the world. *Always the puzzle solver, never the voice of salvation. Ah, Thomas, at least the planet will soon be saved from any more of your selfish predilections.*

Lourds started to rise as two of the men leaped down into the far chamber and yanked at the plug. The gurgling of the water increased in speed and intensity.

'Not you, Professor Lourds. I think you are fine where you are.' Davari kept his weapon directed at him. 'I would like very much for you to stay alive a while longer. In case you are needed.' The colonel smiled a little. 'Who knows? Perhaps the Ayatollah won't mind very much if I leave you here alive.'

Lourds didn't believe him, not after what Davari had done to Professor Namati in Evin Prison. Around him, the guards were distracted enough by the recovery operation that he thought he had a good chance at escape, but he couldn't leave. He was stuck fast. He was also struck by the incongruity that Davari now had *six* followers instead of five.

The first cistern chamber hadn't quite emptied when the partition on the second one was released. Water rushed from the second chamber into the first with thunderous gurgling, and the drain flow increased dramatically. The two other cistern chambers, including the one with the flying beast marking it and the bronze disk at the bottom, were quickly emptied as well.

Davari waved Lourds toward the empty cistern. 'Get down there. Find out what is there.'

Knowing that Davari expected the disk to be booby-trapped in some way, Lourds dropped into the chamber. Even without the gun pointed at him, even without the notion of traps, he was going. He couldn't stay away now if he tried. His boots splashed through the shallow water puddles on the uneven floor.

Reaching for the bronze disk, Lourds felt through the silt that had drifted down over the area. They were lucky that the last thirteen hundred years hadn't filled the cistern entirely with silt, but it meant that the source – whatever it was – was mostly clean. Or perhaps it was filtered through an aquifer at the other end.

'Stop right there.'

Lourds couldn't believe it. One hand held his flashlight and the other hovered only inches from the surface of the bronze disk. He was pinned in the glare of Davari's flashlight and at least three of the others.

'What?'

'There are no traps. I will not have the hands of an infidel on the holy words of God and Mohammad. You will touch the disk and go no farther.'

Helplessly, Lourds watched as one of the men clambered down into the chamber at Davari's direction. The man seized the disk, twisted, then shook his head at the colonel.

'Help him.'

Lourds put his flashlight to one side, then gripped the disk as well and heaved. Grudgingly, the disk turned, the bronze metal grating against the stone. After a few more coordinated heaves, the disk slid from the opening.

The Revolutionary Guardsman pointed his flashlight into the hole. Lourds grabbed his own light and added its beam.

Below, in the musty darkness, was a small room. A stone writing table held two ceramic oil lamps. In the far corner sat an old stone chest covered in tiles. Even in the weak light, Lourds made out the flying beast on the tiles, blue against the white.

'Lourds, look out!'

As Lourds glanced up, the Guardsman beside him started to draw his weapon, but his head burst apart, spilling blood, brains, and bone across the wet floor. The dead man rolled bonelessly to one side.

At the top of the cistern chamber, Davari jerked, and blood jumped from the side of his neck. The colonel threw his light down and dodged for the darkness.

Muzzle flashes strobed the inky blackness that suddenly filled the chamber. The attacker's shots had been silenced, but the Guardsmen's weren't. The hollow booms of their weapons filled the cavern space, deafening Lourds, who clapped his hands over his ears.

Filled with adrenaline and a need to flee, but also overcome with the desire to see what lay within, Lourds grabbed his flashlight and dropped through the opening. He landed on his feet and headed for the stone chest. An inscription was chiseled in Arabic across the top: 'God is great. We shall all meet in Paradise.'

Above, the bullets continued flying, and someone cut loose with an automatic weapon. The gun battle seemed surreal against the solid reality of the chest.

Lourds braced himself and pushed the lid off with a grunt, dropping it gently to the floor. He shined his flashlight inside. A richly decorated book covered in green leather and decorated with gold and silver filigree and precious gems lay beside an ancient roll of parchment.

Unable to stop himself, Lourds opened the parchment. The language was hard to read, but the promises of a global *jihad* and a supernatural fire claiming the world were prominent.

Then another man dropped into the room.

Lourds whirled to face him and realized only then that he had no means of protecting himself.

The man reached up and removed his *keffiyeh*. The bloody face was swollen and barely recognizable, but Lourds recognized him as the bearded man from Evin Prison. He held a machine pistol in one hand, the muzzle pointed at Lourds. He had his other wrapped around his middle.

'Is that Mohammad's Koran and the Scroll?'

'I think so.'

'What does the Scroll say?'

'That Mohammad's people should rise up and declare war on the world.'

The bearded man shook his head. 'That's unacceptable.' He coughed and blood spewed from his mouth and down his chin. 'Your lucky day, Professor. I cannot let that Book and Scroll fall into the hands of the enemies of Saudi Arabia. So I'm going to let you live to steal it from them.' He took his hand from his middle, and it was covered with blood. 'I can't go on. But I can survive long enough to get you out of this place.'

Lourds carefully placed the Book and the Scroll under his robe and tied them into place. He felt fairly confident they would stay put as he moved.

'How?'

'Back out the way you came. I'll give you cover.' The

bearded man coughed more blood and shoved a fresh magazine into his weapon. 'Now we've got to move, or they'll get brave. If they get their wits about them, they'll surround this cistern and either shoot us or starve us out. There are only a couple left. I killed the rest.'

Lourds felt terrified, but he knew what the man said was true. 'All right.' He started for the ladder built into the wall that led to the opening.

'I'll go first, but you'd better be at my heels.' The man pulled himself up the ladder with flagging strength. Just as he reached the top, a Guardsman shoved his gun and his head into the chamber. The bearded man shot the Guardsman point-blank in the face and waited till the falling body cleared the opening. Then, leading with his machine pistol, he pulled himself through.

Lourds followed, switching off his flashlight first because he knew it made him an instant target.

In the cistern, the bearded man grabbed the wall and heaved himself up. He looked back. 'Hurry.' He fired a long burst toward the far end of the cistern cavern.

Lourds climbed up and got his feet under him, instantly focusing on the barely illumined doorway ahead of him. The muzzle flashes, even sustained ones, didn't provide much light.

'Go!' The man removed the magazine from his weapon and inserted a new one. Then he growled as at least one more bullet struck him.

Fighting panic, trying to keep his head clear, Lourds ran. He hated leaving the dying man behind, but the man was . . . dying. That had been evident from his injuries. Automatic fire thundered and filled the chamber, sending out echoes that rolled into the next cavern.

Once he cleared the cistern chamber, Lourds switched on his flashlight and ran for the hole in the wall. Before he reached it, the firing behind him died away. Then Davari's voice filled the silence.

'*Lourds!*'

Scurrying into the hole, Lourds crawled as fast as he was able. His elbows and knees bruised painfully. The Book and Scroll tied to his body made his efforts cumbersome. The sound of running feet followed him, but by then he'd already reached the turns, where a straight shot wouldn't hit him.

Then he was at the hidden entrance by the steps. He slammed a hand into it and pushed it open. Legs under him again, he sprinted up the stairs, driving forward hard.

In the main room, the faithful slowed his pace and blocked his path, but he pushed through them, bumping and jostling and twice just running people down. When the bullets started flying, coming from behind him, the crowd hit the ground like they were practicing for an air raid.

Two men at the far end didn't drop, though. They drew weapons and took up the chase.

Standing tall above the crowd, Lourds leaped over the last few people in his way. He saw bullets splinter the door ahead just before he ran through it. Heart pounding, ears burning, air whistling in his lungs, he took off down the streets.

Sprinting off the curb, he caused a pileup as a driver tried to brake to avoid hitting him and got rear-ended by the vehicle behind it. A taxi parked on the other side of the street. Lourds couldn't change his stride or direction in time, so he leaped forward, sliding across the hood as bullets hammered its body and smashed through the windshield and windows.

As he rose to his feet, a body crashed into him from behind. The impact against the cobblestoned street drove the wind from his lungs and made his senses reel. The Guardsman who had tackled him tried to shove his pistol into Lourds's face, but Lourds caught the man's wrist in both hands. Only then did he realize that the impact had knocked the Book and the Scroll loose.

Horns blared around them, and shouts filled the street. Lourds struggled against his opponent, fueled by adrenaline and his desire to live. The Guardsman snarled curses, promising him God's vengeance. Lourds twisted hard, forcing the man to drop the gun.

Someone else stepped in close to Lourds as he fought for his life. From the corner of his eye, he watched helplessly as Davari picked up the Book and Scroll. Then the colonel pointed his pistol at Lourds.

Panicked, not knowing what else to do, Lourds released his hold on the Guardsman and scrambled for safety. Before he could do more than turn over, the Guardsman hurled himself on top of Lourds again, taking them both back to the ground. Lourds's chin struck the cobblestone, splitting open his skin. He felt warm blood flow as his head went sideways.

Pistol shots boomed and rolled. More blood cascaded down Lourds's neck, and for a frenzied moment he thought it was from his. The Guardsman convulsed above him, though, and Lourds knew Davari had shot his own man in his zeal.

For a moment, Lourds remained still, knowing if he moved, he would be killed. Remaining unmoving, especially with panic racing through him, was almost impossible.

Davari ran, calling to the men that followed him.

Once they had gone, Lourds shoved the dead man off him. For an instant, he stood panting, watching helplessly as Davari got away with the prizes.

Are you going to stand here and let him get away? Lourds thought about Lev and how his friend had given his life to get the Book and the Scroll into safe hands. He thought of all the risks Alice had undertaken for something she didn't even know about. He thought about how Davari had killed Professor Namati.

He thought about how Davari had tortured Miriam.

Davari can't be allowed to take the Book back to Iran. Lourds took off in pursuit, driving his legs hard and feeling the steady drip of blood coming from his chin. His heart labored in his chest, but his stride lengthened and steadied.

Davari ran across the next street while holding a

walkie-talkie to his mouth. Evidently he was trying to put together an alternate exit strategy.

The alley didn't go through the neighborhood, though; Lourds knew that from all his visits with Lev. They'd walked all over Jerusalem, discussing the various historical and biblical events that had taken place there. Apparently Lourds knew the city much better than Davari did.

Angling away from the alley Davari had gone through, Lourds ran left, toward the next alley. The one Davari was in came around in a big U.

At the mouth of the next alley, Lourds dashed into a small tourist shop. The space was filled with T-shirts and souvenirs. A bin next to the doorway held umbrellas and walking sticks.

'May I help you?' A rotund little shopkeeper started from behind the counter.

'Stay back or you're going to get hurt.' Lourds didn't know if it was his bloody face or hearing the shots on the street that persuaded the man to back away, but he did retreat.

The man also snatched up a cell phone and called the police as he dropped behind the counter.

Tense and shaking, Lourds waited as the running footsteps grew louder. Angling his head, Lourds discovered he could see the alley reflected in the glass door that was propped open outside.

Davari was approaching fast, still talking on the walkie-talkie.

Desperate, Lourds reached into the bin and pulled out a curved walking stick. Turning back to the doorway, he stuck it out, caught Davari around the neck, and yanked the man into the shop as if he were he was hauling in a prize marlin.

Surprised and half-choked, Davari stumbled into the shop and slammed into a display rack of T-shirts, taking everything down with him.

Twisting the walking stick free, Lourds swung it into the face of the first Guardsman who tried to come through the door. The wood shattered upon impact, the Guardsman staggered backward, and Lourds's hands went temporarily numb.

Confused and coughing, Davari desperately tried to fight free of the clothing rack. He lifted his pistol and pointed it at Lourds.

Moving on instinct, Lourds kicked the man's gun hand and launched the pistol toward the opposite wall. The gun shattered the window and disappeared into the alley.

Bending down, he gathered up the Book and the Scroll, both of which had spilled across the floor. Lourds ran to the window, hurling himself onto the street as more Guardsmen poured into the room. Bullets chipped the window frame and slammed into the building across the alley. Then Lourds was outside and running for all he was worth.

He dashed down the first alley he came to and followed the twisting path between buildings, trying to figure out some goal, wondering if he had enough gas left in him to outrun his pursuers.

He risked a glance over his shoulder and instantly regretted it. Davari and three men had taken up the chase and were pacing him easily, like a pride of lions stalking an antelope.

Cutting around a corner, Lourds slipped on loose trash from a spilled container behind a restaurant. Spoiled vegetables turned into paste underfoot. He struggled to maintain his balance, couldn't, and skidded across the rough paving stones, losing skin from his chin, his cheek, and his left hand.

He pushed himself up, grabbed the Scroll he'd dropped, managed to get to one knee, and watched helplessly as Davari and his men appeared out of the alley and pointed their weapons at him.

Then a slender figure in a *burqa* came out of nowhere and flung herself at the last Guardsman. She struck the man at the knees and he went down with a cry of alarm. As he dropped his weapon, Miriam scooped it up and came up on one knee with the pistol in both hands.

She pressed the pistol against the head of the fallen man and pulled the trigger. Blood spattered her face, but she didn't even flinch as she brought the pistol up. The last two men turned at the unexpected gunshot. Her bullets caught them in the face and dropped them both where they stood.

Davari swung around, dropping into a crouch. Both of them fired at the same time. Miriam held her ground, and for a moment Lourds thought she'd been hit.

Then Davari sprawled forward, head turning so Lourds could see the bullet hole squarely between his staring eyes.

Miriam ran to him, helping him to his feet. 'You got the Book and the Scroll?'

'Yeah.' Lourds held them up, his left hand torn and bloody.

They stepped out into the street, and a black sedan shrieked to a halt in front of them. The doors opened, and men in dark suits and earpieces opened the back doors. Lourds and Miriam looked at each other.

Aaron Jacob, president of the Hebrew University of Jerusalem, sat in the backseat. 'We meet again, Professor Lourds. I'd get in if I were you.'

Pushing Miriam ahead of him, Lourds fell into the back seat and struggled to get his breath back. He looked at Miriam as she stripped off the *burqa* and *hijab.*

Jacob smiled at Lourds as the car got under way and held out his hands. 'I'll take the Book and Scroll now, please.'

Lourds sighed and handed over both items. 'Mossad?'

Jacob smiled. 'I know some people that are. Reputedly.'

'I don't suppose I'm going to get to read those items, am I?'

'You didn't look at them?'

'I looked at them enough. No one's going to be able to prove that Mohammad himself wrote those documents because we don't have any existing examples of his handwriting, but the message was clear enough to spin the world out of control if it had fallen into the Ayatollah's hands.'

'Thank God that didn't happen. You understand that it would be better if no one ever sees these documents again?'

Lourds nodded. 'It's what Lev would have wanted.'

Jacob smiled in relief. 'I'm glad you see it that way.' He clapped Lourds on the shoulder.

Lourds winced in pain at the friendly contact, then swiveled his gaze to Miriam, relieved that she wasn't hurt. 'I have never had a graduate assistant who helped take work away from me. Especially work that would have impacted the world.'

'You've probably never had a graduate assistant who saved your life before. Especially not as many times as I have these past few days. Starting with that little episode in Namchee Bazaar.'

'That was you?'

'Yes.'

Lourds leaned forward to hug her. 'Thank you.'

She surprised him by turning her face up to be kissed.

When they parted, Lourds looked at her. 'Maybe after this is over we could meet for dinner?'

'To renew the friendship?'

'Whatever you want it to be.'

She looked at him. 'But it'll never be any more than what it is.'

Lourds shook his head. 'I'm a good friend, Miriam, but I'm not good for much more. There's too much work I want to do, too many things I want to see.'

She took his hand. 'I understand. And good friends are a rare pleasure.'

'I've always thought so.'

Epilogue

Covert Operations
Institute for Intelligence and Special Operations (Mossad)
Tel Aviv, Republic of Israel
August 18, 2011

'I appreciate you joining us today, Professor Lourds.'

Leaning back in his chair, Lourds took stock of the old man sitting on the other side of the rectangular table. 'I wasn't exactly given a choice. Your agents came to my hotel room and took me.'

'I'm sure it wasn't as dramatic as that.'

Lourds rubbed his bruised wrists. 'Take my word for it. When I told them I wasn't interested, they handcuffed me and took me into custody.'

'I'll have a word with them.'

'I'm sure that will do all the good in the world.'

The old man grinned and laid his walking stick across his knees as he sat. 'I'll do my best.'

'I don't suppose it would do any good for me to call the US Embassy and protest.'

'No. They already know you're here.'

Lourds grew more irritated but curbed the feeling. 'Did you bring me here to look at the Koran or the Scroll?'

The old man raised an eyebrow. 'What Koran? What Scroll?'

Lourds didn't even bother to reply.

'I don't mean to be facetious, Professor Lourds, but I do want to clarify some things.'

Letting out an angry breath, Lourds waited.

'Under no circumstances will anyone be allowed to see that Koran and Scroll again – even if they did exist, which they most certainly do not.'

'You can't just shut those things away.'

'Of course we can.'

'Think of the history you're hiding.'

The old man's gaze turned wintry. 'Professor Lourds, history has already taken care of itself. It's the future we're protecting now. And I won't have anyone risking the balance in the world over a document that no one can conclusively prove was written by Mohammad. Even if it existed.' He paused. 'Especially not some sensationalism-seeking Harvard linguistics professor that has the libido of a three-balled tomcat. If we hear of such a professor making idle claims about a fictitious document at some later date, Jimmy Hoffa will be easier to find. Do I make myself clear?'

His throat suddenly bone-dry, Lourds nodded and squeaked out, 'Perfectly.'

'Then I'll see to it that you're returned to your hotel room.' The old man got to his feet. 'Enjoy the rest of your stay in Jerusalem, Professor Lourds.'

Givat Shaul Cemetery
Jerusalem, the State of Israel
August 21, 2011

'Sorry I haven't been by sooner, old friend, but as you know, you left me quite a bit of work to do when you left this world.' Hat in hand, Lourds stood at the foot of the recent grave and stared at the simple wooden marker that declared the final resting place of Lev Strauss.

A pile of stones, all deposited by visitors, lay atop the grave. There were a lot of them. Lev was missed by many people.

'Those of us who know what you've done still talk about how you saved the world. I regret that no one's willing to step forward and let everyone know, but even admitting what was at stake is probably enough to launch an attack from the Ayatollah.' Lourds smiled. 'As it turns out, there was an added benefit to having Alice in our camp. Klaus Von Volker left a journal behind that detailed his arms sales. Even as we speak, joint efforts by various intelligence-community strike forces – who shall remain unnamed, of course – are even now dismantling the Ayatollah's stockpiles of nuclear weapons and shutting down Von Volker's clients The message is clear.'

Lourds juggled the stone he held in his bandaged palm. 'I don't have much more to say, old friend, but I will think of you often. And always with respect and much love.' Gently, he added his stone to the pile.

Alice stepped up beside Lourds and left a stone as well. Together, hand in hand, they walked back toward the waiting rental car.

'So what are you going to do, Professor Lourds?'

Lourds shrugged. 'The dean called to remind me I still have a job to do and that he expects me to get back to it – soon. I've got a new class of students waiting. A new book to write. Some more work to do on Scholar's Rock Temple. A lot to do. And I'm still searching for whatever may remain of the Library of Alexandria.'

'You still entertain thoughts of finding that?'

Lourds grinned. 'I seem to have quite a record for finding lost things.'

'And lost loves?'

Lourds stopped and looked into her eyes. 'And lost loves.'

'It's never going to be what I'd hoped it would be, is it?'

Gently, Lourds smiled. 'If I stopped doing what I do, could you still love me in the same way?'

She looked at him. 'No.'

'Then maybe we should remain friends.'

'*Good* friends?'

'*Very good* friends.'

'Like your new *friend*, Miriam?'

'Miriam has been drafted to a new assignment.'

'You never said exactly what it was that she did.'

'Graduate assistantship.'

'Really?' Alice looked surprised. 'She seemed more like the adventurous type.'

'Graduate work can be extremely adventurous.'

'I stand corrected, Professor Lourds. However, it seems that I have recently come into possession of an obscene amount of money. You can take a week or two before you return to the grind. Let me spoil us for a while. Then I promise I'll let you back out into the world to play.'

Lourds grinned. 'I'd like that.'

She snaked his hat from his head and put it on, then leaned her face up to be kissed. And he did.

read more

CHARLES BROKAW

THE ATLANTIS CODE

An ancient artefact is discovered in a dusty antiquities shop in Alexandria, Egypt – the long-forgotten trinket soon becomes the centre of the most deadly race against time in history.

The 20,000-year-old relic is inscribed with what appears to be the long-lost language of Atlantis. Only one man would seem to be able to decode its meaning - the world's foremost linguist, Dr Thomas Lourdes – but only if he can stay alive long enough . . .

Meanwhile, an earthquake in Cadiz, Spain, uncovers a most unexpected site – one which the Vatican rush to be the first to explore . . . Perhaps the lost city of Atlantis is finally ready to be found?

But is the world ready for her secrets?

'The Atlantis Code will take you to a new level of mystery, wonder, adventure and excitement' Deepak Chopra